Vanishing Act

Where the "Black House" had stood—the house in which Ellery himself had set foot only the afternoon before, the old Victorian house built during the Civil War where Sylvester Mayhew had died, where Thorne had barricaded himself with a cutlass for a week—there stood nothing.

No walls. No chimney. No roof. No ruins. No debris. No house. Nothing.

Nothing but empty space covered smoothly and warmly with snow.

THE HOUSE HAD VANISHED DURING THE NIGHT.

Other SIGNET Ellery Queen Titles

The New Adventures of Ellery Queen

by ELLERY QUEEN

A SIGNET BOOK from
NEW AMERICAN LIBRARY
TIMES MIRROR

ACKNOWLEDGMENTS

The author wishes to express his gratitude to *Detective Story,
Red Book, American, Cavalcade,* and *Blue Book* for permission
to include certain copyrighted stories which appeared
in their publications as listed below:

"The Lamp of God," "Treasure Hunt": 1935, *Detective Story*

"The Hollow Dragon": 1936, *Red Book*

"The House of Darkness": 1935, *American*

"The Bleeding Portrait" (under the title "Beauty and
the Beast"): 1937, *Cavalcade*

"Man Bites Dog," "Mind Over Matter," "Long Shot,"
"Trojan Horse": 1939, *Blue Book*

Published by arrangement with the late Manfred B. Lee
and Frederic Dannay.

SECOND PRINTING
THIRD PRINTING
FOURTH PRINTING
FIFTH PRINTING
SIXTH PRINTING
SEVENTH PRINTING
EIGHTH PRINTING
NINTH PRINTING
TENTH PRINTING

Contents

The Lamp of God

A Short Novel

I

IF A STORY began: "Once upon a time in a house cowering in wilderness there lived an old and eremitical creature named Mayhew, a crazy man who had buried two wives and lived a life of death; and this house was known as 'The Black House'"—if a story began in this fashion, it would strike no one as especially remarkable. There are people like that who live in houses like that, and very often mysteries materialize like ectoplasm about their wild-eyed heads.

Now however disorderly Mr. Ellery Queen may be by habit, mentally he is an orderly person. His neckties and shoes may be strewn about his bedroom helter-skelter, but inside his skull hums a perfectly oiled machine, functioning as neatly and inexorably as the planetary system. So if there was a mystery about one Sylvester Mayhew, deceased, and his buried wives and gloomy dwelling, you may be sure the Queen brain would seize upon it and worry it and pick it apart and get it all laid out in neat and shiny rows. Rationality, that was it. No esoteric mumbo-jumbo could fool *that* fellow. Lord, no! His two feet were planted solidly on God's good earth, and one and one made two—always—and that's all there was to that.

Of course, Macbeth had said that stones have been known to move and trees to speak; but, pshaw! for these literary fancies. In this day and age, with its Cominforms, its wars of peace and its rocketry experiments? Nonsense! The truth is, Mr. Queen would have said, there is something about the harsh, cruel world we live in that's very rough on miracles. Miracles just don't happen any more, unless they are miracles of stupidity or miracles of national avarice. Everyone with a grain of intelligence knows that.

"Oh, yes," Mr. Queen would have said; "there are yogis, voodoos, fakirs, shamans, and other tricksters from the effete East and primitive Africa, but nobody pays any attention to such pitiful monkeyshines—I mean, nobody with sense. This is a reasonable world and everything that happens in it must have a reasonable explanation."

You couldn't expect a sane person to believe, for example, that a three-dimensional, flesh-and-blood, veritable human being could suddenly stoop, grab his shoelaces, and fly away. Or that a water-buffalo could change into a golden-haired little boy before your eyes. Or that a man dead one hundred and thirty-seven years could push aside his tombstone, step out of his grave, yawn, and then sing three verses of *Mademoiselle from Armentières*. Or even, for that matter, that a stone could move or a tree speak—yea, though it were in the language of Atlantis or Mu.

Or . . . *could you?*

The tale of Sylvester Mayhew's house is a strange tale. When what happened happened, proper minds tottered on their foundations and porcelain beliefs threatened to shiver into shards. Before the whole fantastic and incomprehensible business was done, God Himself came into it. Yes, God came into the story of Sylvester Mayhew's house, and that is what makes it quite the most remarkable adventure in which Mr. Ellery Queen, that lean and indefatigable agnostic, has ever become involved.

The early mysteries in the Mayhew case were trivial—mysteries merely because certain pertinent facts were lacking; pleasantly provocative mysteries, but scarcely savorous of the supernatural.

Ellery was sprawled on the hearthrug before the hissing fire that raw January morning, debating with himself whether it was more desirable to brave the slippery streets and biting wind on a trip to Centre Street in quest of amusement, or to remain where he was in idleness but comfort, when the telephone rang.

It was Thorne on the wire. Ellery, who never thought of Thorne without perforce visualizing a human monolith—a long-limbed, gray-thatched male figure with marbled cheeks and agate eyes, the whole man coated with a veneer of ebony, was rather startled. Thorne was excited;

8

every crack and blur in his voice spoke eloquently of emotion. It was the first time, to Ellery's recollection, that Thorne had betrayed the least evidence of human feeling.

"What's the matter?" Ellery demanded. "Nothing's wrong with Ann, I hope?" Ann was Thorne's wife.

"No, no." Thorne spoke hoarsely and rapidly, as if he had been running.

"Where the deuce have you been? I saw Ann only yesterday and she said she hadn't heard from you for almost a week. Of course, your wife's used to your preoccupation with those interminable legal affairs, but an absence of six days—"

"Listen to me, Queen, and don't hold me up. I must have your help. Can you meet me at Pier 54 in half an hour? That's North River."

"Of course."

Thorne mumbled something that sounded absurdly like: "Thank God!" and hurried on: "Pack a bag. For a couple of days. And a revolver. Especially a revolver, Queen."

"I see," said Ellery, not seeing at all.

"I'm meeting the Cunarder *Caronia*. Docking this morning. I'm with a man by the name of Reinach, Dr. Reinach. You're my colleague; get that? Act stern and omnipotent. Don't be friendly. Don't ask him—or me—questions. And don't allow yourself to be pumped. Understood?"

"Understood," said Ellery, "but not exactly clear. Anything else?"

"Call Ann for me. Give her my love and tell her I shan't be home for days yet, but that you're with me and that I'm all right. And ask her to telephone my office and explain matters to Crawford."

"Do you mean to say that not even your partner knows what you've been doing?"

But Thorne had hung up.

Ellery replaced the receiver, frowning. It was stranger than strange. Thorne had always been a solid citizen, a successful attorney who led an impeccable private life and whose legal practice was dry and unexciting. To find old Thorne entangled in a web of mystery . . .

Ellery drew a happy breath, telephoned Mrs. Thorne, tried to sound reassuring, yelled for Djuna, hurled some clothes into a bag, loaded his .38 police revolver with a grimace, scribbled a note for Inspector Queen, dashed downstairs and jumped into the cab Djuna had summoned, and landed on Pier 54 with thirty seconds to spare.

There was something terribly wrong with Thorne, Ellery saw at once, even before he turned his attention to the vast fat man by the lawyer's side. Thorne was shrunken within his Scotch-plaid greatcoat like a pupa which had died prematurely in its cocoon. He had aged years in the few weeks since Ellery had last seen him. His ordinarily sleek cobalt cheeks were covered with a straggly stubble. Even his clothing looked tired and uncared-for. And there was a glitter of furtive relief in his bloodshot eyes as he pressed Ellery's hand that was, to one who knew Thorne's self-sufficiency and aplomb, almost pathetic.

But he merely remarked: "Oh, hello, there, Queen. We've a longer wait than we anticipated, I'm afraid. Want you to shake hands with Dr. Herbert Reinach. Doctor, this is Ellery Queen."

" 'D'you do," said Ellery curtly, touching the man's immense gloved hand. If he was to be omnipotent, he thought, he might as well be rude, too.

"Surprise, Mr. Thorne?" said Dr. Reinach in the deepest voice Ellery had ever heard; it rumbled up from the caverns of his chest like the echo of thunder. His little purplish eyes were very, very cold.

"A pleasant one, I hope," said Thorne.

Ellery snatched a glance at his friend's face as he cupped his hands about a cigarette, and he read approval there. If he had struck the right tone, he knew how to act thenceforth. He flipped the match away and turned abruptly to Thorne. Dr. Reinach was studying him in a half-puzzled, half-amused way.

"Where's the *Caronia*?"

"Held up in quarantine," said Thorne. "Somebody's seriously ill aboard with some disease or other and there's been difficulty in clearing her passengers. It will take hours, I understand. Suppose we settle down in the waiting room for a bit."

They found places in the crowded room, and Ellery set his bag between his feet and disposed himself so that he was in a position to catch every expression on his companions' faces. There was something in Thorne's repressed excitement, an even more piquing aura enveloping the fat doctor, that violently whipped his curiosity.

"Alice," said Thorne in a casual tone, as if Ellery knew who Alice was, "is probably becoming impatient. But that's a family trait with the Mayhews, from the little I saw of old Sylvester. Eh, Doctor? It's trying, though, to

10

come all the way from England only to be held up on the threshold."

So they were to meet an Alice Mayhew, thought Ellery, arriving from England on the *Caronia*. Good old Thorne! He almost chuckled aloud. "Sylvester" was obviously a senior Mayhew, some relative of Alice's.

Dr. Reinach fixed his little eyes on Ellery's bag and rumbled politely: "Are you going away somewhere, Mr. Queen?"

Then Reinach did not know Ellery was to accompany them—wherever they were bound for.

Thorne stirred in the depths of his greatcoat, rustling like a sack of desiccated bones. "Queen's coming back with me, Dr. Reinach." There was something brittle and hostile in his voice.

The fat man blinked, his eyes buried beneath half-moons of damp flesh. "Really?" he said, and by contrast his bass voice was tender.

"Perhaps I should have explained," said Thorne abruptly. "Queen is a colleague of mine, Doctor. This case has interested him."

"Case?" said the fat man.

"Legally speaking. I really hadn't the heart to deny him the pleasure of helping me—ah—protect Alice Mayhew's interests. I trust you won't mind?"

This was a deadly game, Ellery became certain. Something important was at stake, and Thorne in his stubborn way was determined to defend it by force or guile.

Reinach's puffy lids dropped over his eyes as he folded his paws on his stomach. "Naturally, naturally not," he said in a hearty tone. "Only too happy to have you, Mr. Queen. A little unexpected, perhaps, but delightful surprises are as essential to life as to poetry. Eh?" And he chuckled.

Samuel Johnson, thought Ellery, recognizing the source of the doctor's remark. The physical analogy struck him. There was iron beneath those layers of fat and a good brain under that dolichocephalic skull. The man sat there on the waiting-room bench like an octopus, lazy and inert and peculiarly indifferent to his surroundings. Indifference —that was it, thought Ellery! the man was a colossal remoteness, as vague and darkling as a storm cloud on an empty horizon.

Thorne said in a weary voice: "Suppose we have lunch. I'm famished."

11

By three in the afternoon Ellery felt old and worn. Several hours of nervous, cautious silence, threading his way smiling among treacherous shoals, had told him just enough to put him on guard. He often felt knotted-up and tight inside when a crisis loomed or danger threatened from an unknown quarter. Something extraordinary was going on.

As they stood on the pier watching the *Caronia*'s bulk being nudged alongside, he chewed on the scraps he had managed to glean during the long, heavy, pregnant hours. He knew definitely now that the man called Sylvester Mayhew was dead, that he had been pronounced paranoic, that his house was buried in an almost inaccessible wilderness on Long Island. Alice Mayhew, somewhere on the decks of the *Caronia* doubtless straining her eyes pierward, was the dead man's daughter, parted from her father since childhood.

And he had placed the remarkable figure of Dr. Reinach in the puzzle. The fat man was Sylvester Mayhew's half-brother. He had also acted as Mayhew's physician during the old man's last illness. This illness and death seemed to have been very recent, for there had been some talk of "the funeral" in terms of fresh if detached sorrow. There was also a Mrs. Reinach glimmering unsubstantially in the background, and a queer old lady who was the dead man's sister. But what the mystery was, or why Thorne was so perturbed, Ellery could not figure out.

The liner tied up to the pier at last. Officials scampered about, whistles blew, gangplanks appeared, passengers disembarked in droves to the accompaniment of the usual howls and embraces.

Interest crept into Dr. Reinach's little eyes, and Thorne was shaking.

"There she is!" croaked the lawyer. "I'd know her anywhere from her photographs. That slender girl in the brown turban!"

As Thorne hurried away Ellery studied the girl eagerly. She was anxiously scanning the crowd, a tall charming creature with an elasticity of movement more esthetic than athletic and a harmony of delicate feature that approached beauty. She was dressed so simply and inexpensively that he narrowed his eyes.

Thorne came back with her, patting her gloved hand and speaking quietly to her. Her face was alight and alive, and there was a natural gaiety in it which convinced El-

12

lery that whatever mystery or tragedy lay before her, it was still unknown to her. At the same time there were certain signs about her eyes and mouth—fatigue, strain, worry, he could not put his finger on the exact cause— which puzzled him.

"I'm so glad," she murmured in a cultured voice, strongly British in accent. Then her face grew grave and she looked from Ellery to Dr. Reinach.

"This is your uncle, Miss Mayhew," said Thorne. "Dr. Reinach. This other gentleman is not, I regret to say, a relative. Mr. Ellery Queen, a colleague of mine."

"Oh," said the girl; and she turned to the fat man and said tremulously: "Uncle Herbert. How terribly odd. I mean—I've felt so all alone. You've been just a legend to me, Uncle Herbert, you and Aunt Sarah and the rest, and now . . ." She choked a little as she put her arms about the fat man and kissed his pendulous cheek.

"My dear," said Dr. Reinach solemnly; and Ellery could have struck him for the Judas quality of his solemnity.

"But you must tell me everything! Father—how is Father? It seems so strange to be . . . to be saying that."

"Don't you think, Miss Mayhew," said the lawyer quickly, "that we had better see you through the Customs? It's growing late and we have a long trip before us. Long Island, you know."

"Island?" Her candid eyes widened. "That sounds so exciting!"

"Well, it's not what you might think—"

"Forgive me. I'm acting the perfect gawk." She smiled. "I'm entirely in your hands, Mr. Thorne. Your letter was more than kind."

As they made their way toward the Customs, Ellery dropped a little behind and devoted himself to watching Dr. Reinach. But that vast lunar countenance was as inscrutable as a gargoyle.

Dr. Reinach drove. It was not Thorne's car; Thorne had a regal new Lincoln limousine and this was a battered if serviceable old Buick sedan.

The girl's luggage was strapped to the back and sides; Ellery was puzzled by the scantness of it—three small suitcases and a tiny steamer trunk. Did these four pitiful containers hold all of her worldly possessions?

Sitting beside the fat man, Ellery strained his ears. He paid little attention to the road Reinach was taking.

The two behind were silent for a long time. Then

13

Thorne cleared his throat with an oddly ominous finality. Ellery saw what was coming; he had often heard that throat-clearing sound emanate from the mouths of judges pronouncing sentence of doom.

"We have something sad to tell you, Miss Mayhew. You may as well learn it now."

"Sad?" murmured the girl after a moment. "Sad? Oh, it's not—"

"Your father," said Thorne inaudibly. "He's dead."

She cried: "Oh!" in a small helpless voice; and then she grew quiet.

"I'm dreadfully sorry to have to greet you with such news," said Thorne in the silence. "We'd anticipated. . . . And I realize how awkward it must be for you. After all, it's quite as if you had never known him at all. Love for a parent, I'm afraid, lies in direct ratio to the degree of childhood association. Without any association at all . . ."

"It's a shock, of course," Alice said in a muffled voice. "And yet, as you say, he was a stranger to me, a mere name. As I wrote you, I was only a toddler when Mother got her divorce and took me off to England. I don't remember Father at all. And I've not seen him since, or heard from him."

"Yes," muttered the attorney.

"I might have learned more about Father if Mother hadn't died when I was six; but she did, and my people— her people—in England . . . Uncle John died last fall. He was the last one. And then I was left all alone. When your letter came I was—I was so glad, Mr. Thorne. I didn't feel lonely any more. I was really happy for the first time in years. And now—" She broke off to stare out the window.

Dr. Reinach swiveled his massive head and smiled benignly. "But you're not alone, my dear. There's my unworthy self, and your Aunt Sarah, and Milly—Milly's my wife, Alice; naturally you wouldn't know anything about her—and there's even a husky young fellow named Keith who works about the place—bright lad who's come down in the world." He chuckled. "So you see there won't be a dearth of companionship for you."

"Thank you, Uncle Herbert," she murmured. "I'm sure you're all terribly kind. Mr. Thorne, how did Father . . . When you replied to my letter you wrote me he was ill, but—"

"He fell into a coma unexpectedly nine days ago. You

14

hadn't left England yet and I cabled you at your antique-shop address. But somehow it missed you."

"I'd sold the shop by that time and was flying about, patching up things. When did he . . . die?"

"A week ago Thursday. The funeral . . . Well, we couldn't wait, you see. I might have caught you by cable or telephone on the *Caronia*, but I didn't have the heart to spoil your voyage."

"I don't know how to thank you for all the trouble you've taken." Without looking at her Ellery knew there were tears in her eyes. "It's good to know that someone—"

"It's been hard for all of us," rumbled Dr. Reinach.

"Of course, Uncle Herbert. I'm sorry." She fell silent. When she spoke again, it was as if there were a compulsion expelling the words. "When Uncle John died, I didn't know where to reach Father. The only American address I had was yours, Mr. Thorne, which some patron or other had given me. It was the only thing I could think of. I was sure a solicitor could find Father for me. That's why I wrote to you in such detail, with photographs and all."

"Naturally we did what we could." Thorne seemed to be having difficulty with his voice. "When I found your father and went out to see him the first time and showed him your letter and photographs, he . . . I'm sure this will please you, Miss Mayhew. He wanted you badly. He'd apparently been having a hard time of late years—ah, mentally, emotionally. And so I wrote you at his request. On my second visit, the last time I saw him alive, when the question of the estate came up—"

Ellery thought that Dr. Reinach's paws tightened on the wheel. But the fat man's face bore the same bland, remote smile.

"Please," said Alice wearily. "Do you greatly mind, Mr. Thorne? I—I don't feel up to discussing such matters now."

The car was fleeing along the deserted road as if it were trying to run away from the weather. The sky was gray lead; a frowning, gloomy sky under which the countryside lay cowering. It was growing colder, too, in the dark and drafty tonneau; the cold seeped in through the cracks and their overclothes.

Ellery stamped his feet a little and twisted about to glance at Alice Mayhew. Her oval face was a glimmer in the murk; she was sitting stiffly, her hands clenched into

15

tight little fists in her lap. Thorne was slumped miserably by her side, staring out the window.

"By George, it's going to snow," announced Dr. Reinach with a cheerful puff of his cheeks.

No one answered.

The drive was interminable. There was a dreary sameness about the landscape that matched the weather's mood. They had long since left the main highway to turn into a frightful byroad, along which they jolted in an unsteady eastward curve between ranks of leafless woods. The road was pitted and frozen hard; the woods were tangles of dead trees and underbrush densely packed but looking as if they had been repeatedly seared by fire. The whole effect was one of widespread and oppressive desolation.

"Looks like No Man's Land," said Ellery at last from his bouncing seat beside Dr. Reinach. "And feels like it, too."

Dr. Reinach's cetaceous back heaved in a silent mirth. "Matter of fact, that's exactly what it's called by the natives. Land-God-forgot, eh? But then Sylvester always swore by the Greek unities."

The man seemed to live in a dark and silent cavern, out of which he maliciously emerged at intervals to poison the atmosphere.

"It isn't very inviting-looking, is it?" remarked Alice in a low voice. It was clear she was brooding over the strange old man who had lived in this wasteland, and of her mother who had fled from it so many years before.

"It wasn't always this way," said Dr. Reinach, swelling his cheeks like a bullfrog. "Once it was pleasant enough; I remember it as a boy. Then it seemed as if it might become the nucleus of a populous community. But progress has passed it by, and a couple of uncontrollable forest fires did the rest."

"It's horrible," murmured Alice, "simply horrible."

"My dear Alice, it's your innocence that speaks there. All life is a frantic struggle to paint a rosy veneer over the ugly realities. Why not be honest with yourself? Everything in this world is stinking rotten; worse than that, a bore. Hardly worth living, in any impartial analysis. But if you have to live, you may as well live in surroundings consistent with the rottenness of everything."

The old attorney stirred beside Alice, where he was

16

buried in his greatcoat. "You're quite a philosopher, Doctor," he snarled.

"I'm an honest man."

"Do you know, Doctor," murmured Ellery, despite himself, "you're beginning to annoy me."

The fat man glanced at him. Then he said: "And do you agree with this mysterious friend of yours, Thorne?"

"I believe," snapped Thorne, "that there is a platitude extant which says that actions speak with considerably more volume than words. I haven't shaved for six days, and today has been the first time I left Sylvester Mayhew's house since his funeral."

"Mr. Thorne!" cried Alice, turning to him. "Why?"

The lawyer muttered: "I'm sorry, Miss Mayhew. All in good time, in good time."

"You wrong us all," smiled Dr. Reinach, deftly skirting a deep rut in the road. "And I'm afraid you're giving my niece quite the most erroneous impression of her family. We're odd, no doubt, and our blood is presumably turning sour after so many generations of cold storage; but then don't the finest vintages come from the deepest cellars? You've only to glance at Alice to see my point. Such vital loveliness could only have been produced by an old family."

"My mother," said Alice, with a faint loathing in her glance, "had something to do with that, Uncle Herbert."

"Your mother, my dear," replied the fat man, "was merely a contributory factor. You have the typical Mayhew features."

Alice did not reply. Her uncle, whom until today she had not seen, was an obscene enigma; the others, waiting for them at their destination, she had never seen at all, and she had no great hope that they would prove better. A livid streak ran through her father's family; he had been a paranoiac with delusions of persecution. The Aunt Sarah in the dark distance, her father's surviving sister, was apparently something of a character. As for Aunt Milly, Dr. Reinach's wife, whatever she might have been in the past, one had only to glance at Dr. Reinach to see what she undoubtedly was in the present.

Ellery felt prickles at the nape of his neck. The farther they penetrated this wilderness the less he liked the whole adventure. It smacked vaguely of a foreordained theatricalism, as if some hand of monstrous power were setting the stage for the first act of a colossal tragedy. . . . He

17

shrugged this sophomoric foolishness off, settling deeper into his coat. It was queer enough, though. Even the life-lines of the most indigent community were missing; there were no telephone poles and, so far as he could detect, no electric cables. That meant candles. He detested candles.

The sun was behind them, leaving them. It was a feeble sun, shivering in the pallid cold. Feeble as it was, Ellery wished it would stay.

They crashed on and on, endlessly, shaken like dolls. The road kept lurching toward the east in a stubborn curve. The sky grew more and more leaden. The cold seeped deeper and deeper into their bones.

When Dr. Reinach finally rumbled: "Here we are," and steered the jolting car leftward off the road into a narrow, wretchedly graveled driveway, Ellery came to with a start of surprise and relief. So their journey was really over, he thought. Behind him he heard Thorne and Alice stirring; they must be thinking the same thing.

He roused himself, stamping his icy feet, looking about. The same desolate tangle of woods to either side of the byroad. He recalled now that they had not once left the main road nor crossed another road since turning off the highway. No chance, he thought grimly, to stray off this path to perdition.

Dr. Reinach twisted his fat neck and said: "Welcome home, Alice."

Alice murmured something incomprehensible; her face was buried to the eyes in the moth-eaten laprobe Reinach had flung over her. Ellery glanced sharply at the fat man; there had been a note of mockery, of derision, in that heavy rasping voice. But the face was smooth and damp and bland, as before.

Dr. Reinach ran the car up the driveway and brought it to a rest a little before, and between, two houses. These structures flanked the drive, standing side by side, separated by only the width of the drive, which led straight ahead to a ramshackle garage. Ellery caught a glimpse of Thorne's glittering Lincoln within its crumbling walls.

The three buildings huddled in a ragged clearing, surrounded by the tangle of woods, like three desert islands in an empty sea.

"That," said Dr. Reinach heartily, "is the ancestral mansion, Alice. To the left."

The house to the left was of stone; once gray, but now so tarnished by the elements and perhaps the ravages of fire that it was almost black. Its face was blotched and streaky, as if it had succumbed to an insensate leprosy. Rising three stories, elaborately ornamented with stone flora and gargoyles, it was unmistakably Victorian in its architecture. The façade had a neglected, granular look that only the art of great age could have etched. The whole structure appeared to have thrust its roots immovably into the forsaken landscape.

Ellery saw Alice Mayhew staring at it with a sort of speechless horror; it had nothing of the pleasant hoariness of old English mansions. It was simply old, old with the dreadful age of this seared and blasted countryside. He cursed Thorne beneath his breath for subjecting the girl to such a shocking experience.

"Sylvester called it 'the Black House,'" said Dr. Reinach cheerfully as he turned off the ignition. "Not pretty, I admit, but as solid as the day it was built, seventy-five years ago."

"Black House," grunted Thorne. "Rubbish."

"Do you mean to say," whispered Alice, "that Father ... Mother lived here?"

"Yes, my dear. Quaint name, eh, Thorne? Another illustration of Sylvester's preoccupation with the morbidly colorful. Built by your grandfather, Alice. The old gentleman built this one, too, later; I believe you'll find it considerably more habitable. Where the devil is everyone?"

He descended heavily and held the rear door open for his niece. Mr. Ellery Queen slipped down to the driveway on the other side and glanced about with the sharp, uneasy sniff of a wild animal. The old mansion's companion house was a much smaller and less pretentious dwelling, two stories high and built of an originally white stone which had turned gray. The front door was shut and the curtains at the lower windows were drawn. But there was a fire burning somewhere inside; he caught the tremulous glimmers. In the next moment they were blotted out by the head of an old woman, who pressed her face to one of the panes for a single instant and then vanished. But the door remained shut.

"You'll stop with us, of course," he heard the doctor say genially; and Ellery circled the car. His three companions were standing in the driveway, Alice pressed close to old Thorne as if for protection. "You won't want to sleep in the Black House, Alice. No one's there, it's in rather a mess; and a house of death, y'know ..."

19

"Stop it," growled Thorne. "Can't you see the poor child is half-dead from fright as it is? Are you trying to scare her away?"

"Scare me away?" repeated Alice, dazedly.

"Tut, tut," smiled the fat man. "Melodrama doesn't become you at all, Thorne. I'm a blunt old codger, Alice, but I mean well. It will really be more comfortable in the White House." He chuckled suddenly again. "White House. That's what *I* named it to preserve a sort of atmospheric balance."

"There's something frightfully wrong here," said Alice in a tight voice. "Mr. Thorne, what is it? There's been nothing but innuendo and concealed hostility since we met at the pier. And just why *did* you spend six days in Father's house after the funeral? I think I've a right to know."

Thorne licked his lips. "I shouldn't—"

"Come, come, my dear," said the fat man. "Are we to freeze here all day?"

Alice drew her thin coat more closely about her. "You're all being beastly. Would you mind, Uncle Herbert? I should like to see the inside—where Father and Mother . . ."

"I don't think so, Miss Mayhew," said Thorne hastily.

"Why not?" said Dr. Reinach tenderly, and he glanced once over his shoulder at the building he had called the White House. "She may as well do it now and get it over with. There's still light enough to see by. Then we'll go over, wash up, have a hot dinner, and you'll feel worlds better." He seized the girl's arm and marched her toward the dark building, across the dead, twig-strewn ground. "I believe," continued the doctor blandly, as they mounted the steps of the stone porch, "that Mr. Thorne has the keys."

The girl stood quietly waiting, her dark eyes studying the faces of the three men. The attorney was pale, but his lips were set in a stubborn line. He did not reply. Taking a bunch of large rusty keys out of a pocket, he fitted one into the lock of the front door. It turned over with a creak.

Then Thorne pushed open the door and they stepped into the house.

It was a tomb. It smelled of must and damp. The furniture, ponderous pieces which once no doubt had been

20

regal, was uniformly dilapidated and dusty. The walls were peeling, showing broken, discolored laths beneath. There was dirt and débris everywhere. It was inconceivable that a human being could once have inhabited this grubby den.

The girl stumbled about, her eyes a blank horror, Dr. Reinach steering her calmly. How long the tour of inspection lasted Ellery did not know; even to him, a stranger, the effect was so oppressive as to be almost unendurable. They wandered about, silent, stepping over trash from room to room, impelled by something stronger than themselves.

Once Alice said in a strangled voice: "Uncle Herbert, didn't anyone . . . take care of Father? Didn't anyone ever clean up this horrible place?"

The fat man shrugged. "Your father had notions in his old age, my dear. There wasn't much anyone could do with him. Perhaps we had better not go into that."

The sour stench filled their nostrils. They blundered on, Thorne in the rear, watchful as an old cobra. His eyes never left Dr. Reinach's face.

On the middle floor they came upon a bedroom in which, according to the fat man, Sylvester Mayhew had died. The bed was unmade; indeed, the impress of the dead man's body on the mattress and tumbled sheets could still be discerned.

It was a bare and mean room, not as filthy as the others, but infinitely more depressing. Alice began to cough.

She coughed and coughed, hopelessly, standing still in the center of the room and staring at the dirty bed in which she had been born.

Then suddenly she stopped coughing and ran over to a lopsided bureau with one foot missing. A large, faded chromo was propped on its top against the yellowed wall. She looked at it for a long time without touching it. Then she took it down.

"It's Mother," she said slowly. "It's really Mother. I'm glad now I came. He did love her, after all. He's kept it all these years."

"Yes, Miss Mayhew," muttered Thorne. "I thought you'd like to have it."

"I've only one portrait of Mother, and that's a poor one. This—why, she was beautiful, wasn't she?"

She held the chromo up proudly, almost laughing in

21

her hysteria. The time-dulled colors revealed a stately young woman with her hair worn high. The features were piquant and regular. There was little resemblance between Alice and the woman in the picture.

"Your father," said Dr. Reinach with a sigh, "often spoke of your mother toward the last, and of her beauty."

"If he had left me nothing but this, it would have been worth the trip from England." Alice trembled a little. Then she hurried back to them, the chromo pressed to her breast. "Let's get out of here," she said in a shriller voice. "I—I don't like it here. It's ghastly. I'm . . . afraid."

They left the house with half-running steps, as if someone were after them. The old lawyer turned the key in the lock of the front door with great care, glaring at Dr. Reinach's back as he did so. But the fat man had seized his niece's arm and was leading her across the driveway to the White House, whose windows were now flickeringly bright with light and whose front door stood wide open.

As they crunched along behind, Ellery said sharply to Thorne: "Thorne. Give me a clue. A hint. Anything. I'm completely in the dark."

Thorne's unshaven face was haggard in the setting sun. "Can't talk now," he muttered. "Suspect everything, everybody. I'll see you tonight, in your room. Or wherever they put you, if you're alone. . . . Queen, for God's sake, be careful!"

"Careful?" frowned Ellery.

"As if your life depended on it." Thorne's lips made a thin, grim line. "For all I know, it does."

Then they were crossing the threshold of the White House.

Ellery's impressions were curiously vague. Perhaps it was the effect of the sudden smothering heat after the hours of cramping cold outdoors; perhaps he thawed out too suddenly, and the heat went to his brain.

He stood about for a while in a state of almost semi-consciousness, basking in the waves of warmth that eddied from a roaring fire in a fireplace black with age. He was only dimly aware of the two people who greeted them, and of the interior of the house. The room was old, like everything else he had seen, and its furniture might have come from an antique shop. They were standing in a large living room, comfortable enough; strange to his senses only because it was so old-fashioned in its appointments. There were actually antimacassars on the overstuffed chairs! A wide staircase with worn brass treads wound from one corner to the sleeping quarters above.

One of the two persons awaiting them was Mrs. Reinach, the doctor's wife. The moment Ellery saw her, even as she embraced Alice, he knew that this was inevitably the sort of woman the fat man would choose for a mate. She was a pale and wizened midge, almost fragile in her delicacy of bone and skin; and she was plainly in a silent convulsion of fear. She wore a hunted look on her dry and bluish face; and over Alice's shoulder she glanced timidly, with the fascinated obedience of a whipped bitch, at her husband.

"So, you're Aunt Milly," sighed Alice, pushing away. "You'll forgive me if I . . . It's all so very new to me."

"You must be exhausted, poor darling," said Mrs. Reinach in the chirping twitter of a bird; and Alice smiled wanly and looked grateful. "And I quite understand. After all, we're no more than strangers to you. Oh!" she said, and stopped. Her faded eyes were fixed on the chromo in the girl's hands. "Oh," she said again. "I see you've been over to the other house *already*."

"Of course she has," said the fat man; and his wife grew even paler at the sound of his bass voice. "Now, Alice, why don't you let Milly take you upstairs and get you comfortable?"

"I am rather done in," confessed Alice; and then she looked at her mother's picture and smiled again. "I suppose you think I'm very silly, dashing in this way with just—" She did not finish; instead, she went to the fireplace. There was a broad flame-darkened mantel above it, crowded with gew-gaws of a vanished era. She set the chromo of the handsome Victorian-garbed woman among them. "There! Now I feel ever so much better."

"Gentlemen, gentlemen," said Dr. Reinach. "Please don't stand on ceremony. Nick! Make yourself useful. Miss Mayhew's bags are strapped to the car."

A gigantic young man, who had been leaning against the wall, nodded in a surly way. He was studying Alice Mayhew's face with a dark absorption. He went out.

"Who," murmured Alice, flushing, "is that?"

"Nick Keith." The fat man slipped off his coat and went to the fire to warm his flabby hands. "My morose protégé. You'll find him pleasant company, my dear, if you can

23

pierce that thick defensive armor he wears. Does odd jobs about the place, as I believe I mentioned, but don't let that hold you back. This is a democratic country."

"I'm sure he's very nice. Would you excuse me? Aunt Milly, if you'd be kind enough to . . ."

The young man reappeared under a load of baggage, clumped across the living room, and plodded up the stairs. And suddenly, as if at a signal, Mrs. Reinach broke out into a noisy twittering and took Alice's arm and led her to the staircase. They disappeared after Keith.

"As a medical man," chuckled the fat man, taking their wraps and depositing them in a hall closet, "I prescribe a large dose of . . . this, gentlemen." He went to a sideboard and brought out a decanter of brandy. "Very good for chilled bellies." He tossed off his own glass with an amazing facility, and in the light of the fire the finely etched capillaries in his bulbous nose stood out clearly. "Ah-h! One of life's major compensations. Warming, eh? And now I suppose you feel the need of a little sprucing up yourselves. Come along, and I'll show you to your rooms."

Ellery shook his head in a dogged way, trying to clear it. "There's something about your house, Doctor, that's unusually soporific. Thank you, I think both Thorne and I would appreciate a brisk wash."

"You'll find it brisk enough," said the fat man, shaking with silent laughter. "This is the forest primeval, you know. Not only haven't we any electric light or gas or telephone, but we've no running water, either. Well behind the house keeps us supplied. The simple life, eh? Better for you than the pampering influences of modern civilization. Our ancestors may have died more easily of bacterial infections, but I'll wager they had a greater body immunity to coryza! . . . Well, well, enough of this prattle. Up you go."

The chilly corridor upstairs made them shiver, but the very shiver revived them; Ellery felt better at once. Dr. Reinach, carrying candles and matches, showed Thorne into a room overlooking the front of the house, and Ellery into one on the side. A fire burned crisply in the large fireplace in one corner, and the basin on the old-fashioned washstand was filled with icy-looking water.

"Hope you find it comfortable," drawled the fat man, lounging in the doorway. "We were expecting only Thorne

24

and my niece, but one more can always be accommodated. Ah—colleague of Thorne's, I believe he said?"

"Twice," replied Ellery. "If you don't mind—"

"Not at all." Reinach lingered, eyeing Ellery with a smile. Ellery shrugged, stripped off his coat, and made his ablutions. The water *was* cold; it nipped his fingers like the mouths of little fishes. He scrubbed his face vigorously.

"That's better," he said, drying himself. "Much. I wonder why I felt so peaked downstairs."

"Sudden contrast of heat after cold, no doubt." Dr. Reinach made no move to go.

Ellery shrugged again. He opened his bag with pointed nonchalance. There, plainly revealed on his haberdashery, lay the .38 police revolver. He tossed it aside.

"Do you always carry a gun, Mr. Queen?" murmured Dr. Reinach.

"Always." Ellery picked up the revolver and slipped it into his hip pocket.

"Charming!" The fat man stroked his triple chin. "Charming. Well, Mr. Queen, if you'll excuse me I'll see how Thorne is getting on. Stubborn fellow, Thorne. He could have taken pot luck with us this past week, but he insisted on isolating himself in that filthy den next door."

"I wonder," murmured Ellery, "why."

Dr. Reinach eyed him. Then he said: "Come downstairs when you're ready. Mrs. Reinach has an excellent dinner prepared and if you're as hungry as I am, you'll appreciate it." Still smiling, the fat man vanished.

Ellery stood still for a moment, listening. He heard the fat man pause at the end of the corridor; a moment later the heavy tread was audible again, this time descending the stairs.

Ellery went swiftly to the door on tiptoe. He had noticed that the instant he had come into the room.

There was no lock. Where a lock had been there was a splintery hole, and the splinters had a newish look about them. Frowning, he placed a rickety chair against the doorknob and began to prowl.

He raised the mattress from the heavy wooden bedstead and poked beneath it, searching for he knew not what. He opened closets and drawers; he felt the worn carpet for wires.

But after ten minutes, angry with himself, he gave up and went to the window. The prospect was so dismal

25

that he scowled in sheer misery. Just brown stripped woods and the leaden sky; the old mansion picturesquely known as the Black House was on the other side, invisible from this window.

A veiled sun was setting; a bank of storm clouds slipped aside for an instant and the brilliant rim of the sun shone directly into his eyes, making him see colored, dancing balls. Then other clouds, fat with snow, moved up and the sun slipped below the horizon. The room darkened rapidly.

Lock taken out, eh? Someone had worked fast. They could not have known he was coming, of course. Then someone must have seen him through the window as the car stopped in the drive. The old woman who had peered out for a moment? Ellery wondered where she was. At any rate, a few minutes' work by a skilled hand at the door . . . He wondered, too, if Thorne's door had been similarly mutilated. And Alice Mayhew's.

Thorne and Dr. Reinach were already seated before the fire when Ellery came down, and the fat man was rumbling: "Just as well. Give the poor girl a chance to return to normal. With the shock she's had today, it might be the finisher. I've told Mrs. Reinach to break it to Sarah gently. . . . Ah, Queen. Come over here and join us. We'll have dinner as soon as Alice comes down."

"Dr. Reinach was just apologizing," said Thorne casually, "for this Aunt Sarah of Miss Mayhew's—Mrs. Fell, Sylvester Mayhew's sister. The excitement of anticipating her niece's arrival seems to have been a bit too much for her."

"Indeed," said Ellery, sitting down and planting his feet on the nearest firedog.

"Fact is," said the fat man," "my poor half-sister is cracked. The family paranoia. She's off-balance; not violent, you know, but it's wise to humor her. She isn't normal, and for Alice to see her—"

"Paranoia," said Ellery. "An unfortunate family, it seems. Your half-brother Sylvester's weakness seems to have expressed itself in rubbish and solitude. What's Mrs. Fell's delusion?"

"Common enough—she thinks her daughter is still alive. As a matter of fact, poor Olivia was killed in an automobile accident three years ago. It shocked Sarah's maternal instinct out of plumb. Sarah's been looking forward to seeing Alice, her brother's daughter, and it may prove

26

awkward. Never can tell how a diseased mind will react to an unusual situation."

"For that matter," drawled Ellery, "I should have said the same remark might be made about any mind, diseased or not."

Dr. Reinach laughed silently. Thorne, hunched by the fire, said: "This Keith boy."

The fat man set his glass down slowly. "Drink, Queen?"

"No, thank you."

"This Keith boy," said Thorne again.

"Eh? Oh, Nick. Yes, Thorne? What about him?"

The lawyer shrugged. Dr. Reinach picked up his glass again. "Am I imagining things, or is there the vaguest hint of hostility in the circumambient ether?"

"Reinach—" began Thorne harshly.

"Don't worry about Keith, Thorne. We let him pretty much alone. He's sour on the world, which demonstrates his good sense; but I'm afraid he's unlike me in that he hasn't the emotional buoyancy to rise above his wisdom. You'll probably find him anti-social. . . . Ah, there you are, my dear! Lovely, lovely."

Alice was wearing a different gown, a simple unfrilled frock, and she had freshened up. There was color in her cheeks and her eyes were sparkling with a light and tinge they had not had before. Seeing her for the first time without her hat and coat, Ellery thought she looked different, as all women contrive to look different divested of their outer clothing and refurbished by the mysterious activities which go on behind the closed doors of feminine dressing rooms. Apparently the ministrations of another woman, too, had cheered her; there were still rings under her eyes, but her smile was more cheerful.

"Thank you, Uncle Herbert." Her voice was slightly husky. "But I do think I've caught a nasty cold."

"Whisky and hot lemonade," said the fat man promptly. "Eat lightly and go to bed early."

"To tell the truth, I'm famished."

"Then eat as much as you like. I'm one hell of a physician, as no doubt you've already detected. Shall we go in to dinner?"

"Yes," said Mrs. Reinach in a frightened voice. "We shan't wait for Sarah or Nicholas."

Alice's eyes dulled a little. Then she sighed and took the fat man's arm and they all trooped into the dining room.

27

Dinner was a failure. Dr. Reinach divided his energies between gargantuan inroads on the viands and copious drinking. Mrs. Reinach donned an apron and served, scarcely touching her own food in her haste to prepare the next course and clear the plates; apparently the household employed no domestic. Alice gradually lost her color, the old strained look reappearing on her face; occasionally she cleared her throat. The oil lamp on the table flickered badly, and every mouthful Ellery swallowed was flavored with the taste of oil. Besides, the *pièce de résistance* was curried lamb; if there was one dish he detested, it was lamb, and if there was one culinary style that sickened him, it was curry. Thorne ate stolidly, not raising his eyes from his plate.

As they returned to the living room the old lawyer managed to drop behind. He whispered to Alice: "Is everything all right? Are you?"

"I'm a little scarish, I think," she said quietly. "Mr. Thorne, please don't think me a child, but there's something so strange about—everything. . . . I wish now I hadn't come."

"I know," muttered Thorne. "And yet it was necessary, quite necessary. If there was any way to spare you this, I should have taken it. But you obviously couldn't stay in that horrible hole next door—"

"Oh, no," she shuddered.

"And there isn't a hotel for miles and miles. Miss Mayhew, has any of these people—"

"No, no. It's just that they're so strange to me. I suppose it's my imagination and this cold. Would you greatly mind if I went to bed? Tomorrow will be time enough to talk."

Thorne patted her hand. She smiled gratefully, murmured an apology, kissed Dr. Reinach's cheek, and went upstairs with Mrs. Reinach again.

They had just settled themselves before the fire again and were lighting cigarettes when feet stamped somewhere at the rear of the house.

"Must be Nick," wheezed the doctor. "Now where's *he* been?"

The gigantic young man appeared in the living-room archway, glowering. His boots were soggy with wet. He growled, "Hello," in his surly manner and went to the fire to toast his big reddened hands. He paid no attention whatever to Thorne, although he glanced once, swiftly, at Ellery in passing.

"Where've you been, Nick? Go in and have your dinner."

"I ate before you came."

"What's been keeping you?"

"I've been hauling in firewood. Something you didn't think of doing." Keith's tone was truculent, but, Ellery noticed that his hands were shaking. Damnably odd! His manner was noticeably not that of a servant, and yet he was apparently employed in a menial capacity. "It's snowing."

"Snowing?"

They crowded to the front windows. The night was moonless and palpable, and big fat snowflakes were sliding down the panes.

"Ah, snow," sighed Dr. Reinach; and for all the sigh there was something in his tone that made the nape of Ellery's neck prickle. " 'The whited air hides hills and woods, the river, and the heaven, and veils the farmhouse at the garden's end.' "

"You're quite the countryman, Doctor," said Ellery.

"I like Nature in her more turbulent moods. Spring is for milksops. Winter brings out the fundamental iron." The doctor slipped his arm about Keith's broad shoulders. "Smile, Nick. Isn't God in His heaven?"

Keith flung the arm off without replying.

"Oh, you haven't met Mr. Queen. Queen, this is Nick Keith. You know Mr. Thorne already." Keith nodded shortly. "Come, come, my boy, buck up. You're too emotional, that's the trouble with you. Let's all have a drink. The disease of nervousness is infectious."

Nerves! thought Ellery grimly. His nostrils were pinched, sniffing the little mysteries in the air. They tantalized him. Thorne was tied up in knots, as if he had cramps; the veins at his temples were pale blue swollen cords and there was sweat on his forehead. Above their heads the house was soundless. Dr. Reinach went to the sideboard and began hauling out bottles—gin, bitters, rye, vermouth. He busied himself mixing drinks, talking incessantly. There was a purr in his hoarse undertones, a vibration of pure excitement. What in Satan's name, thought Ellery in a sort of agony, was going on here?

Keith passed the cocktails around, and Ellery's eyes warned Thorne. Thorne nodded slightly; they had two drinks apiece and refused more. Keith drank doggedly, as if he were anxious to forget something.

"Now that's better," said Dr. Reinach, settling his bulk into an easy chair. "With the women out of the way and a fire and liquor, life becomes almost endurable."

"I'm afraid," said Thorne, "that I shall prove an unpleasant influence, Doctor. I'm going to make it unendurable."

Dr. Reinach blinked. "Well, now," he said. "Well, now." He pushed the brandy decanter carefully out of the way of his elbow and folded his pudgy paws on his stomach. His purple little eyes shone.

Thorne went to the fire and stood looking down at the flames, his back to them. "I'm here in Miss Mayhew's interests, Dr. Reinach," he said, without turning. "In her interests alone. Sylvester Mayhew died last week very suddenly. Died while waiting to see the daughter whom he hadn't seen since his divorce from her mother almost twenty years ago."

"Factually exact," rumbled the doctor, without stirring.

Thorne spun about. "Dr. Reinach, you acted as Mayhew's physician for over a year before his death. What was the matter with him?"

"A variety of things. Nothing extraordinary. He died of cerebral hemorrhage."

"So your certificate claimed." The lawyer leaned forward. "I'm not entirely convinced," he said slowly, "that your certificate told the truth."

The doctor stared at him for an instant, then he slapped his bulging thigh. "Splendid!" he roared. "Splendid! a man after my own heart. Thorne, for all your desiccated exterior you have juicy potentialities." He turned on Ellery, beaming. "You heard that, Mr. Queen? Your friend openly accuses me of murder. This is becoming quite exhilarating. So! Old Reinach's a fratricide. What do you think of that, Nick? Your patron accused of cold-blooded murder. Dear, dear."

"That's ridiculous, Mr. Thorne," growled Nick Keith. "You don't believe it yourself."

The lawyer's gaunt cheeks sucked in. "Whether I believe it or not is immaterial. The possibility exists. But I'm more concerned with Alice Mayhew's interests at the moment than with a possible homicide. Sylvester Mayhew is dead, no matter by what agency—divine or human; but Alice Mayhew is very much alive."

"And so?" asked Reinach softly.

"And so I say," muttered Thorne, "it's damnably queer her father should have died when he did. Damnably."

For a long moment there was silence. Keith put his elbows on his knees and stared into the flames, his shaggy boyish hair over his eyes. Dr. Reinach sipped a glass of brandy with enjoyment.

Then he set his glass down and said with a sigh: "Life is too short, gentlemen, to waste in cautious skirmishings. Let us proceed without feinting movements to the major engagement. Nick Keith is in my confidence and we may speak freely before him." The young man did not move. "Mr. Queen, you're very much in the dark, aren't you?" went on the fat man with a bland smile.

Ellery did not move, either. "And how," he murmured, "did you know that?"

Reinach kept smiling. "Pshaw. Thorne hadn't left the Black House since Sylvester's funeral. Nor did he receive or send any mail during his self-imposed vigil last week. This morning he left me on the pier to telephone someone. You showed up shortly after. Since he was gone only a minute or two, it was obvious that he hadn't had time to tell you much, if anything. Allow me to felicitate you, Mr. Queen, upon your conduct today. It's been exemplary. An air of omniscience covering a profound and desperate ignorance."

Ellery removed his pince-nez and began to polish their lenses. "You're a psychologist as well as a physician, I see."

Thorne said abruptly: "This is all beside the point."

"No, no, it's all very much *to* the point," replied the fat man in a sad bass. "Now the canker annoying your friend, Mr. Queen—since it seems a shame to keep you on tenterhooks any longer—is roughly this: My half-brother Sylvester, God rest his troubled soul, was a miser. If he'd been able to take his gold with him to the grave—with any assurance that it would remain there—I'm sure he would have done it."

"Gold?" asked Ellery, raising his brows.

"You may well titter, Mr. Queen. There was something medieval about Sylvester; you almost expected him to go about in a long black velvet gown muttering incantations in Latin. At any rate, unable to take his gold with him to the grave, he did the next best thing. He hid it."

31

"Oh, lord," said Ellery. "You'll be pulling clanking ghosts out of your hat next."

"Hid," beamed Dr. Reinach, "the filthy lucre in the Black House."

"And Miss Alice Mayhew?"

"Poor child, a victim of circumstances. Sylvester never thought of her until recently, when she wrote from London that her last maternal relative had died. Wrote to friend Thorne, he of the lean and hungry eye, who had been recommended by some friend as a trustworthy lawyer. As he is, as he is! You see, Alice didn't even know if her father was alive, let alone where he was. Thorne, good Samaritan, located us, gave Alice's exhaustive letters and photographs to Sylvester, and has acted as liaison officer ever since. And a downright circumspect one, too, by thunder!"

"This explanation is wholly unnecessary," said the lawyer stiffly. "Mr. Queen knows—"

"Nothing," smiled the fat man, "to judge by the attentiveness with which he's been following my little tale. Let's be intelligent about this, Thorne." He turned to Ellery again, nodding very amiably. "Now, Mr. Queen, Sylvester clutched at the thought of his new-found daughter with the pertinacity of a drowning man clutching a life preserver. I betray no secret when I say that my half-brother, in his paranoiac dotage, suspected his own family—imagine!—of having evil designs on his fortune."

"A monstrous slander, of course."

"Neatly put, neatly put! Well, Sylvester told Thorne in my presence that he had long since converted his fortune into specie, that he'd hidden this gold somewhere in the house next door, and that he wouldn't reveal the hiding place to anyone but Alice, his daughter, who was to be his sole heir. You see?"

"I see," said Ellery.

"He died before Alice's arrival, unfortunately. Is it any wonder, Mr. Queen, that Thorne thinks dire things of us?"

"This is fantastic," snapped Thorne, coloring. "Naturally, in the interests of my client, I couldn't leave the premises unguarded with that mass of gold lying about loose somewhere—"

"Naturally not," nodded the doctor.

"If I may intrude my still, small voice," murmured Ellery, "isn't this a battle of giants over a mouse? The possession of gold is a clear violation of the law in this country, and has been for several years. Even if you found it, wouldn't the government confiscate it?"

"There's a complicated legal situation, Queen," said Thorne; "but one which cannot come into existence before the gold is found. Therefore my efforts to—"

"And successful efforts, too," grinned Dr. Reinach. "Do you know, Mr. Queen, your friend has slept behind locked, barred doors, with an old cutlass in his hand—one of Sylvester's prized mementoes of a grandfather who was in the Navy? It's terribly amusing."

"I don't find it so," said Thorne shortly. "If you insist on playing the buffoon—"

"And yet—to go back to this matter of your little suspicions, Thorne—have you analyzed the facts? Whom do you suspect, my dear fellow? Your humble servant? I assure you that I am spiritually an ascetic—"

"An almighty fat one!" snarled Thorne.

"—and that money, *per se*, means nothing to me," went on the doctor imperturbably. "My half-sister Sarah? An anile wreck living in a world of illusion, quite as antediluvian as Sylvester—they were twins, you know—who isn't very long for this world. Then that leaves my estimable Milly and our saturnine young friend Nick. Milly? Absurd; she hasn't had an idea, good or bad, for two decades. Nick? Ah, an outsider—we may have struck something there. Is it Nick you suspect, Thorne?" chuckled Dr. Reinach.

Keith got to his feet and glared down into the bland, damp, lunar countenance of the fat man. He seemed quite drunk. "You damned porker," he said thickly.

Dr. Reinach kept smiling, but his little porcine eyes were wary. "Now, now, Nick," he said in a soothing rumble.

It all happened very quickly. Keith lurched forward, snatched the heavy cut-glass brandy decanter, and swung it at the doctor's head. Thorne cried out and took an instinctive forward step; but he might have spared himself the exertion. Dr. Reinach jerked his head back like a fat snake and the blow missed. The violent effort pivoted Keith's body completely about; the decanter slipped from his fingers and flew into the fireplace, crashing to pieces. The fragments splattered all over the fireplace, strewing the hearth, too; the little brandy that remained in the bottle hissed into the fire, blazing with a blue flame.

33

"That decanter," said Dr. Reinach angrily, "was almost a hundred and fifty years old!"

Keith stood still, his broad back to them. They could see his shoulders heaving.

Ellery sighed with the queerest feeling. The room was shimmering as in a dream, and the whole incident seemed unreal, like a scene in a play on a stage. Were they acting? Had the scene been carefully planned? But, if so, why? What earthly purpose could they have hoped to achieve by pretending to quarrel and come to blows? The sole result had been the wanton destruction of a lovely old decanter. It didn't make sense.

"I think," said Ellery, struggling to his feet, "that I shall go to bed before the Evil One comes down the chimney. Thank you for an altogether extraordinary evening, gentlemen. Coming, Thorne?"

He stumbled up the stairs, followed by the lawyer, who seemed as weary as he. They separated in the cold corridor, without a word, to stumble to their respective bedrooms. From below came a heavy silence.

It was only as he was throwing his trousers over the footrail of his bed that Ellery recalled hazily Thorne's whispered intention hours before to visit him that night and explain the whole fantastic business. He struggled into his dressing gown and slippers and shuffled down the hall to Thorne's room. But the lawyer was already in bed, snoring stertorously.

Ellery dragged himself back to his room and finished undressing. He knew he would have a head the next morning; he was a notoriously poor drinker. His brain spinning, he crawled between the blankets and fell asleep almost instantly.

He opened his eyes after a tossing, tiring sleep with the uneasy conviction that something was wrong. For a moment he was aware only of the ache in his head and the fuzzy feel of his tongue; he did not remember where he was. Then, as his glance took in the faded wallpaper, the pallid patches of sunlight on the worn blue carpet, his trousers tumbled over the footrail where he had left them the night before, memory returned; and, shivering, he consulted his wristwatch, which he had forgotten to take off on going to bed. It was five minutes to seven. He raised his head from the pillow in the frosty air of the bedroom; his nose was half-frozen. But he could detect

34

nothing wrong; the sun looked brave if weak in his eyes; the room was quiet and exactly as he had seen it on retiring; the door was closed. He snuggled between the blankets again.

Then he heard it. It was Thorne's voice. It was Thorne's voice raised in a thin faint cry, almost a wail, coming from somewhere outside the house.

He was out of bed and at the window in his bare feet in one leap. But Thorne was not visible at this side of the house, upon which the dead woods encroached directly; so he scrambled back to slip shoes on his feet and his gown over his pajamas, darted toward the footrail and snatched his revolver out of the hip pocket of his trousers, and ran out into the corridor, heading for the stairs, the revolver in his hand.

"What's the matter?" grumbled someone, and he turned to see Dr. Reinach's vast skull protruding nakedly from the room next to his.

"Don't know. I heard Thorne cry out," and Ellery pounded down the stairs and flung open the front door.

He stopped within the doorway, gaping.

Thorne, fully dressed, was standing ten yards in front of the house, facing Ellery obliquely, staring at something outside the range of Ellery's vision with the most acute expression of terror on his gaunt face Ellery had ever seen on a human countenance. Beside him crouched Nicholas Keith, only half-dressed; the young man's jaws gaped foolishly and his eyes were enormous glaring discs.

Dr. Reinach shoved Ellery roughly aside and growled: "What's the matter? What's wrong?" The fat man's feet were encased in carpet slippers and he had pulled a raccoon coat over his nightshirt, so that he looked like a particularly obese bear.

Thorne's Adam's apple bobbed nervously. The ground, the trees, the world were blanketed with snow of a peculiarly unreal texture; and the air was saturated with warm woolen flakes, falling softly. Deep drifts curved upwards to clamp the boles of trees.

"Don't move," croaked Thorne as Ellery and the fat man stirred. "Don't move, for the love of God. Stay where you are." Ellery's grip tightened on the revolver and he tried perversely to get past the doctor; but he might have been trying to budge a stone wall. Thorne stumbled through the snow to the porch, paler than his background, leaving two deep ruts behind him. "Look at me," he shouted. *"Look at me. Do I* seem all right? Have I gone mad?"

"Pull yourself together, Thorne," said Ellery sharply. "What's the matter with you? I don't see anything wrong."

"Nick!" bellowed Dr. Reinach. "Have you gone crazy, too?"

The young man covered his sunburned face suddenly with his hands; then he dropped his hands and looked again.

He said in a strangled voice: "Maybe we all have. This is the most— Take a look yourself."

Reinach moved then, and Ellery squirmed by him to land in the soft snow beside Thorne, who was trembling violently. Dr. Reinach came lurching after. They plowed through the snow toward Keith, squinting, straining to see.

They need not have strained. What was to be seen was plain for any seeing eye to see. Ellery felt his scalp crawl as he looked; and at the same instant he was aware of the sharp conviction that this was inevitable, this was the only possible climax to the insane events of the previous day. The world had turned topsy-turvy. Nothing in it meant anything reasonable or sane.

Dr. Reinach gasped once; and then he stood blinking like a huge owl. A window rattled on the second floor of the White House. None of them looked up. It was Alice Mayhew in a wrapper, staring from the window of her bedroom, which was on the side of the house facing the driveway. She screamed once; and then she, too, fell silent.

There was the house from which they had just emerged, the house Dr. Reinach had dubbed the White House, with its front door quietly swinging open and Alice Mayhew at an upper side window. Substantial, solid, an edifice of stone and wood and plaster and glass and the patina of age. It was everything a house should be. That much was real, a thing to be grasped.

But beyond it, beyond the driveway and the garage, where the Black House had stood, the house in which Ellery himself had set foot only the afternoon before, the house of the filth and the stench, the house of the equally stone walls, wooden facings, glass windows, chimneys, gargoyles, porch; the house of the blackened look; the old Victorian house built during the Civil War where Sylvester Mayhew had died, where Thorne had

36

barricaded himself with a cutlass for a week; the house which they had all seen, touched, smelled . . . there, *there stood nothing.*

No walls. No chimney. No roof. No ruins. No débris. No house. Nothing.

Nothing but empty space covered smoothly and warmly with snow.

The house had vanished during the night.

II

"There's even," thought Mr. Ellery Queen dully, "a character named Alice."

He looked again. The only reason he did not rub his eyes was that it would have made him feel ridiculous; besides, his sight, all his senses, had never been keener.

He simply stood there in the snow and looked and looked and looked at the empty space where a three-story stone house seventy-five years old had stood the night before.

"Why, it isn't there," said Alice feebly from the upper window. "It . . . isn't . . . there."

"Then I'm not insane." Thorne stumbled toward them. Ellery watched the old man's feet sloughing through the snow, leaving long tracks. A man's weight still counted for something in the universe, then. Yes, and there was his own shadow; so material objects still cast shadows. Absurdly, the discovery brought a certain faint relief.

"It *is* gone!" said Thorne in a cracked voice.

"Apparently." Ellery found his own voice thick and slow; he watched the words curl out on the air and become nothing. "Apparently, Thorne." It was all he could find to say.

Dr. Reinach arched his fat neck, his wattles quivering like a gobbler's. "Incredible. Incredible!"

"Incredible," said Thorne in a whisper.

"Unscientific. It can't be. I'm a man of sense. Of senses. My mind is clear. Things like this—damn it, they just don't happen!"

"As the man said who saw a giraffe for the first time," sighed Ellery. "And yet . . . there it was."

Thorne began wandering helplessly about in a circle. Alice stared, bewitched into stone, from the upper window. And Keith cursed and began to run across the snow-covered driveway toward the invisible house, his hands outstretched before him like a blind man's.

"Hold on," said Ellery. "Stop where you are."

The giant halted, scowling. "What d'ye want?"

Ellery slipped his revolver back into his pocket and sloshed through the snow to pause beside the young man in the driveway. "I don't know precisely. Something's wrong. Something's out of kilter either with us or with the world. It isn't the world as we know it. It's almost . . . almost a matter of transposed dimensions. Do you suppose the solar system has slipped out of its niche in the universe and gone stark crazy in the uncharted depths of space-time? I suppose I'm talking nonsense."

"You know best," shouted Keith. "I'm not going to let this screwy business stampede *me*. There was a solid house on that plot last night, by God, and nobody can convince me it still isn't there. Not even my own eyes. We've—we've been hypnotized! The hippo could do it here—he could do anything. Hypnotized. You hypnotized us, Reinach!"

The doctor mumbled: "What?" and kept glaring at the empty lot.

"I tell you it's there!" cried Keith angrily.

Ellery sighed and dropped to his knees in the snow; he began to brush aside the white, soft blanket with chilled palms. When he had laid the ground bare, he saw wet gravel and a rut.

"This *is* the driveway, isn't it?" he asked without looking up.

"The driveway," snarled Keith, "or the road to hell. You're as mixed up as we are. Sure it's the driveway! Can't you see the garage? Why shouldn't it be the driveway?"

"I don't know." Ellery got to his feet, frowning. "I don't know anything. I'm beginning to learn all over again. Maybe—maybe it's a matter of gravitation. Maybe we'll all fly into space any minute now."

Thorne groaned: "My God."

"All I can be sure of is that something very strange happened last night."

"I tell you," growled Keith, "it's an optical illusion!"

"Something strange." The fat man stirred. "Yes, decidedly. What an inadequate word! A house has disappeared. Something strange." He began to chuckle in a choking, mirthless way.

"Oh that," said Ellery impatiently. "Certainly. Certainly, Doctor. That's a *fact*. As for you, Keith, you don't really believe this mass-hypnosis bilge. The house is gone, right enough. . . . It's not the fact of its being gone that bothers me. It's the agency, the *means*. It smacks of—of —" He shook his head. "I've never believed in . . . this sort of thing, damn it all!"

Dr. Reinach threw back his vast shoulders and glared, red-eyed, at the empty snow-covered space. "It's a trick," he bellowed. "A rotten trick, that's what it is. That house is right there in front of our noses. Or—or—They can't fool *me!*"

Ellery looked at him. "Perhaps," he said, "Keith has it in his pocket?"

Alice clattered out on the porch in high-heeled shoes over bare feet, her hair streaming, a cloth coat flung over her night clothes. Behind her crept little Mrs. Reinach. The women's eyes were wild.

"Talk to them," muttered Ellery to Thorne. "Anything; but keep their minds occupied. We'll all go balmy if we don't preserve at least an air of sanity. Keith, get me a broom."

He shuffled up the driveway, skirting the invisible house very carefully and not once taking his eyes off the empty space. The fat man hesitated; then he lumbered along in Ellery's tracks. Thorne stumbled back to the porch and Keith strode off, disappearing behind the White House.

There was no sun now. A pale and eerie light filtered down through the cold clouds. The snow continued its soft, thick fall.

They looked like dots, small and helpless, on a sheet of blank paper.

Ellery pulled open the folding doors of the garage and peered. A healthy odor of raw gasoline and rubber assailed his nostrils. Thorne's car stood within, exactly as Ellery had seen it the afternoon before, black monster with glittering chrome work. Beside it, apparently parked by Keith after their arrival, stood the battered Buick in which Dr. Reinach had driven them from the city. Both cars were perfectly dry.

He shut the doors and turned back to the driveway. Aside from the catenated links of their footprints in the snow, made a moment before, the white covering on the driveway was virgin.

39

"Here's your broom," said the giant. "What are you going to do—ride it?"

"Hold your tongue, Nick," growled Dr. Reinach.

Ellery laughed. "Let him alone, Doctor. His angry sanity is infectious. Come along, you two. This may be the Judgment Day, but we may as well go through the motions."

"What do you want with a broom, Queen?"

"It's hard to decide whether the snow was an accident or part of the plan," murmured Ellery. "Anything may be true today. Literally anything."

"Rubbish," snorted the fat man. "Abracadabra. *Om mani padme hum*. How could a man have planned a snowfall? You're talking gibberish."

"I didn't say a human plan, Doctor."

"Rubbish, rubbish, rubbish!"

"You may as well save your breath. You're a badly scared little boy whistling in the dark—for all your bulk, Doctor."

Ellery gripped the broom tightly and stamped out across the driveway. He felt his own foot shrinking as he tried to make it step upon the white rectangle. His muscles were gathered in, as if in truth he expected to encounter the adamantine bulk of a house which was still there but unaccountably impalpable. When he felt nothing but cold air, he laughed a little self-consciously and began to wield the broom on the snow in a peculiar manner. He used the most delicate of sweeping motions, barely brushing the surface crystals away, so that layer by layer he reduced the depth of the snow. He scanned each layer with anxiety as it was uncovered. And he continued to do this until the ground itself lay revealed; and at no depth did he come across the minutest trace of a human imprint.

"Elves," he complained. "Nothing less than elves. I confess it's beyond me."

"Even the foundation—" began Dr. Reinach heavily.

Ellery poked the tip of the broom at the earth. It was hard as corundum.

The front door slammed as Thorne and the two women crept into the White House. The three men outside stood still, doing nothing.

"Well," said Ellery at last, "this is either a bad dream or the end of the world." He made off diagonally across the plot, dragging the broom behind him like a tired charwoman, until he reached the snow-covered drive; and then he trudged down the drive towards the invisible road, disappearing around a bend under the stripped white-dripping trees.

It was a short walk to the road. Ellery remembered it well. It had curved steadily in a long arc all the way from the turn-off at the main highway. There had been no crossroad in all the jolting journey.

He went out into the middle of the road, snow-covered now but plainly distinguishable between the powdered tangles of woods as a gleaming, empty strip. There was the long curve exactly as he remembered it. Mechanically he used the broom again, sweeping a small area clear. And there were the pits and ruts of the old Buick's journeys.

"What are you looking for," said Nick Keith quietly, "gold?"

Ellery straightened up by degrees, turning about slowly until he was face to face with the giant. "So you thought it was necessary to follow me? Or—no, I beg your pardon. Undoubtedly it was Dr. Reinach's idea."

The sun-charred features did not change expression.

"You're crazy as a bat. Follow you? I've got all I can do to follow myself."

"Of course," said Ellery. "But did I understand you to ask me if I was looking for gold, my dear young Prometheus?"

"You're a queer one," said Keith as they made their way back toward the house.

"Gold," repeated Ellery. "Hmm. There was gold in that house, and now the house is gone. In the shock of the discovery that houses fly away like birds, I'd quite forgotten that little item. Thank you, Mr. Keith," said Ellery grimly, "for reminding me."

"Mr. Queen," said Alice. She was crouched in a chair by the fire, white to the lips. "What's happened to us? What are we to do? Have we . . . Was yesterday a dream? Didn't we walk into that house, go through it, touch things? . . . I'm frightened."

"If yesterday *was* a dream," smiled Ellery, "then we may expect that tomorrow will bring a vision; for that's what holy Sanskrit says, and we may as well believe in parables as in miracles." He sat down, rubbing his hands briskly. "How about a fire, Keith? It's arctic in here."

"Sorry," said Keith with surprising amiability, and he went away.

"We could see a vision," shivered Thorne. "My brain is—sick. It just isn't possible. It's horrible." His hands slapped his side and something jangled in his pocket.

"Keys," said Ellery, "and no house. It *is* staggering."

Keith came back under a mountain of firewood. He grimaced at the litter in the fireplace, dropped the wood, and began sweeping together the fragments of glass, the remains of the brandy decanter he had smashed against the brick wall the night before. Alice glanced from his broad back to the chromo of her mother on the mantel. As for Mrs. Reinach, she was as silent as a sacred bird; she stood in a corner like a wizened little gnome, her wrapper drawn about her, her stringy sparrow-colored hair hanging down her back, and her glassy eyes fixed on the face of her husband.

"Milly," said the fat man.

"Yes, Herbert, I'm going," said Mrs. Reinach instantly, and she crept up the stairs and out of sight.

"Well, Mr. Queen, what's the answer? Or is this riddle too esoteric for your taste?"

"No riddle is esoteric," muttered Ellery, "unless it's the riddle of God; and that's no riddle—it's a vast blackness. Doctor, is there any way of reaching assistance?"

"Not unless you can fly."

"No phone," said Keith without turning, "and you saw the condition of the road for yourself. You'd never get a car through those drifts."

"If you had a car," chuckled Dr. Reinach. Then he seemed to remember the disappearing house, and his chuckle died.

"What do you mean?" demanded Ellery. "In the garage are—"

"Two useless products of the machine age. Both cars are out of fuel."

"And mine," said old Thorne suddenly, with a resurrection of grim personal interest, "mine has something wrong with it besides. I left my chauffeur in the city, you know, Queen, when I drove down last time. Now I can't get the engine running on the little gasoline that's left in the tank."

Ellery's fingers drummed on the arm of his chair. "Bother! Now we can't even call on the other eyes to test whether we've been bewitched or not. By the way,

Doctor, how far is the nearest community? I'm afraid I didn't pay attention on the drive down."

"Over fifteen miles by road. If you're thinking of footing it, Mr. Queen, you're welcome to the thought."

"You'd never get through the drifts," muttered Keith. The drifts appeared to trouble him.

"And so we find ourselves snowbound," said Ellery, "in the middle of the fourth dimension—or perhaps it's the fifth. A pretty kettle! Ah there, Keith, that feels considerably better."

"You don't seem bowled over by what's happened," said Dr. Reinach, eyeing him curiously. "I'll confess it's given even me a shock."

Ellery was silent for a moment. Then he said lightly: "There wouldn't be any point to losing our heads, would there?"

"I fully expect dragons to come flying over the house," groaned Thorne. He eyed Ellery a bit bashfully. "Queen . . . perhaps we had better . . . try to get out of here."

"You heard Keith, Thorne."

Thorne bit his lips. "I'm frozen," said Alice, drawing nearer the fire. "That was well done, Mr. Keith. It—it —a fire like this makes me think of home, somehow." The young man got to his feet and turned around. Their eyes met for an instant.

"It's nothing," he said shortly. "Nothing at all."

"You seem to be the only one who— *Oh!*"

An enormous old woman with a black shawl over her shoulders was coming downstairs. She might have been years dead, she was so yellow and emaciated and mummified. And yet she gave the impression of being very much alive, with a sort of ancient, ageless life; her black eyes were young and bright and cunning, and her face was extraordinarily mobile. She was sidling down stiffly, feeling her way with one foot and clutching the banister with two dried claws, while her lively eyes remained fixed on Alice's face. There was a curious hunger in her expression, the flaring of a long-dead hope suddenly, against all reason.

"Who—who—" began Alice, shrinking back.

"Don't be alarmed," said Dr. Reinach quickly. "It's unfortunate that she got away from Milly. . . . Sarah!" In a twinkling he was at the foot of the staircase, barring the old woman's way. "What are you doing up at this hour? You should take better care of yourself, Sarah."

43

She ignored him, continuing her snail's pace down the stairs until she reached his pachyderm bulk. "Olivia," she mumbled, with a vital eagerness. "It's Olivia come back to me. Oh, my sweet, sweet darling . . ."

"Now, Sarah," said the fat man, taking her hand gently. "Don't excite yourself. This isn't Olivia, Sarah. It's Alice—Alice Mayhew, Sylvester's girl, come from England. You remember Alice, little Alice? Not Olivia, Sarah."

"Not Olivia?" The old woman peered across the banister, her wrinkled lips moving. "Not Olivia?"

The girl jumped up. "I'm Alice, Aunt Sarah. Alice—"

Sarah Fell darted suddenly past the fat man and scurried across the room to seize the girl's hand and glare into her face. As she studied those shrinking features her expression changed to one of despair. "Not Olivia. Olivia's beautiful black hair . . . Not Olivia's voice. Alice? Alice?" She dropped into Alice's vacated chair, her skinny broad shoulders sagging, and began to weep. They could see the yellow skin of her scalp through the sparse gray hair.

Dr. Reinach roared: "Milly!" in an enraged voice. Mrs. Reinach popped into sight like a jack-in-the-box. "Why did you let her leave her room?"

"B-but I thought she was—" began Mrs. Reinach, stammering.

"Take her upstairs at once!"

"Yes, Herbert," whispered the sparrow, and Mrs. Reinach hurried downstairs in her wrapper and took the old woman's hand and, unopposed, led her away. Mrs. Fell kept repeating, between sobs: "Why doesn't Olivia come back? Why did they take her away from her mother?" until she was out of sight.

"Sorry," panted the fat man, mopping himself. "One of her spells. I knew it was coming on from the curiosity she exhibited the moment she heard you were coming, Alice. There *is* a resemblance; you can scarcely blame her."

"She's—she's horrible," said Alice faintly. "Mr. Queen —Mr. Thorne, must we stay here? I'd feel so much easier in the city. And then my cold, these frigid rooms—"

"By heaven," burst out Thorne, "I feel like chancing it on foot!"

"And leave Sylvester's gold to our tender mercies?" smiled Dr. Reinach. Then he scowled.

44

"I don't want Father's legacy," said Alice desperately. "At this moment I don't want anything but to get away. I—I can manage to get along all right. I'll find work to do—I can do so many things. I want to go away. Mr. Keith, couldn't you possibly—"

"*I'm* not a magician," said Keith rudely; and he buttoned his mackinaw and strode out of the house. They could see his tall figure stalking off behind a veil of snowflakes.

Alice flushed, turning back to the fire.

"Nor are any of us," said Ellery. "Miss Mayhew, you'll simply have to be a brave girl and stick it out until we can find a means of getting out of here."

"Yes," murmured Alice, shivering; and stared into the flames.

"Meanwhile, Thorne, tell me everything you know about this case, especially as it concerns Sylvester Mayhew's house. There may be a clue in your father's history, Miss Mayhew. If the house has vanished, so has the gold *in* the house; and whether you want it or not, it belongs to you. Consequently we must make an effort to find it."

"I suggest," muttered Dr. Reinach, "that you find the house first. House!" he exploded, waving his furred arms. And he made for the sideboard.

Alice nodded listlessly. Thorne mumbled: "Perhaps, Queen, you and I had better talk privately."

"We made a frank beginning last night; I see no reason why we shouldn't continue in the same candid vein. You needn't be reluctant to speak before Dr. Reinach. Our host is obviously a man of parts—unorthodox parts."

Dr. Reinach did not reply. His globular face was dark as he tossed off a water goblet full of gin.

Through air metallic with defiance, Thorne talked in a hardening voice; not once did he take his eyes from Dr. Reinach.

His first suspicion that something was wrong had been germinated by Sylvester Mayhew himself.

Hearing by post from Alice, Thorne had investigated and located Mayhew. He had explained to the old invalid his daughter's desire to find her father, if he still lived. Old Mayhew, with a strange excitement, had acquiesced; he was eager to be reunited with his daughter;

45

and he seemed to be living, explained Thorne defiantly, in mortal fear of his relatives in the neighboring house.

"Fear, Thorne?" The fat man sat down, raising his brows. "You know he was afraid, not of us, but of poverty. He was a miser."

Thorne ignored him. Mayhew had instructed Thorne to write Alice and bid her come to America at once; he meant to leave her his entire estate and wanted her to have it before he died. The repository of the gold he had cunningly refused to divulge, even to Thorne; it was "in the house," he had said, but he would not reveal its hiding place to anyone but Alice herself. The "others," he had snarled, had been looking for it ever since their "arrival."

"By the way," drawled Ellery, "how long have you good people been living in this house, Dr. Reinach?"

"A year or so. You certainly don't put any credence in the paranoiac ravings of a dying man? There's no mystery about our living here. I looked Sylvester up over a year ago after a long separation and found him still in the old homestead, and this house boarded up and empty. The White House, this house, incidentally, was built by my stepfather—Sylvester's father—on Sylvester's marriage to Alice's mother; Sylvester lived in it until my stepfather died, and then moved back to the Black House. I found Sylvester, a degenerated hulk of what he'd once been, living on crusts, absolutely alone and badly in need of medical attention."

"Alone—here, in this wilderness?" said Ellery incredulously.

"Yes. As a matter of fact, the only way I could get his permission to move back to this house, which belonged to him, was by dangling the bait of free medical treatment before his eyes. I'm sorry, Alice; he was quite unbalanced. . . . And so Milly and Sarah and I—Sarah had been living with us ever since Olivia's death—moved in here."

"Decent of you," remarked Ellery. "I suppose you had to give up your medical practice to do it, Doctor?"

Dr. Reinach grimaced. "I didn't have much of a practice to give up, Mr. Queen."

"But it was an almost pure brotherly impulse, eh?"

"Oh, I don't deny that the possibility of falling heir to some of Sylvester's fortune had crossed our minds. It was rightfully ours, we believed, not knowing anything about Alice. As it's turned out—" he shrugged his fat shoulders. "I'm a philosopher."

"And don't deny, either," shouted Thorne, "that when I came back here at the time Mayhew sank into that fatal coma you people watched me like a—like a band of spies! I was in your way!"

"Mr. Thorne," whispered Alice, paling.

"I'm sorry, Miss Mayhew, but you may as well know the truth. Oh, you didn't fool me, Reinach! You wanted that gold, Alice or no Alice. I shut myself up in that house just to keep you from getting your hands on it!"

Dr. Reinach shrugged again; his rubbery lips compressed.

"You want candor; here it is!" rasped Thorne. "I was in that house, Queen, for six days after Mayhew's funeral and before Miss Mayhew's arrival, *looking for the gold.* I turned that house upside down. And I didn't find the slightest trace of it. I tell you it isn't there." He glared at the fat man. "I tell you it was stolen before Mayhew died!"

"Now, now," sighed Ellery. "That makes less sense than the other. Why then has somebody intoned an incantation over the house and caused it to disappear?"

"I don't know," said the old lawyer fiercely. "I know only that the most dastardly thing's happened here, that everything is unnatural, veiled in that—that false creature's smile! Miss Mayhew, I'm sorry I must speak this way about your own family. But I feel it my duty to warn you that you've fallen among human wolves. Wolves!"

"I'm afraid," said Reinach sourly, "that I shouldn't come to you, my dear Thorne, for a reference."

"I wish," said Alice in a very low tone, "I truly wish I were dead."

But the lawyer was past control. "That man Keith," he cried. "Who is he? What's he doing here? He looks like a gangster. I suspect him, Queen—"

"Apparently," smiled Ellery, "you suspect everybody."

"Mr. Keith?" murmured Alice. "Oh, I'm sure not. I—I don't think he's that sort at all, Mr. Thorne. He looks as if he's had a hard life. As if he's suffered terribly from something."

Thorne threw up his hands, turning to the fire.

"Let us," said Ellery amiably, "confine ourselves to the problem at hand. We were, I believe, considering the

47

problem of a disappearing house. Do any architect's plans of the so-called Black House exist?"

"Lord, no," said Dr. Reinach.

"Who has lived in it since your stepfather's death besides Sylvester Mayhew and his wife?"

"Wives," corrected the doctor, pouring himself another glassful of gin. "Sylvester married twice; I suppose you didn't know that, my dear." Alice shivered by the fire. "I dislike raking over old ashes, but since we're at confessional . . . Sylvester treated Alice's mother abominably."

"I—guessed that," whispered Alice.

"She was a woman of spirit and she rebelled; but when she'd got her final decree and returned to England, the reaction set in and she died very shortly afterward, I understand. Her death was recorded in the New York papers."

"When I was a baby," whispered Alice.

"Sylvester, already unbalanced, although not so anchoretic in those days as he became later, then wooed and won a wealthy widow and brought her out here to live. She had a son, a child by her first husband, with her. Father'd died by this time, and Sylvester and his second wife lived in the Black House. It was soon evident that Sylvester had married the widow for her money; he persuaded her to sign it over to him—a considerable fortune for those days—and promptly proceeded to devil the life out of her. Result: the woman vanished one day, taking her child with her."

"Perhaps," said Ellery, seeing Alice's face, "we'd better abandon the subject, Doctor."

"We never did find out what actually happened—whether Sylvester drove her out or whether, unable to stand his brutal treatment any longer, she left voluntarily. At any rate, I discovered by accident, a few years later, through an obituary notice, that she died in the worst sort of poverty."

Alice was staring at him with a wrinklenosed nausea. "Father . . . did that?"

"Oh, stop it," growled Thorne. "You'll have the poor child gibbering in another moment. What has all this to do with the house?"

"Mr. Queen asked," said the fat man mildly. Ellery was studying the flames as if they fascinated him.

"The real point," snapped the lawyer, "is that you've watched me from the instant I set foot here, Reinach.

48

Afraid to leave me alone for a moment. Why, you even had Keith meet me in your car on both my visits—to 'escort' me here! And I didn't have five minutes alone with the old gentleman—you saw to that. And then he lapsed into the coma and was unable to speak again before he died. Why? Why all this surveillance? God knows I'm a forbearing man; but you've given me every ground for suspecting your motives."

"Apparently," chuckled Dr. Reinach, "you don't agree with Caesar."

"I beg your pardon?"

"'Would,'" quoted the fat man, "'he were fatter.' Well, good people, the end of the world may come, but that's no reason why we shouldn't have breakfast. Milly!" he bellowed.

Thorne awoke sluggishly, like a drowsing old hound dimly aware of danger. His bedroom was cold; a pale morning light was struggling in through the window. He groped under his pillow.

"Stop where you are!" he said harshly.

"So you have a revolver, too?" murmured Ellery. He was dressed and looked as if he had slept badly. "It's only I, Thorne, stealing in for a conference. It's not so hard to steal in here, by the way."

"What do you mean?" grumbled Thorne, sitting up and putting his old-fashioned revolver away.

"I see your lock has gone the way of mine, Alice's, the Black House, and Sylvester Mayhew's elusive gold."

Thorne drew the patchwork comforter about him, his old lips blue. "Well, Queen?"

Ellery lit a cigarette and for a moment stared out Thorne's window at the streamers of crêpy snow still dropping from the sky. The snow had fallen without a moment's let-up the entire previous day. "This is a curious business all round, Thorne. The queerest medley of spirit and matter. I've just reconnoitered. You'll be interested to learn that our young friend the Colossus is gone."

"Keith gone?"

"His bed hasn't been slept in at all. I looked."

"And he was away most of yesterday, too!"

"Precisely. Our surly Crichton, who seems afflicted by a particularly acute case of *Weltschmerz,* periodically

49

vanishes. Where does he go? I'd give a good deal to know the answer to that question."

"He won't get far in those nasty drifts," mumbled the lawyer.

"It gives one, as the French say, to think. Comrade Reinach is gone, too." Thorne stiffened. "Oh, yes; his bed's been slept in, but briefly, I judge. Have they eloped together? Separately? Thorne," said Ellery thoughtfully, "this becomes an increasingly subtle devilment."

"It's beyond me," said Thorne with another shiver. "I'm just about ready to give up. I don't see that we're accomplishing a thing here. And then there's always that annoying, incredible fact . . . the house—vanished."

Ellery sighed and looked at his wristwatch. It was a minute past seven.

Thorne threw back the comforter and groped under the bed for his slippers. "Let's go downstairs," he snapped.

"Excellent bacon, Mrs. Reinach," said Ellery. "I suppose it must be a trial carting supplies up here."

"We've the blood of pioneers," said Dr. Reinach cheerfully, before his wife could reply. He was engulfing mounds of scrambled eggs and bacon. "Luckily, we've enough in the larder to last out a considerable siege. The winters are severe out here—we learned that last year."

Keith was not at the breakfast table. Old Mrs. Fell was. She ate voraciously, with the unconcealed greed of the very old, to whom nothing is left of the sensual satisfactions of life but the filling of the belly. Nevertheless, although she did not speak, she contrived as she ate to keep her eyes on Alice, who wore a haunted look.

"I didn't sleep very well," said Alice, toying with her coffee cup. Her voice was huskier. "This abominable snow! Can't we manage somehow to get away today?"

"Not so long as the snow keeps up, I'm afraid," said Ellery gently. "And you, Doctor? Did you sleep badly, too? Or hasn't the whisking away of a whole house from under your nose affected your nerves at all?"

The fat man's eyes were red-rimmed and his lids sagged. Nevertheless, he chuckled and said: "I? I always sleep well. Nothing on my conscience. Why?"

"Oh, no special reason. Where's friend Keith this morning? He's a seclusive sort of chap, isn't he?"

Mrs. Reinach swallowed a muffin whole. Her husband

glanced at her and she rose and fled to the kitchen. "Lord knows," said the fat man. "He's as unpredictable as the ghost of Banquo. Don't bother yourself about the boy; he's harmless."

Ellery sighed and pushed back from the table. "The passage of twenty-four hours hasn't softened the wonder of the event. May I be excused? I'm going to have another peep at the house that isn't there any more." Thorne started to rise. "No, no, Thorne; I'd rather go alone."

He put on his warmest clothes and went outdoors. The drifts reached the lower windows now; and the trees had almost disappeared under the snow. A crude path had been hacked by someone from the front door for a few feet; already it was half refilled with snow.

Ellery stood still in the path, breathing deeply of the raw air and staring off to the right at the empty rectangle where the Black House had once stood. Leading across that expanse to the edge of the woods beyond were barely discernible tracks. He turned up his coat collar against the cutting wind and plunged into the snow waist-deep.

It was difficult going, but not unpleasant. After a while he began to feel quite warm. The world was white and silent—a new, strange world.

When he had left the open area and struggled into the woods, it was with a sensation that he was leaving even that new world behind. Everything was so still and white and beautiful, with a pure beauty not of the earth; the snow draping the trees gave them a fresh look, making queer patterns out of old forms.

Occasionally a clump of snow fell from a low branch, pelting him.

Here, where there was a roof between ground and sky, the snow had not filtered into the mysterious tracks so quickly. They were purposeful tracks, unwandering, striking straight as a dotted line for some distant goal. Ellery pushed on more rapidly, excited by a presentiment of discovery.

Then the world went black.

It was a curious thing. The snow grew gray, and grayer, and finally very dark gray, becoming jet black at the last instant, as if flooded from underneath by ink. And with some surprise he felt the cold wet kiss of the drift on his cheek.

51

He opened his eyes to find himself flat on his back in the snow and Thorne in the greatcoat stooped over him, nose jutting from blued face like a winter thorn.

"Queen!" cried the old man, shaking him. "Are you all right?"

Ellery sat up, licking his lips. "As well as might be expected," he groaned. "What hit me? It felt like one of God's angrier thunderbolts." He caressed the back of his head, and staggered to his feet. "Well, Thorne, we seem to have reached the border of the enchanted land."

"You're not delirious?" asked the lawyer anxiously.

Ellery looked about for the tracks which should have been there. But except for the double line at the head of which Thorne stood, there were none. Apparently he had lain unconscious in the snow for a long time.

"Farther than this," he said with a grimace, "we may not go. Hands off. Nose out. Mind your own business. Beyond this invisible boundary line lie Sheol and Domdaniel and Abaddon. *Lasciate ogni speranza voi ch'entrate.* . . . Forgive me, Thorne. Did you save my life?"

Thorne jerked about, searching the silent woods. "I don't know. I think not. At least I found you lying here, alone. Gave me quite a start—thought you were dead."

"As well," said Ellery with a shiver, "I might have been."

"When you left the house Alice went upstairs, Reinach said something about a catnap, and I wandered out of the house. I waded through the drifts on the road for a spell, and then I thought of you and made my way back. Your tracks were almost obliterated; but they were visible enough to take me across the clearing to the edge of the woods, and I finally blundered upon you. By now the tracks are gone."

"I don't like this at all," said Ellery, "and yet in another sense I like it very much."

"What do you mean?"

"I can't imagine," said Ellery, "a divine agency stooping to such a mean assault."

"Yes, it's open war now," muttered Thorne. "Whoever it is—he'll stop at nothing."

"A benevolent war, at any rate. I was quite at his mercy, and he might have killed me as easily as—"

He stopped. A sharp report, like a pine-knot snapping in a fire or an ice-stiffened twig breaking in two, but greatly magnified, had come to his ears. Then the echo came to them, softer but unmistakable.

It was the report of a gun.

"From the house!" yelled Ellery. "Come on!"

Thorne was pale as they scrambled through the drifts. "Gun . . . I forgot. I left my revolver under the pillow in my bedroom. Do you think——?"

Ellery scrabbled at his own pocket. "Mine's still here. . . . No, by George, I've been scotched!" His cold fingers fumbled with the cylinder. "Bullets taken out. And I've no spare ammunition." He fell silent, his mouth hardening.

They found the women and Reinach running about like startled animals, searching for they knew not what.

"Did you hear it, too?" cried the fat man as they burst into the house. He seemed extraordinarily excited. "Someone fired a shot!"

"Where?" asked Ellery, his eyes on the rove. "Keith?"

"Don't know where he is. Milly says it might have come from behind the house. I was napping and couldn't tell. Revolvers! At least he's come out in the open."

"Who has?" asked Ellery.

The fat man shrugged. Ellery went through to the kitchen and opened the back door. The snow outside was smooth, untrodden. When he returned to the living room Alice was adjusting a scarf about her neck with fingers that shook.

"I don't know how long you people intend to stay in this ghastly place," she said in a passionate voice. "But I've had *quite* enough, thank you. Mr. Thorne, I insist you take me away at once. At once! I shan't stay another instant."

"Now, now, Miss Mayhew," said Thorne in a distressed way, taking her hands. "I should like nothing better. But can't you see——"

Ellery, on his way upstairs three steps at a time, heard no more. He made for Thorne's room and kicked the door open, sniffing. Then, with rather a grim smile, he went to the tumbled bed and pulled the pillow away. A long-barreled, old-fashioned revolver lay there. He examined the cylinder; it was empty. Then he put the muzzle to his nose.

"Well?" said Thorne from the doorway. The English girl was clinging to him.

"Well," said Ellery, tossing the gun aside, "we're facing fact now, not fancy. It's war, Thorne, as you said. The shot was fired from your revolver. Barrel's still warm, muzzle still reeks, and you can smell the burned gunpowder if you sniff this cold air hard enough. *And* the bullets are gone."

"But what does it mean?" moaned Alice.

"It means that somebody's being terribly cute. It was a harmless trick to get Thorne and me back to the house. Probably the shot was a warning as well as a decoy."

Alice sank into Thorne's bed. "You mean we—"

"Yes," said Ellery, "from now on we're prisoners, Miss Mayhew. Prisoners who may not stray beyond the confines of the jail. I wonder," he added with a frown, "precisely why."

The day passed in a timeless haze. The world of outdoors became more and more choked in the folds of the snow. The air was a solid white sheet. It seemed as if the very heavens had opened to admit all the snow that ever was, or ever would be.

Young Keith appeared suddenly at noon, taciturn and leaden-eyed, gulped down some hot food, and without explanation retired to his bedroom. Dr. Reinach shambled about quietly for some time; then he disappeared, only to show up, wet, grimy, and silent, before dinner. As the day wore on, less and less was said. Thorne in desperation took up a bottle of whisky. Keith came down at eight o'clock, made himself some coffee, drank three cups, and went upstairs again. Dr. Reinach appeared to have lost his good nature; he was morose, almost sullen, opening his mouth only to snarl at his wife.

And the snow continued to fall.

They all retired early, without conversation.

At midnight the strain was more than even Ellery's iron nerves could bear. He had prowled about his bedroom for hours, poking at the brisk fire in the grate, his mind leaping from improbability to fantasy until his head throbbed with one great ache. Sleep was impossible.

Moved by an impulse which he did not attempt to analyze, he slipped into his coat and went out into the frosty corridor.

Thorne's door was closed; Ellery heard the old man's bed creaking and groaning. It was pitch-dark in the hall as he groped his way about. Suddenly Ellery's toe caught in a rent in the carpet and he staggered to regain his balance, coming up against the wall with a thud, his

54

heels clattering on the bare planking at the bottom of the baseboard.

He had no sooner straightened up than he heard the stifled exclamation of a woman. It came from across the corridor; if he guessed right, from Alice Mayhew's bedroom. It was such a weak, terrified exclamation that he sprang across the hall, fumbling in his pockets for a match as he did so. He found match and door in the same instant; he struck one and opened the door and stood still, the tiny light flaring up before him.

Alice was sitting up in bed, quilt drawn about her shoulders, her eyes gleaming in the quarter-light. Before an open drawer of a tallboy across the room, one hand arrested in the act of scattering its contents about, loomed Dr. Reinach, fully dressed. His shoes were wet; his expression was blank; his eyes were slits.

"Please stand still, Doctor," said Ellery softly as the match sputtered out. "My revolver is useless as a percussion weapon, but it still can inflict damage as a blunt instrument." He moved to a nearby table, where he had seen an oil-lamp before the match went out, struck another match, lighted the lamp, and stepped back again to stand against the door.

"Thank you," whispered Alice.

"What happened, Miss Mayhew?"

"I . . . don't know. I slept badly. I came awake a moment ago when I heard the floor creak. And then you dashed in." She cried suddenly: "Bless you!"

"You cried out."

"Did I?" She sighed like a tired child. "I . . . Uncle Herbert!" she said suddenly, fiercely. "What's the meaning of this? What are you doing in my room?"

The fat man's eyes came open, innocent and beaming; his hand withdrew from the drawer and closed it; and he shifted his elephantine bulk until he was standing erect. "Doing, my dear?" he rumbled. "Why, I came in to see if you were all right." His eyes were fixed on a patch of her white shoulders visible above the quilt. "You were so overwrought today. Purely an avuncular impulse, my child. Forgive me if I startled you."

"I think," sighed Ellery, "that I've misjudged you, Doctor. That's not clever of you at all. Downright clumsy, in fact; I can only attribute it to a certain understandable confusion of the moment. Miss Mayhew isn't normally to be found in the top drawer of a tallboy, no matter how

55

capacious it may be." He said sharply to Alice: "Did this fellow touch you?"

"Touch me?" Her shoulders twitched with repugnance. "No. If he had, in the dark, I—I think I should have died."

"What a charming compliment," said Dr. Reinach ruefully.

"Then what," demanded Ellery, *"were* you looking for, Dr. Reinach?"

The fat man turned until his right side was toward the door. "I'm notoriously hard of hearing," he chuckled, "in my right ear. Good night, Alice; pleasant dreams. May I pass, Sir Launcelot?"

Ellery kept his gaze on the fat man's bland face until the door closed. For some time after the last echo of Dr. Reinach's chuckle died away they were silent.

Then Alice slid down in the bed and clutched the edge of the quilt. "Mr. Queen, please! Take me away tomorrow. I mean it. I truly do. I—can't tell you how frightened I am of . . . all this. Every time I think of that—that. . . . How can such things be? We're not in a place of sanity, Mr. Queen. We'll all go mad if we remain here much longer. Won't you take me away?"

Ellery sat down on the edge of her bed. "Are you really so upset, Miss Mayhew?" he asked gently.

"I'm simply terrified," she whispered.

"Then Thorne and I will do what we can tomorrow." He patted her arm through the quilt. "I'll have a look at his car and see if something can't be done with it. He said there's some gas left in the tank. We'll go as far as it will take us and walk the rest of the way."

"But with so little petrol . . . Oh, I don't care!" She stared up at him wide-eyed. "Do you think . . . he'll let us?"

"He?"

"Whoever it is that . . ."

Ellery rose with a smile. "We'll cross that bridge when it gets to us. Meanwhile, get some sleep; you'll have a strenuous day tomorrow."

"Do you think I'm—he'll—"

"Leave the lamp burning and set a chair under the doorknob when I leave." He took a quick look about. "By the way, Miss Mayhew, is there anything in your possession which Dr. Reinach might want to appropriate?"

"That's puzzled me, too. I can't imagine what I've got

he could possibly want. I'm so poor, Mr. Queen—quite the Cinderella. There's nothing; just my clothes, the things I came with."

"No old letters, records, mementoes?"

"Just one very old photograph of Mother."

"Hmm, Dr. Reinach doesn't strike me as that sentimental. Well, good night. Don't forget the chair. You'll be quite safe, I assure you."

He waited in the frigid darkness of the corridor until he heard her creep out of bed and set a chair against the door. Then he went into his own room.

And there was Thorne in a shabby dressing gown, looking like an ancient and disheveled specter of gloom.

"What ho! The ghost walks. Can't you sleep, either?"

"Sleep!" The old man shuddered. "How can an honest man sleep in this God-forsaken place? I notice you seem rather cheerful."

"Not cheerful. Alive." Ellery sat down and lit a cigarette. "I heard you tossing about your bed a few minutes ago. Anything happen to pull you out into this cold?"

"No. Just nerves." Thorne jumped up and began to pace the floor. "Where have you been?"

Ellery told him. "Remarkable chap, Reinach," he concluded. "But we mustn't allow our admiration to overpower us. We'll really have to give this thing up, Thorne, at least temporarily. I had been hoping. . . . But there! I've promised the poor girl. We're leaving tomorrow as best we can."

"And be found frozen stiff next March by a rescue party," said Thorne miserably. "Pleasant prospect! And yet even death by freezing is preferable to this abominable place." He looked curiously at Ellery. "I must say I'm a trifle disappointed in you, Queen. From what I'd heard about your professional cunning . . ."

"I never claimed," shrugged Ellery, "to be a magician. Or even a theologian. What's happened here is either the blackest magic or palpable proof that miracles can happen."

"It would seem so," muttered Thorne. "And yet, when you put your mind to it . . . It goes against reason, by thunder!"

"I see," said Ellery dryly, "the man of law is recovering from the initial shock. Well, it's a shame to have to leave here now, in a way. I detest the thought of giving up—especially at the present time."

"At the present time? What do you mean?"

"I dare say, Thorne, you haven't emerged far enough from your condition of shock to have properly analyzed this little problem. I gave it a lot of thought today. The goal eludes me—but I'm near it," he said softly, "very near it."

"You mean," gasped the lawyer, "you mean you actually—"

"Remarkable case," said Ellery. "Oh, extraordinary—there isn't a word in the English language or any other, for that matter, that properly describes it. If I were religiously inclined . . ." He puffed away thoughtfully. "It gets down to the very simple elements, as all truly great problems do. A fortune in gold exists. It is hidden in a house. The house disappears. To find the gold, then, you must first find the house. I believe. . . ."

"Aside from that mumbo-jumbo with Keith's broom the other day," cried Thorne, "I can't recall that you've made a single effort in that direction. Find the house!—why, you've done nothing but sit around and wait."

"Exactly," murmured Ellery.

"What?"

"Wait. That's the prescription, my lean and angry friend. That's the sigil that will exorcise the spirit of the Black House."

"Sigil?" Thorne stared. "Spirit?"

"Wait. Precisely. Lord, how I'm waiting!"

Thorne looked puzzled and suspicious, as if he suspected Ellery of a contrary midnight humor. But Ellery sat soberly smoking. "Wait! For what, man? You're more exasperating than that fat monstrosity! What are you waiting for?"

Ellery looked at him. Then he rose and flung his butt into the dying fire and placed his hand on the old man's arm. "Go to bed, Thorne. You wouldn't believe me if I told you."

"Queen, you *must.* I'll go mad if I don't see daylight on this thing soon!"

Ellery looked shocked, for no reason that Thorne could see. And then, just as inexplicably, he slapped Thorne's shoulder and began to chuckle.

"Go to bed," he said, still chuckling.

"But you must tell me!"

Ellery sighed, losing his smile. "I can't. You'd laugh."

"I'm not in a laughing mood!"

"Nor is it a laughing matter. Thorne, I began to say a moment ago that if I, poor sinner that I am, possessed religious susceptibilities, I should have become permanently devout in the past three days. I suppose I'm a hopeless case. But even I see a power not of earth in this."

"Play-actor," growled the old lawyer. "Professing to see the hand of God in . . . Don't be sacrilegious, man. We're not all heathen."

Ellery looked out his window at the moonless night and the glimmering grayness of the snow-swathed world.

"Hand of God?" he murmured. "No, not hand, Thorne. If this case is ever solved, it will be by . . . a lamp."

"Lamp?" said Thorne faintly. "Lamp?"

"In a manner of speaking. *The lamp of God.*"

III

The next day dawned sullenly, as ashen and hopeless a morning as ever was. Incredibly, it still snowed in the same thick fashion, as if the whole sky were crumbling bit by bit.

Ellery spent the better part of the day in the garage, tinkering at the big black car's vitals. He left the doors wide open, so that anyone who wished might see what he was about. He knew little enough of automotive mechanics, and he was engaged in a futile business.

But in the late afternoon, after hours of vain experimentation, he suddenly came upon a tiny wire which seemed to him to be out of joint with its environment. It simply hung, a useless thing. Logic demanded a connection. He experimented. He found one.

As he stepped on the starter and heard the cold motor sputter into life, a shape darkened the entrance of the garage. He turned off the ignition quickly and looked up.

It was Keith, a black mass against the background of snow, standing with widespread legs, a large can hanging from each big hand.

"Hello, there," murmured Ellery. "You've assumed human shape again I see. Back on one of your infrequent jaunts to the world of men, Keith?"

Keith said quietly: "Going somewhere, Mr. Queen?"

"Certainly. Why—do you intend to stop me?"

59

"Depends on where you're going."

"Ah, a treat. Well, suppose I tell *you* where to go?"

"Tell all you want. You don't get off these grounds until I know where you're bound for."

Ellery grinned. "There's a naive directness about you, Keith, that draws me in spite of myself. Well, I'll relieve your mind. Thorne and I are taking Miss Mayhew back to the city."

"In that case it's all right." Ellery studied his face; it was worn deep with ruts of fatigue and worry. Keith dropped the cans to the cement floor of the garage. "You can use these, then. Gas."

"Gas! Where on earth did you get it?"

"Let's say," said Keith grimly, "I dug it up out of an old Indian tomb."

"Very well."

"You've fixed Thorne's car, I see. Needn't have. I could have done it."

"Then why didn't you?"

"Because nobody asked me to." The giant swung on his heel and vanished.

Ellery sat still, frowning. Then he got out of the car, picked up the cans, and poured their contents into the tank. He reached into the car again, got the engine running, and leaving it to purr away like a great cat he went back to the house.

He found Alice in her room, a coat over her shoulders, staring out her window. She sprang up at his knocks.

"Mr. Queen, you've got Mr. Thorne's car going!"

"Success at last," smiled Ellery. "Are you ready?"

"Oh, yes! I feel so much better, now that we're actually to leave. Do you think we'll have a hard time? I saw Mr. Keith bring those cans in. Petrol, weren't they? Nice of him. I never did believe such a nice young man—" She flushed. There were hectic spots in her cheeks and her eyes were brighter than they had been for days. Her voice seemed less husky, too.

"It may be hard going through the drifts, but the car is equipped with chains. With luck we should make it. It's a powerful—"

Ellery stopped very suddenly indeed, his eyes fixed on the worn carpet at his feet, stony yet startled.

"Whatever is the matter, Mr. Queen?"

"Matter?" Ellery raised his eyes and drew a deep,

deep breath. "Nothing at all. God's in His heaven and all's right with the world."

She looked down at the carpet. "Oh . . . the sun!" With a little squeal of delight she turned to the window. "Why, Mr. Queen, it's stopped snowing. There's the sun setting—at last!"

"And high time, too," said Ellery briskly. "Will you please get your things on? We leave at once." He picked up her bags and left her, walking with a springy vigor that shook the old boards. He crossed the corridor to his room opposite hers and began, whistling, to pack his bag.

The living room was noisy with a babble of adieus. One would have said that this was a normal household, with normal people in a normal human situation. Alice was positively gay, quite as if she were not leaving a fortune in gold for what might turn out to be all time.

She set her purse down on the mantel next to her mother's chromo, fixed her hat, flung her arms about Mrs. Reinach, pecked gingerly at Mrs. Fell's withered cheek, and even smiled forgivingly at Dr. Reinach. Then she dashed back to the mantel, snatched up her purse, threw one long enigmatic glance at Keith's drawn face, and hurried outdoors as if the devil himself were after her.

Thorne was already in the car, his old face alight with incredible happiness, as if he had been reprieved at the very moment he was to set foot beyond the little green door. He beamed at the dying sun.

Ellery followed Alice more slowly. The bags were in Thorne's car; there was nothing more to do. He climbed in, raced the motor, and then released the brake.

The fat man filled the doorway, shouting: "You know the road, now, don't you? Turn to the right at the end of this drive. Then keep going in a straight line. You can't miss. You'll hit the main highway in about. . . ."

His last words were drowned in the roar of the engine. Ellery waved his hand. Alice, in the tonneau beside Thorne, twisted about and laughed a little hysterically. Thorne sat beaming at the back of Ellery's head.

The car, under Ellery's guidance, trundled unsteadily out of the drive and made a right turn into the road.

It grew dark rapidly. They made slow progress. The big machine inched its way through the drifts, slipping

61

and lurching despite its chains. As night fell, Ellery turned the powerful headlights on.

He drove with unswerving concentration.

None of them spoke.

It seemed hours before they reached the main highway. But when they did the car leaped to life on the road, which had been partly cleared by snowplows, and it was not long before they were entering the nearby town.

At the sight of the friendly electric lights, the paved streets, the solid blocks of houses, Alice gave a cry of sheer delight. Ellery stopped at a gasoline station and had the tank filled.

"It's not far from here, Miss Mayhew," said Thorne reassuringly. "We'll be in the city in no time. The Triborough Bridge . . ."

"Oh, it's wonderful to be alive!"

"Of course you'll stay at my house. My wife will be delighted to have you. After that . . ."

"You're so kind, Mr. Thorne. I don't know how I shall ever be able to thank you enough." She paused, startled. "Why, what's the matter, Mr. Queen?"

For Ellery had done a strange thing. He had stopped the car at a traffic intersection and asked the officer on duty something in a low tone. The officer stared at him and replied with gestures. Ellery swung the car off into another street. He drove slowly.

"What's the matter?" asked Alice again, leaning forward.

Thorne said, frowning: "You can't have lost your way. There's a sign which distinctly says. . . ."

"No, it's not that," said Ellery in a preoccupied way. "I've just thought of something."

The girl and the old man looked at each other, puzzled. Ellery stopped the car at a large stone building with green lights outside and went in, remaining there for fifteen minutes. He came out whistling.

"Queen!" said Thorne abruptly, eyes on the green lights. "What's up?"

"Something that must be brought down." Ellery swung the car about and headed it for the traffic intersection. When he reached it he turned left.

"Why, you've taken the wrong turn," said Alice nervously. "This is the direction from which we've just come. I'm sure of that."

"And you're quite right, Miss Mayhew. It is." She

sank back, pale, as if the very thought of returning terrified her. "We're going back, you see," said Ellery.

"Back!" exploded Thorne, sitting up straight.

"Oh, can't we just forget all those horrible people?" moaned Alice.

"I've a viciously stubborn memory. Besides, we have reinforcements. If you'll look back you'll see a car following us. It's a police car, and in it are the local Chief of Police and a squad of picked men."

"But why, Mr. Queen?" cried Alice. Thorne said nothing; his happiness had quite vanished, and he sat gloomily staring at the back of Ellery's neck.

"Because," said Ellery grimly, "I have my own professional pride. Because I've been on the receiving end of a damnably cute magician's trick."

"Trick?" she repeated dazedly.

"Now I shall turn magician myself. You saw a house disappear." He laughed softly. "I shall make it appear again!"

They could only stare at him, too bewildered to speak.

"And then," said Ellery, his voice hardening, "even if we chose to overlook such trivia as dematerialized houses, in all conscience we can't overlook . . . *murder.*"

IV

And there was the Black House again. Not a wraith. A solid house, a strong dirty time-encrusted house, looking as if it would never dream of taking wings and flying off into space.

It stood on the other side of the driveway, where it had always stood.

They saw it even as they turned into the drive from the drift-covered road, its bulk looming black against the brilliant moon, as substantial a house as could be found in the world of sane things.

Thorne and the girl were incapable of speech; they could only gape, dumb witnesses of a miracle even greater than the disappearance of the house in the first place.

As for Ellery, he stopped the car, sprang to the ground, signaled to the car snuffling up behind, and darted across the snowy clearing to the White House, whose windows were bright with lamp- and fire-light. Out of the police car swarmed men, and they ran after Ellery like hounds. Thorne and Alice followed in a daze.

Ellery kicked open the White House door. There was a revolver in his hand and there was no doubt, from the way he gripped it, that its cylinder had been replenished.

"Hello again," he said, stalking into the living room. "Not a ghost; Inspector Queen's little boy in the too, too solid flesh. Nemesis, perhaps. I bid you good evening. What—no welcoming smile, Dr. Reinach?"

The fat man had paused in the act of lifting a glass of Scotch to his lips. It was wonderful how the color seeped out of his pouchy cheeks, leaving them gray. Mrs. Reinach whimpered in a corner, and Mrs. Fell stared stupidly. Only Nick Keith showed no great astonishment. He was standing by a window, muffled to the ears; and on his face there was bitterness and admiration and, strangely, a sort of relief.

"Shut the door." The detectives behind Ellery spread out silently. Alice stumbled to a chair, her eyes wild, studying Dr. Reinach with a fierce intensity. . . . There was a sighing little sound and one of the detectives lunged toward the window at which Keith had been standing. But Keith was no longer there. He was bounding through the snow toward the woods like a huge deer.

"Don't let him get away!" cried Ellery. Three men dived through the window after the giant, their guns out. Shots began to sputter. The night outside was streaked with orange lightning.

Ellery went to the fire and warmed his hands. Dr. Reinach slowly, very slowly, sat down in the armchair. Thorne sank into a chair, too, putting his hands to his head.

Ellery turned around and said: "I've told you, Captain, enough of what's happened since our arrival to allow you an intelligent understanding of what I'm about to say." A stocky man in uniform nodded curtly.

"Thorne, last night for the first time in my career," continued Ellery whimsically, "I acknowledged the assistance of . . . Well, I tell you, who are implicated in this extraordinary crime, that had it not been for the good God above you would have succeeded in your plot against Alice Mayhew's inheritance."

"I'm disappointed in you," said the fat man from the depths of the chair.

"A loss I keenly feel." Ellery looked at him, smiling.

"Let me show you, skeptic. When Mr. Thorne, Miss Mayhew and I arrived the other day, it was late afternoon. Upstairs, in the room you so thoughtfully provided, I looked out the window and saw the sun setting. This was nothing and meant nothing, surely: sunset. Mere sunset. A trivial thing, interesting only to poets, meteorologists, and astronomers. But this was the one time when the sun was vital to a man seeking truth . . . a veritable lamp of God shining in the darkness.

"For, see. Miss Mayhew's bedroom that first day was on the opposite side of the house from mine. If the sun set in my window, then I faced west and she faced east. So far, so good. We talked, we retired. The next morning I awoke at seven—shortly after sunrise in this winter month—and what did I see? *I saw the sun streaming into my window*."

A knot hissed in the fire behind him. The stocky man in the blue uniform stirred uneasily.

"Don't you understand?" cried Ellery. "The sun had *set* in my window, and now it was *rising* in my window!"

Dr. Reinach was regarding him with a mild ruefulness. The color had come back to his fat cheeks. He raised the glass he was holding in a gesture curiously like a salute. Then he drank, deeply.

And Ellery said: "The significance of this unearthly reminder did not strike me at once. But much later it came back to me; and I dimly saw that chance, cosmos, God, whatever you may choose to call it, had given me the instrument for understanding the colossal, the mind-staggering phenomenon of a house which vanished overnight from the face of the earth."

"Good lord," muttered Thorne.

"But I was not sure; I did not trust my memory. I needed another demonstration from heaven, a bulwark to bolster my own suspicions. And so, as it snowed and snowed and snowed, the snow drawing a blanket across the face of the sun through which it could not shine, I waited. I waited for the snow to stop, and for the sun to shine again."

He sighed. "When it shone again, there could no longer be any doubt. It appeared first to me in Miss Mayhew's room, which had faced the east the afternoon of our arrival. But what was it I saw in Miss Mayhew's room late this afternoon? I saw the sun *set*."

65

"Good lord," said Thorne again; he seemed incapable of saying anything else.

"Then her room faced west today. How could her room face west today when it had faced east the day of our arrival? How could my room face west the day of our arrival and face east today? Had the sun stood still? Had the world gone mad? Or was there another explanation—one so extraordinarily simple that it staggered the imagination?"

Thorne muttered: "Queen, this is the most—"

"Please," said Ellery, "let me finish. The only logical conclusion, the only conclusion that did not fly in the face of natural law, of science itself, was that while the house we were in today, the rooms we occupied, *seemed* to be identical with the house and the rooms we had occupied on the day of our arrival, *they were not*. Unless this solid structure had been turned about on its foundation like a toy on a stick, which was palpably absurd, then *it was not the same house*. It looked the same inside and out, it had identical furniture, identical carpeting, identical decorations . . . but it was not the same house. It was another house. It was another house exactly like the first in every detail except one: and that was its terrestrial position in relation to the sun."

A detective outside shouted a message of failure, a shout carried away by the wind under the bright cold moon.

"See," said Ellery softly, "how everything fell into place. If this White House we were in was not the same White House in which we had slept that first night, but was a twin house in a different position in relation to the sun, then the Black House, which apparently had vanished, had not vanished at all. It was where it had always been. It was not the Black House which had vanished, but we who had vanished. It was not the Black House which had moved away, but we who had moved away. We had been transferred during that first night to a new location, where the surrounding woods looked similar, where there was a similar driveway with a similar garage at its terminus, where the road outside was similarly old and pitted, where everything was similar except that there was no Black House, only an empty clearing.

"So we must have been moved, body and baggage, to this twin White House during the time we retired the first night and the time we awoke the next morning. We, Miss Mayhew's chromo on the mantel, the holes in our doors where locks had been, even the fragments of a brandy decanter which had been shattered the night before in a cleverly staged scene against the brick wall of the fireplace at the original house . . . all, all transferred to the twin house to further the illusion that we were still in the original house the next morning."

"Drivel," said Dr. Reinach, smiling. "Such pure drivel that it smacks of phantasmagoria."

"It was beautiful," said Ellery. "A beautiful plan. It had symmetry, the polish of great art. And it made a beautiful chain of reasoning, too, once I was set properly at the right link. For what followed? Since we had been transferred without our knowledge during the night, it must have been while we were unconscious. I recalled the two drinks Thorne and I had had, and the fuzzy tongue and head that resulted the next morning. Mildly drugged, then; and the drinks had been mixed the night before by Dr. Reinach's own hand. Doctor—drugs; very simple." The fat man shrugged with amusement, glancing sidewise at the stocky man in blue. But the stocky man in blue wore a hard, unchanging mask.

"But Dr. Reinach alone?" murmured Ellery. "Oh, no, impossible. One man could never have accomplished all that was necessary in the scant few hours available . . . fix Thorne's car, carry us and our clothes and bags from the one White House to its duplicate—by machine—put Thorne's car out of commission again, put us to bed again, arrange our clothing identically, transfer the chromo, the fragments of the cut-glass decanter in the fireplace, perhaps even a few knickknacks and ornaments not duplicated in the second White House, and so on. A prodigious job, even if most of the preparatory work had been done before our arrival. Obviously the work of a whole group. Of accomplices. Who but everyone in the house? With the possible exception of Mrs. Fell, who in her condition could be swayed easily enough, with no clear perception of what was occurring."

Ellery's eyes gleamed. "And so I accuse you all—including young Mr. Keith who has wisely taken himself off—of having aided in the plot whereby you would prevent the rightful heiress of Sylvester Mayhew's fortune from taking possession of the house in which it was hidden."

67

Dr. Reinach coughed politely, flapping his paws together like a great seal. "Terribly interesting, Queen, terribly. I don't know when I've been more captivated by sheer fiction. On the other hand, there are certain personal allusions in your story which, much as I admire their ingenuity, cannot fail to provoke me." He turned to the stocky man in blue. "Certainly, Captain," he chuckled, "you don't credit this incredible story? I believe Mr. Queen has gone a little mad from sheer shock."

"Unworthy of you, Doctor," sighed Ellery. "The proof of what I say lies in the very fact that we are here, at this moment."

"You'll have to explain that," said the police chief, who seemed out of his depth.

"I mean that we are now in the original White House. I led you back here, didn't I? And I can lead you back to the twin White House, for now I know the basis of the illusion. After our departure this evening, incidentally, all these people returned to this house. The other White House had served its purpose and they no longer needed it.

"As for the geographical trick involved, it struck me that this side road we're on makes a steady curve for miles. Both driveways lead off this same road, one some six miles farther up the road; although, because of the curve, which is like a number 9, the road makes a wide sweep and virtually doubles back on itself, so that as the crow flies the two settlements are only a mile or so apart, although by the curving road they are six miles apart.

"When Dr. Reinach drove Thorne and Miss Mayhew and me out here the day the *Caronia* docked, he deliberately passed the almost imperceptible drive leading to the substitute house and went on until he reached this one, the original. We didn't notice the first driveway.

"Thorne's car was put out of commission deliberately to prevent his driving. The driver of a car will observe landmarks when his passengers notice little or nothing. Keith even met Thorne on both Thorne's previous visits to Mayhew—ostensibly 'to lead the way,' actually to prevent Thorne from familiarizing himself with the road. And it was Dr. Reinach who drove the three of us here that first day. They permitted me to drive away tonight for what they hoped was a one-way trip because we started from the substitute house—of the two, the one on the road nearer to town. We couldn't possibly, then, pass the tell-tale second drive and become suspicious.

68

And they knew the relatively shorter drive would not impress our consciousness."

"But even granting all that, Mr. Queen," said the policeman, "I don't see what these people expected to accomplish. They couldn't hope to keep you folks fooled forever."

"True," cried Ellery, "but don't forget that by the time we caught on to the various tricks involved they hoped to have laid hands on Mayhew's fortune and disappeared with it. Don't you see that the whole illusion was planned *to give them time?* Time to dismantle the Black House without interference, raze it to the ground if necessary, to find that hidden hoard of gold? I don't doubt that if you examine the house next door you'll find it a shambles and a hollow shell. That's why Reinach and Keith kept disappearing. They were taking turns at the Black House, picking it apart, stone by stone, in a frantic search for the cache, while we were occupied in the duplicate White House with an apparently supernatural phenomenon. That's why someone—probably the worthy doctor here—slipped out of the house behind your back, Thorne, and struck me over the head when I rashly attempted to follow Keith's tracks in the snow. I could not be permitted to reach the original settlement, for if I did the whole preposterous illusion would be revealed."

"How about that gold?" growled Thorne.

"For all I know," said Ellery with a shrug, "they've found it and salted it away again."

"Oh, but we didn't," whimpered Mrs. Reinach, squirming in her chair. "Herbert, I *told* you not to—"

"Idiot," said the fat man. "Stupid swine." She jerked as if he had struck her.

"If you hadn't found the loot," said the police chief to Dr. Reinach brusquely, "why did you let these people go tonight?"

Dr. Reinach compressed his blubbery lips; he raised his glass and drank quickly.

"I think I can answer that," said Ellery in a gloomy tone. "In many ways it's the most remarkable element of the whole puzzle. Certainly it's the grimmest and least excusable. The other illusion was child's play compared to it. For it involves two apparently irreconcilable elements —Alice Mayhew and a murder."

"A murder!" exclaimed the policeman, stiffening.

"Me?" said Alice in bewilderment.

Ellery lit a cigarette and flourished it at the policeman. "When Alice Mayhew came here that first afternoon, she went into the Black House with us. In her father's bedroom she ran across an old chromo—I see it's not here, so it's still in the other White House—portraying her long-dead mother as a girl. Alice Mayhew fell on the chromo like a Chinese refugee on a bowl of rice. She had only one picture of her mother, she explained, and that a poor one. She treasured this unexpected discovery so much that she took it with her, then and there, to the White House—this house. And she placed it on the mantel over the fireplace here in a prominent position."

The stocky man frowned; Alice sat very still; Thorne looked puzzled. And Ellery put the cigarette back to his lips and said: "Yet when Alice Mayhew fled from the White House in our company tonight for what seemed to be the last time, *she completely ignored her mother's chromo,* that treasured memento over which she had gone into such raptures the first day! She could not have failed to overlook it in, let us say, the excitement of the moment. She had placed her purse on the mantel, a moment before, next to the chromo. She returned to the mantel for her purse. And yet she passed the chromo up without a glance. Since its sentimental value to her was overwhelming, by her own admission, it's the one thing in all this property she would not have left. *If she had taken it in the beginning, she would have taken it on leaving.*"

Thorne cried: "What in the name of heaven are you saying, Queen?" His eyes glared at the girl, who sat glued to her chair, scarcely breathing.

"I am saying," said Ellery curtly, "that we were blind. I am saying that not only was a house impersonated, but a woman as well. *I am saying that this woman is not Alice Mayhew.*"

The girl raised her eyes after an infinite interval in which no one, not even the policemen present, so much as stirred a foot.

"I thought of everything," she said with the queerest sigh, and quite without the husky tone, "but that. And it was going off so beautifully."

"Oh, you fooled me very neatly," drawled Ellery. "That pretty little bedroom scene last night. . . . I know now what happened. This precious Dr. Reinach of yours had stolen into your room at midnight to report to you on

70

the progress of the search at the Black House, perhaps to urge you to persuade Thorne and me to leave today—at any cost. I happened to pass along the hall outside your room, stumbled, and fell against the wall with a clatter; not knowing who it might be or what the intruder's purpose, you both fell instantly into that cunning deception. . . . Actors! Both of you missed a career on the stage."

The fat man closed his eyes; he seemed asleep. And the girl murmured, with a sort of tired defiance: "Not missed, Mr. Queen. I spent several years in the theater."

"You were devils, you two. Psychologically this plot has been the conception of evil genius. You knew that Alice Mayhew was unknown to anyone in this country except by her photographs. Moreover, there was a startling resemblance between the two of you, as Miss Mayhew's photographs showed. And you knew Miss Mayhew would be in the company of Thorne and me for only a few hours, and then chiefly in the murky light of a sedan."

"Good lord," groaned Thorne, staring at the girl in horror.

"Alice Mayhew," said Ellery grimly, "walked into this house and was whisked upstairs by Mrs. Reinach. *And Alice Mayhew, the English girl, never appeared before us again.* It was you who came downstairs; you, who had been secreted from Thorne's eyes during the past six days deliberately, so that he would not even suspect your existence; you who probably conceived the entire plot when Thorne brought the photographs of Alice Mayhew here, and her gossipy, informative letters; you, who looked enough like the real Alice Mayhew to get by with an impersonation in the eyes of two men to whom Alice Mayhew was a total stranger. I did think you looked different, somehow, when you appeared for dinner that first night; but I put it down to the fact that I was seeing you for the first time refreshed, brushed up, and without your hat and coat. Naturally, after that, the more I saw of you the less I remembered the details of the real Alice Mayhew's appearance and so became more and more convinced, unconsciously, that you were Alice Mayhew. As for the husky voice and the excuse of having caught cold on the long automobile ride from the pier, that was a clever ruse to disguise the inevitable difference between your voices. The only danger that existed lay in Mrs. Fell, who gave us the answer to the whole riddle the first time we met her.

71

She thought you were her own daughter Olivia. Of course. *Because that's who you are!"*

Dr. Reinach was sipping brandy now with a steady indifference to his surroundings. His little eyes were fixed on a point miles away. Old Mrs. Fell sat gaping stupidly at the girl.

"You even covered that danger by getting Dr. Reinach to tell us beforehand that trumped-up story of Mrs. Fell's 'delusion' and Olivia Fell's 'death' in an automobile accident several years ago. Oh, admirable! Yet even this poor creature, in the frailty of her anile faculties, was fooled by a difference in voice and hair—two of the most easily distinguishable features. I suppose you fixed up your hair at the time Mrs. Reinach brought the real Alice Mayhew upstairs and you had a living model to go by. . . . I could find myself moved to admiration if it were not for one thing."

"You're so clever," said Olivia Fell coolly. "Really a fascinating monster. What do you mean?"

Ellery went to her and put his hand on her shoulder. "Alice Mayhew vanished and you took her place. Why did you take her place? For two possible reasons. One—to get Thorne and me away from the danger zone as quickly as possible, and to keep us away by 'abandoning' the fortune or dismissing us, which as Alice Mayhew would be your privilege: in proof, your vociferous insistence that we take you away. Two—of infinitely greater importance to the scheme: if your confederates did not find the gold at once, you were still Alice Mayhew in our eyes. You could then dispose of the house when and as you saw fit. Whenever the gold was found, it would be yours and your accomplices'.

"But the real Alice Mayhew vanished. For you, her impersonator, to be in a position to go through the long process of taking over Alice Mayhew's inheritance, it was necessary that Alice Mayhew remain *permanently invisible*. For you to get possession of her rightful inheritance and live to enjoy its fruits, it was necessary that Alice Mayhew die. And that, Thorne," snapped Ellery, gripping the girl's shoulder hard, "is why I said that there was something besides a disappearing house to cope with tonight. Alice Mayhew was murdered."

There were three shouts from outside which rang with tones of great excitement. And then they ceased, abruptly.

"Murdered," went on Ellery, "by the only occupant of the house who was not *in* the house when this imposter came downstairs that first evening—Nicholas Keith. A hired killer. Although these people are all accessories to that murder."

A voice said from the window: "Not a hired *killer*."

They wheeled sharply, and fell silent. The three detectives who had sprung out of the window were there in the background, quietly watchful. Before them were two people.

"Not a killer," said one of them, a woman. "That's what he was supposed to be. Instead, and without their knowledge, he saved my life . . . dear Nick."

And now the pall of grayness settled over the faces of Mrs. Fell, and of Olivia Fell, and of Mrs. Reinach, and of the burly doctor. For by Keith's side stood Alice Mayhew. She was the same woman who sat near the fire only in general similitude of feature. Now that both women could be compared in proximity, there were obvious points of difference. She looked worn and grim, but happy withal; and she was holding to the arm of bitter-mouthed Nick Keith with a grip that was quite possessive.

ADDENDUM

Afterwards, when it was possible to look back on the whole amazing fabric of plot and event, Mr. Ellery Queen said: "The scheme would have been utterly impossible except for two things: the character of Olivia Fell and the —in itself—fantastic existence of that duplicate house in the woods."

He might have added that both of these would in turn have been impossible except for the aberrant strain in the Mayhew blood. The father of Sylvester Mayhew—Dr. Reinach's stepfather—had always been erratic, and he had communicated his unbalance to his children. Sylvester and Sarah, who became Mrs. Fell, were twins, and they had always been insanely jealous of each other's prerogatives. When they married in the same month, their father avoided trouble by presenting each of them with a specially built house, the houses being identical in every detail. One he had erected next to his own house and presented to Mrs. Fell as a wedding gift; the other he built on a piece of property he owned some miles away and gave to Sylvester.

Mrs. Fell's husband died early in her married life; and she moved away to live with her half-brother Herbert. When old Mayhew died, Sylvester boarded up his own house and moved into the ancestral mansion. And there the twin houses stood for many years, separated by only a few miles by road, completely and identically furnished inside—fantastic monuments to the Mayhew eccentricity.

The duplicate White House lay boarded up, waiting, idle, requiring only the evil genius of an Olivia Fell to be put to use. Olivia was beautiful, intelligent, accomplished, and as unscrupulous as Lady Macbeth. It was she who had influenced the others to move back to the abandoned house next to the Black House for the sole purpose of coercing or robbing Sylvester Mayhew. When Thorne appeared with the news of Sylvester's long-lost daughter, she recognized the peril to their scheme and, grasping her own resemblance to her English cousin from the photographs Thorne brought, conceived the whole extraordinary plot.

Then obviously the first step was to put Sylvester out of the way. With perfect logic, she bent Dr. Reinach to her will and caused him to murder his patient before the arrival of Sylvester's daughter. (A later exhumation and autopsy revealed traces of poison in the corpse.) Meanwhile, Olivia perfected the plans of the impersonation and illusion.

The house illusion was planned for the benefit of Thorne, to keep him sequestered and bewildered while the Black House was being torn down in the search for gold. The illusion would perhaps not have been necessary had Olivia felt certain that her impersonation would succeed perfectly.

The illusion was simpler, of course, than appeared on the surface. The house was there, completely furnished, ready for use. All that was necessary was to take the boards down, air the place out, clean up, put fresh linen in. There was plenty of time before Alice's arrival for this preparatory work.

The one weakness of Olivia Fell's plot was objective, not personal. That woman would have succeeded in anything. But she made the mistake of selecting Nick Keith for the job of murdering Alice Mayhew. Keith had originally insinuated himself into the circle of plotters, posing as a desperado prepared to do anything for sufficient pay. Actually, he was the son of Sylvester Mayhew's second wife, who had been so brutally treated by Mayhew and driven off to die in poverty.

Before his mother expired she instilled in Keith's mind a hatred for Mayhew that waxed, rather than waned, with the ensuing years. Keith's sole motive in joining the conspirators was to find his stepfather's fortune and take that part of it which Mayhew had stolen from his mother. He had never intended to murder Alice—his ostensible role. When he carried her from the house that first evening under the noses of Ellery and Thorne, it was not to strangle and bury her, as Olivia had directed, but to secrete her in an ancient shack in the nearby woods known only to himself.

He had managed to smuggle provisions to her while he was ransacking the Black House. At first he had held her frankly prisoner, intending to keep her so until he found the money, took his share, and escaped. But as he came to know her, he came to love her, and he soon confessed the whole story to her in the privacy of the shack. Her sympathy gave him new courage; concerned now with her safety above everything else, he prevailed upon her to remain in hiding until he could find the money and outwit his fellow-conspirators. Then they both intended to unmask Olivia.

The ironical part of the whole affair, as Mr. Ellery Queen was to point out, was that the goal of all this plotting and counterplotting—Sylvester Mayhew's gold—remained as invisible as the Black House apparently had been. Despite the most thorough search of the building and grounds no trace of it had been found.

"I've asked you to visit my poor diggings," smiled Ellery a few weeks later, "because something occurred to me that simply cried out for investigation."

Keith and Alice glanced at each other blankly; and Thorne, looking clean, rested, and complacent for the first time in weeks, sat up straighter in Ellery's most comfortable chair.

"I'm glad something occurred to somebody," said Nick Keith with a grin. "I'm a pauper; and Alice is only one jump ahead of me."

"You haven't the philosophic attitude towards wealth," said Ellery dryly, "that's so charming a part of Dr. Reinach's personality. Poor Colossus! I wonder how he likes our jails. . . ." He poked a log into the fire. "By this time, Miss Mayhew, our common friend Thorne has had your father's house virtually annihilated. No gold. Eh, Thorne?"

"Nothing but dirt," said the lawyer sadly. "Why, we've taken that house apart stone by stone."

"Exactly. Now there are two possibilities, since I am incorrigibly categorical: either your father's fortune exists, Miss Mayhew, or it does not. If it does not and he was lying, there's an end to the business, of course, and you and your precious Keith will have to put your heads together and agree to live either in noble, rugged individualistic poverty or by the grace of the Relief Administration. But suppose there was a fortune, as your father claimed, and suppose he did secrete it somewhere in that house. What then?"

"Then," sighed Alice, "it's flown away."

Ellery laughed. "Not quite; I've had enough of vanishments for the present, anyway. Let's tackle the problem differently. Is there anything which was in Sylvester Mayhew's house before he died which is not there now?"

Thorne stared. "If you mean the—er—the body . . ."

"Don't be gruesome, Literal Lyman. Besides, there's been an exhumation. No, guess again."

Alice looked slowly down at the package in her lap. "So that's why you asked me to fetch this with me today!"

"You mean," cried Keith, "the fellow was deliberately putting everyone off the track when he said his fortune was gold?"

Ellery chuckled and took the package from the girl. He unwrapped it and for a moment gazed appreciatively at the large old chromo of Alice's mother.

And then, with the self-assurance of the complete logician, he stripped away the back of the frame.

Gold-and-green documents cascaded into his lap.

"Converted into bonds," grinned Ellery. "Who said your father was cracked, Miss Mayhew? A very clever gentleman! Come, come, Thorne, stop rubbernecking and let's leave these children of fortune alone!"

The Adventure of the
Treasure Hunt

"DISMOUNT!" roared Major-General Barrett gaily, scrambling off his horse. "How's that for exercise before breakfast, Mr. Queen?"

"Oh, lovely," said Ellery, landing on *terra firma* somehow. The big bay tossed his head, visibly relieved. "I'm afraid my cavalry muscles are a little atrophied, General. We've been riding since six-thirty, remember." He limped to the cliff's edge and rested his racked body against the low stone parapet.

Harkness uncoiled himself from the roan and said: "You lead a life of armchair adventure, Queen? It must be embarrassing when you poke your nose out into the world of men." He laughed. Ellery eyed the man's yellow mane and nervy eyes with the unreasoning dislike of the chronic shut-in. That broad chest was untroubled after the gallop.

"Embarrassing to the horse," said Ellery. "Beautiful view, General. You couldn't have selected this site blindly. Must be a streak of poetry in your make-up."

"Poetry your foot, Mr. Queen! I'm a military man." The old gentleman waddled to Ellery's side and gazed down over the Hudson River, a blue-grass reflector under the young sun. The cliff was sheer; it fell cleanly to a splinter of beach far below, where Major-General Barrett had his boathouse. A zigzag of steep stone steps in the face of the cliff was the only means of descent.

An old man was seated on the edge of a little jetty below, fishing. He glanced up, and to Ellery's astonishment sprang to his feet and snapped his free hand up in a stiff salute. Then he very placidly sat down and resumed his fishing.

"Braun," said the General, beaming. "Old pensioner of mine. Served under me in Mexico. He and Magruder, the old chap at the caretaker's cottage. You see? Discipline, that's it. . . . Poetry?" He snorted. "Not for me, Mr. Queen. I like this ledge for its military value. Commands the river. Miniature West Point, b'gad!"

Ellery turned and looked upward. The shelf of rock on which the General had built his home was surrounded on its other three sides by precipitous cliffs, quite unscalable, which towered so high that their crests were swimming in mist. A steep road had been blasted in the living rock of the rearmost cliff; it spiraled down from the top of the mountain, and Ellery still remembered with vertigo the automobile descent the evening before.

"You command the river," he said dryly, "but an enemy could shoot the hell out of you by commanding that road up there. Or are my tactics infantile?"

The old gentleman spluttered: "Why, I could hold that gateway to the road against an army, man!"

"And the artillery," murmured Ellery. "Heavens, General, you *are* prepared." He glanced with amusement at a small sleek cannon beside the nearby flagpole, its muzzle gaping over the parapet.

"General's getting ready for the revolution," said Harkness with a lazy laugh. "We live in parlous times."

"You sportsmen," snapped the General, "have no respect whatever for tradition. You know very well this is a sunset gun—you don't sneer at the one on the Point, do you? That's the only way Old Glory," he concluded in a parade-ground voice, "will ever come down on *my* property, Harkness—to the boom of a cannon salute!"

"I suppose," smiled the big-game hunter, "my elephant gun wouldn't serve the same purpose? On safari I—"

"Ignore the fellow, Mr. Queen," said the General testily. "We just tolerate him on these weekends because he's a friend of Lieutenant Fiske's. . . . Too bad you arrived too late last night to see the ceremony. Quite stirring! You'll see it again at sunset today. Must keep up the old traditions. Part of my life, Mr. Queen . . . I guess I'm an old fool."

"Oh, indeed not," said Ellery hastily. "Traditions are the backbone of the nation; anybody knows that." Harkness chuckled, and the General looked pleased. Ellery knew the type—retired army man, too old for service, pining for the military life. From what Dick Fiske, the General's prospective son-in-law, had told him on the way down the night before, Barrett had been a passionate and single-

78

tracked soldier; and he had taken over with him into civilian life as many mementoes of the good old martial days as he could carry. Even his servants were old soldiers; and the house, which bristled with relics of three wars, was run like a regimental barracks.

A groom led their horses away, and they strolled back across the rolling lawns toward the house. Major-General Barrett, Ellery was thinking, must be crawling with money; he had already seen enough to convince him of that. There was a tiled swimming pool outdoors; a magnificent solarium; a target range; a gun room with a variety of weapons that . . .

"General," said an agitated voice; and he looked up to see Lieutenant Fiske, his uniform unusually disordered, running toward them. "May I see you a moment alone, sir?"

"Of course, Richard. Excuse me, gentlemen?"

Harkness and Ellery hung back. The Lieutenant said something, his arms jerking nervously; and the old gentleman paled. Then, without another word, both men broke into a run, the General waddling like a startled grandfather gander toward the house.

"I wonder what's eating Dick," said Harkness, as he and Ellery followed more decorously.

"Leonie," ventured Ellery. "I've known Fiske for a long time. That ravishing daughter of the regiment is the only unsettling influence the boy's ever encountered. I hope there's nothing wrong."

"Pity if there is," shrugged the big man. "It promised to be a restful weekend. I had my fill of excitement on my last expedition."

"Ran into trouble?"

"My boys deserted, and a flood on the Niger did the rest. Lost everything. Lucky to have escaped with my life . . . Ah, there, Mrs. Nixon. Is anything wrong with Miss Barrett?"

A tall pale woman with red hair and amber eyes looked up from the magazine she was reading. "Leonie? I haven't seen her this morning. Why?" She seemed not too interested. "Oh, Mr. Queen! That dreadful game we played last night kept me awake half the night. How *can* you sleep with all those murdered people haunting you?"

"My difficulty," grinned Ellery, "is not in sleeping too little, Mrs. Nixon, but in sleeping too much. The original sluggard. No more imagination than an amoeba.

Nightmare? You must have something on your conscience."

"But was it necessary to take our *fingerprints*, Mr. Queen? I mean, a game's a game. . . ."

Ellery chuckled. "I promise to destroy my impromptu little Bureau of Identification at the very first opportunity. No thanks, Harkness; don't care for any this early in the day."

"Queen," said Lieutenant Fiske from the doorway. His brown cheeks were muddy and mottled, and he held himself very stiffly. "Would you mind—?"

"What's wrong, Lieutenant?" demanded Harkness.

"Has something happened to Leonie?" asked Mrs. Nixon.

"Wrong? Why, nothing at all." The young officer smiled, took Ellery's arm, and steered him to the stairs. He was smiling no longer. "Something rotten's happened, Queen. We're—we don't quite know what to do. Lucky you're here. You might know. . . ."

"Now, now," said Ellery gently. "What's happened?"

"You remember that rope of pearls Leonie wore last night?"

"Oh," said Ellery.

"It was my engagement gift to her. Belonged to my mother." The Lieutenant bit his lip. "I'm not—well, a lieutenant in the United States Army can't buy pearls on his salary. I wanted to give Leonie something—expensive. Foolish of me, I suppose. Anyway, I treasured mother's pearls for sentimental reasons, too, and—"

"You're trying to tell me," said Ellery as they reached the head of the stairs, "that the pearls are gone."

"Damn it, yes!"

"How much are they worth?"

"Twenty-five thousand dollars. My father was wealthy —once."

Ellery sighed. In the workshop of the cosmos it had been decreed that he should stalk with open eyes among the lame, the halt, and the blind. He lit a cigarette and followed the officer into Leonie Barrett's bedroom.

There was nothing martial in Major-General Barrett's bearing now; he was simply a fat old man with sagging shoulders. As for Leonie, she had been crying; and Ellery thought irrelevantly that she had used the hem of her *peignoir* to stanch her tears. But there was also a set to her chin and a gleam in her eye; and she pounced upon

Ellery so quickly that he almost threw his arm up to defend himself.

"Someone's stolen my necklace," she said fiercely. "Mr. Queen, you must get it back. You *must*, do you hear?"

"Leonie, my dear," began the General in a feeble voice.

"No, father! I don't care *who's* going to be hurt. That—that rope of pearls meant a lot to Dick, and it means a lot to me, and I don't propose to sit by and let some *thief* snatch it right from under my nose!"

"But, darling," said the Lieutenant miserably. "After all, your guests . . ."

"Hang my guests, and yours, too," said the young woman with a toss of her head. "I don't think there's anything in Mrs. Post's book which says a thief gathers immunity simply because he's present on an invitation."

"But it's certainly more reasonable to suspect that one of the servants—"

The General's head came up like a shot. "My dear Richard," he snorted, "put that notion out of your head. There isn't a man in my employ who hasn't been with me for at least twenty years. I'd trust any one of 'em with anything I have. I've had proof of their honesty and loyalty a hundred times."

"Since I'm one of the guests," said Ellery cheerfully, "I think I'm qualified to pass an opinion. Murder will out, but it was never hindered by a bit of judicious investigation, Lieutenant. Your fiancée's quite right. When did you discover the theft, Miss Barrett?"

"A half-hour ago, when I awoke." Leonie pointed to the dressing table beside her four-posted bed. "Even before I rubbed the sleep out of my eyes I saw that the pearls were gone. Because the lid of my jewel box was up, as you see."

"And the box was closed when you retired last night?"

"Better than that. I awoke at six this morning feeling thirsty. I got out of bed for a glass of water, and I distinctly remember that the box was closed at that time. Then I went back to sleep."

Ellery strolled over and glanced down at the box. Then he blew smoke and said: "Happy chance. It's a little after eight now. You discovered the theft, then, at a quarter of eight or so. Therefore the pearls were stolen between six and seven-forty-five. Didn't you hear anything, Miss Barrett?"

Leonie smiled ruefully. "I'm a disgustingly sound sleeper, Mr. Queen. That's something you'll learn, Dick. And then for years I've suspected that I snore, but nobody ever—"

The Lieutenant blushed. The General said: "Leonie," not very convincingly, and Leonie made a face and began to weep again, this time on the Lieutenant's shoulder.

"What the deuce are we to do?" snarled the General. "We can't—well, hang it all, you just can't *search* people. Nasty business! If the pearls weren't so valuable I'd say forget the whole ruddy thing."

"A body search is scarcely necessary, General," said Ellery. "No thief would be so stupid as to carry the loot about on his person. He'd expect the police to be called; and the police, at least, are notoriously callous to the social niceties."

"Police," said Leonie in a damp voice, raising her head. "Oh, goodness. Can't we—"

"I think," said Ellery, "we can struggle along without them for the proverbial nonce. On the other hand, a search of the premises . . . Any objection to my prowling about?"

"None whatever," snapped Leonie. "Mr. Queen, you prowl!"

"I believe I shall. By the way, who besides the four of us—and the thief—knows about this?"

"Not another soul."

"Very good. Now, discretion is our shibboleth today. Please pretend nothing's happened. The thief will know we're acting, but he'll be constrained to act, too, and perhaps . . ." He smoked thoughtfully. "Suppose you dress and join your guests downstairs, Miss Barrett. Come, come, get that Wimpole Street expression off your face, my dear!"

"Yes, sir," said Leonie, trying out a smile.

"You gentlemen might co-operate. Keep everyone away from this floor while I go into my prowling act. I shouldn't like to have Mrs. Nixon, for example, catch me red-handed among her brassières."

"Oh," said Leonie suddenly. And she stopped smiling.

"What's the matter?" asked the Lieutenant in an anxious voice.

"Well, Dorothy Nixon is up against it. Horribly short of funds. No, that's a—a rotten thing to say." Leonie flushed. "Goodness, I'm half-naked! Now, *please*, clear out."

82

"Nothing," said Ellery in an undertone to Lieutenant Fiske after breakfast. "It isn't anywhere in the house."

"Damnation," said the officer. "You're positive?"

"Quite. I've been through all the rooms. Kitchen. Solarium. Pantry. Armory. I've even visited the General's cellar."

Fiske gnawed his lower lip. Leonie called gaily: "Dorothy and Mr. Harkness and I are going into the pool for a plunge. Dick! Coming?"

"Please go," said Ellery softly; and he added: "And while you're plunging, Lieutenant, search that pool."

Fiske looked startled. Then he nodded rather grimly and followed the others.

"Nothing, eh?" said the General glumly. "I saw you talking to Richard."

"Not yet." Ellery glanced from the house, into which the others had gone to change into bathing costume, to the riverside. "Suppose we stroll down there, General. I want to ask your man Braun some questions."

They made their way cautiously down the stone steps in the cliff to the sliver of beach below, and found the old pensioner placidly engaged in polishing the brasswork of the General's launch.

"Mornin', sir," said Braun, snapping to attention.

"At ease," said the General moodily. "Braun, this gentleman wants to ask you some questions."

"Very simple ones," smiled Ellery. "I saw you fishing, Braun, at about eight this morning. How long had you been sitting on the jetty?"

"Well, sir," replied the old man, scratching his left arm, "on and off since ha'-past five. Bitin' early, they are. Got a fine mess."

"Did you have the stairs there in view all the time?"

"Sure thing, sir."

"Has anyone come down this morning?" Braun shook his gray thatch. "Has anyone approached from the river?"

"Not a one, sir."

"Did anyone drop or throw anything down here or into the water from the cliff up there?"

"If they'd had, I'd 'a' heard the splash, sir. No, sir."

"Thank you. Oh, by the way, Braun, you're here all day?"

"Well, only till early afternoon, unless someone's usin' the launch, sir."

"Keep your eyes open, then. General Barrett is especially anxious to know if anyone comes down this afternoon. If someone does, watch closely and report."

"General's orders, sir?" asked Braun, cocking a shrewd eye.

"That's right, Braun," sighed the General. "Dismissed."

"And now," said Ellery, as they climbed to the top of the cliff, "let's see what friend Magruder has to say."

Magruder was a gigantic old Irishman with leathery cheeks and the eyes of a top sergeant. He occupied a rambling little cottage at the only gateway to the estate.

"No, sir," he said emphatically, "ain't been a soul near here all mornin'. Nob'dy, in or out."

"But how can you be sure, Magruder?"

The Irishman stiffened. "From a quarter to six till seven-thirty I was a-settin' right there in full view o' the gate a cleanin' some o' the Gin'ral's guns, sir. And afther I was trimmin' the privets."

"You may take Magruder's word as gospel," snapped the General.

"I do, I do," said Ellery soothingly. "This is the only vehicular exit from the estate, of course, sir?"

"As you see."

"Yes, yes. And the cliffside . . . Only a lizard could scale those rocky side walls. Very interesting. Thanks, Magruder."

"Well, what now?" demanded the General, as they walked back toward the house.

Ellery frowned. "The essence of any investigation, General, is the question of how many possibilities you can eliminate. This little hunt grows enchanting on that score. You say you trust your servants implicitly?"

"With anything."

"Then round up as many as you can spare and have them go over every inch of the grounds with a fine comb. Fortunately your estate isn't extensive, and the job shouldn't take long."

"Hmm." The General's nostrils quivered. "B'gad, there's an idea! I see, I see. Splendid, Mr. Queen. You may trust my lads. Old soldiers, every one of 'em; they'll love it. And the trees?"

"I beg your pardon?"

"The trees, man, the trees! Crotches of 'em; good hiding-places."

"Oh," said Ellery gravely, "the trees. By all means search them."

"Leave that to me," said the General fiercely; and he trotted off breathing fire.

Ellery sauntered over to the pool, which churned with vigorous bodies, and sat down on a bench to watch. Mrs. Nixon waved a shapely arm and dived under, pursued by a bronzed giant who turned out to be Harkness when his dripping curls reappeared. A slim slick figure shot out of the water almost at Ellery's feet and in the same motion scaled the edge of the pool.

"I've done it," murmured Leonie, smiling and preening as if to invite Ellery's admiration.

"Done what?" mumbled Ellery, grinning back.

"Searched them."

"Searched—! I don't understand."

"Oh, are *all* men fundamentally stupid?" Leonie leaned back and shook out her hair. "Why d'ye think I suggested the pool? So that everyone would have to take his clothes off! All I did was slip into a bedroom or two before going down myself. I searched *all* our clothes. It was possible the—the thief had slipped the pearls into some unsuspecting pocket, you see. Well . . . nothing."

Ellery looked at her. "My dear young woman, *I'd* like to play Browning to your Ba, come to think of it. . . . But their bathing suits—"

Leonie colored. Then she said firmly: "That was a long, six-stranded rope. If you think Dorothy Nixon has it on her person *now*, in *that* bathing suit . . ." Ellery glanced at Mrs. Nixon.

"I can't say," he chuckled, "that any of you in your present costumes could conceal an object larger than a fly's wing. Ah, there, Lieutenant! How's the water?"

"No good," said Fiske, thrusting his chin over the pool's edge.

"Why, Dick!" exclaimed Leonie. "I thought you liked—"

"Your fiancé," murmured Ellery, "has just informed me that your pearls are nowhere in the pool, Miss Barrett."

Mrs. Nixon slapped Harkness's face, brought up her naked leg, set her rosy heel against the man's wide chin, and shoved. Harkness laughed and went under.

"Swine," said Mrs. Nixon pleasantly, climbing out.

"It's your own fault," said Leonie. "I *told* you not to wear that bathing suit."

"Look," said the Lieutenant darkly, "who's talking."

"If you *will* invite Tarzan for a weekend," began

85

Mrs. Nixon, and she stopped. "What on earth are those men doing out there? They're crawling!'"

Everybody looked. Ellery sighed. "I believe the General is tired of our company and is directing some sort of wargame with his veterans. Does he often get that way, Miss Barrett?"

"Infantry maneuvers," said the Lieutenant quickly.

"That's a silly game," said Mrs. Nixon with spirit, taking off her cap. "What's on for this afternoon, Leonie? Let's do something exciting!"

"I think," grinned Harkness, clambering out of the pool like a great monkey, "I'd like to play an exciting game, Mrs. Nixon, if you're going to be in it." The sun gleamed on his wet torso.

"Animal," said Mrs. Nixon. "What shall it be? Suggest something, Mr. Queen."

"Lord," said Ellery. "*I* don't know. Treasure hunt? It's a little *passé*, but at least it isn't too taxing on the brain."

"That," said Leonie, "has all the earmarks of a nasty crack. But I think it's a glorious idea. You arrange things, Mr. Queen."

"Treasure hunt?" Mrs. Nixon considered it. "Mmm. Sounds nice. Make the treasure something worth while, won't you? I'm stony."

Ellery paused in the act of lighting a cigarette. Then he threw his match away. "If I'm elected . . . When shall it be—after luncheon?" He grinned. "May as well do it up brown. I'll fix the clues and things. Keep in the house, the lot of you. I don't want any spying. Agreed?"

"We're in your hands," said Mrs. Nixon gaily.

"Lucky dog," sighed Harkness.

"See you later, then." Ellery strolled off toward the river. He heard Leonie's fresh voice exhorting her guests to hurry into the house to dress for luncheon.

Major-General Barrett found him at noon standing by the parapet and gazing absently at the opposite shore, half a mile away. The old gentleman's cheeks were bursting with blood and perspiration, and he looked angry and tired.

"Damn all thieves for black-hearted scoundrels!" he exploded, mopping his bald spot. Then he said inconsistently: "I'm beginning to think Leonie simply mislaid it."

"You haven't found it?"

"No sign of it."

"Then where did she mislay it?"

"Oh, thunderation, I suppose you're right. I'm sick of the whole blasted business. To think that a guest under my roof—"

"Who said," sighed Ellery, "anything about a guest, General?"

The old gentleman glared. "Eh? What's that? What d'ye mean?"

"Nothing at all. You don't know. *I* don't know. Nobody but the thief knows. Shouldn't jump to conclusions, sir. Now, tell me. The search has been thorough?" Major-General Barrett groaned. "You've gone through Magruder's cottage, too?"

"Certainly, certainly."

"The stables?"

"My dear sir—"

"The trees?"

"*And* the trees," snapped the General. "Every last place."

"Good!"

"What's good about it?"

Ellery looked astonished. "My dear General, it's superb! I'm prepared for it. In fact, I anticipated it. Because we're dealing with a very clever person."

"You know—" gasped the General.

"Very little concretely. But I see a glimmer. Now will you go back to the house, sir, and freshen up? You're fatigued, and you'll need your energies for this afternoon. We're to play a game."

"Oh, heavens," said the General; and he trudged off toward the house, shaking his head. Ellery watched him until he disappeared.

Then he squatted on the parapet and gave himself over to thought.

"Now, ladies and gentlemen," began Ellery after they had assembled on the veranda at two o'clock, "I have spent the last two hours hard at work—a personal sacrifice which I gladly contribute to the gaiety of nations, and in return for which I ask only your lusty co-operation."

"Hear," said the General gloomily.

"Come, come, General, don't be antisocial. Of course, you all understand the game?" Ellery lit a cigarette. "I have hidden the 'treasure' somewhere. I've left a trail to it—a winding trail, you understand, which you must follow step by step. At each step I've dropped a clue which,

87

correctly interpreted, leads to the next step. The race is, naturally, to the mentally swift. This game puts a premium on brains."

"That," said Mrs. Nixon ruefully, "lets me out." She was dressed in tight sweater and tighter slacks, and she had bound her hair with a blue ribbon.

"Poor Dick," groaned Leonie. "I'm sure I shall have to pair up with him. He wouldn't get to first base by himself."

Fiske grinned, and Harkness drawled: "As long as we're splitting up, I choose Mrs. N. Looks as if you'll have to go it alone, General."

"Perhaps," said the General hopefully, "you young people would like to play by yourselves. . . ."

"By the way," said Ellery, "all the clues are in the form of quotations, you know."

"Oh, dear," said Mrs. Nixon. "You mean such things as 'First in war, first in peace'?"

"Ah—yes. Yes. Don't worry about the source; it's only the words themselves that concern you. Ready?"

"Wait a minute," said Harkness. "What's the treasure?"

Ellery threw his cigarette, which had gone out, into an ashtray. "Mustn't tell. Get set, now! Let me quote you the first clue. It comes from the barbed quill of our old friend, Dean Swift—but disregard that. The quotation is"—he paused, and they leaned forward eagerly—" *'First (a fish) should swim in the sea.'* "

The General said: "Hrrumph! Damned silly," and settled in his chair. But Mrs. Nixon's amber eyes shone and she jumped up.

"Is *that* all?" she cried. "Goodness, that isn't the least bit difficult, Mr. Queen. Come on, Tarzan," and she sped away over the lawns, followed by Harkness, who was grinning. They made for the parapet.

"Poor Dorothy," sighed Leonie. "She means well, but she isn't exactly blessed with brains. She's taking the wrong tack, of course."

"You'd put her hard a-port, I suppose?" murmured Ellery.

"*Mr.* Queen! You obviously didn't mean us to search the entire Hudson River. Consequently it's a more restricted body of water you had in mind." She sprang off the veranda.

"The pool!" cried Lieutenant Fiske, scrambling after her.

"Remarkable woman, your daughter, sir," said Ellery, following the pair with his eyes. "I'm beginning to think Dick Fiske is an extraordinarily fortunate young man."

"Mother's brain," said the General, beaming suddenly. "B'gad, I *am* interested." He waddled rapidly off the porch.

They found Leonie complacently deflating a large rubber fish which was still dripping from its immersion in the pool.

"Here it is," she said. "Come on, Dick, pay attention. *Not* now, silly! Mr. Queen's looking. What's this? *'Then it should swim in butter.'* Butter, butter . . . Pantry, of course!" And she was off like the wind for the house, the Lieutenant sprinting after.

Ellery replaced the note in the rubber fish, inflated it, stoppered the hole, and tossed the thing back into the pool.

"The others will be here soon enough. There they are! I think they've caught on already. Come along, General."

Leonie was on her knees in the pantry, before the huge refrigerator, digging a scrap of paper out of a butter tub. "Goo," she said, wrinkling her nose. "Did you have to use butter? Read it, Dick. I'm filthy."

Lieutenant Fiske declaimed: " *'And at last, sirrah, it should swim in good claret.'* "

"Mr. Queen! I'm ashamed of you. This is too easy."

"It gets harder," said Ellery dryly, "as it goes along." He watched the young couple dash through the doorway to the cellar, and then replaced the note in the tub. As he and the General closed the cellar door behind them, they heard the clatter of Mrs. Nixon's feet in the pantry.

"Damned if Leonie hasn't forgotten all about that necklace of hers," muttered the General as they watched from the stairs. "Just like a woman!"

"I doubt very much if she has," murmured Ellery.

"Whee!" cried Leonie. "Here it is. . . . What's this, Mr. Queen—Shakespeare?" She had pried a note from between two dusty bottles in the wine cellar and was frowning over it.

"What's it say, Leonie?" asked Lieutenant Fiske.

" *'Under the greenwood tree'* . . . Greenwood tree." She replaced the note slowly. "It *is* getting harder. Have we any greenwood trees, father?"

The General said wearily: "Blessed if I know. Never heard of 'em. You, Richard?" The Lieutenant looked dubious.

"All I know about the greenwood tree," frowned Leonie, "is that it's something in *As You Like It* and a novel by Thomas Hardy. But—"

"Come *on*, Tarzan!" shrieked Mrs. Nixon from above them. "They're still here. Out of the way, you two men! No fair setting up hazards."

Leonie scowled. Mrs. Nixon came flying down the cellar stairs followed by Harkness, who was still grinning, and snatched the note from the shelf. Her face fell. "Greek to me."

"Let me see it." Harkness scanned the note, and laughed aloud. "Good boy, Queen," he chuckled. "*Chlorosplenium aeruginosum*. You need a little botany in jungle work. I've seen that tree any number of times on the estate." He bounded up the stairs, grinned once more at Ellery and Major-General Barrett, and vanished.

"Damn!" said Leonie, and she led the charge after Harkness.

When they came up with him, the big man was leaning against the bark of an ancient and enormous shade tree, reading a scrap of paper and scratching his handsome chin. The bole of the tree was a vivid green which looked fungoid in origin.

"Green wood!" exclaimed Mrs. Nixon. "That *was* clever, Mr. Queen."

Leonie looked chagrined. "A man would take the honors. I'd never have thought it of you, Mr. Harkness. What's in the note?"

Harkness read aloud: " '*And . . . seeks that which he lately threw away. . . .*' "

"Which who lately threw away?" complained the Lieutenant. "That's ambiguous."

"Obviously," said Harkness, "the pronoun couldn't refer to the finder of the note. Queen couldn't possibly have known who would track it down. Consequently . . . Of course!" And he sped off in the direction of the house, thumbing his nose.

"I don't *like* that man," said Leonie. "Dickie, haven't you any brains at all? And now we have to follow him again. I think you're mean, Mr. Queen."

"I leave it to you, General," said Ellery. "Did *I* want to play games?" But they were all streaming after Harkness, and Mrs. Nixon was in the van, her red hair flowing behind her like a pennon.

Ellery reached the veranda, the General puffing behind

him, to find Harkness holding something aloft out of reach of Mrs. Nixon's clutching fingers. "No, you don't. To the victor—"

"But how did you know, you nasty man?" cried Leonie.

Harkness lowered his arm; he was holding a half-consumed cigarette. "Stood to reason. The quotation had to refer to Queen himself. And the only thing I'd seen him 'lately' throw away was this cigarette butt just before we started." He took the cigarette apart; imbedded in the tobacco near the tip there was a tiny twist of paper. He smoothed it out and read its scribbled message.

Then he read it again, slowly.

"Well, for pity's sake!" snapped Mrs. Nixon. "Don't be a *pig*, Tarzan. If you don't know the answer, give the rest of us a chance." She snatched the paper from him and read it. " '*Seeking . . . even in the cannon's mouth.*' "

"Cannon's mouth?" panted the General. "Why—"

"Why, that's *pie!*" giggled the red-haired woman, and ran.

She was seated defensively astride the sunset gun overlooking the river when they reached her. "This is a fine how-d'ye-do," she complained. "Cannon's mouth! How the deuce can you look into the cannon's mouth when the cannon's mouth is situated in thin air seventy-five feet over the Hudson River? Pull this foul thing back a bit, Lieutenant!"

Leonie was helpless with laughter. "You *idiot!* How do you think Magruder loads this gun—through the muzzle? There's a chamber in the back."

Lieutenant Fiske did something expertly to the mechanism at the rear of the sunset gun, and in a twinkling had swung back the safelike little door of the breech block and revealed a round orifice. He thrust his hand in, and his jaw dropped. "It's the treasure!" he shouted. "By George, Dorothy, you've won!"

Mrs. Nixon slid off the cannon, gurgling: "Gimme, gimme!" like an excited *gamine*. She bumped him rudely aside and pulled out a wad of oily cotton batting.

"What is it?" cried Leonie, crowding in.

"I . . . Why, Leonie, you *darling!*" Mrs. Nixon's face fell. "I knew it was too good to be true. Treasure! I should say so."

"*My pearls!*" screamed Leonie. She snatched the rope of snowy gems from Mrs. Nixon, hugging them to her bosom; and then she turned to Ellery with the oddest look of inquiry.

"Well, I'll be—be blasted," said the General feebly. "Did *you* take 'em, Queen?"

"Not exactly," said Ellery. "Stand still, please. That means everybody. We have Mrs. Nixon and Mr. Harkness possibly at a disadvantage. You see, Miss Barrett's pearls were stolen this morning."

"Stolen?" Harkness lifted an eyebrow.

"Stolen!" gasped Mrs. Nixon. "So that's why—"

"Yes," said Ellery. "Now, perceive. Someone filches a valuable necklace. Problem: to get it away. Was the necklace still on the premises? It was; it had to be. There are only two physical means of egress from the estate: by the cliffroad yonder, at the entrance to which is Magruder's cottage; and by the river below. Everywhere else there are perpendicular cliffs impossible to climb. And their crests are so high that it was scarcely feasible for an accomplice, say, to let a rope down and haul the loot up. . . . Now, since before six Magruder had the land exit under observation and Braun the river exit. Neither had seen a soul; and Braun said that nothing had been thrown over the parapet to the beach or water, or he would have heard the impact or splash. Since the thief had made no attempt to dispose of the pearls by the only two possible routes, it was clear then that the pearls were still on the estate."

Leonie's face was pinched and pale now, and she kept her eyes steadfastly on Ellery. The General looked embarrassed.

"But the thief," said Ellery, "must have had a plan of disposal, a plan that would circumvent all normal contingencies. Knowing that the theft might be discovered at once, he would expect an early arrival of the police and plan accordingly; people don't take the loss of a twenty-five-thousand-dollar necklace without a fight. If he expected police, he expected a search; and if he expected a search, he could not have planned to hide his loot in an obvious place—such as on his person, in his luggage, in the house, or in the usual places on the estate. Of course, he might have meant to dig a hole somewhere and bury the pearls; but I didn't think so, because he would in that case still have the problem of disposal, with the estate guarded.

"As a matter of fact, I myself searched every inch of the house; and the General's servants searched every inch of the grounds and outbuildings . . . just to make sure. We called no police, but acted as police ourselves. And the pearls weren't found."

"But—" began Lieutenant Fiske in a puzzled way.

"Please, Lieutenant. It was plain, then, that the thief, whatever his plan, had discarded any *normal* use of either the land or water route as a means of getting the pearls off the estate. Had he intended to walk off with them himself, or mail them to an accomplice? Hardly, if he anticipated a police investigation and surveillance. Besides, remember that he deliberately planned and committed his theft with the foreknowledge that a detective was in the house. And while I lay no claim to exceptional formidability, you must admit it took a daring, clever thief to concoct and carry out a theft under the circumstances. I felt justified in assuming that, whatever his plan was, it was itself daring and clever; not stupid and commonplace.

"But if he had discarded the *normal* means of disposal, he must have had in mind an extraordinary means, still using one of the only two possible routes. And then I recalled that there was one way the river route could be utilized to that end which was so innocent in appearance that it would probably be successful even if a whole regiment of infantry were on guard. And I knew that must be the answer."

"The sunset gun," said Leonie in a low voice.

"Precisely, Miss Barrett, the sunset gun. By preparing a package with the pearls inside, opening the breech block of the gun and thrusting the package into the chamber and walking away, he disposed very simply of the bothersome problem of getting the pearls away. You see, anyone with a knowledge of ordnance and ballistics would know that this gun, like all guns which fire salutes, uses 'blank' ammunition. That is, there is no explosive shell; merely a charge of powder which goes off with a loud noise and a burst of smoke.

"Now, while this powder is a noise-maker purely, it still possesses a certain propulsive power—not much, but enough for the thief's purpose. Consequently Magruder would come along at sundown today, slip the blank into the breech, pulling the firing cord, and—boom! away go the pearls in a puff of concealing smoke, to be hurled the scant twenty feet or so necessary to make it clear the little beach below and fall into the water."

"But how—" spluttered the General, red as a cherry.

"Obviously, the container would have to float. Aluminum, probably, or something equally strong yet light. Then an accomplice must be in the scheme—someone to idle along in the Hudson below in a boat at sunset, pick up the container, and cheerfully sail away. At that time Braun is not on duty, as he told me; but even if he were, I doubt if he would have noticed anything in the noise and smoke of the gun."

"Accomplice, eh?" roared the General. "I'll phone—"

Ellery sighed. "Already done, General. I telephoned the local police at one o'clock to be on the lookout. Our man will be waiting at sundown, and if you stick to schedule with your salute to the dying sun, they'll nab him red-handed."

"But where's this container, or can?" asked the Lieutenant.

"Oh, safely hidden away," said Ellery dryly. "Very safely."

"You hid it? But why?"

Ellery smoked peacefully for a moment. "You know, there's a fat-bellied little god who watches over such as me. Last night we played a murder game. To make it realistic, and to illustrate a point, I took everyone's fingerprints with the aid of that handy little kit I carry about. I neglected to destroy the exhibits. This afternoon, before our treasure hunt, I found the container in the gun here—naturally, having reasoned out the hiding place, I went straight to it for confirmation. And what do you think I found on the can? Fingerprints!" Ellery grimaced. "Disappointing, isn't it? But then our clever thief was so sure of himself he never dreamed anyone would uncover his cache before the gun was fired. And so he was careless. It was child's play, of course, to compare the prints on the can with the master sets from last night's game." He paused. *"Well?"* he said.

There was silence for as long as one can hold a breath; and in the silence they heard the flapping of the flag overhead.

Then, his hands unclenching, Harkness said lightly: "You've got me, pal."

"Ah," said Ellery. "So good of you, Mr. Harkness."

They stood about the gun at sunset, and old Magruder yanked the cord, and the gun roared as the flag came down, and Major-General Barrett and Lieutenant Fiske stood rigidly at attention. The report echoed and re-echoed, filling the air with hollow thunder.

"Look at the creature," gurgled Mrs. Nixon a moment later, leaning over the parapet and staring down. "He looks like a bug running around in circles."

They joined her silently. The Hudson below was a steel mirror reflecting the last copper rays of the sun. Except for a small boat with an outboard motor the river was free of craft; and the man was hurling his boat this way and that in puzzled parabolas, scanning the surface of the river anxiously. Suddenly he looked up and saw the faces watching him; and with ludicrous haste frantically swept his boat about and shot it for the opposite shore.

"I still don't understand," complained Mrs. Nixon, "why you called the law off that person, Mr. Queen. He's a criminal, isn't he?"

Ellery sighed. "Only in intent. And then it was Miss Barrett's idea, not mine. I can't say I'm sorry. While I hold no brief for Harkness and his accomplice, who's probably some poor devil seduced by our dashing friend into doing the work of disposal, I'm rather relieved Miss Barrett hasn't been vindictive. Harkness has been touched and spoiled by the life he leads; it's really not his fault. When you spend half your life in jungles, the civilized moralities lose their edge. He needed the money, and so he took the pearls."

"He's punished enough," said Leonie gently. "Almost as much as if we'd turned him over to the police instead of sending him packing. He's through socially. And since I've got my pearls back—"

"Interesting problem," said Ellery dreamily. "I suppose you all saw the significance of the treasure hunt?"

Lieutenant Fiske looked blank. "I guess I'm thick. *I* don't."

"Pshaw! At the time I suggested the game I had no ulterior motive. But when the reports came in, and I deduced that the pearls were in the sunset gun, I saw a way to use the game to trap the thief." He smiled at Leonie, who grinned back. "Miss Barrett was my accomplice. I asked her privately to start brilliantly—in order to lull suspicion—and slow up as she went along. The mere use of the gun had made me suspect Harkness, who knows guns; I wanted to test him.

"Well, Harkness came through. As Miss Barrett slowed up he forged ahead; and he displayed cleverness in detecting the clue of the 'greenwood' tree. He displayed acute observation in spotting the clue of the cigarette. Two rather difficult clues, mind you. Then, at the easiest of all, he becomes puzzled! He didn't 'know' what was meant by the cannon's mouth! Even Mrs. Nixon—forgive me—spotted that one. Why had Harkness been reluctant to go to the gun? It could only have been because he knew what was in it."

"But it all seems so unnecessary," objected the Lieutenant. "If you had the fingerprints, the case was solved. Why the rigmarole?"

Ellery flipped his butt over the parapet. "My boy," he said, "have you ever played poker?"

"Of course I have."

Leonie cried: "You fox! Don't tell me—"

"Bluff," said Ellery sadly. "Sheer bluff. There *weren't* any fingerprints on the can."

The Adventure of the

Hollow Dragon

MISS MERRIVEL always said (she said) that the Lord took care of everything, and she affirmed it now with undiminished faith, although she was careful to add in her vigorous contralto that it didn't hurt to help Him out if you could.

"And can you?" asked Mr. Ellery Queen a trifle rebelliously, for he was a notorious heretic, besides having been excavated from his bed without ceremony by Djuna at an obscene hour to lend ear to Miss Merrivel's curiously inexplicable tale. Morpheus still beckoned plaintively, and if this robust and bountiful young woman—she was as healthy-looking and overflowing as a cornucopia—had come only to preach Ellery firmly intended to send her about her business and return to bed.

"Can I?" echoed Miss Merrivel grimly. "*Can* I!" and she took off her hat. Aside from a certain rakish im-

11 murders by the cream of crime writers $1.

Gardner

1. The Case of the Irate Witness and other stories by Erle Stanley Gardner. Unless Perry Mason can pull a miracle, ex-convict Harvey Corbin is certain to be nailed for the hundred grand heist. *Never before available in book form.* (Publ. Ed. $4.95)

2. The Case of the Fabulous Fake by Erle Stanley Gardner. 36-24-36 is her only I.D. Can Perry Mason find her before she's accused of murder? (Publ. Ed. $4.95)

3. The Case of the Careless Cupid by Erle Stanley Gardner. A well-to-do widow is doomed unless Perry finds out who put arsenic in her husband's last

Queen

4. The Case of the Crimson Kiss and other stories by Erle Stanley Gardner. The murder victim is found with lipstick on his forehead and it matches the shade Perry's client uses. (Publ. Ed. $4.95)

5. The Case of the Crying Swallow and other stories by Erle Stanley Gardner. Perry's client is a war hero whose wife has vanished. The police suspect the husband of murdering her. (Publ. Ed. $4.95)

Christie

6. Nemesis by Agatha Christie. Miss Marple gets a letter asking her to investigate a forgotten crime. But the man who wrote it is already dead!

7. A Fine and Private Place by Ellery Queen. The clues point to the victim's young wife and her lover—or do they? (Publ. Ed. $5.95)

Creasey

8. The Kidnaped Child by John Creasey as Gordon Ashe. A mother and baby at the mercy of a blackmailer and a murderess. (Publ. Ed. $4.50)

9. Gideon's Art by J.J. Marric. The priceless Velásquez painting has completely vanished without a trace. England's only hope is the deductive art of The New Scotland Yard and

Eberhart

10. Two Little Rich Girls by Mignon Eberhart. New York Society is shocked to learn the killer is the beautiful Van Seidem heiress. Or is she? (Publ. Ed. $4.95)

The Saint

11. The Saint and the People Importers by Leslie Charteris. Immigrants are smuggled into England, then blackmailed by their benefactors. Or murdered. (Publ. Ed. $4.95)

The Detective Book Club,

Please enroll me as a member and send at once the 4 double volumes of full-length Gardner thrillers and 4 more great mysteries. Plus a specially selected triple volume including a newly published Perry Mason and 2 more by Eberhart and Creasey.

I enclose *no money in advance*. Within a week after receiving my books, I will either return them and owe nothing, or keep all 5 volumes for the special new member price of only \$1 (plus shipping charges).

As a member, I am to receive advance descriptions of all future selections, but I'm not obligated to buy any. For each 3-in-1 volume I keep, I will send you only \$3.39 (plus shipping charges). I may reject any volume before or after I receive it and can cancel my membership at any time. **DKM 5**

Mr.
Ms. _____
(Please print plainly)

Address _____

City, State _____ Zip _____ 34-2A

In Canada: Enclose this reply card in an envelope and mail to D.B.C. of Canada, Pendragon House Ltd., 71 Bathurst Street, Toronto 135, Ontario

Erle Stanley Gardner · John Creasey (as Gordon Ashe)
THE CASE OF THE FABULOUS FAKE CHILD · **THE KIDNAPED**

Erle Stanley Gardner · Agatha Christie
THE CASE OF THE CRYING SWALLOW · **NEMESIS**

Erle Stanley Gardner · Leslie Charteris
THE CASE OF THE CRIMSON KISS · **THE SAINT AND THE PEOPLE IMPORTERS**

Erle Stanley Gardner · Ellery Queen
THE CASE OF THE CARELESS CUPID · **A FINE AND PRIVATE PLACE**

Gideon's Art J. J. MARRIC

Two Little Rich Girls MIGNON G. EBERHART

The Case of The Irate Witness ERLE STANLEY GARDNER

(See other side for further details.)

each month's selections. You may
reject any volume before or after

Send the card to get these
11 mysteries for $1.

**With this card
and $1, you can
get away with
11 murders.**

(See other side
for further
details.)

The Case
Of The
Irate
Witness
ERLE STANLEY
GARDNER

Two L...
Rich
Gita
MIGNON
EBERH...

Gia
J. J.

probability in the hat's design, which looked like a soup plate, Ellery could see nothing remarkable in it; and he blinked wearily at her. "Look at this!"

She lowered her head, and for a horrified instant Ellery thought she was praying. But then her long brisk fingers came up and parted the reddish hair about her left temple, and he saw a lump beneath the titian strands that was the shape and size of a pigeon's egg and the color of spoiled meat.

"How on earth," he cried, sitting up straight, "did you acquire *that* awful thing?"

Miss Merrivel winced stoically as she patted her hair down and replaced the soup plate. "I don't know."

"You don't know!"

"It's not so bad now," said Miss Merrivel, crossing her long legs and lighting a cigarette. "The headache's almost gone. Cold applications and pressure . . . you know the technique? I sat up half the night trying to bring the swelling down. You should have seen it at one o'clock this morning! It looked as if someone had put a bicycle pump in my mouth and forgotten to stop pumping."

Ellery scratched his chin. "There's no error, I trust? I'm—er—not a physician, you know. . . ."

"What I need," snapped Miss Merrivel, "is a detective."

"But how in mercy's name—"

The broad shoulders under the tweeds shrugged. "It's not important, Mr. Queen. I mean my being struck on the head. I'm a brawny wench, as you can see, and I haven't been a trained nurse for six years without gathering a choice assortment of scratches and bruises on my lily-white body. I once had a patient who took the greatest delight in kicking my shins." She sighed; a curious gleam came into her eye and her lips compressed a little. "It's something else, you see. Something—funny."

A little silence swept over the Queens' living room and out the window, and Ellery was annoyed to feel his skin crawling. There was something in the depths of Miss Merrivel's voice that suggested a hollow moaning out of a catacomb.

"Funny?" he repeated, reaching for the solace of his cigarette case.

"Queer. Prickly. You feel it in that house. I'm not a nervous woman, Mr. Queen, but I declare if I weren't ashamed of myself I'd have quit my job weeks ago." Looking into her calm eyes, Ellery fancied it would go hard with any ordinary ghost who had the temerity to mix with her.

"You're not taking this circuitous method of informing me," he said lightly, "that the house in which you're currently employed is haunted?"

She sniffed. "Haunted! I don't believe in that nonsense, Mr. Queen. You're pulling my leg—"

"My dear Miss Merrivel, what a charming thought!"

"Besides, who ever heard of a ghost raising bumps on people's heads?"

"An excellent point."

"It's something different," continued Miss Merrivel thoughtfully. "I can't quite describe it. It's just as if something were going to happen, and you waited and waited without knowing where it would strike—or, for that matter, what it would be."

"Apparently the uncertainty has been removed," remarked Ellery dryly, glancing at the soup plate. "Or do you mean that what you anticipated *wasn't* an assault on yourself?"

Miss Merrivel's calm eyes opened wide. "But, Mr. Queen, no one has assaulted me!"

"I beg your pardon?" Ellery said in a feeble voice.

"I mean to say I *was* assaulted, but I'm sure not intentionally. I just happened to get in the way."

"Of what?" asked Ellery wearily, closing his eyes.

"I don't know. That's the horrible part of it."

Ellery pressed his fingers delicately to his temples, groaning. "Now, now, Miss Merrivel, suppose we organize? I confess to a vast bewilderment. Just why are you here? Has a crime been committed—"

"Well, you see," cried Miss Merrivel with animation, "Mr. Kagiwa is such an odd little man, so helpless and everything. I do feel sorry for the poor old creature. And when they stole that fiendish little doorstop of his with the tangled-up animal on it . . . Well, it was enough to make anyone suspicious, don't you think?" And she paused to dab her lips with a handkerchief that smelled robustly of disinfectant, smiling triumphantly as she did so, as if her extraordinary speech explained everything.

Ellery puffed four times on his cigarette before trusting himself to speak. "Did I understand you to say *doorstop?*"

"Certainly. You know, one of those thingamabobs you put on the floor to keep a door open."

"Yes, yes. Stolen, you say?"

"Well, it's gone. And it was there before they hit me on the head last night; I saw it myself, right by the study door, as innocent as you please. Nobody ever paid much attention to it, and—"

"Incredible," sighed Ellery. "A doorstop. Pretty taste in petit larceny, I must say! Er—animal? I believe you mentioned something about its being 'tangled up'? I'm afraid I don't visualize the beast from your epithet, Miss Merrivel."

"Snaky sort of monster. They're all over the house. Dragons, I suppose you'd call them. Although *I've* never heard of anyone actually seeing them, except in *delirium tremens*."

"I begin," said Ellery with a reflective nod, "to see. This old gentleman, Kagiwa—I take it he's your present patient?"

"That's right," said Miss Merrivel brightly, nodding at this acute insight. "A chronic renal case. Dr. Sutter of Polyclinic took out one of Mr. Kagiwa's kidneys a couple of months ago, and the poor man is just convalescing. He's quite old, you see, and it's a marvel he's alive to tell the tale. Surgery was risky, but Dr. Sutter had to—"

"Spare the technical details, Miss Merrivel. I believe I understand. Of course, your uni-kidneyed convalescent is Japanese?"

"Yes. My first."

"You say that," remarked Ellery with a chuckle, "like a young female after her initial venture into maternity. . . . Well, Miss Merrivel, your Japanese and your unstable doorstop and that bump on your charming noddle interest me hugely. If you'll be kind enough to wait, I'll throw some clothes on and go a-questing with you. And on the way you can tell me all about it in something like sane sequence."

In Ellery's ugly but voracious Duesenberg, Miss Merrivel watched the city miles devoured, drew a powerful breath, and plunged into her narrative. She had been recommended by Dr. Sutter to nurse Mr. Jito Kagiwa, the aged Japanese gentleman, back to health on his Westchester estate. From the moment she had set foot in the house—which from Miss Merrivel's description was a lovely old non-Nipponese place that rambled over several acres and at the rear projected on stone piles into the waters of the Sound—she had been oppressed by the most annoying and tantalizing feeling of apprehension.

She could not put her finger on the source. It might have come from the manner in which the outwardly Colonial house was furnished: inside it was like an Oriental museum, she said, full of queer alien furniture and pottery and pictures and things.

"It even smells foreign," she explained with a handsome frown. "That sticky-sweet smell . . ."

"The effluvium of sheer age?" murmured Ellery; he was occupied between driving at his customary breakneck speed and listening intently. "We seem up to our respective ears in intangibles, Miss Merrivel. Or perhaps it's merely incense?"

Miss Merrivel did not know. She was slightly psychic, she explained; that might account for her sensitivity to impressions. Then again, she continued, it might have been merely the *people*. Although the Lord Himself knew, she said piously, they were nice enough on the surface; all but Letitia Gallant. Mr. Kagiwa was an extremely wealthy importer of Oriental curios; he had lived in the United States for over forty years and was quite American-ized. So much so that he had actually married an American divorcee who had subsequently died, bequeathing her Oriental widower a host of fragrant memories, a big blond footballish son, and a vinegary and hard-bitten spinster sister. Bill, Mr. Kagiwa's stepson, who retained his dead mother's maiden name of Gallant, was very fond of his ancient little Oriental stepfather and for the past several years, according to Miss Merrivel, had practically run the old Japanese's business for him.

As for Letitia Gallant, Bill's aunt, she made life miserable for everyone, openly bewailing the cruel fate which had thrown her on "the tender mercies of the heathen," as she expressed it, and treating her gentle benefactor with a contempt and sharp-tongued scorn which, said Miss Merrivel with a snap of her strong teeth, were "little short of scandalous."

"Heathen," said Ellery thoughtfully, sliding the Duesenberg into the Pelham highway. "Perhaps that's it, Miss Merrivel. Alien atmospheres generally affect us disagreeably. . . . By the way, was this doorstop valuable?" The theft of that commonplace object was nibbling away at his brain cells.

"Oh, no. Just a few dollars; I once heard Mr. Kagiwa say so." And Miss Merrivel brushed the doorstop aside with a healthy swoop of her arm and sailed into the more

100

dramatic portion of her story, glowing with its reflected vitality and investing it with an aura of suspense and horror.

On the previous night she had tucked her aged charge into his bed upstairs at the rear of the house, waited until he fell asleep, and then—her duties for the day over—had gone downstairs to the library, which adjoined the old gentleman's study, for a quiet hour of reading. She recalled how hushed the house had been and how loudly the little Japanese clock had ticked away on the mantel over the fireplace. She had been busy with her patient since after dinner and had no idea where the other members of the household were; she supposed they were sleeping, for it was past eleven o'clock. . . . Miss Merrivel's calm eyes were no longer calm; they reflected something unpleasant and yet exciting.

"It was so cozy in there," she said in a low, troubled voice. "And so still. I had the lamp over my left shoulder and was reading *White Woman*—all about a beautiful young nurse who went on a case and fell in love with the secretary of . . . Well, I was reading it," she went on quickly, with a faint flush, "and the house began to get creepy. Simply—creepy. It shouldn't have, from the book. It's an awfully nice book, Mr. Queen. And the clock went ticking away, and I could hear the water splashing against the piles down at the rear of the house, and suddenly I began to shiver. I don't know why. I felt cold all over. I looked around, but there was nothing; the door to the study was open but it was pitch dark in there. I—I think I got to feeling a little silly. Me hearing things!"

"Just what do you think you heard?" asked Ellery patiently.

"I really don't know. I can't describe it. A slithery sound, like a—a—" She hesitated, and then burst out: "Oh, I know you'll laugh, Mr. Queen, but it was like a *snake!*"

Ellery did not laugh. Dragons danced on the macadam road. Then he sighed and said, "Or like a dragon, if you can imagine what a dragon would sound like; eh, Miss Merrivel? By the way, have you ever heard sounds like that over the radio? An aspirin dropped into a glass of water becomes a beautiful girl diving into the sea. Powerful thing, imagination . . . And where did this remarkable sound come from?"

"From Mr. Kagiwa's study. From the dark." Miss

Merrivel's pink skin was paler now, and her eyes were luminous with half-glimpsed terrors, impervious to such sane analogies. "I was annoyed with myself for making up things in my head and I got out of the chair to investigate. And—and the door of the study suddenly swung shut!"

"Oh," said Ellery in a vastly different tone. "And despite everything you opened the door and investigated?"

"It was silly of me," breathed Miss Merrivel. "Foolhardy, really. There was danger there. But I've always been a fool and I did open the door, and the moment I opened it and gawped like an idiot into the darkness something hit me on the head. I really saw stars, Mr. Queen." She laughed, but it was a mirthless, desperate sort of laugh; and her eyes looked sidewise at him, as if for comfort.

"Nevertheless," murmured Ellery, "that was very brave, Miss Merrivel. And then?" They had swung into the Post Road and were heading north.

"I was unconscious for about an hour. When I came to I was lying on the threshold, half in the library, half in the study. The study was still dark. Nothing had changed. . . . I put the light on in the study and looked around. It seemed the same, you know. All except the doorstop; that was gone, and I knew then why the door had swung shut so suddenly. Funny, isn't it? . . . I spent most of the rest of the night bringing the swelling down."

"Then you haven't told anyone about last night?"

"Well, no." She screwed up her features and peered through the windshield with a puckered concentration. "I didn't know that I should. If there's anyone in that house who's—who's homicidally inclined, let him think I don't know what it's all about. Matter of fact, I don't." Ellery said nothing. "They all looked the same to me this morning," continued Miss Merrivel after a pause. "It's my morning off, you see, and I was able to come to town without exciting comment. Not that anyone would care! It's all very silly, isn't it, Mr. Queen?"

"Precisely why it interests me. We turn here, I believe?"

Two things struck Mr. Ellery Queen as a maid with frightened eyes opened the front door for them and ushered them into a lofty reception hall. One was that this house was not like other houses in his experience, and the other that there was something queerly wrong in it. The first impression arose from the boldly Oriental character of the furnishings—a lush rug on the floor brilliant and soft with the vivid technique of the East, a mother-of-pearl-inlaid teak table, an overhead lamp that was a miniature pagoda, a profusion of exotic chrysanthemums, silk hangings embroidered with colored dragons. . . . The second troubled him. Perhaps it arose from the scared pallor of the maid, or the penetrating aroma. A sticky-sweet odor, even as Miss Merrivel had described it, hung heavily in the air, cloying his senses and instantly making him wish for the open air.

"Miss Merrivel!" cried a man's voice, and Ellery turned quickly to find a tall young man with thin cheeks and intelligent eyes advancing upon them from a doorway which led, from what he could see beyond it, to the library Miss Merrivel had mentioned. He turned back to the young woman and was astonished to see that her cheeks were a flaming crimson.

"Good morning, Mr. Cooper," she said with a catch of her breath. "I want you to meet Mr. Ellery Queen, a friend of mine. I happened to run into him—" They had cooked up a story between them to account for Ellery's visit, but it was destined never to be served.

"Yes, yes," said the young man excitedly, scarcely glancing at Ellery. He pounced upon Miss Merrivel, seizing her hands; and her cheeks burned even more brightly. "Merry, where on earth is old Jito?"

"Mr. Kagiwa? Why, isn't he upstairs in his—"

"No, he isn't. He's gone!"

"Gone?" gasped the nurse, sinking into a chair. "Why, I put him to bed myself last night! When I looked into his room this morning, before I left the house, he was still sleeping. . . ."

"No, he wasn't. You only thought he was. He'd rigged up a crude dummy of sorts—I suppose it was he—and covered it with the bedclothes." Cooper paced up and down, worrying his fingernails. "I simply don't understand it."

"I beg your pardon," said Ellery mildly. "I have some experience in these matters." The tall young man stopped short, flinging him a startled glance. "I understand that your Mr. Kagiwa is an old man. He may have crossed the line. It's conceivable that he's playing a senile prank on all of you."

"Lord, no! He's keen as a whippet. And the Japanese don't indulge in childish tomfoolery. There's something

103

up; no question about it, Mr. Queen. . . . Queen!" Cooper glared at Ellery with sudden suspicion. "By George, I've heard that name before—"

"Mr. Queen," said Miss Merrivel in a damp voice, "is a detective."

"Of course! I remember now. You mean you—" The young man became very still as he looked at Miss Merrivel. Under his steady inspection she grew red again. "Merry, you know something!"

"The merest tittle," murmured Ellery. "She's told me what she knows, and it's skimpy enough to whet my curiosity. Were you aware, Mr. Cooper, that Mr. Kagiwa's doorstop is missing?"

"Doorstop. . . . Oh, you mean that monstrosity he keeps in his study. It can't be. I saw it myself only last night—"

"Oh, it is!" wailed Miss Merrivel. "And—and somebody hit me over the head, Mr. C-Cooper, and t-took it. . . ."

The young man paled. "Why, Merry. I mean—that's perfectly barbarous! Are you hurt?"

"Oh, Mr. Cooper . . ."

"Now, now," said Ellery sternly, "let's not get maudlin. By the way, Mr. Cooper, just what factor do you represent in this bizarre equation? Miss Merrivel neglected to mention your name in her statement of the problem."

Miss Merrivel blushed again, positively glowing, and this time Ellery looked at her very sharply indeed. It occurred to him suddenly that Miss Merrivel had been reading a romance in which the beautiful young nurse fell in love with the secretary of her patient.

"I'm old Jito's secretary," said Cooper abstractedly. "Look here, old man. What has that confounded doorstop to do with Kagiwa's disappearance?"

"That," said Ellery, "is what I propose to find out." There was a little silence, and Miss Merrivel sent a liquidly pleading glance at Ellery, as if to beg him to keep her secret. "Is anything else missing?"

"I don't know what business it is of yours, young man," snapped a female from the library doorway, "but, praise be; the heathen is gone, bag and baggage, and good riddance, I say. I always said that slinky yellow devil would come to no good."

"Miss Letitia Gallant, I believe?" sighed Ellery, and from the stiffening backbones and freezing faces of Miss Mer-

104

rivel and Mr. Cooper it was evident that truth had prevailed.

"Stow it, Aunt Letty, for heaven's sake," said a man worriedly from behind her, and she swept her long skirts aside with a sniff that had something Airedale-ish about it. Bill Gallant was a giant with a red face and bloodshot eyes in sacs. He looked as if he had not slept and his clothes were rumpled and droopy. His aunt in the flesh was all that Miss Merrivel had characterized her, and more. Thin to the point of emaciation, she seemed composed of whalebone, tough rubber, and acid—a tall she-devil of fifty, with slightly mad eyes, dressed in the height of pre-War fashion. Ellery fully expected to find that her tongue was forked; but she shut her lips tightly and, with a cunning perversity, persisted in keeping quiet thenceforward and glaring at him with a venomous intensity that made him uncomfortable inside.

"Baggage?" he said, after he had introduced himself and they had repaired to the library.

"Well, his suitcase is gone," said Gallant hoarsely, "and his clothes are missing—not all, but several suits and plenty of haberdashery. I've questioned all the servants and no one saw him leave the house. We've searched every nook and cranny in the house, and every foot of the grounds. He's just vanished into thin air. . . . Lord, what a mess! He must have gone crazy."

"Ducked out during the night?" Cooper passed his hand over his hair. "But he isn't crazy, Mr. Gallant; you know that. If he's gone, there was a thumping good reason for it."

"Have you looked for a note?" asked Ellery absently, glancing about. The heavy odor had followed them into the library and it bathed the Oriental furnishings with a peculiar fittingness. The door to what he assumed was the missing Japanese's study was closed, and he crossed the room and opened it. There was another door in the study; apparently it led to an extension of the main hall. Miss Merrivel's assailant of the night before, then, had probably entered the study through that door. But why had he stolen the doorstop?

"Of course," said Gallant; they had followed Ellery into the study and were watching him with puzzled absorption. "But there isn't any. He's left without a word."

Ellery nodded; he was kneeling on the thick Oriental rug a few feet behind the library door, scrutinizing a

105

rectangular depression in the nap. Something heavy, about six inches wide and a foot long, had rested on that very spot for a long time; the nap was crushed to a uniform flatness as if from great and continuous pressure. The missing doorstop, obviously; and he rose and lit a cigarette and perched himself on the arm of a huge mahogany chair, carved tortuously in a lotus and dragon motif and inlaid with mother-of-pearl.

"Don't you think," suggested Miss Merrivel timidly, "that we ought to telephone the police?"

"No hurry," said Ellery with a cheerful wave of his hand. "Let's sit down and talk things over. There's nothing criminal in a man's quitting his own castle without explanation—even, Miss Gallant, a heathen. I'm not even sure anything's wrong. The yellow people are a subtle race with thought-processes worlds removed from ours. This business of the pilfered doorstop, however, is provocative. Will someone please describe it to me?"

Miss Merrivel looked helpful; the others glanced at one another, however, with a sort of inert helplessness.

Then Bill Gallant hunched his thick shoulders and growled: "Now, look here, Queen, you're evading the issue." He looked worried and haggard, as if a secret maggot were nibbling at his conscience. "This is certainly a matter for old Jito's attorney, if not for the police. I must call—"

"You must follow the dictates of your own conscience, of course," said Ellery gently, "but if you will take my advice someone will describe the doorstop for my edification."

"I can tell you exactly," said young Cooper, brushing his thin hair back again with his white musician's fingers, "because I've handled the thing a number of times and, in fact, signed the express receipt when it was delivered. It's six inches wide, six inches high, and an even foot long. Perfectly regular in shape, you see, except for the decorative bas-reliefs—the dragons. Typical conventionalized Japanese craftsmanship, by the way. Nothing really remarkable."

"Heathen idolatry," said Miss Letitia distinctly; her ophidian eyes glared their chronic hate with a fanatical fire. "Devil!"

Ellery glanced at her. Then he said: "Miss Merrivel has told me that the doorstop isn't valuable." Cooper and Gallant nodded. "What's its composition?"

106

"Natural soapstone," said Gallant; his expression was still worried. "You know, that smooth and slippery mineral that's used so much in the Orient—steatite, technically. It's a talc. Jito imports hundreds of gadgets made out of it."

"Oh, this doorstop was something from his curio establishment?"

"No. It was sent to the old man four or five months ago as a gift by some friend traveling in Japan."

"A white man?" asked Ellery suddenly.

They all looked blank. Then Cooper said with an uneasy smile: "I don't believe Mr. Kagiwa ever mentioned his name, or said anything about him, Mr. Queen."

"I see," said Ellery, and he smoked for a moment in silence. "Sent, eh? By express?" Cooper nodded. "You're a man of method, Mr. Cooper?"

The secretary looked surprised. "I beg your pardon?"

"Obviously, obviously. Secretaries have a deplorable habit of saving things. May I see that express receipt, please? Evidence is always better than testimony, as any lawyer will tell you. The receipt may provide us with a clue—sender's name may indicate . . ."

"Oh," said Cooper. "So that's your notion? I'm sorry, Mr. Queen. There was no sender's name on the receipt. I remember very clearly."

Ellery looked pained. He blew out a curtain of smoke, communing with his thoughts in its folds. When he spoke again it was with abruptness, as if he had decided to take a plunge. "How many dragons are there on this doorstop, Mr. Cooper?"

"Idolatry," repeated Miss Letitia venomously.

Miss Merrivel paled a little. "You think—"

"Five," said Cooper. "The bottom face, of course, is blank. Five dragons, Mr. Queen."

"Pity it isn't seven," said Ellery without smiling. "The mystic number." And he rose and took a turn about the room, smoking and frowning in the sweet heavy air at the coils of a golden monster embroidered on a silk wall-hanging. Miss Merrivel shivered suddenly and moved closer to the tall thin-faced young man. "Tell me," continued Ellery with a snap of his teeth, turning on his heel and squinting at them through the smoke haze. "Is your little Jito Kagiwa a Christian?"

Only Miss Letitia was not startled; that woman would

have outstared Beelzebub himself. "Lord preserve us!" she cried in a shrill voice. "That devil?"

"Now why," asked Ellery patiently, "do you persist in calling your brother-in-law a devil, Miss Gallant?"

She set her metallic lips and glared. Miss Merrivel said in a warm tone: "He is not. He's a nice kind old gentleman. He may not be a Christian, Mr. Queen, but he isn't a heathen, either. He doesn't believe in anything like that. He's often said so."

"Then he certainly isn't a heathen, strictly speaking," murmured Ellery. "A heathen, you know, is a person belonging to a nation or race neither Christian, Jewish, nor Mohammedan who has not abandoned the original creed of his people."

Miss Letitia looked baffled. But then she shrilled triumphantly: "He is, too! I've often heard him talk of some outlandish belief called—called . . ."

"Shinto," muttered Cooper. "It's not true, Merry, that Mr. Kagiwa doesn't believe in anything. He believes in the essential goodness of mankind, in each man's conscience being his best guide. That's the moral essence of Shinto, isn't it, Mr. Queen?"

"Is it?" murmured Ellery in an absent way. "I suppose so. Most interesting. He wasn't a cultist? Shinto is rather primitive, you know."

"Idolater," said Miss Letitia nastily, like a phonograph needle caught in one groove.

They looked uneasily about them. On the study desk there was a fat-bellied little idol of shiny black obsidian. In a corner stood a squat and powerful suit of Samurai armor. The silk of the dragon rippled a little on the wall under the push of the sea breeze coming in through the open window.

"He didn't belong to some ancient secret Japanese society?" persisted Ellery. "Has he had much correspondence from the East? Has he received slant-eyed visitors? Did he seem afraid of anything?"

His voice died away, and the dragon stirred again wickedly, and the Samurai looked on with his sightless, enigmatic, invisible face. The sickly-sweet odor seemed to grow stronger, filling their heads with dizzying, horrid fancies. They looked at Ellery mutely and helplessly, caught in the grip of vague primeval fears.

"And was this doorstop *solid* soapstone?" murmured Ellery, gazing out the window at the heaving Sound.

Everything heaved and swayed; the house itself seemed afloat in an endless ocean, bobbing to the breathing of the sea. He waited for their reply, but none came. Big Bill Gallant shuffled his feet; he looked even more worried than before. "It couldn't have been, you know," continued Ellery thoughtfully, answering his own question. He wondered what they were thinking.

"What makes you say that, Mr. Queen?" asked Miss Merrivel in a subdued voice.

"Common sense. The piece being valueless from a practical standpoint, why was it stolen last night? For sentimental reasons? The only one for whom it might have possessed such an attachment is Mr. Kagiwa, and I scarcely think he would have struck you over the head, Miss Merrivel, to retrieve his own property if he merely had a fondness for it." Aunt and nephew looked startled. "Oh, you didn't know that, of course. Yes, we had a case of simple but painful assault here last night. Gave Miss Merrivel quite a headache. The bump is, take my word for it, a thing of singular beauty. . . . Did the doorstop possess an esoteric meaning? Was it a symbol of something, a sign, a portent, a *warning*?" Again the breeze stirred the dragon, and they shuddered; the hatred had vanished from Miss Letitia's mad eyes, to be replaced by the naked fear of a small and malicious soul trapped in the filthy den of its own malice at last.

"It—" began Cooper, shaking his head. Then he licked his dry lips and said: "This is the twentieth century, Mr. Queen."

"So it is," said Ellery, nodding, "wherefore we shall confine ourselves to sane and demonstrable matters. The practical alternative is that, since the doorstop *was* taken, it was valuable to the taker. But not, obviously, for itself alone. Deduction: It *contained* something valuable. That's why I said it couldn't have been a solid chunk of soapstone."

"That's the most—" said Gallant; his shoulders hunched, and he stopped and stared at Ellery in a fascinated way.

"I beg your pardon?" said Ellery softly.

"Nothing. I was just thinking—"

"That I had shot straight to the mark, Mr. Gallant?"

The big man dropped his gaze and flushed; and he began to pace up and down with his hands loosely behind his back, the worried expression more evident than ever. Miss

Merrivel bit her lip and sank into the nearest chair. Cooper looked restive, and Letitia Gallant's stiff clothing made rustling little sounds, like furtive animals in underbrush at night. Then Gallant stopped pacing and said in a rush: "I suppose I may as well come out with it. Yes, you guessed it, Queen, you guessed it." Ellery looked pained. "The doorstop isn't solid. There's a hollow space inside."

"Ah! And what did it contain, Mr. Gallant?"

"Fifty thousand dollars in hundred-dollar bills."

It is proverbial that money works miracles. In Jito Kagiwa's study it lived up to its reputation.

The dragon died. The Samurai became an empty shell of crumbling leather and metal. The house ceased rocking and stood firmly on its foundation. The very air freshened and crept into its normal niche and was noticed no more. Money talked in familiar accents and before the logic of its speech the specter of dread, creeping things vanished in a snuffed instant. They sighed with relief in unison and their eyes cleared again with that peculiar blankness which passes for sanity in the social world. There had been mere money in the doorstop! Miss Merrivel giggled a little.

"Fifty thousand dollars in hundred-dollar bills," nodded Mr. Ellery Queen, looking both envious and disappointed in the same instant. "That's an indecent number of hundred-dollar bills, Mr. Gallant. Elucidate."

Bill Gallant elucidated—rapidly, his expression vastly comforted, as if a great weight had been lifted from his mind. Old Kagiwa's business, there was no concealing it longer, was on the verge of bankruptcy. But against his stepson's advice old Kagiwa, with the serene, silent, and unconquerable will of his race, had refused to alter his lifelong business policies. Only when ruin stared him in the eyes did his resolution waver, and then it was too late to do more than salvage the battered wreck.

"He did it on the q.t.," said Gallant, shrugging, "and the first I knew about it was the other day when he called me into this room, locked the door, picked up the doorstop—he'd left it on the floor all the time!—unscrewed one of the dragons. . . . Came out like a plug. He told me he'd found the secret cavity in the doorstop by accident right after he received it. Nothing in it, he said, and went into some long-winded explanation about the probable origin of the piece. It hadn't been a doorstop originally, of course—don't suppose the Japanese have such things. Well

110

. . . there was the money, in a tight wad, which he'd stowed away in the hole. I told him he was a fool to leave it lying around that way, but he said no one knew except him and me. Naturally—" He flushed.

"I see now," said Ellery mildly, "why you were reluctant to tell me about it. It looks bad for you, obviously."

The big young man spread his hands in a helpless gesture. "I didn't steal the damned thing, but who'd believe me?" He sat down, fumbling for a cigarette.

"There's one thing in your favor," murmured Ellery. "Or at least I suppose there is. Are you his heir?"

Gallant looked up wildly. "Yes!"

"Yes, he is," said Cooper in a slow, almost reluctant, voice. "I witnessed the old man's will myself."

"Tut, tut. Much ado about nothing. You naturally wouldn't steal what belongs to you anyway. Buck up, Mr. Gallant; you're safe enough." Ellery sighed and began to button up his coat. "Well, ladies and gentlemen, my interest in the case, I fear, is dissipated. I had foreseen something *outré*. . . ." He smiled and picked up his hat. "This is a matter for the police, after all. Of course, I'll help if I can, but it's been my experience that local officers prefer to work alone. And really, there's nothing more that I can do."

"But what do you think happened?" asked Miss Merrivel in hushed stones. "Do you think poor Mr. Kagiwa—"

"I'm not a psychologist, Miss Merrivel. Even a psychologist, as a matter of fact, might be baffled by the inner workings of an Oriental's mind. Your policeman doesn't worry about such subtle matters, and I don't doubt the local men will clear this business up in short order. Good day."

Miss Letitia sniffed and swept by Ellery with a disdainful swish of her skirts. Miss Merrivel wearily followed, tugging at her hat. Cooper went to the telephone and Gallant frowned out of the window at the Sound.

"Headquarters?" said Cooper, clearing his throat. "I want to speak to the Chief."

A little of the old heavy-scented, alien silence crept back as they waited.

"One moment," said Ellery from the doorway. "One moment, please." The men turned, surprised. Ellery was smiling apologetically. "I've just discovered something. The human mind is a fearful thing. I've been criminally negligent, gentlemen. There's still another possibility."

111

"Hold the wire, hold the wire," said Cooper. "Possibility?"

Ellery waved an airy hand. "I may be wrong," he admitted handsomely. "Can either of you gentlemen direct me to an almanac?"

"Almanac?" repeated Gallant, bewildered. "Why, certainly. I don't— There's one on the library table, Queen. Here, I'll get it for you." He disappeared into the adjoining room and returned a moment later with a fat paperbacked volume.

Ellery seized it and riffled pages, humming. Cooper and Gallant exchanged glances; and then Cooper shrugged and hung up.

"Ah," said Ellery, dropping his aria like a hot coal. "Ah. Hmm. Well, well. Mind over matter. The pen is mightier . . . I may be wrong," he said quietly, closing the book and taking off his coat, "but the odds are now superbly against it. Useful things, almanacs . . . Mr. Cooper," he said in a new voice, "let me see that express receipt."

The metallic quality of the tone brought them both up, stiffening. The secretary got to his feet, his face suffused with blood. "Look here," he growled, "are you insinuating that I've lied to you?"

"Tut, tut," said Ellery. "The receipt, Mr. Cooper, quickly."

Bill Gallant said uneasily: "Of course, Cooper. Do as Mr. Queen says. But I don't see what possible value there can be. . . ."

"Value is in the mind, Mr. Gallant. The hand may be quicker than the eye, but the brain is quicker than both of them."

Cooper glared, but he pulled open a drawer of the carved desk and began to rummage about. Finally he came up with a sheaf of motley papers and went through them with reluctance until he found a small yellow slip.

"Here," he said, scowling. "Damned impertinence, *I* think."

"It's not a question," said Ellery gently, "of what *you* think, Mr. Cooper." He picked up the slip and scanned the yellow paper with the painful scrupulosity of an archeologist. It was an ordinary express receipt, describing the contents of the package delivered, the date, the sending point, charges, and similar information. The name of the sender was missing. The package had been shipped by a

Nippon Yusen Kaisha steamer from Yokohama, Japan, had been picked up in San Francisco by the express company, and forwarded to its consignee, Jito Kagiwa, at his Westchester address. Shipping and expressage charges had been prepaid in Yokohama, it appeared, on the basis of the 44-pound weight of the doorstop, which was sketchily described as being of soapstone, 6 by 6 by 12 inches in dimensions, and decorated with dragons in bas-relief.

"Well," said Cooper with a sneer, "I suppose that mess of statistics means something to you."

"This mess of statistics," said Ellery gravely, pocketing the receipt, "means everything to me. Pity if it had been lost. It's like the Rosetta Stone—it's the key to an otherwise mystifying set of facts." He looked pleased with himself, and at the same time his gray eyes were watchful. "The old adage was wrong. It isn't safety that you find in numbers, but enlightenment."

Gallant threw up his hands. "You're talking gibberish, Queen."

"I'm talking sense." Ellery stopped smiling. "You gentlemen are excused. By all means the Chief of Police must be called—but it's I who'll call him and, by your leave . . . alone."

"I was not to be cheated of my tidbit of *bizarrerie*," announced Mr. Ellery Queen that evening, "after all." He was serene and self-contained. He was perched on the edge of the study desk, and his hand played with the belly of the obsidian image.

Cooper, Miss Merrivel, the two Gallants stared at him. They were all in the last stages of nervousness. The house was rocking again, and the dragon quivered in all his coils in the wind coming through the open window; and the Samurai had magically taken watchful life unto himself once more. The sky through the window was dark and dappled with blacker clouds; the moon had not yet slipped from under the hem of the sea.

Ellery had departed from the Kagiwa mansion after his telephonic conversation with the Chief of Police, to be seen no more by interested mortal eyes until evening. When he had returned, there were men with him. These men, quiet and solid creatures, had not come into the house. No one had approached the Gallants, the secretary, the nurse, the servants. Instead the deputation had disappeared, swallowed up by the darkness. Now strange

113

clankings and swishings were audible from the sea outside the study window, but no one dared rise and look.

And Ellery said: " 'What a world were this, how un-endurable its weight, if they whom Death had sundered did not meet again.' A moving thought. And very apt on this occasion. We shall meet Death tonight, my friends; and even more strangely, the weight shall be lifted. As Southey predicted."

They gaped, utterly bewildered. From the night outside the clankings and swishings continued, and occasionally there was the far shout of a man.

Ellery lit a cigarette. "I find," he said, inhaling deeply, "that once more I have been in error. I demonstrated to you this morning that the most likely reason for the theft of the doorstop was that it was stolen for its contents. I was wrong. It was not stolen for its contents. It was never intended that the belly of the dragon should be ravished."

"But the fifty thousand dollars—" began Miss Merrivel weakly.

"Mr. Queen," cried Bill Gallant, "what's going on here? What are those policemen doing outside? What are those noises? You owe us—"

"Logic," murmured Ellery, "has a way of being slip-pery. Quite like soapstone, Mr. Gallant. It eluded my fingers today. I pointed out that the doorstop could *not* have been stolen for itself. I was wrong again. It could have been stolen for itself in one remote contingency. There was one value possible to the doorstop beyond its worth in dollars and cents, or in a sentiment attached to it, or in its significance as a symbol. And that was—*its utility.*"

"Utility?" gasped Cooper. "You mean somebody stole it to use as a doorstop?"

"That's absurd, of course. But there is still another pos-sible utility, Mr. Cooper. What are the characteristics of this piece of carved stone which might be made use of? Well, what are its chief points physically? Its substance and weight. It is stone, and it weighs forty-four pounds."

Gallant made a queer brushing-aside gesture with one hand and rose as if under compulsion and went to the win-dow. The others wavered, and then they too rose and went to the window, pressing eagerly toward the last, their pent-up fears and curiosity urging them on. Ellery watched them quietly.

The moon was rising now. The scene below was blue-

114

black and sharp, a miniature etching in motion. A large rowboat was anchored a few yards from the rear of the Kagiwa house. There were men in it, and apparatus. Someone was leaning overside, gazing intently into the water. The surface suddenly quickened into concentric life, becoming violently agitated. A man's dripping head appeared, open mouth sucking in air. And then, half-nude, he climbed into the boat and said something, and the apparatus creaked, and a rope emerged from the blue-black water and began to wind about a small winch.

"But why," came Ellery's voice from behind them, "should an object be stolen because it is stone and weighs forty-four pounds? Regarded in this light, the view became brilliantly clear. A man was mysteriously and inexplicably missing—a sick, defenseless, wealthy old man. A heavy stone was missing. And there was the sea at his back door. Put one, two, and three together and you have—"

Someone shouted hoarsely from the boat. In the full moon a dripping mass emerged from the water at the end of the rope. As it was pulled into the boat the silver light revealed it as a mass made up of three parts. One was a suitcase. Another was a small rectangular chunk of stone with carving on it. And the third was the stiff naked body of a little old man with yellow skin and slanted eyes.

"And you have," continued Ellery sharply, slipping from the edge of the desk and poking the muzzle of an automatic into the small of Bill Gallant's rigid back, "the murderer of Jito Kagiwa!"

The shouts of the triumphant fishers made meaningless sound in the old Japanese's study, and Bill Gallant without turning or moving a muscle said in a dead voice: "You damned devil. How did you know?"

Miss Letitia's bitter mouth opened and closed without achieving the dignity of speech.

"I knew," said Ellery, holding the automatic quite still, "because I knew that the doorstop had no hollow at all, that it was a piece of solid stone."

"You couldn't have known that. You never saw it. You were guessing. Besides, you said—"

"That's the second time you have accused me of guessing," said Ellery in an aggrieved tone. "I assure you, my dear Mr. Gallant, that I did nothing of the sort. But knowing that the doorstop was solid, I knew that you had lied when you maintained that you had seen with your

115

own eyes Kagiwa's withdrawal of the dragon 'plug,' that you had seen the 'cavity' and the 'money' in it. And so I asked myself why such an obviously distressed and charming gentleman had lied. And I saw that it could only have been because you had something to conceal and were sure the doorstop would never be found to give you the lie."

The waters were stilling under the moon.

"But to be sure that the doorstop would never be found, you had to know where the doorstop was. To know where it was, you had to be the person who had disposed of it after striking Miss Merrivel over the head and stealing it from this room, unconsciously making that slithery, dragonish sound in the process which was merely the scuffing of your shoes in the thick pile of this rug. But the person who disposed of the doorstop was the person who disposed of the carcass of gentle little Jito Kagiwa; which is to say, the murderer. No, no, my dear Gallant; be fair. It wasn't precisely guesswork."

Miss Merrivel said in a ghastly voice: "Mr. Gallant. I can't—But why did you do this awful—awful . . ."

"I think I can tell you that," sighed Ellery. "It was apparent to me, when I saw that his story of the cache in the doorstop was a lie, that he had probably planned to tell that ingenious story from the beginning. Why? One reason might have been to cover up the real motive for the theft of the carved piece; divert the trail from its use as a mere weight for a dead body to a fabricated use as the receptacle of a fortune, and its theft for that reason. But why the lie about the fifty thousand dollars? Why so detailed, so specific, so careful? Was it because you had embezzled fifty thousand dollars from your stepfather's business, Mr. Gallant, knew that the discovery of this shortage was imminent, and therefore created a figmentary thief who last night stole the money which you had stolen and dissipated possibly months ago?"

Bill Gallant was silent.

"And so you built up a series of events," murmured Ellery. "You arranged the old gentleman's bedclothes during the night to form a human figure, as if he had done it himself. You threw some clothes of his in one of his suitcases, as if he had planned to flee. In fact, you arranged the whole thing to give the impression that Mr. Kagiwa, whose business I have no doubt is shaky—largely due to your peculations—had cut loose from his Occidental surroundings once and for all time and vanished into the mysterious Orient from which he had come . . . with the remnants of his fortune. In this way there would be no body to look for, no murder, indeed, to suspect; and you yourself would escape the consequences of your original crime of grand larceny. For you knew that, like all honorable and gentle men, your stepfather, who had given you everything, would forgive everything except your crime against honor. Had Mr. Kagiwa discovered your larceny, all would have been lost."

But Bill Gallant said nothing to these inexorable words; he was still staring out the window where nothing more was to be seen except the quieting water. The rowboat, the stone, the suitcase, the dead body, the men had vanished.

And Ellery nodded at that paralyzed back with something like sad satisfaction.

"And the inheritance," muttered Cooper. "Of course, he was the heir. Clever, clever."

"Stupid," said Ellery gently, "stupid. All crime is stupid."

Gallant said in the same dead voice: "I still think you were guessing about the doorstop being solid," as if he were engaged in a polite difference of opinion. Ellery was not fooled. His grip tightened on the automatic. The window was open and the water might look inviting to a desperate man, for whom even death would be an escape.

"No, no," said Ellery, almost protesting. "Please give the devil his due. It was all obscure to me, you know, until on my way out I thought of the fact that the doorstop was made of soapstone. I knew soapstone to be fairly heavy. I knew the piece was almost perfectly regular in shape, and therefore admissible to elementary calculation. It was conceivable that I could test the accuracy of your statement that the doorstop was hollow. And so I came back and asked to consult an almanac. Once I had run across in such a reference book a list of the weights of common minerals. I looked up soapstone. And there it was."

"There what was?" asked Gallant almost with curiosity.

"The almanac said that 1 cubic foot of soapstone weighs between 162 and 175 pounds. The doorstop was of soapstone; what were its dimensions? Six by six by twelve inches, or 432 cubic inches. In other words, one-quarter of a cubic foot. Or, by computing from the almanac's figures and allowing for the small additional weight of the shallow

117

bas-relief dragons, the doorstop should weigh one-quarter of the cubic-foot poundage, which is forty-four pounds."

"But that's what the receipt said," muttered Cooper.

"Quite so. But what do these forty-four pounds represent? They represent forty-four pounds of *solid* soapstone! Mr. Gallant had said the doorstop was *not* solid, had a hollow inside large enough to hold fifty thousand dollars in hundred-dollar bills. That's five hundred bills. Any space large enough to contain five hundred bills, no matter how tightly rolled or compressed, would make the total weight of the doorstop considerably *less* than forty-four pounds. And so I knew that the doorstop was solid and that Mr. Gallant had lied."

Heavy feet tramped outside. Suddenly the room was full of men. The corpse of Jito Kagiwa was deposited on a divan, naked and yellow as old marble, where it dripped quietly, almost apologetically. Bill Gallant was turned about, still frozen, and they saw that his eyes, too, were dead as they regarded the corpse . . . as if for the first time the enormity of what he had done had struck home.

Ellery took the heavy doorstop, glistening from the sea, from the hand of a policeman and turned it over in his fingers. And he looked up at the wall and smiled in friendly fashion at the dragon, which was now obviously a pretty thing of silk and golden threads and nothing more.

The Adventure of the
House of Darkness

"AND THIS," proclaimed Monsieur Dieudonné Duval with a deprecatory twirl of his mustache, "is of an ingenuity incomparable, my friend. It is not that I should say so, perhaps. But examine it. Is it not the—how do you say—the pip?"

Mr. Ellery Queen wiped his neck and sat down on a bench facing the little street of amusements. "It is indeed," he sighed, "the pip, my dear Duval. I quite share your creative enthusiasm. . . . Djuna, for the love of mercy! Sit still." The afternoon sun was tropical and his whites had long since begun to cling.

"Let's go on it," suggested Djuna hopefully.

"Let's not and say we did," groaned Mr. Queen, stretching his weary legs. He had promised Djuna this lark all summer, but he had failed to reckon with the Law of Diminishing Returns. He had already—under the solicitous wing of Monsieur Duval, that tireless demon of the scenic-designing art; one of the variegated hundreds of his amazing acquaintanceship—partaken of the hectic allurements of Joyland Amusement Park for two limb-rending hours, and they had taken severe toll of his energy. Djuna, of course, what with excitement, sheer pleasure, and indefatigable youth, was a law unto himself; he was still as fresh as the breeze blowing in from the sea.

"You will find it of the most amusing," said Monsieur Duval eagerly, showing his white teeth. "It is my *chef-d'oeuvre* in Joyland." Joyland was something new to the county, a model amusement park meticulously landscaped and offering a variety of ingenious entertainments and mechanical divertissements—planned chiefly by Duval— not to be duplicated anywhere along the Atlantic. "A house of darkness . . . That, my friend, was an inspiration!"

"I think it's swell," said Djuna craftily, glancing at Ellery.

"A mild word, Djun'," said Mr. Queen, wiping his neck again. The House of Darkness which lay across the thoroughfare did not look too diverting to a gentleman of even catholic tastes. It was a composite of all the haunted houses of fact and fiction. A diabolic imagination had planned its crazy walls and tumbledown roofs. It reminded Ellery—although he was tactful enough not to mention it to Monsieur Duval—of a set out of a German motion picture he had once seen, *The Cabinet of Dr. Caligari*. It wound and leaned and stuck out fantastically and had broken false windows and doors and decrepit balconies. Nothing was normal or decent. Constructed in a huge rectangle, its three wings overlooked a court which had been fashioned into a nightmarish little street with broken cobbles and tired lampposts; and its fourth side was occupied by the ticket-booth and a railing. The street in the open court was atmosphere only; the real dirty

119

work, thought Ellery disconsolately, went on behind those grim surrealistic walls.

"Alors," said Monsieur Duval, rising, "if it is permitted that I excuse myself? For a moment only. I shall return. Then we shall visit . . . *Pardon!"* He bowed his trim little figure away and went quickly toward the booth, near which a young man in park uniform was haranguing a small group.

Mr. Queen sighed and closed his eyes. The park was never crowded; but on a hot summer's afternoon it was almost deserted, visitors preferring the adjoining bathhouses and beach. The camouflaged loud-speakers concealed all over the park played dance music to almost empty aisles and walks.

"That's funny," remarked Djuna, crunching powerfully upon a pink, conic section of popcorn.

"Eh?" Ellery opened a bleary eye.

"I wonder where *he's* goin'. 'N awful hurry."

"Who?" Ellery opened the other eye and followed the direction of Djuna's absent nod. A man with a massive body and thick gray hair was striding purposefully along up the walk. He wore a slouch hat pulled down over his eyes and dark clothes, and his heavy face was raw with perspiration. There was something savagely decisive in his bearing.

"Ouch," murmured Ellery with a wince. "I sometimes wonder where people get the energy."

"Funny, all right," mumbled Djuna, munching.

"Most certainly is," said Ellery sleepily, closing his eyes again. "You've put your finger on a nice point, my lad. Never occurred to me before, but it's true that there's something unnatural in a man's hurrying in an amusement park of a hot afternoon. Chap might be the White Rabbit, eh, Djuna? Running about so. But the *genus* Joylander is, like all such orders, a family of inveterate strollers. Well, well! A distressing problem." He yawned.

"He must be crazy," said Djuna.

"No, no, my son, that's the conclusion of a sloppy thinker. The proper deduction begins with the observation that Mr. Rabbit hasn't come to Joyland to dabble in the delights of Joyland *per se*, if you follow me. Joyland is, then, merely a means to an end. In a sense Mr. Rabbit— note the cut of his wrinkled clothes, Djuna; he's a distinguished bunny—is oblivious to Joyland. It doesn't exist for him. He barges past Dante's Inferno and the perilous

120

Dragonfly and the popcorn and frozen custard as if he is blind or they're invisible. . . . The diagnosis? A date, I should say, with a lady. And the gentleman is late. *Quod erat demonstrandum.* . . . Now for heaven's sake, Djuna, eat your petrified shoddy and leave me in peace."

"It's all gone," said Djuna wistfully, looking at the empty bag.

"I am here!" cried a gay Gallic voice, and Ellery suppressed another groan at the vision of Monsieur Duval bouncing toward them. "Shall we go, my friends? I promise you entertainment of the most divine. . . . *Ouf!*" Monsieur Duval expelled his breath violently and staggered backward. Ellery sat up in alarm. But it was only the massive man with the slouch hat, who had collided with the dapper little Frenchman, almost upsetting him, muttered something meant to be conciliatory, and hurried on. *"Cochon,"* said Monsieur Duval softly, his black eyes glittering. Then he shrugged his slim shoulders and looked after the man.

"Apparently," said Ellery dryly, "our White Rabbit can't resist the lure of your *chef-d'oeuvre,* Duval. I believe he's stopped to listen to the blandishments of your barker!"

"White Rabbit?" echoed the Frenchman, puzzled. "But yes, he is a customer. *Voilà!* One does not fight with such, *hein?* Come, my friends!"

The massive man had halted abruptly in his tracks and pushed into the thick of the group listening to the attendant. Ellery sighed, and rose, and they strolled across the walk.

The young man was saying confidentially: "Ladies and gentlemen, you haven't visited Joyland if you haven't visited The House of Darkness. There's never been a thrill like it! It's new, different. Nothing like it in any amusement park in the *world!* It's grim. It's shivery. It's terrifying. . . ."

A tall young woman in front of them laughed and said to the old gentleman leaning on her arm: "Oh, Daddy, let's try it! It's sure to be loads of fun." Ellery saw the white head under its leghorn nod with something like amusement, and the young woman edged forward through the crowd, eagerly. The old man did not release her arm. There was a curious stiffness in his carriage, a slow shuffle in his walk, that puzzled Ellery. The young woman purchased two tickets at the booth and led the old man along a fenced lane inside.

"The House of Darkness," the young orator was declaiming in a dramatic whisper, "is . . . just . . . that. There's not a light you can see by in the whole place! You have to feel your way, and if you aren't *feeling* well . . . ha, ha! Pitch dark. Ab-so-lutely *black* . . . I see the gentleman in the brown tweeds is a little frightened. Don't be afraid. We've taken care of even the faintest hearted—"

"Ain't no sech thing," boomed an indignant bass voice from somewhere in the van of the crowd. There was a mild titter. The faintheart addressed by the attendant was a powerful young Negro, attired immaculately in symphonic brown, his straw hat dazzling against the sooty carbon of his skin. A pretty colored girl giggled on his arm. "C'mon, honey, we'll show 'em! Heah—two o' them theah tickets, mistuh!" The pair beamed as they hurried after the tall young woman and her father.

"You could wander around in the dark inside," cried the young man enthusiastically, "for *hours,* looking for the way out. But if you can't stand the suspense there's a little green arrow, every so often along the route, that points to an invisible door, and you just go through that door and you'll find yourself in a dark passage that runs *all* around the house in the back and leads to the—uh—ghostly cellar, the assembly room, downstairs there. Only *don't* go out any of those green-arrow doors unless you want to *stay* out, because they open only one way—into the hall, ha, ha! You can't get back into The House of Darkness proper again, you see. But nobody uses that *easy* way out. Everybody follows the little *red* arrows. . . ."

A man with a full, rather untidy black beard, shabby broad-brimmed hat, a soft limp tie, and carrying a flat case which looked like an artist's box, purchased a ticket and hastened down the lane. His cheekbones were flushed with self-consciousness as he ran the gantlet of curious eyes.

"Now what," demanded Ellery, "is the idea of *that,* Duval?"

"The arrows?" Monsieur Duval smiled apologetically. "A concession to the old, the infirm, and the apprehensive. It is really of the most blood-curdling, my masterpiece, Mr. Queen. So—" He shrugged. "I have planned a passage to permit of exit at any time. Without it one could, as the admirable young man so truly says, wander about for hours. The little green and red arrows are nonluminous; they do not disturb the blackness."

122

The young man asserted: "But if you follow the red arrows you are bound to come out. Some of them go the right way, others don't. But eventually . . . After exciting adventures on the way . . . Now, ladies and gentlemen, for the price of—"

"Come *on*," panted Djuna, overwhelmed by this salesmanship. "Boy, I bet that's *fun*."

"I bet," said Ellery gloomily as the crowd began to shuffle and mill about. Monsieur Duval smiled with delight and with a gallant bow presented two tickets.

"I shall await you, my friends, here," he announced. "I am most curious to hear of your reactions to my little *maison des ténèbres*. Go," he chuckled, "with God."

As Ellery grunted, Djuna led the way in prancing haste down the fenced lane to a door set at an insane angle. An attendant took the tickets and pointed a solemn thumb over his shoulder. The light of day struggled down a flight of tumbledown steps. "Into the crypt, eh?" muttered Ellery. "Ah, the young man's 'ghostly cellar.' Dieudonné, I could cheerfully strangle you!"

They found themselves in a long narrow cellar-like chamber dimly illuminated by bulbs festooned with spurious spiderwebs. The chamber had a dank appearance and crumbly walls, and it was presided over by a courteous skeleton who took Ellery's hat, gave him a brass disc, and deposited the hat in one of the partitions of a long wooden rack. Most of the racks were empty, although Ellery noticed the artist's box in one of the partitions and the white-haired old man's leghorn in another. The rite was somehow ominous, and Djuna shivered with ecstatic anticipation. An iron grating divided the cellar in two, and Ellery reasoned that visitors to the place emerged after their adventures into the division beyond the grating, redeemed their checked belongings through the window in the grate, and climbed to blessed daylight through another stairway in the righthand wing.

"Come *on*," said Djuna again, impatiently. "Gosh, you're slow. Here's the way in." And he ran toward a crazy door on the left which announced ENTRANCE. Suddenly he halted and waited for Ellery, who was ambling reluctantly along behind. "I saw *him*," he whispered.

"Eh? Whom?"

"*Him*. The Rabbit!"

Ellery started. "Where?"

"He just went inside there." Djuna's passionate gamin-eyes narrowed. "Think he's got his date in *here?*"

"Pesky queer place to have one, I'll confess," murmured Ellery, eyeing the crazy door with misgivings. "And yet logic . . . Now, Djuna, it's no concern of ours. Let's take our punishment like men and get the devil out of here. I'll go first."

"I wanna go first!"

"Over my dead body. I promised Dad Queen I'd bring you back—er—alive. Hold on to my coat—tightly, now! Here we go."

What followed is history. The Queen clan, as Inspector Richard Queen has often pointed out, is made of the stuff of heroes. And yet while Ellery was of the unpolluted and authentic blood, it was not long before he was feeling his way with quivering desperation and wishing himself at least a thousand light-years away.

The place was fiendish. From the moment they stepped through the crazy doorway to fall down a flight of padded stairs and land with a gentle bump on something which squealed hideously and fled from beneath them, they knew the tortures of the damned. There was no conceivable way of orienting themselves; they were in the deepest, thickest, blackest darkness Ellery had ever had the misfortune to encounter. All they could do was grope their way, one shrinking foot at a time, and pray for the best. It was literally impossible to see their hands before their faces.

They collided with walls which retaliated ungratefully with an electric shock. They ran into things which were all rattling bones and squeaks. Once they followed a tiny arrow of red light which had no sheen, and found a hole in a wall just large enough to admit a human form if its owner crawled like an animal. They were not quite prepared for what they encountered on the other side: a floor which tipped precariously under their weight and, to Ellery's horror, slid them gently downward toward the other side of the room—if it was a room—and through a gap to a padded floor three feet below. . . . Then there was the incident of the flight of steps which made you mount rapidly and get nowhere, since the steps were on a tread-mill going the other way; the wall which fell on your head; the labyrinth where the passage was just wide enough for a broad man's shoulders and just high enough for a gnome walking erect; the grating which blew blasts of frigid air up your legs; the earthquake room; and such abodes of pleasantry. And, to frazzle already frayed nerves, the air was filled with rumbles, gratings, clankings, whistlings, crashes, and explosions in a symphony of noises which would have done credit to the inmates of Bedlam.

"Some fun eh, kid?" croaked Ellery feebly, landing on his tail after an unexpected slide. Then he said some unkind things about Monsieur Dieudonné Duval under his breath. "Where are we now?"

"Boy, is it *dark*," said Djuna with satisfaction, clutching Ellery's arm. "I can't see a thing, can you?"

Ellery grunted and began to grope. "This looks promising." His knuckles had rapped on a glassy surface. He felt it all over; it was a narrow panel, but taller than he. There were cracks along the sides which suggested that the panel was a door or window. But search as he might he could find no knob or latch. He bared a blade of his penknife and began to scratch away at the glass, which reason told him must have been smeared with thick opaque paint. But after several minutes of hot work he had uncovered only a faint and miserable sliver of light.

"That's not it," he said wearily. "Glass door or window here, and that pinline of light suggests it opens onto a balcony or something, probably overlooking the court. We'll have to find—"

"*Ow!*" shrieked Djuna from somewhere behind him. There was a scraping sound, followed by a thud.

Ellery whirled. "For heaven's sake, Djuna, what's the matter?"

The boy's voice wailed from a point close at hand in the darkness. "I was lookin' for how to get out an'—an' I slipped on somethin' an' fell!"

"Oh." Ellery sighed with relief. "From the yell you unloosed I thought a banshee had attacked you. Well, pick yourself up. It's not the first fall you've taken in this confounded hole."

"B-but it's *wet*," blubbered Djuna.

"Wet?" Ellery groped toward the anguished voice and seized a quivering hand. "Where?"

"On the f-floor. I got some of it on my hand when I slipped. My other hand. It—it's wet an' sticky an'—an' warm."

"Wet and sticky and wa . . ." Ellery released the boy's hand and dug about in his clothes until he found his tiny pencil-flashlight. He pressed the button with the most curious feeling of drama. There was something tangibly un-

125

real, and yet, final, in the darkness. Djuna panted by his side. . . .

It was a moderately sane door with only a suggestion of cubistic outline, a low lintel, and a small knob. The door was shut. Something semiliquid and dark red in color stained the floor, emanating from the other side of the crack.

"Let me see your hand," said Ellery tonelessly. Djuna, staring, tendered a small, thin fist. Ellery turned it over and gazed at the palm. It was scarlet. He raised it to his nostrils and sniffed. Then he took out his handkerchief almost absently and wiped the scarlet away. "Well! That hasn't the smell of paint, eh, Djuna? And I scarcely think Duval would have so far let enthusiasm run away with better sense as to pour anything else on the floor as atmosphere." He spoke soothingly, divided between the stained floor and the dawning horror on Djuna's face. "Now, now, son. Let's open this door."

He shoved. The door stirred a half-inch, stuck. He set his lips and rammed, pushing with all his strength. There was something obstructing the door, something large and heavy. It gave way stubbornly, an inch at a time. . . .

He blocked Djuna's view deliberately, sweeping the flashlight's thin finger about the room disclosed by the opening of the door. It was perfectly octagonal, devoid of fixtures. Just eight walls, a floor, and a ceiling. There were two other doors besides the one in which he stood. Over one there was a red arrow, over the other a green. Both doors were shut. . . . Then the light swept sidewise and down to the door he had pushed open, seeking the obstruction.

The finger of light touched something large and dark and shapeless on the floor and quite still. It sat doubled up like a jackknife, rump to the door. The finger fixed itself on four blackish holes in the middle of the back, from which a ragged cascade of blood had gushed, soaking the coat on its way to the floor.

Ellery growled something to Djuna and knelt, raising the head of the figure. It was the massive White Rabbit, and he was dead.

When Mr. Queen rose he was pale and abstracted. He swept the flash slowly about the floor. A trail of red led to the dead man from across the room. Diagonally op-

126

posite lay a short-barreled revolver. The smell of powder still lay heavily over the room.

"Is he—is he—?" whispered Djuna.

Ellery grabbed the boy's arm and hustled him back into the room they had just left. His flashlight illuminated the glass door on whose surface he had scratched. He kicked high, and the glass shivered as the light of day rushed in. Hacking out an aperture large enough to permit passage of his body, he wriggled past the broken glass and found himself on one of the fantastic little balconies overlooking the open inner court of The House of Darkness. A crowd was collecting below, attracted by the crash of falling glass. He made out the dapper figure of Monsieur Duval by the ticketbooth, in agitated conversation with the khaki-clad special officer, one of the regular Joyland police.

"Duval!" he shouted. "Who's come out of the House?"

"Eh?" gulped the little Frenchman.

"Since I went in? Quick, man, don't stand there gaping!"

"Who has come out?" Monsieur Duval licked his lips, staring up with scared black eyes. "But no one has come out, Mr. Queen. . . . What is it that is the matter? Have you—your head—the sun—"

"Good!" yelled Ellery. "Then he's still in this confounded labyrinth. Officer, send in an alarm for the regular county police. See that nobody leaves. Arrest 'em as soon as they try to come out. A man has been murdered up here!"

The note, in a woman's spidery scrawl said: "Darling Anse—I *must* see you. It's important. Meet me at the old place, Joyland, Sunday afternoon, three o'clock, in that House of Darkness. I'll be awfully careful not to be seen. Especially this time. *He suspects*. I don't know what to do. I love you, love you!!!—Madge."

Captain Ziegler of the county detectives cracked his knuckles and barked: "That's the payoff, Mr. Queen. Fished it out of his pocket. Now who's Madge, and who the hell's the guy that 'suspects'? Hubby, d'ye suppose?"

The room was slashed with a dozen beams. Police crisscrossed flashlights in a pattern as bizarre as the shape of the chamber, with the shedding lantern held high by a policeman over the dead man as their focal point. Six people were lined up against one of the eight walls; five of them glared, mesmerized, at the still heap in the center of

127

the rays. The sixth—the white-haired old man, still leaning on the arm of the tall young woman—was looking directly before him.

"Hmm," said Ellery; he scanned the prisoners briefly. "You're sure there's no one else skulking in the House, Captain Ziegler?"

"That's the lot of 'em. Mr. Duval had the machinery shut off. He led us through himself, searched every nook and cranny. And, since nobody left this hellhole, the killer must be one o' these six." The detective eyed them coldly; they all flinched—except the old man.

"Duval," murmured Ellery. Monsieur Duval started; he was deadly pale. "There's no 'secret' method of getting out of here unseen?"

"Ah, no, no, Mr. Queen! Here, I shall at once secure a copy of the plans myself, show you. . . ."

"Scarcely necessary."

"The—the assembly chamber is the sole means of emerging," stammered Duval. "Eh, that this should happen to—"

Ellery said quietly to a dainty woman, somberly gowned, who hugged the wall: "You're Madge, aren't you?" He recalled now that she was the only one of the six prisoners he had not seen while listening with Djuna and Monsieur Duval to the oration of the barker outside. She must have preceded them all into the House. The five others were here—the tall young woman and her old father, the bearded man with his artist's tie, and the burly young Negro and his pretty mulatto companion. "Your name, please—your last name?"

"I—I'm not Madge," she whispered, edging, shrinking away. There were half-moons of violet shadow under her tragic eyes. She was perhaps thirty-five, the wreck of a once beautiful woman. Ellery got the curious feeling that it was not age, but fear, which had ravaged her.

"That's Dr. Hardy," said the tall young woman suddenly in a choked voice. She gripped her father's arm as if she were already sorry she had spoken.

"Who?" asked Captain Ziegler quickly.

"The . . . dead man. Dr. Anselm Hardy, the eye specialist. Of New York City."

"That's right," said the small, quiet man kneeling by the corpse. He tossed something over to the detective. "Here's one of his cards."

"Thanks, Doc. What's *your* name, Miss?"

"Nora Reis." The tall young woman shivered. "This is my father, Matthew Reis. We don't know anything about this—this horrible thing. We've just come out to Joyland today for some fun. If we'd known—"

"Nora, my dear," said her father gently; but neither his eyes nor his head moved from their fixed position.

"So you know the dead man, hey?" Ziegler's disagreeable face expressed heavy suspicion.

"If I may," said Matthew Reis. There was a soft musical pitch to his voice. "We knew Dr. Hardy, my daughter and I, only in his professional capacity. That's a matter of record, Captain Ziegler. He treated me for over a year. Then he operated upon my eyes." A spasm of pain flickered over his waxy features. "Cataracts, he said. . . ."

"Hmm," said Ziegler. "Was it—"

"I am totally blind."

There was a shocked silence. Ellery shook his head with impatience at his own blindness. He should have known. The old man's helplessness, the queer fixed stare, that vague smile, the shuffling walk . . . "This Dr. Hardy was responsible for your blindness, Mr. Reis?" he demanded abruptly.

"I didn't say that," murmured the old man. "It was no doubt the hand of God. He did what he could. I have been blind for over two years."

"Did you know Dr. Hardy was here, in this place, today?"

"No. We haven't seen him for two years."

"Where were you people when the police found you?"

Matthew Reis shrugged. "Somewhere ahead. Near the exit, I believe."

"And you?" asked Ellery of the colored couple.

"M'name is—is," stuttered the Negro, "Juju Jones, suh. Ah'm a prizefighter. Light-heavy, suh. Ah don't know nothin' 'bout this doctuh man. Me an' Jessie we been havin' a high ol' time down yonduh in a room that bounded 'n' jounced all roun'. We been—"

"Lawd," moaned the pretty mulatto, hanging on to her escort's arm.

"And how about you?" demanded Ellery of the bearded man.

He raised his shoulders in an almost Gallic gesture. "How about me? This is all Classical Greek to me. I've been out on the rocks at the Point most of the day doing a couple of sea pictures and a landscape. I'm an artist—

James Oliver Adams, at your service." There was something antagonistic, almost sneering, in his attitude. "You'll find my paint box and sketches in the checkroom downstairs. Don't know this dead creature, and I wish to God I'd never been tempted by this atrocious gargoyle of a place."

"Garg—" gasped Monsieur Duval; he became furious. "Do you know of whom you speak?" he cried, advancing upon the bearded man. "I am Dieudonné Du—"

"There, there, Duval," said Ellery soothingly. "We don't want to become involved in an altercation between clashing artistic temperaments; not now, anyway. Where were you, Mr. Adams, when the machinery stopped?"

"Somewhere ahead." The man had a harsh cracked voice, as if there was something wrong with his vocal cords. "I was looking for a way out of the hellish place. *I'd* had a bellyful. I—"

"That's right," snapped Captain Ziegler. "I found this bird myself. He was swearin' to himself like a trooper, stumblin' around in the dark. He says to me: 'How the hell do you get out of here? The barker said you've got to follow the green lights, but they don't get you anywhere except in another silly hole of a monkeyshine room, or somethin' like that.' Now why'd you want to get out so fast, Mr. Adams? What do you know? Come on, spill it!"

The artist snorted his disgust, disdaining to reply. He shrugged again and set his shoulders against the wall in an attitude of resignation.

"I should think, Captain," murmured Ellery, studying the faces of the six against the wall, "that you'd be much more concerned with finding the one who 'suspects' in Madge's note. Well, Madge, are you going to talk? It's perfectly silly to hold out. This is the sort of thing that can't be kept secret. Sooner or later—"

The dainty woman moistened her lips; she looked faint. "I suppose you're right. It's bound to come out," she said in a low empty voice. "I'll talk. Yes, my name *is* Madge— Madge Clarke. It's true. I wrote that note to—to Dr. Hardy." Then her voice flamed passionately. "But I didn't write it of my own free will! *He* made me. It was a trap. I knew it. But I couldn't—"

"*Who* made you?" growled Captain Ziegler.

"My husband. Dr. Hardy and I had been friends . . . well, friends, quietly. My husband didn't know at first. Then he—he did come to know. He must have followed us

130

—many times. We—we've met here before. My husband is very jealous. He made me write the note. He threatened to—to kill me if I didn't write it. Now I don't care. Let him! He's a murderer!" And she buried her face in her hands and began to sob.

Captain Ziegler said gruffly: "Mrs. Clarke." She looked up and then down at the snub-nosed revolver in his hand. "Is that your husband's gun?"

She shrank from it, shuddering. "No. He has a revolver, but it's got a long barrel. He's a—a good shot."

"Pawnshop," muttered Ziegler, putting the gun in his pocket; and he nodded gloomily to Ellery.

"You came here, Mrs. Clarke," said Ellery gently, "in the face of your husband's threats?"

"Yes. Yes. I—I couldn't stay away. I thought I'd warn—"

"That was very courageous. Your husband—did you see him in Joyland, in the crowd before this place?"

"No. I didn't. But it must have been Tom. He *told* me he'd kill Ansel!"

"Did you meet Dr. Hardy in here, before he was dead?"

She shivered. "No. I couldn't find—"

"Did you meet your husband here?"

"No . . ."

"Then where is he?" asked Ellery dryly. "He couldn't have vanished in a puff of smoke. The age of miracles is past. . . . Do you think you can trace that revolver, Captain Ziegler?"

"Try." Ziegler shrugged. "Manufacturer's number has been filed off. It's an old gun, too. And no prints. Bad for the D.A."

Ellery clucked irritably and stared down at the quiet man by the corpse. Djuna held his breath a little behind him. Suddenly he said: "Duval, isn't there some way of illuminating this room?"

Monsieur Duval started, his pallor deeper than before in the sword-thrusts of light crossing his face. "There is not an electrical wire or fixture in the entire structure. Excepting for the assembly room, Mr. Queen."

"How about the arrows pointing the way? They're visible."

"A chemical. I am desolated by this—"

"Naturally; murder's rarely an occasion for hilarity. But this Stygian pit of yours complicates matters. What do you think, Captain?"

131

"Looks open and shut to *me*. I don't know how he got away, but this Clarke's the killer. We'll find him and sweat it out of him. He shot the doctor from the spot where you found the gun layin' "—Ellery frowned—"and then dragged the body to the door of the preceding room and set it up against the door to give him time for his getaway. Blood trail tells that. The shots were lost in the noise of this damn' place. He must have figured on that."

"Hmm. That's all very well, except for the manner of Clarke's disappearance . . . if it *was* Clarke." Ellery sucked his fingernail, revolving Ziegler's analysis in his mind. There was one thing wrong. . . . "Ah, the coroner's finished. Well, Doctor?"

The small quiet man rose from his knees in the light of the lantern. The six against the wall were incredibly still. "Simple enough. Four bullets within an area of inches. Two of them pierced the heart from behind. Good shooting, Mr. Queen."

Ellery blinked. "Good shooting," he repeated. "Yes, very good shooting indeed, Doctor. How long has he been dead?"

"About an hour. He died instantly, by the way."

"That means," muttered Ellery, "that he must have been shot only a few minutes before I found him. His body was still warm." He looked intently at the empurpled dead face. "But you're wrong, Captain Ziegler, about the position of the killer when he fired the shots. He couldn't have stood so far away from Dr. Hardy. In fact, as I see it, he must have been very close to Hardy. There are powder marks on the dead man's body of course, Doctor?"

The county coroner looked puzzled. "Powder marks? Why, no. Of course not. Not a trace of burned powder. Captain Ziegler's right."

Ellery said in a strangled voice: "No powder marks? Why, that's impossible! You're positive? There *must* be powder marks!"

The coroner and Captain Ziegler exchanged glances. "As something of an expert in these matters, Mr. Queen," said the little man icily, "let me assure you that the victim was shot from a distance of at least twelve feet, probably a foot or two more."

The most remarkable expression came over Ellery's face. He opened his mouth to speak, closed it again, blinked once more, and then took out a cigarette and lit it, puffing slowly. "Twelve feet. No powder marks," he said in a hushed voice. "Well, well. Now, that's downright amazing. That's a lesson in the illogicalities that would interest Professor Dewey himself. I can't believe it. Simply can't."

The coroner eyed him hostilely. "I'm a reasonably intelligent man, Mr. Queen, but you're talking nonsense as far as I'm concerned."

"What's on your mind?" demanded Captain Ziegler.

"Don't *you* know, either?" Then Ellery said abstractedly: "Let's have a peep at the contents of his clothes, please."

The detective jerked his head toward a pile of miscellaneous articles on the floor. Ellery went down on his haunches, indifferent to his staring audience. When he rose he was mumbling to himself almost with petulance. He had not found what he was seeking, what logic told him should be there. There were not even smoking materials of any kind. And there was no watch; he even examined the dead man's wrists for marks.

He strode about the room, nose lowered, searching the floor with an absorption that was oblivious to the puzzled looks directed at him. The flashlight in his hand was a darting, probing finger.

"But we've searched this room!" exploded Captain Ziegler. "What in the name of heaven are you looking for, Mr. Queen?"

"Something," murmured Ellery grimly, "that must be here if there's any sanity in this world. Let's see what your men have scraped together from the floors of all the rooms, Captain."

"But they didn't find anything!"

"I'm not talking of things that would strike a detective as possibly 'important.' I'm referring to trivia: a scrap of paper, a sliver of wood—anything."

A broad-shouldered man said respectfully: "I looked myself, Mr. Queen. There wasn't even dust."

"*S'il vous plaît*," said Monsieur Duval nervously. "Of that we have taken care with ingenuity. There is here both a ventilation system and another, a vacuum system, which sucks in the dust and keeps *la maison des ténèbres* of a cleanliness immaculate."

"Vacuum!" exclaimed Ellery. "A sucking process . . . It's possible! Is this vacuum machine in operation all the time, Duval?"

"But no, my friend. Only in the night, when The House

133

of Darkness is empty and—how do you say?—inoperative. But that is why your *gendarmes* found nothing, not even the dust."

"Foiled," muttered Ellery whimsically, but his eyes were grave. "The machine doesn't operate in the daytime. So that's out. Captain, forgive my persistence. But *everything's* been searched? The assembly room downstairs, too? Someone here might have—"

Captain Ziegler's face was stormy. "I can't figure you out. How many times do I have to say it? The man on duty in the cellar says no one even popped in there and went back during the period of the murder. So what?"

"Well, then," sighed Ellery, "I'll have to ask you to search each of these people, Captain." There was a note of desperation in his voice.

Mr. Ellery Queen's frown was a thing of beauty when he put down the last personal possession of the six prisoners. He had picked them apart to the accompaniment of a chorus of protests, chiefly from the artist Adams and Miss Reis. But he had not found what should have been there. He rose from his squatting position on the floor and silently indicated that the articles might be returned to their owners.

"Parbleu!" cried Monsieur Duval suddenly. "I do not know what is it for which you seek, my friend; but it is possible that it has been secretly placed upon the person of one of us, *n'est-ce pas?* If it is of a nature damaging, that would be—"

Ellery looked up with a faint interest. "Good for you, Duval. I hadn't thought of that."

"We shall see," said Monsieur Duval excitedly, beginning to turn out his pockets, "if the brain of Dieudonné Duval is not capable . . . *Voici!* Will you please examine, Mr. Queen?"

Ellery looked over the collection of odds and ends briefly. "No dice. That was generous, Duval." He began to poke about in his own pockets.

Djuna announced proudly: "I've got everything *I* ought to."

"Well, Mr. Queen?" asked Ziegler impatiently.

Ellery waved an absent hand. "I'm through, Captain. . . . Wait!" He stood still, eyes lost in space. "Wait here. It's still possible—" Without explanation he plunged through the doorway marked with the green arrow, found himself in a narrow passageway as black as the rooms leading off from it, and flashed his light about. Then he ran back to the extreme end of the corridor and began a worm's progress, scrutinizing each inch of the corridor floor as if his life depended upon his thoroughness. Twice he turned corners, and at last he found himself at a dead end confronted by a door marked EXIT: ASSEMBLY ROOM. He pushed the door in and blinked at the lights of the cellar. A policeman touched his cap to him; the attendant skeleton looked scared.

"Not even a bit of wax, or a few crumbs of broken glass, or a burned matchstick," he muttered. A thought struck him. "Here, officer, open this door in the grating for me, will you?"

The policeman unlocked a small door in the grating and Ellery stepped through to the larger division of the room. He made at once for the rack on the wall, in the compartments of which were the things the prisoners— and he himself—had checked before plunging into the main body of the House. He inspected these minutely. When he came to the artist's box he opened it, glanced at the paints and brushes and palette and three small daubs —a landscape and two seascapes—which were quite orthodox and uninspired, closed it. . . .

He paced up and down under the dusty light of the bulbs, frowning fiercely. Minutes passed. The House of Darkness was silent, as if in tribute to its unexpected dead. The policeman gaped.

Suddenly Ellery halted and the frown faded, to be replaced by a grim smile. "Yes, yes, that's it," he muttered. "Why didn't I think of it before? Officer! Take all this truck back to the scene of the crime. I'll carry this small table back with me. We've all the paraphernalia, and in the darkness we should be able to conduct a very thrilling séance!"

When he knocked on the door of the octagonal room from the corridor, it was opened by Captain Ziegler himself.

"You back?" growled the detective. "We're just ready to scram. Stiff's crated—"

"Not for a few moments yet, I trust," said Ellery smoothly, motioning the burdened policeman to precede him. "I've a little speech to make."

"Speech!"

135

"A speech fraught with subtleties and cleverness, my dear Captain. Duval, this will delight your Gallic soul. Ladies and gentlemen, you will please remain in your places. That's right, officer; on the table. Now, gentlemen, if you will kindly focus the rays of your flashes upon me and the table, we can begin our demonstration."

The room was very still. The body of Dr. Anselm Hardy lay in a wickerwork basket, brown-covered, invisible. Ellery presided like a swami in the center of the room, the nucleus of thin beams. Only the glitter of eyes was reflected back to him from the walls.

He rested one hand on the small table, cluttered with the belongings of the prisoners. *"Alors, mesdames et messieurs,* we begin. We begin with the extraordinary fact that the scene of this crime is significant for one thing above all: its darkness. Now, that's a little out of the usual run. It suggests certain disturbing nuances before you think it out. This is literally a house of darkness. A man has been murdered in one of its unholy chambers. In the house itself—excluding, of course, the victim, myself, and my panting young charge—we find six persons presumably devoting themselves to enjoyment of Monsieur Duval's satanic creation. No one during the period of the crime was observed to emerge from the only possible exit, if we are to take the word of the structure's own architect, Monsieur Duval. It is inevitable, then, that one of these six is the killer of Dr. Hardy."

There was a mass rustle, a rising sigh, which died almost as soon as it was born.

"Now observe," continued Ellery dreamily, "what pranks fate plays. In this tragedy of darkness, the cast includes at least three characters associated with darkness. I refer to Mr. Reis, who is blind; and to Mr. Juju Jones and his escort, who are Negroes. Isn't that significant? Doesn't it mean something to you?"

Juju Jones groaned: "Ah di'n't do it, Mistuh Queen."

Ellery said: "Moreover, Mr. Reis has a possible motive; the victim treated his eyes, and in the course of this treatment Mr. Reis became blind. And Mrs. Clarke offered us a jealous husband. Two motives, then. So far, so good. . . . But all this tells us nothing vital about the crime itself."

"Well," demanded Ziegler harshly, "what does?"

"The darkness, Captain, the darkness," replied Ellery in gentle accents. "I seem to have been the only one who was disturbed by that darkness." A brisk note sprang into his voice. "This room is totally black. There is no electricity, no lamp, no lantern, no gas, no candle, no window, in its equipment. Its three doors open onto places as dark as itself. The green and red lights above the doors are nonluminous, radiate no light visible to the human eye beyond the arrows themselves. . . . *And yet, in this blackest of black rooms, someone was able at a distance of at least twelve feet to place four bullets within an area of inches in this invisible victim's back!*"

Someone gasped. Captain Ziegler muttered: "By damn . . ."

"How?" asked Ellery softly. "Those shots were accurate. They couldn't have been accidents—not four of them. I had assumed in the beginning that there must be powder burns on the dead man's coat, that the killer must have stood directly behind Dr. Hardy, touching him, even holding him steady, jamming the muzzle of the revolver into his back and firing. But the coroner said no! It seemed impossible. In a totally dark room? At twelve feet? The killer couldn't have hit Hardy by ear alone, listening to movements, footsteps; the shots were too accurately placed for that theory. Besides, the target must have been moving, however slowly. I couldn't understand it. The only possible answer was that *the murderer had light to see by.* And yet there was no light."

Matthew Reis said musically: "Very clever, sir."

"Elementary, rather, Mr. Reis. There was no light in the room itself. . . . Now, thanks to Monsieur Duval's vacuum-suction system, there is never any débris in this place. That meant that if we found something it might belong to one of the suspects. But the police had searched minutely and found literally nothing. I myself fine-combed this room looking for a flashlight, a burned match, a wax taper—anything that might have indicated the light by which the murderer shot Dr. Hardy. Since I had analyzed the facts, I knew what to look for, as would anyone who had analyzed them. When I found nothing in the nature of a light-giver, I was flabbergasted.

"I examined the contents of the pockets of our six suspects; still no clue to the source of the light. A single matchstick would have helped, although I realized that that would hardly have been the means employed; for this had been a trap laid in advance. The murderer had apparently enticed his victim to The House of Darkness.

He had planned the murder to take place here. Undoubtedly he had visited it before, seen its complete lack of lighting facilities. He therefore would have planned in advance to provide means of illumination. He scarcely would have relied on matches; certainly he would have preferred a flashlight. But there was nothing, nothing, not even the improbable burned match. If it was not on his person, had he thrown it away? But where? It has not been found. Nowhere in the rooms or corridor."

Ellery paused over a cigarette. "And so I came to the conclusion," he drawled, puffing smoke, "that *the light must have emanated from the victim himself.*"

"But no!" gasped Monsieur Duval. "No man would so foolish be—"

"Not consciously, of course. But he might have provided light unconsciously. I looked over the very dead Dr. Hardy. He wore dark clothing. There was no watch which might possess radial hands. He had no smoking implements on his person; a nonsmoker, obviously. No matches or lighter, then. And no flashlight. Nothing of a luminous nature which might explain how the killer saw where to aim. That is," he murmured, "nothing but one last possibility."

"What—"

"Will you gentlemen please put the lantern and your flashes out?"

For a moment there was uncomprehending inaction; and then lights began to snap off, until finally the room was steeped in the same thick palpable darkness that had existed when Ellery had stumbled into it. "Keep your places, please," said Ellery curtly. "Don't move, anyone."

There was no sound at first except the quick breaths of rigid people. The glow of Ellery's cigarette died, snuffed out. Then there was a slight rustling and a sharp click. And before their astonished eyes a roughly rectangular blob of light no larger than a domino, misty and nacreous, began to move across the room. It sailed in a straight line, like a homing pigeon, and then another blob detached itself from the first and touched something, and lo! there was still a third blob of light.

"Demonstrating," came Ellery's cool voice, "the miracle of how Nature provides for her most wayward children. Phosphorus, of course. Phosphorus in the form of paint. If, for example, the murderer had contrived to daub the back of the victim's coat before the victim entered

138

The House of Darkness—perhaps in the press of a crowd —he insured himself sufficient light for his crime. In a totally black place he had only to search for the phosphorescent patch. Then four shots in the thick of it from a distance of twelve feet—no great shakes to a good marksman—the bullet holes obliterate most of the light patch, any bit that remains is doused in gushing blood . . . and the murderer's safe all around. . . . Yes, yes, very clever. *No, you don't!*"

The third blob of light jerked into violent motion, lunging forward, disappearing, appearing, making progress toward the green-arrowed door. . . . There was a crash and a clatter, the sounds of a furious struggle. Lights flicked madly on, whipping across one another. They illuminated an area on the floor in which Ellery lay entwined with a man who fought in desperate silence. Beside them lay the paint box, open.

Captain Ziegler jumped in and rapped the man over the head with his billy. He dropped back with a groan, unconscious. It was the artist, Adams.

"But how did you know it was Adams?" demanded Ziegler a few moments later, when some semblance of order had been restored. Adams lay on the floor, manacled; the others crowded around, relief on some faces, fright on others.

"By a curious fact," panted Ellery, brushing himself off. "Djuna, stop pawing me! I'm quite all right. . . . You yourself told me, Captain, that when you found Adams blundering around in the dark he was complaining that he wanted to get out but couldn't find the exit. (Naturally he would!) He said that he knew he should follow the green lights, but when he did he only got deeper into the labyrinth of rooms. But how could that have been if he *had* followed the green lights? Any one of them would have taken him directly into the straight, monkeyshineless corridor leading to the exit. Then he *hadn't* followed the green lights. Since he could have no reason to lie about it, it must simply have meant, I reasoned, that he *thought* he had been following the green lights but had been following the red lights instead, since he continued to blunder from room to room."

"But how—"

"Very simple. Color blindness. He's afflicted with the common type of color blindness in which the subject confuses red and green. Unquestionably he didn't know that he had such an affliction; many color-blind persons don't. He had expected to make his escape quickly, before the body was found, depending on the green light he had previously heard the barker mention to insure his getaway.

"But that's not the important point. The important point is that *he claimed to be an artist*. Now, it's almost impossible for an artist to work in color and still be color blind. The fact that he had found himself trapped, misled by the red lights, proved that he was not conscious of his red-green affliction. But I examined his landscape and seascapes in the paint box and found them quite orthodox. I knew, then, that they weren't his; that he was masquerading, that he was not an artist at all. But if he was masquerading, he became a vital suspect!

"Then, when I put that together with the final deduction about the source of light, I had the whole answer in a flash. Phosphorus paint—paint box. And he had directly preceded Hardy into the House. . . . The rest was pure theatre. He felt that he wasn't running any risk with the phosphorus, for whoever would examine the paint box would naturally open it *in the light,* where the luminous quality of the chemical would be invisible. And there you are."

"Then my husband—" began Mrs. Clarke in a strangled voice, staring down at the unconscious murderer.

"But the motive, my friend," protested Monsieur Duval, wiping his forehead. "The motive! A man does not kill for nothing. Why—"

"The motive?" Ellery shrugged. "You already know the motive, Duval. In fact, you know—" He stopped and knelt suddenly by the bearded man. His hand flashed out and came away—with the beard. Mrs. Clarke screamed and staggered back. "He even changed his voice. This, I'm afraid, is your vanishing Mr. Clarke!"

The Adventure of the
Bleeding Portrait

NATCHITAUK is the sort of place where the Gramatons
and Eameses and Angerses of this world may be found
when the barns are freshly red and the rambler roses begin
to sprinkle the winding roadside fences. In summer its
careless hills seethe with large children who paint vistas
and rattle typewriters under trees and mumble unperfected
lines to the rafters of a naked backstage. These colonials
prefer rum to rye, and applejack to rum; and most of
them are famous and charming and great talkers.

Mr. Ellery Queen, who was visiting Natchitauk at Pearl
Angers' invitation to taste her scones and witness her
Candida, had hardly more than shucked his coat and
seated himself on the porch with an applejack highball
when the great lady told him the story of how Mark
Gramaton met his Mimi.

It seems that Gramaton had been splashing away at a
watercolor of the East River from a point high above
Manhattan when a dark young woman appeared on a
roof below him, spread a Navajo blanket, removed her
clothes, and lay down to sun herself.

The East River fluttered fifteen stories to the street.

And after a while Gramaton bellowed down: "You!
You woman, there!"

Mimi sat up, scared. There was Gramaton straining
over the parapet, his thick blond hair in tufts and his ugly
face the color of an infuriated persimmon.

"Turn over!" roared Gramaton in a terrible voice. "I'm
finished with that side!"

Ellery laughed. "He sounds amusing."

"But that's not the point of the story," protested the
Angers. "For when Mimi spied the paintbrush in his hand
she did meekly turn over. And when Gramaton saw her

141

dark back under the sun—well, he divorced his wife, who was a sensible woman, and married the girl."

"Ah, impulsive, too."

"You don't know Mark! He's a frustrated Botticelli. To him Mimi is beauty incarnate." It appeared, too, that no Collatinus had a more faithful Lucrece. At least four unsuccessful Tarquins of the Natchitauk aristocracy were —if not publicly prepared—at least privately in a position to attest Mimi's probity. "Besides, they're essentially gentlemen," said the actress, "and Gramaton is such a large and muscular man."

"Gramaton," said Ellery. "That's an odd name."

"English. His father was a yachtsman who clung barnaclelike to the tail of a long line of lords, and his mother's epidermis was so incrusted with tradition that she considered Queen Anne's death without surviving issue a major calamity to the realm, inasmuch as it ended the Stuart succession. At least, that's what Mark says!" The Angers sighed emotionally.

"Wasn't he a little hard on his first wife?" asked Ellery, who was inclined to be strait-laced.

"Oh, not really! She knew she couldn't hold him, and besides she had her own career to think of. They're still friends."

The next evening, taking his seat in the Natchitauk Playhouse, Ellery found himself staring at the loveliest female back within his critical memory. No silkworm spun, nor oyster strained, that dared aspire to that perfect flesh. The nude dark glowing skin quite obliterated the stage and Miss Angers and Mr. Shaw's aged dialogue.

When the lights came on Ellery awoke from his rhapsodizing to find that the seat in front of him had been vacated; and he rose with a purpose. Shoulders like that enter a man's life only once.

On the sidewalk he spied Emilie Eames, the novelist.

"Look," said Ellery. "I was introduced to you once at a party. How are you, and all that. Miss Eames, you know everybody in America, don't you?"

"All except a family named Radewicz," replied Miss Eames.

"I didn't see her face, curse it. But she has hazel shoulders, a tawny, toasty, nutty sort of back that . . . You *must* know her!"

"That," said Miss Eames reflectively, "would be Mimi."

"Mimi!" Ellery became glum.

"Well, come along. We'll find her where the cummer-bunds are thickest."

And there was Mimi in the lounge, surrounded by seven speechless young men. Against the red plush of the chair, with her lacquered hair, child's eyes, and soft tight back-less gown, she looked like a Polynesian queen. And she was altogether beautiful.

"Out of the way, you cads." Miss Eames dispersed the courtiers. "Mimi darling, here's somebody named Queen. Mrs. Gramaton."

"Gramaton," groaned Ellery. "My *bête blonde*."

"And this," added Miss Eames through her teeth, "is the foul fiend. Its name is Borcca."

It seemed a curious introduction. Ellery shook hands with Mr. Borcca, wondering if a smile or a cough were called for. Mr. Borcca was a sallow swordblade of a man with an antique Venetian face, looking as if he needed only a pitchfork.

Mr. Borcca smiled, showing a row of sharp vulpine teeth. "Miss Eames is my indefatigable admirer."

Miss Eames turned her back on him. "Queen has fallen in love with you, darling."

"How nice." Mimi looked down modestly. "And do you know my husband, Mr. Queen?"

"Ouch," said Ellery.

"My dear sir, it is not of the slightest use," said Mr. Borcca, showing his teeth again. "Mrs. Gramaton is that *rara avis*, a beautiful lady who cannot be dissuaded from adoring her husband."

The beautiful lady's beautiful back arched.

"Go away," said Miss Eames coldly. "You annoy me." Mr. Borcca did not seem to mind; he bowed as if at a compliment and Mrs. Gramaton sat very still.

Candida was a success; the Angers was radiant; Ellery soaked in the sun and rambled over the countryside and consumed mountains of brook trout and scones; and several times he saw Mimi Gramaton, so the week passed pleasantly.

The second time he saw her he was sprawled on the Angers jetty, fishing in the lake for dreams. One came, fortunately escaping his hook—she bobbed up under the line, wet and seal brown and clad in something shimmery, scant, and adhesive.

Mimi laughed at him, twisted, coiled against the jetty,

143

and shot off toward the large island in the middle of the lake. A fat hairy-chested man fishing from a rowboat she hailed joyously; he grinned back at her; and she streaked on, her bare back incandescent under the sun.

And then, as if she had swum into a net, she stopped. Ellery saw her jerk; tread water, blink through wet lashes at the island.

Mr. Borcca stood on the island's beach, leaning upon a curiously shaped walking stick.

Mimi dived. When she reappeared she was swimming on a tangent, headed for the cove at the eastern tip of the island. Mr. Borcca started to walk toward the eastern tip of the island. Mimi stopped again. . . . After a moment, with a visible resignation, she swam slowly for the beach again. When she emerged dripping from the lake, Mr. Borcca was before her. He merely stood still, and she went by him as if he were invisible. He followed her eagerly up the path into the woods.

"Who," demanded Ellery that evening, "is this Borcca?"

"Oh, you've met him?" The Angers paused. "One of Mark Gramaton's pets. A political refugee—he's been vague about it. Gramaton collects such people the way old ladies collect cats. . . . Borcca is—rather terrifying. Let's not talk about him."

The next day, at Emilie Eames's place, Ellery saw Mimi again. She wore linen shorts and a gay halter, and she had just finished three sets of tennis with a wiry gray man, Dr. Varrow, the local leech. She sauntered off the court, laughing, waved to Ellery and Miss Eames, who were lying on the lawn, and began to stroll toward the lake swinging her racket.

Suddenly she began to run. Ellery sat up.

She ran desperately. She cut across a cloverfield. She dropped her racket and did not stop to pick it up.

There was Mr. Borcca following her flight with rapid strides along the edge of the woods, his curiously-shaped stick under his arm.

"It strikes me," said Ellery slowly, "that *someone* ought to teach that fellow—"

"Please lie down again," said Miss Eames.

Dr. Varrow came off the court swabbing his neck, and stopped short. He saw Mimi running; he saw Mr. Borcca striding. Dr. Varrow's mouth tightened and he followed. Ellery got to his feet.

144

Miss Eames plucked a daisy. "Gramaton," she said softly, "doesn't know, you see. And Mimi is a brave child who is terribly in love with her husband."

"Bosh," said Ellery, watching the three figures. "If the man's a menace Gramaton should be told. How can he be so blind? Apparently everyone in Natchitauk—"

"Mark's peculiar. As many faults as virtues. When it is aroused he has the most jealous temper in the world."

"Will you excuse me?" said Ellery.

He strode toward the woods. Under the trees he stopped, listening. A man was crying out somewhere, thickly, helplessly, and yet defiantly. Ellery nodded, feeling his knuckles.

On his way back he saw Mr. Borcca stumble out of the woods. The man's medallion face was convulsed; he blundered into a rowboat and rowed off toward Gramaton's island with choppy strokes. And then Dr. Varrow and Mimi Gramaton strolled into view as if nothing had happened.

"I suppose every able-bodied man in Natchitauk," remarked Miss Eames calmly when Ellery rejoined her, "has had a crack at Borcca this summer."

"Why doesn't somebody run him out of town?"

"He's a queer animal. Complete physical coward, never defends himself, and yet undiscourageable. His seems to be an epic passion." Miss Eames shrugged. "If you noticed, Johnny Varrow didn't leave any marks on him. If his pet were mussed up Mark might ask inescapable questions."

"I don't understand it," muttered Ellery.

"Well, if he found out, you see," said Miss Eames in a light tone, "Mark would kill the beast."

Ellery met Gramaton and first encountered the phenomenon of the fourth Lord Gramaton's leaky breast at one of those carefully spontaneous entertainments with which the colonial *illuminati* periodically amuse themselves. There were charades, Guggenheim, Twenty Questions, and some sparkling pasquinade; and it all took place Sunday evening at Dr. Varrow's.

The doctor was gravely exhibiting a contraption. It was a tubular steel frame in which, suspended by invisible cords, hung a glistening cellophane heart filled with a fluid that looked like blood and was obviously tomato juice. Varrow announced in a sepulchral voice: "She is unfaithful," and squeezed a rubber ball. Whereupon the heart pursed itself and squirted a red stream that was caught uncannily by a brass cuspidor on the floor. Everyone folded up with laughter.

"Surrealism?" asked Ellery politely, wondering if he was mad.

The Angers collapsed. "It's Gramaton's bleeder," she gasped. "The *nerve* of Johnny! Of course, he's Gramaton's best friend."

"What has that to do with it?" asked Ellery, bewildered.

"You poor thing! Don't you know the story of the Bleeding Heart?"

She pulled him toward a very large and ugly blond man who was leaning helplessly on Mimi Gramaton's bare shoulders from behind, burying his face in her hair and laughing in gusts.

"Mark," said the Angers, "this is Ellery Queen. And he never heard the story of the Bleeding Heart!"

Gramaton released his wife, wiping his eyes with one hand and groping for Ellery with the other.

"Hullo there. That Johnny Varrow! He's the only man I know who can exhibit bad taste so charmingly it becomes good. . . . Queen? Don't believe I've seen you in Natchitauk before."

"Naturally not," said Mimi, poking her hair, "since Mr. Queen's only been staying with Pearl a few days and you've been shut up with that mural of yours."

"So you've met, you two," grinned Gramaton, but he placed his enormous arm about his wife's shoulders.

"Mark," pleaded the Angers, "tell him the story."

"Oh, he must see the portrait first. Artist?"

"Ellery writes murder stories," said Pearl. "Most people say 'How quaint' and he gets furious, so don't say it."

"Then you certainly must see the fourth Lord Gramaton. Murder stories? By George, this should be material for you." Gramaton chuckled. "Are you irrevocably committed to Pearl?"

"Certainly not," said the Angers. "He's eating me out of house and home. Do go, Ellery," she said. "He's going to ask you; he always does."

"Besides," said Gramaton, "I like your face."

"He means," murmured Mimi, "that he wants to use it on his mural."

"But—" began Ellery, rather helplessly.

"Of course you'll come," said Mimi Gramaton.

146

"Of course," beamed Ellery.

Mr. Queen found himself being borne across the lake under the stars to Gramaton's island, his suitcase under his feet, trying to recall exactly how he had got there as he watched the big man row. Mimi faced him bewitchingly from the stern, with Gramaton's huge shoulders spread between them, rising and falling like the flails of time; and Ellery shivered a little.

It was queer, because Gramaton seemed the friendliest fellow. He had stopped at Pearl's and fetched Ellery's bag himself, he chattered on, promising Ellery peace, rabbit-shooting, intelligent arguments about Communism, 16-millimeter views of Tibet, Tanganyika, and the Australian bush, and all manner of pleasant diversions.

"Simple life," chuckled Gramaton. "We're primitive here, you know—no bridge to the island, no motorboats . . . a bridge would spoil our natural isolation and I've a horror of things that make noise. Interested in art?"

"I don't know much about it," admitted Ellery.

"Appreciation doesn't necessarily require knowledge, despite what the academicians say." They landed on the beach; a figure rose, dark and fat against the sands, and took the boat. "Jeff," explained Gramaton, as they entered the woods. "Professional hobo; like him hanging around. . . . Appreciation? You could appreciate Mimi's back without knowing the least thing about the geometric theory of esthetics."

"He makes me exhibit it," complained Mimi, not very convincingly, "like a freak. Why, he selects my clothes! I feel naked half the time."

They came to the house and stopped to let Ellery admire it. Fat Jeff, the hairy man, came up from behind and took Ellery's bag and silently carried it off. The house was odd, all angles, ells, and wings, built of hewn logs on a rough stone foundation.

"It's just a house," said Gramaton. "Come along to my studio; I'll introduce you to Lord Gramaton."

The studio occupied the second story of a far wing. The north wall was completely glass, in small panes, and the other walls were covered with oils, watercolors, pastels, etchings, plasters, and carvings in wood.

"Good evening," bowed Mr. Borcca. He was standing before a large covered framework, and he had just turned around.

"Oh, there's Borcca," smiled Gramaton. "Inhaling art, you pagan? Queen, meet—"

"I've had the pleasure," said Ellery politely. He was wondering what the framework concealed; the cover was askew and it seemed to him that Mr. Borcca had been examining what lay under it with passionate absorption when they had surprised him.

"I think," said Mimi in a small voice, "I'll see about Mr. Queen's room."

"Nonsense. Jeff's doing that. Here's my mural," Gramaton said, ripping the cover off the framework. "Just the preliminary work on one corner—it's to go over the lobby entrance of the New Arts building. Of course you recognize Mimi."

And indeed Ellery did. The central motif of a throng of curious masculine faces was a gargantuan female back, dark and curved and womanly. He glanced at Mr. Borcca; but Mr. Borcca was looking at Mrs. Gramaton.

"And this is His Nibs."

The ancient portrait had been placed where the north light tactfully did not venture—a life-size canvas the color of gloomy molasses, set flush with the floor. The fourth Lord Gramaton glared down out of the habiliments of the seventeenth century, remarkable only for the diameter of his belly and flare of his nose. Ellery thought he had never seen a more repulsive daub.

"Isn't he a beauty?" grinned Gramaton. "Shove an armful, of those canvases off that chair. . . . Done by some earnest but, as you can see, horny-handed forerunner of Hogarth."

"But what's the connection between Lord Gramaton and Dr. Varrow's little pleasantry?" demanded Ellery.

"Come here, darling." Mimi went to her husband and sat down on his lap, resting her dark head against his shoulder. Mr. Borcca turned away, stumbling over a sharp-pointed palette knife on the floor. "Borcca, pour Mr. Queen a drink.

"Well, my noble ancestor married a carefully preserved Lancashire lass who'd never been two miles from her father's hayrick. The old pirate was very proud of his wife because of her beauty; and he exhibited her at Court much as he had exhibited his blacks in the African slave markets. Lady Gramaton quickly became the ambition of London's more buckety buckos."

"Scotch, Mr. Queen?" mumbled Mr. Borcca.

"No."

Gramaton kissed his wife's neck, and Mr. Borcca helped himself to two quick drinks. "It seems," continued Gramaton, "that, conscious of his responsibility to posterity, Lord Gramaton soon after his marriage commissioned some pot-slinger to paint his portrait, with the foul result you see.

"The old chap was terribly pleased with it, though, and hung it over the fireplace in the great hall of his castle, in the most conspicuous place. Well, the story says that one night—he was gouty, too—unable to sleep, he hobbled downstairs for something and was horrified to see blood dripping from the waistcoat of his own portrait."

"Oh, no," protested Ellery. "Or was it some Restoration joke?"

"No, it was blood," chuckled the artist. "The old cut-throat knew blood when he saw it! Well, he hobbled upstairs to his wife's chamber to inform her of the miracle and caught the poor girl enjoying a bit of life with one of the young bucks I mentioned. Naturally, he skewered them both with his sword, and as I recall it lived to be ninety and remarried and had five children by his second wife."

"But—blood," said Ellery, staring at Lord Gramaton's immaculate waistcoat. "What did that have to do with his wife's infidelity?"

"Nobody understands that," said Mimi in a muffled voice. "That's why it's a story."

"And when he went downstairs again," said Gramaton, fondling his wife's ear, "wiping his sword, the blood on the portrait had vanished. Typical British symbolism, you know—mysteriously dull. Ever after the tradition has persisted that the fourth Lord Gramaton's heart would bleed every time a Gramaton wife strayed to greener pastures."

"Sort of domestic tattletale," remarked Ellery dryly.

Mimi jumped off her husband's lap. "Mark, I'm simply weary."

"Sorry." Gramaton stretched his long arms. "Rum sort of thing, eh? Use it if you like. . . . Shall I show you your room? Borcca, be a good chap and turn off the lights."

Mimi went out quickly, like a woman pursued. And indeed she was—by Mr. Borcca's eyes, as they left him standing by the sideboard with the decanter of Scotch in his hand.

"Awkward," said Gramaton at breakfast. "Will you forgive me? I've had a telegram from the architect and I must run into the city this afternoon."

"I'll go with you," suggested Ellery. "You've been so kind—"

"Won't hear of it. I'll be back tomorrow morning and we'll have some sport."

Ellery strolled into the woods for a trampling survey of Gramaton's island. It was, he found, shaped like a peanut; a densely wooded place except in the middle, covering at least thirty acres. The sky was overcast and he felt chilled, despite his leather jacket. But whether it was from the natural elements or not he did not know. The place depressed him.

Finding himself following an old, almost obliterated path, he pursued it with curiosity. It led across a rocky neck and vanished near the eastern end of the island in an overgrown clearing in which stood a wooden hut, its roof half fallen in and its wall timbers sticking out like broken bones.

"Some deserted squatter's shack," he thought; and it caught his fancy to explore it. One found things in old places.

But what Ellery found was a dilemma. Stepping upon the crumbly stone doorstep he heard voices from the gloom inside. And at the same instant, faintly from the wood behind, rose Gramaton's voice calling: "Mimi!"

Ellery stood still.

Mimi's voice came passionately from the shack. "Don't you dare. Don't touch me. I didn't ask you here for that."

Mr. Borcca's plaintive voice said: "Mimi. Mimi. Mimi," like a grooved phonograph record.

"Here's money. Take it and get out of here. Take it!" She seemed hysterical.

But Mr. Borcca merely repeated: "Mimi," and his feet scuffed across the rough floor.

"Borcca! You're a mad animal. Borcca! I'll scream! My husband—"

"I shall kill you," said Mr. Borcca in a tired voice. "I cannot stand this—"

"Gramaton!" shouted Ellery, as the big man came into view. The voices in the shack ceased. "Don't look so concerned. I've kidnaped Mrs. Gramaton and made her show me your forest."

"Oh," said Gramaton, wiping his head. "Mimi!"

150

Mimi appeared, smiling, and her arm, close to Ellery's jacket, shook. "I've just been showing Mr. Queen the shack. Were you worried about me, darling?" She ran past Ellery and linked her arms about her husband's neck.

"But, Mimi, you know I needed you to pose this morning." Gramaton seemed uneasy; his big blond head jerked from side to side. Then his head stopped jerking.

"I forgot, Mark. Don't look so grumpy!" She took his arm, turned him around and, laughing, walked him off.

"Lovely place," called Ellery fatuously, standing still.

Gramaton smiled back at him, but the gray eyes were intent. Mimi drew him into the woods.

Ellery looked down. Mr. Borcca's curiously-shaped walking stick lay on the path. Gramaton had seen it.

He took up the stick and went into the hut. It was empty.

He came out, broke the stick over his knee, pitched the pieces into the lake, and slowly followed the Gramatons down the path.

When Mimi returned from the village after seeing Gramaton off she was accompanied by Emilie Eames and Dr. Varrow.

"I spend more time with a paintbrush than a stethoscope," explained the doctor to Ellery. "I find art catching. And people here are so depressingly healthy."

"We'll swim and things," announced Mimi, "and tonight we'll toast wieners and marshmallows outdoors. We do owe you something, Mr. Queen." But she did not look at him. It seemed to Ellery that she was unnaturally animated; her cheeks were dark red.

While they played in the lake Mr. Borcca appeared on the beach and quietly sat down. Mimi stopped being gay. Later, when they came out of the lake, Mr. Borcca rose and went away.

After dinner Jeff built a fire. Mimi sat very close to Miss Eames, snuggling as if she were cold. Dr. Varrow unexpectedly produced a guitar and sang some obscure sailors' chanteys. It turned out that Mimi possessed a clear, sweet soprano voice; she sang, too, until she caught sight of a pair of iridescent eyes regarding her from the underbrush. Then she abruptly stopped, and Ellery observed to himself that at night Mr. Borcca might easily turn into a wolf. There was such a feral glare in those orbs that his muscles tightened.

A light rain began to fall; they scampered for the house gratefully, Jeff trampling out the fire.

"Do stay over," urged Mimi. "With Mark away—"

"You couldn't drive me home," said Dr. Varrow cheerfully. "I like your beds."

"Do you want me to sleep with you, Mimi?" asked Miss Eames.

"No," said Mimi slowly. "That won't be—necessary."

Ellery was just removing his jacket when someone tapped on his door. "Mr. Queen," whispered a voice.

Ellery opened the door. Mimi stood there in the semi-darkness clad in a gauzy backless negligee. She said nothing more, but her large eyes begged.

"Perhaps," suggested Ellery, "it would be more discreet if we talked in your husband's studio."

He retrieved his jacket and she led him in silence to the studio, turning on a single bulb. Details sprang up— the fourth Lord Gramaton glowering, the sheen of the unbroken north wall windows, the palette knife lying on the floor.

"I owe you an explanation," whispered Mimi, sinking into a chair. "And such terribly important thanks that I can't ever—"

"You owe me nothing," said Ellery gently. "But you owe yourself a good deal. How long do you think you can keep this up?"

"So you know, too!" She began to weep without sound into her hands. "That animal has been here since May, and . . . what am I to do?"

"Tell your husband."

"No, oh, no! You don't know Mark. It's not myself, but Mark . . . he'd strangle Borcca slowly. He'd—he'd break his arms and legs and . . . He'd kill the creature! Don't you see I've got to protect Mark from that?"

Ellery was silent, for the excellent reason that he could think of nothing to say. Short of killing Borcca himself, he was helpless. Mimi sat collapsed in the chair, crying again.

"Please go," she sobbed. "And I do thank you."

"Do you think it's wise to stay here alone?"

She did not reply. Feeling a perfect fool, Ellery left. Outside the house the roly-poly figure of Jeff separated itself from a tree.

"It's all right, Mr. Queen," said Jeff.

Ellery went to bed, reassured.

Gramaton was red-eyed and grayish the next morning, as if he had spent a sleepless night in the city. But he seemed cheerful enough.

"I promise you I shan't run off again," he said, over the eggs. "What's the matter, Mimi—are you cold?"

It was an absurd thing to suggest, because the morning was hot, with every sign of growing hotter. And yet Mimi wore a heavy gown of some unflattering stuff and a long camel's-hair coat. Her face was oddly drawn.

"I don't feel awfully well," she said with a pale smile. "Did you have a nice trip, Mark?"

He made a face. "There's been a change in the plans; the design must be altered. I'll have to pose your back all over again."

"Oh . . . darling." Mimi put down her toast. "Would you be terribly cross if . . . if I didn't pose for you?"

"Bother! Well, all right, dear. We'll begin tomorrow."

"I mean," murmured Mimi, picking up her fork, "I— I'd rather not pose at all . . . any more."

Gramaton set his cup down very, very slowly, as if he had suddenly developed a griping ache in his arm. No one said anything.

"Of course, Mimi."

Ellery felt the need of fresh air.

Emilie Eames said lightly: "You've done something to the man, Mimi. When he was my husband he'd have thrown something."

It was all very confusing to Ellery. Gramaton smiled, and Mimi pecked at her omelet, and Dr. Varrow folded his napkin with absorption. When Jeff lumbered in, scratching his stubble, Ellery could have embraced him.

"Can't find the skunk nowheres," Jeff growled. "He didn't sleep in his bed last night, Mr. Gramaton."

"Who?" said Gramaton absently. "What?"

"Borrca. Didn't you want him for paintin'? He's gone."

Gramaton drew his blond brows together, concentrating. Miss Eames exclaimed hopefully: "Do you suppose he fell into the lake and was drowned?"

"This seems to be my morning for disappointments," said Gramaton, rising. "Would you care to come up to my shop, Queen? I'd be grateful if you'd allow me to sketch your head into the group." He walked out without looking back.

"I think," said Mimi faintly, "I have a headache."

When Ellery reached the studio he found Gramaton

153

standing wide-legged, hands clenched behind his back. The room was curiously disordered; two chairs were over-turned, and canvases cluttered the floor. Gramaton was glaring at the portrait of his ancestor. A hot breeze ruffled his hair; one of the windows on the glass wall stood open.

"This," said Gramaton in a gravelly voice, "is simply intolerable." Then his voice swelled into a roar; he sounded like a lion in agony. "Varrow! Emilie! Jeff!"

Ellery went to the portrait and squinted into the shadow. He stared, unbelieving.

Sometime during the night, the fourth Lord Gramaton's heart had bled.

There was a smear of brownish stuff directly over the painted left breast. Some of it, while in a liquid state, had trickled in drops an inch or two. More of it was splattered down Lord Gramaton's waistcoat and over his belly. Whatever it was, there had been a good deal of it.

Gramaton made a whimpering noise, ripped the portrait from the wall, and flung it to the floor in the full light.

"Who did this?" he asked huskily.

Mimi covered her mouth. Dr. Varrow smiled. "Little boys have a habit of smearing filth on convenient walls, Mark."

Gramaton looked at him, breathing heavily. "Don't act so tragic, Mark," said Miss Eames. "It's just some moron's idea of a practical joke. Goodness knows there's enough paint lying around here."

Ellery stooped over the prostrate, wounded nobleman and sniffed. Then he rose and said: "But it isn't paint."

"Not paint?" echoed Miss Eames feebly. Gramaton paled, and Mimi closed her eyes and felt for a chair.

"I'm rather familiar with the concomitants of violence, and this looks remarkably like dry blood to me."

"Blood!"

Gramaton laughed. He ground his heels very deliber-ately into Lord Gramaton's face. He jumped up and down on the frame, cracking it in a dozen places. He crumpled the canvas and kicked the remains into the fireplace. He ignited a whole packet of matches and carefully pushed it under the débris. Then he stumbled out.

Ellery smiled apologetically. He bent over and managed to rip away a sample of brown-stained canvas before Lord Gramaton suffered complete cremation. When he rose, only Dr. Varrow remained in the room.

"Borcca," said Dr. Varrow thickly. "Borcca."

"These English," mumbled Ellery. "Old saws are true saws. No sense of humor at all. Could you test this for me at once, Dr. Varrow?"

When the doctor had gone Ellery, finding himself alone and the house wonderfully quiet, sat down in Gramaton's studio to think. While he thought, he looked. It seemed to him that something which had been on the studio floor the day before was no longer there. And then he remembered. It had been Gramaton's sharp-pointed palette knife.

He went over to the north wall and stuck his head out of the open section of the window.

"He ain't anywheres," said Jeff, from behind him.

"Still looking for Borcca? Very sensible, Jeff."

"Aw, he's just skipped. And good riddance, the dog."

"Nevertheless, would you show me his room, please?"

The fat man blinked his shrewd eyes and scratched his hairy breast. Then he led the way to a room on the first floor of the same wing. The silence hummed.

"No," decided Ellery after a while, "Mr. Borcca didn't just skip out, Jeff. Until the moment he vanished he had every intention of staying, to judge from the undisturbed condition of his belongings. Nervous, though—look at those cigarette butts."

Closing Mr. Borcca's door softly, he left the house and tramped around until he stood below the north window of Gramaton's studio. There were flower beds here, and the soft loam was gay with pansies.

But someone or something had been very brutal with the pansies. Below Gramaton's studio window they lay crushed and broken, and imbedded in the earth, as if a considerable weight had landed heavily on them. Where the devastated area began, near the wall, there were two deep trenches in the loam, parallel and narrow scoops, with the impressions of a man's shoe at the lowest depth of each scoop.

The toes pointed away from the wall and were queerly turned inwards toward each other.

"Borcca wore shoes like that," muttered Ellery. He sucked his lower lip, standing still. Beyond the pansy bed lay a gravel walk; snaking across the walk from the two trenches led a faint trail, rough and irregular, about the width of a human body.

Jeff flapped his arms suddenly, as if he wanted to fly away. But he merely clumped off, shoulders sagging.

155

Pearl Angers and Emilie Eames came hurrying around the house. The actress was very pale.

"I came over to be neighborly, and Emilie told me the frightful—"

"How," asked Ellery absently, "is Mrs. Gramaton?"

"How would you think!" cried Miss Eames. "Oh, Mark's still the big stupid fool I know! Prowling his room like a bear thrashing up his temper. You'd think that, since it's his pet story, he'd appreciate the joke, anyway."

"Blood," said the Angers damply. "Blood, Emilie."

"Mimi's simply prostrated," said Miss Eames furiously. "Oh, Mark's an idiot! That cock-and-bull story! Joke!"

"I'm afraid," said Ellery, "that it isn't as much a joke as you seem to think." He pointed at the pansy bed.

"What," faltered the Angers, shrinking against her friend and pointing to the dim trail, "is—that?"

Ellery did not reply. He turned and slowly began to follow the trail, bent over and peering.

Miss Eames moistened her lips and stared from the open window of Gramaton's studio two stories above to the crushed area in the pansy bed directly below.

The actress giggled hysterically, staring at the trail Ellery was pursuing. "Why, it looks," she said in a stricken voice, "as if—someone—dragged a . . . body. . . ."

The two women joined hands like children and stumbled along behind.

The erratic trail meandered across the garden in zigzags and arcs; in its course it revealed a narrower track of thin parallel scrapings, as if shoes had dragged. When it entered the woods it became harder to follow, for the ground here was a confusion of leaf mold, roots and twigs.

The women followed Ellery like sleepwalkers, making no sound. Somewhere along the route Mark Gramaton caught up with them; he stalked behind on stiff iron legs.

It was very hot in the woods. Sweat dripped off their noses. And after a while Mimi, bundled up as if she were cold, crept up to her husband. He paid no attention. She dropped behind, whimpering.

As the underbrush grew more tangled the trail became even more difficult to trace. Ellery, leading the voiceless procession, had to skirt several places and skip over rotting logs. At one point the trail led under a tangle of bramble so wide and thick and impenetrable that it was impossible to accompany it, even on hands and knees. For a time Ellery lost the scent altogether. His eyes were unnaturally bright. Then, after a detour by way of a broad grove, he picked up the trail again.

Not long after, he stopped; they all stopped. In the center of the trail lay a gold cuff link. Ellery examined it —it was initialed exquisitely *B*—and dropped it in his pocket.

Gramaton's island pinched up near the middle. The pinched area was extensive, completely rock—a dangerous, boulder-strewn ankle-trap. The lake hemmed it in on two sides.

Here Ellery lost the trail again. He searched among the boulders for a while, but only a bloodhound could have retained hope there. So he stepped thoughtfully, with a curious lack of interest.

"Oh, look," said Pearl Angers in a shocked voice.

Miss Eames had her arms about Mimi, holding her up. Gramaton stood alone, staring stonily. Ellery picked his way to the Angers, who was perched perilously on a jutting bone of the rocky neck, pointing with horror into the lake.

The water was shallow there. Gleaming on the sandy bottom, at arm's length, lay Gramaton's palette knife, patently hurled away.

Ellery seated himself on a boulder and lit a cigarette. He made no attempt to retrieve the knife; the lake had long since washed away any clues it might last night have betrayed.

The Angers restlessly eyed the lake, repelled and yet eager, searching, searching for something larger than a knife.

"Queen!" shouted a faraway voice. "Queen!"

Ellery called: "Here!" several times in a loud but weary voice, and resumed his cigarette.

Soon they heard someone thrashing toward them through the woods. In a few minutes Dr. Varrow appeared on the dead run.

"Queen," he panted. "It—*is*—blood! Human blood!" Seeing Gramaton, he stopped, as if abashed.

Ellery nodded.

"Blood," repeated the Angers in a loathing voice. "And Borcca's missing. And you found his cuff link on that hideous trail." She shivered.

"Someone stabbed him to death in the studio last night," whispered Miss Eames, "and in the struggle his blood got on the portrait."

"And then either threw his body out the window," said the actress, barely audible, "or he fell out during the fight. And then, whoever it was—came down and dragged the body all the way through the woods to—to this horrible place, and . . ."

"We could probably," said Dr. Varrow thickly, "find the body ourselves, right here in the lake."

Gramaton said very slowly: "We ought to send for the police."

They all looked at Ellery, stricken by the word. But Ellery continued to smoke without saying anything.

"I don't suppose," faltered Miss Eames finally, "you can hope to *conceal* a—murder, can you?"

Gramaton began to trudge back in the direction of his house.

"Oh, just a moment," Ellery said, flinging his cigarette into the lake. Gramaton stopped, without turning around. "Gramaton, you're a fool."

"What do you mean?" growled the artist. But he still did not turn around.

"Are you the nice chap you seem to be," demanded Ellery, "or are you what your wife and ex-wife and friends seem to think you are—a homicidal maniac?"

Gramaton wheeled then, his ugly face crimson. "All right!" he yelled. "I killed him!"

"No," cried Mimi, half-rising from her stone. "Mark, no!"

"Pshaw," said Ellery, "there's no need to be so vehement, Gramaton. A child could see you're protecting your wife—or think you are." Gramaton sank onto a boulder. "That," continued Ellery equably, "gives you a character. You don't know what to believe about your wife, but you're willing to confess to a murder you think she committed—just the same."

"I killed him, I say," said Gramaton sullenly.

"Killed whom, Gramaton?"

They all looked at him then. "Mr. Queen," cried Mimi. "No!"

"It's no use, Mrs. Gramaton," said Ellery. "All this would have been avoided if you'd been sensible enough to trust your husband in the first place. That's what husbands, poor saps, are for."

"But Borcca—" began Dr. Varrow.

"Ah, yes, Borcca. Yes, indeed, we must discuss Mr.

Borcca. But first we must discuss our hostess's charming back."

"My back?" said Mimi faintly.

"What about my wife's back?" shouted Gramaton.

"Everything, or nearly," smiled Ellery, lighting another cigarette. "Smoke? You need one badly. . . . You see, your wife's back is not only beautiful, Gramaton; it's eloquent, too.

"I've been in Natchitauk over a week; I've had the pleasure of observing it on several precious occasions; it's always been bared to the world, as beautiful things should be; and in fact Mrs. Gramaton told me herself that you were so proud of it you selected her clothes—with an eye, I suppose, to keeping it constantly on exhibition."

Miss Eames made a muffled noise, and Mimi looked sick.

"This morning," drawled Ellery, "Mrs. Gramaton suddenly appears garbed in a heavy, all-concealing gown; she wears a long, all-concealing coat; she announces she will no longer pose for your mural, in which her nude back is the central motif. This despite these facts: first, that it is an extremely hot day; second, that up to late last night I myself saw her back bare and beautiful as ever; third, that she is well aware what it must mean to you to be denied suddenly, and without explanation, the inspiration of her charms in such an ambitious artistic undertaking as the New Arts mural. Yet," said Ellery, "she suddenly covers her back and refuses to pose. Why?"

Gramaton looked at his wife, his brow contorted.

"Shall I tell you why, Mrs. Gramaton?" said Ellery gently. "Because obviously you are *concealing* your back. Because obviously something happened between the time I left you last night and breakfast this morning that *forced* you to conceal your back. Because obviously something happened to your back last night which you don't want your husband to see, and which he would have to see if as usual you posed for him this morning. Am I right?"

Mimi Gramaton's lips moved, but she said nothing. Gramaton and the others stared at Ellery, bewildered.

"Of course I am," smiled Ellery. "Well, I said to myself, what could have happened to your back last night? Was there any clue? There certainly was—the portrait of the fourth Lord Gramaton!"

"The portrait?" repeated Miss Eames, wrinkling her nose.

"For, mark you, last night Lord Gramaton's breast bled again. Ah, what a story! I left you in the studio, and the noble lord bled, and this morning you concealed your back. . . . Surely it makes sense? The bleeding picture might have been a bad joke; it might have been—forgive me—a supernatural phenomenon; but at least it *was* blood—human blood, Dr. Varrow has established. Well, human blood has to flow, and that means a wound. Whose wound? Lord Gramaton's? Pshaw! Blood is blood, and canvas doesn't wound easily. *Your* blood, Mrs. Gramaton, and *your* wound, to be sure; otherwise why were you afraid to display your back?"

"Oh Lord," said Gramaton. "Mimi—darling—" Mimi began to weep and Gramaton buried his ugly face in his hands.

"It was easy to reconstruct what must have happened. It was in the studio; there are signs there of a tussle. You were attacked—with the palette knife, of course; we found it thrown away. You backed against the portrait, the wound in your back streaming blood: Lord Gramaton was set flush with the floor, and was life-size, so your back wound smeared Lord Gramaton's breast in just the right place, happily for the ghost story. I assumed you fainted, and Jeff—he was outside when I left, so he must have been attracted by the sounds of the struggle—found you, carried you to your room, and treated your wound and kept his mouth shut like the loyal soul he is, because you begged him to." Mimi nodded, sobbing.

"Mimi!" Gramaton sprang to her.

"But—Borcca," muttered Dr. Varrow. "I don't see—"

Ellery flicked ashes. "It's wonderful what the imagination is," he grinned. "Blood—Borcca missing—plenty of motive for murder—the trail of a human body through the woods . . . murder! How very illogical, and how very human."

He puffed. "I saw, of course, that Borcca must have been the attacker: the man threatened to kill Mrs. Gramaton yesterday in my hearing, and he was plainly insane with jealousy and a deep thwarted passion. What happened to Borcca? Ah, the open window. It had been shut when I saw it the night before. Now it was open. Below, in the pansy bed, the plain sign of a fallen body, two deep trenches in the soil showing where his feet must have landed. . . . In short, panicky, a coward, perhaps thinking he had committed murder, hearing Jeff lumbering upstairs, Borcca jumped out of Gramaton's window in a blind impulse to escape—and fell two stories."

"But how can you know he jumped?" frowned the Angers. "How do you know—Jeff, say, didn't catch and kill him and throw his dead body out and then drag it. . . ."

"No," smiled Ellery. "The dragging marks stretched out a considerable distance through these woods. In one place, as you saw, it led under some brambles so thick that I couldn't have gone through it except on my belly; yet the trail went right through, didn't it? If Borcca was dead, and his body was being dragged, how did the murderer get the body through those brambles? In fact, why should he want to? Surely he wouldn't crawl himself at that point, hauling the body after him. It would have been easier to go by an unobstructed path nearby, as we did.

"So," said Ellery, rising and beginning to pick his way across the rocky neck, "it was evident that Borcca had *not* been dragged, *that Borcca had dragged himself,* crawling on his stomach. Therefore he was alive, and no murder had been committed at all, you see."

Slowly they began to follow. Gramaton had his arm about Mimi, humbly, his big chin on his breast.

"But why should he crawl all that distance?" demanded Dr. Varrow. "He might crawl *to* the woods to escape being seen, but once in the woods, at night, surely he didn't have to. . . ."

"Exactly; he didn't have to," said Ellery. "But he crawled nevertheless. Then he *must* have had to. . . . He had jumped two stories. He had landed feet first, and from the turning-in of the toemarks in the pansy bed his feet had twisted inward in landing. So, I said to myself, he must have broken his ankles. You see?"

He stopped. They stopped. Ellery had led them to the end of the path on the eastward part of the island. They could see the abandoned shack through the trees.

"A man with two broken feet—both were broken, because the trail showed two parallel shoe marks dragging, indicating that he could not use even one leg for pushing—cannot swim, without foot leverage he can hardly be conceived as rowing, and there is neither a motorboat nor a bridge on this island. I felt sure," he said in a low voice, "that he was therefore still on the island."

Gramaton growled deep in his throat, like a bloodhound.

"And in view of Jeff's inability to find our Mr. Borcca this morning, it also seemed probable that he had taken refuge in that shack." Ellery looked into Gramaton's gray eyes. "For more than twelve hours the creature has been cowering in there, in intense pain, thinking himself a murderer, waiting to be routed out for the capital punishment he believes he's earned. I imagine he's been punished enough, don't you, Gramaton?"

The big man's eyes blinked. Then, without a word, he said: "Mimi?" in a low voice, and she looked up at him and took his arm and he turned her carefully around and began to walk her back to the western end of the island.

Offshore, resting on his oars like a watchful Buddha, sat Jeff.

"You may as well go back, too," said Ellery gently to the two women. He waved his arm at Jeff. "Dr. Varrow and I have a nasty job to—finish."

Man Bites Dog

ANYONE observing the tigerish pacings, the gnawings of lip, the contortions of brow, and the fierce melancholy which characterized the conduct of Mr. Ellery Queen, the noted sleuth, during those early October days in Hollywood, would have said reverently that the great man's intellect was once more locked in titanic struggle with the forces of evil.

"Paula," Mr. Queen said to Paula Paris, "I'm going mad."

"I hope," said Miss Paris tenderly, "it's love."

Mr. Queen paced, swathed in yards of thought. Queenly Miss Paris observed him with melting eyes. When he had first encountered her, during his investigation of the double murder of Blythe Stuart and Jack Royle, the famous motion-picture stars,* Miss Paris had been in the grip of a morbid psychology. She had been in a deathly terror of crowds. "Crowd phobia" the doctors called it. Mr. Queen, stirred by a nameless emotion, determined to cure the lady of her psychological affliction. The therapy, he conceived, must be both shocking and compensatory; and so he made love to her.

And lo! although Miss Paris recovered, to his horror Mr. Queen found that the cure may sometimes present a worse problem than the affliction. For the patient promptly fell in love with her healer; and the healer did not himself escape certain excruciating emotional consequences.

"Is it?" asked Miss Paris, her heart in her eyes.

"Eh?" said Mr. Queen. "What? Oh, no. I mean—it's the World Series." He looked savage. "Don't you realize what's happening? The New York Giants and the New York Yankees are waging mortal combat to determine the baseball championship of the world, and I'm three thousand miles away!"

"Oh," said Miss Paris. Then she said cleverly: "You poor darling."

"Never missed a New York series before," wailed Mr. Queen. "Driving me cuckoo. And what a battle! Greatest series ever played. Moore and DiMaggio have done miracles in the outfield. Giants have pulled a triple play. Goofy Gomez struck out fourteen men to win the first game. Hubbell's pitched a one-hit shutout. And today Dickey came up in the ninth inning with the bases loaded, two out, and the Yanks three runs behind, and slammed a homer over the right-field stands!"

"Is that good?" asked Miss Paris.

"Good!" howled Mr. Queen. "It merely sent the series into a seventh game."

"Poor darling," said Miss Paris again, and she picked up her telephone. When she set it down she said: "Weather's threatening in the East. Tomorrow the New York Weather Bureau expects heavy rains."

Mr. Queen stared wildly. "You mean—"

"I mean that you're taking tonight's plane for the East. And you'll see your beloved seventh game day after tomorrow."

---

*Related in *The Four of Hearts*, by Ellery Queen. Frederick A. Stokes Company, 1938.

"Paula, you're a genius!" Then Mr. Queen's face fell. "But the studio, tickets . . . *Bigre!* I'll tell the studio I'm down with elephantiasis, and I'll wire Dad to snare a box. With his pull at City Hall, he ought to—Paula, I don't know what I'd do. . . ."

"You might," suggested Miss Paris, "kiss me . . . goodbye."

Mr. Queen did so, absently. The he started. "Not at all! You're coming with me!"

"That's what I had in mind," said Miss Paris contentedly.

And so Wednesday found Miss Paris and Mr. Queen at the Polo Grounds, ensconced in a field box behind the Yankees' dugout.

Mr. Queen glowed, he reveled, he was radiant. While Inspector Queen, with the suspiciousness of all fathers, engaged Paula in exploratory conversation, Ellery filled his lap and Paula's with peanut hulls, consumed frankfurters and soda pop immoderately, made hypercritical comments on the appearance of the various athletes, derided the Yankees, extolled the Giants, evolved complicated fifty-cent bets with Detective-Sergeant Velie, of the Inspector's staff, and leaped to his feet screaming with fifty thousand other maniacs as the news came that Carl Hubbell, the beloved Meal Ticket of the Giants, would oppose Señor El Goofy Gomez, the ace of the Yankee staff, on the mound.

"Will the Yanks murder that apple today!" predicted the Sergeant, who was an incurable Yankee worshiper. "And will Goofy mow 'em down!"

"Four bits," said Mr. Queen coldly, "say the Yanks don't score three earned runs off Carl."

"It's a pleasure!"

"I'll take a piece of that, Sergeant," chuckled a handsome man to the front of them, in a rail seat. "Hi, Inspector. Swell day for it, eh?"

"Jimmy Connor!" exclaimed Inspector Queen. "The old Song-and-Dance Man in person. Say, Jimmy, you never met my son, Ellery, did you? Excuse me. Miss Paris, this is the famous Jimmy Connor, God's gift to Broadway."

"Glad to meet you, Miss Paris," smiled the Song-and-Dance Man, sniffing at his orchidaceous lapel. "Read your *Seeing Stars* column, every day. Meet Judy Starr."

Miss Paris smiled, and the woman beside Jimmy Connor smiled back, and just then three Yankee players strolled over to the box and began to jeer at Connor for having had to take seats behind that hated Yankee dugout.

Judy Starr was sitting oddly still. She was the famous Judy Starr who had been discovered by Florenz Ziegfeld—a second Marilyn Miller, the critics called her; dainty and pretty, with a perky profile and great honey-colored eyes, who had sung and danced her way into the heart of New York. Her day of fame was almost over now. Perhaps, thought Paula, staring at Judy's profile, that explained the pinch of her little mouth, the fine lines about her tragic eyes, the singing tension of her figure.

Perhaps. But Paula was not sure. There was immediacy, a defense against a palpable and present danger, in Judy Starr's tautness. Paula looked about. And at once her eyes narrowed.

Across the rail of the box, in the box at their left, sat a very tall, leather-skinned, silent and intent man. The man, too, was staring out at the field, in an attitude curiously like that of Judy Starr, whom he could have touched by extending his big, ropy, muscular hand across the rail. And on the man's other side there sat a woman whom Paula recognized instantly. Lotus Verne, the motion-picture actress!

Lotus Verne was a gorgeous, full-blown redhead with deep mercury-colored eyes who had come out of Northern Italy Ludovica Vernicchi, changed her name, and flashed across the Hollywood skies in a picture called *Woman of Bali,* a color film in which loving care had been lavished on the display possibilities of her dark, full, dangerous body. With fame, she had developed a passion for press agentry, borzois in pairs, and tall brown men with muscles. She was arrayed in sun yellow, and she stood out among the women in the field boxes like a butterfly in a mass of grubs. By contrast little Judy Starr, in her flame-colored outfit, looked almost old and dowdy.

Paula nudged Ellery, who was critically watching the Yankees at batting practice. "Ellery," she said softly, "who is that big, brown, attractive man in the next box?"

Lotus Verne said something to the brown man, and suddenly Judy Starr said something to the Song-and-Dance Man; and then the two women exchanged the kind of glance women use when there is no knife handy.

Ellery said absently: "Who? Oh! That's Big Bill Tree."

"Tree!" repeated Paula. "Big Bill Tree?"

"Greatest left-handed pitcher major-league baseball ever saw," said Mr. Queen, staring reverently at the brown man. "Six feet three inches of bull whip and muscle, with a temper as sudden as the hook on his curve ball and a change of pace that fooled the greatest sluggers of baseball for fifteen years. What a man!"

"Yes, isn't he?" smiled Miss Paris.

"Now what does that mean?" demanded Mr. Queen.

"It takes greatness to escort a lady like Lotus Verne to a ball game," said Paula, "to find your wife sitting within spitting distance in the next box, and to carry it off as well as your muscular friend Mr. Tree is doing."

"That's right," said Queen softly. "Judy Starr *is* Mrs. Bill Tree."

He groaned as Joe DiMaggio hit a ball to the clubhouse clock.

"Funny," said Miss Paris, her clever eyes inspecting in turn the four people before her: Lotus Verne, the Hollywood siren; Big Bill Tree, the ex-baseball pitcher; Judy Starr, Tree's wife; and Jimmy Connor, the Song-and-Dance Man, Mrs. Tree's escort. Two couples, two boxes . . . and no sign of recognition. "Funny," murmured Miss Paris. "From the way Tree courted Judy you'd have thought the marriage would outlast eternity. He snatched her from under Jimmy Connor's nose one night at the Winter Garden, drove her up to Greenwich at eighty miles an hour, and married her before she could catch her breath."

"Yes," said Mr. Queen politely. "Come on, you Giants!" he yelled, as the Giants trotted out for batting practice.

"And then something happened," continued Miss Paris reflectively. "Tree went to Hollywood to make a baseball picture, met Lotus Verne, and the wench took the overgrown country boy the way the overgrown country boy had taken Judy Starr. What a fall was there, my baseball-minded friend."

"What a wallop!" cried Mr. Queen enthusiastically, as Mel Ott hit one that bounced off the right-field fence.

"And Big Bill yammered for a divorce, and Judy refused to give it to him because she loved him, I suppose," said Paula softly. "And now this. How interesting."

Big Bill Tree twisted in his seat a little; and Judy Starr was still and pale, staring out of her tragic, honey-colored eyes at the Yankee bat boy and giving him unwarranted delusions of grandeur. Jimmy Connor continued to exchange sarcastic greetings with Yankee players, but his

166

eyes kept shifting back to Judy's face. And beautiful Lotus Verne's arm crept about Tree's shoulders.

"I don't like it," murmured Miss Paris a little later.

"You don't like it?" said Mr. Queen. "Why, the game hasn't even started."

"I don't mean your game, silly. I mean the quadrangular situation in front of us."

"Look, darling," said Mr. Queen. "I flew three thousand miles to see a ball game. There's only one angle that interests me—the view from this box of the greatest li'l ol' baseball tussle within the memory of gaffers. I yearn, I strain, I hunger to see it. Play with your quadrangle, but leave me to my baseball."

"I've always been psychic," said Miss Paris, paying no attention. "This is—bad. Something's going to happen."

Mr. Queen grinned. "I know what. The deluge. See what's coming."

Someone in the grandstand had recognized the celebrities, and a sea of people was rushing down on the two boxes. They thronged the aisle behind the boxes, waving pencils and papers, and pleading. Big Bill Tree and Lotus Verne ignored their pleas for autographs; but Judy Starr with a curious eagerness signed paper after paper with the yellow pencils thrust at her by people leaning over the rail. Good-naturedly Jimmy Connor scrawled his signature, too.

"Little Judy," sighed Miss Paris, setting her natural straw straight as an autograph-hunter knocked it over her eyes, "is flustered and unhappy. Moistening the tip of your pencil with your tongue is scarcely a mark of poise. Seated next to her Lotus-bound husband, she hardly knows what she's doing, poor thing."

"Neither do I," growled Mr. Queen, fending off an octopus which turned out to be eight pleading arms offering scorecards.

Big Bill sneezed, groped for a handkerchief, and held it to his nose, which was red and swollen. "Hey, Mac," he called irritably to a red-coated usher. "Do somethin' about this mob, huh?" He sneezed again. "Damn this hay fever!"

"The touch of earth," said Miss Paris. "But definitely attractive."

"Should 'a' seen Big Bill the day he pitched that World Series final against the Tigers," chuckled Sergeant Velie.

"He was sure attractive that day. Pitched a no-hit shut-out!"

Inspector Queen said: "Ever hear the story behind that final game, Miss Paris? The night before, a gambler named Sure Shot McCoy, who represented a betting syndicate, called on Big Bill and laid down fifty grand in spot cash in return for Bill's promise to throw the next day's game. Bill took the money, told his manager the whole story, donated the bribe to a fund for sick ball players, and the next day shut out the Tigers without a hit."

"Byronic, too," murmured Miss Paris.

"So then Sure Shot, badly bent," grinned the Inspector, "called on Bill for the payoff. Bill knocked him down two flights of stairs."

"Wasn't that dangerous?"

"I guess," smiled the Inspector, "you could say so. That's why you see that plug-ugly with the smashed nose sitting over there right behind Tree's box. He's Mr. Terrible Turk, late of Cicero, and since that night Big Bill's shadow. You don't see Mr. Turk's right hand, because Mr. Turk's right hand is holding onto an automatic under his jacket. You'll notice, too, that Mr. Turk hasn't for a second taken his eyes off that pasty-cheeked customer eight rows up, whose name is Sure Shot McCoy."

Paula stared. "But what a silly thing for Tree to do!"

"Well, yes," drawled Inspector Queen, "seeing that when he popped Mr. McCoy Big Bill snapped two of the carpal bones of his pitching wrist and wrote finis to his baseball career."

Big Bill Tree hauled himself to his feet, whispered something to the Verne woman, who smiled coyly, and left his box. His bodyguard, Turk, jumped up; but the big man shook his head, waved aside a crowd of people, and vaulted up the concrete steps toward the rear of the grandstand.

And then Judy Starr said something bitter and hot and desperate across the rail to the woman her husband had brought to the Polo Grounds. Lotus Verne's mercurial eyes glittered, and she replied in a careless, insulting voice that made Bill Tree's wife sit up stiffly. Jimmy Connor began to tell the one about Walter Winchell and the Seven Dwarfs . . . loudly and fast.

The Verne woman began to paint her rich lips with short, vicious strokes of her orange lipstick; and Judy

Starr's flame kid glove tightened on the rail between them.

And after a while Big Bill returned and sat down again. Judy said something to Jimmy Connor, and the Song-and-Dance Man slid over one seat to his right, and Judy slipped into Connor's seat; so that between her and her husband there was now not only the box rail but an empty chair as well.

Lotus Verne put her arm about Tree's shoulders again.

Tree's wife fumbled inside her flame suède bag. She said suddenly: "Jimmy, buy me a frankfurter."

Connor ordered a dozen. Big Bill scowled. He jumped up and ordered some, too. Connor tossed the vendor two one-dollar bills and waved him away.

A new sea deluged the two boxes, and Tree turned round, annoyed. "All right, all right, Mac," he growled at the red-coat struggling with the pressing mob. "We don't want a riot here. I'll take six. Just six. Let's have 'em."

There was a rush that almost upset the attendant. The rail behind the boxes was a solid line of fluttering hands, arms, and scorecards.

"Mr. Tree—said—six!" panted the usher; and he grabbed a pencil and card from one of the outstretched hands and gave them to Tree. The overflow of pleaders spread to the next box. Judy Starr smiled her best professional smile and reached for a pencil and card. A group of players on the field, seeing what was happening, ran over to the field rail and handed her scorecards, too, so that she had to set her half-consumed frankfurter down on the empty seat beside her. Big Bill set his frankfurter down on the same empty seat; he licked the pencil long and absently and began to inscribe his name in the stiff, laborious hand of a man unused to writing.

The attendant howled: "That's six, now! Mr. Tree said just six, so that's all!" as if God himself had said six; and the crowd groaned, and Big Bill waved his immense paw and reached over to the empty seat in the other box to lay hold of his half-eaten frankfurter. But his wife's hand got there first and fumbled round; and it came up with Tree's frankfurter. The big brown man almost spoke to her then; but he did not, and he picked up the remaining frankfurter, stuffed it into his mouth, and chewed away, but not as if he enjoyed its taste.

Mr. Ellery Queen was looking at the four people before him with a puzzled, worried expression. Then he caught Miss Paula Paris's amused glance and blushed angrily.

The groundkeepers had just left the field and the senior umpire was dusting off the plate to the roar of the crowd when Lotus Verne, who thought a double play was something by Eugene O'Neill, flashed a strange look at Big Bill Tree.

"Bill! Don't you feel well?"

The big ex-pitcher, a sickly blue beneath his tanned skin, put his hand to his eyes and shook his head as if to clear it.

"It's the hot dog," snapped Lotus. "No more for you!"

Tree blinked and began to say something, but just then Carl Hubbell completed his warming-up, Crosetti marched to the plate, Harry Danning tossed the ball to his second-baseman, who flipped it to Hubbell and trotted back to his position yipping like a terrier.

The voice of the crowd exploded in one ear-splitting burst. And then silence.

And Crosetti swung at the first ball Hubbell pitched and smashed it far over Joe Moore's head for a triple.

Jimmy Connor gasped as if someone had thrust a knife into his heart. But Detective-Sergeant Velie was bellowing: "Wha'd I tell you? It's gonna be a massacree!"

"What is everyone shouting for?" asked Paula.

Mr. Queen nibbled his nails as Danning strolled halfway to the pitcher's box. But Hubbell pulled his long pants up, grinning. Red Rolfe was waving a huge bat at the plate. Danning trotted back. Manager Bill Terry had one foot up on the edge of the Giant dugout, his chin on his fist, looking anxious. The infield came in to cut off the run.

Again fifty thousand people made no single little sound. And Hubbell struck out Rolfe, DiMaggio, and Gehrig.

Mr. Queen shrieked his joy with the thousands as the Giants came whooping in. Jimmy Connor did an Indian war-dance in the box. Sergeant Velie looked aggrieved. Señor Gomez took his warm-up pitches, the umpire used his whisk-broom on the plate again, and Jo-Jo Moore, the Thin Man, ambled up with his war club.

He walked. Bartell fanned. But Jeep Ripple singled off Flash Gordon's shins on the first pitch; and there were Moore on third and Ripple on first, one out, and Little Mel Ott at bat.

170

Big Bill Tree got half out of his seat, looking surprised, and then dropped to the concrete floor of the box as if somebody had slammed him behind the ear with a fast ball.

Lotus screamed. Judy, Bill's wife, turned like a shot, shaking. People in the vicinity jumped up. Three red-coated attendants hurried down, preceded by the hard-looking Mr. Turk. The bench-warmers stuck their heads over the edge of the Yankee dugout to stare.

"Fainted," growled Turk, on his knees beside the prostrate athlete.

"Loosen his collar," moaned Lotus Verne. "He's so p-pale!"

"Have to git him outa here."

"Yes. Oh, yes!"

The attendants and Turk lugged the big man off, long arms dangling in the oddest way. Lotus stumbled along beside him, biting her lips nervously.

"I think," began Judy in a quivering voice, rising.

But Jimmy Connor put his hand on her arm, and she sank back.

And in the next box Mr. Ellery Queen, on his feet from the instant Tree collapsed, kept looking after the forlorn procession, puzzled, mad about something; until somebody in the stands squawked: "SIDDOWN!" and he sat down.

"Oh, I knew something would happen," whispered Paula.

"Nonsense!" said Mr. Queen shortly. "Fainted, that's all."

Inspector Queen said: "There's Sure Shot McCoy not far off. I wonder if—"

"Too many hot dogs," snapped his son. "What's the matter with you people? Can't I see my ball game in peace?" And he howled: "Come o-o-on, Mel!"

Ott lifted his right leg into the sky and swung. The ball whistled into right field, a long long fly, Selkirk racing madly back after it. He caught it by leaping four feet into the air with his back against the barrier. Moore was off for the plate like a streak and beat the throw to Bill Dickey by inches.

"Yip-ee!" Thus Mr. Queen.

The Giants trotted out to their positions at the end of the first inning leading one to nothing.

Up in the press box the working gentlemen of the press

tore into their chores, recalling Carl Hubbell's similar feat in the All-Star game when he struck out the five greatest batters of the American League in succession; praising Twinkle-toes Selkirk for his circus catch; and incidentally noting that Big Bill Tree, famous ex-hurler of the National League, had fainted in a field box during the first inning. Joe Williams of the *World-Telegram* said it was excitement, Hype Igoe opined that it was a touch of sun —Big Bill never wore a hat—and Frank Graham of the *Sun* guessed it was too many frankfurters.

Paula Paris said quietly: "I should think, with your detective instincts, Mr. Queen, you would seriously question the 'fainting' of Mr. Tree."

Mr. Queen squirmed and finally mumbled: "It's coming to a pretty pass when a man's instincts aren't his own. Velie, go see what really happened to him."

"I wanna watch the game," howled Velie. "Why don't you go yourself, maestro?"

"And possibly," said Mr. Queen, "you ought to go too, Dad. I have a hunch it may lie in your jurisdiction."

Inspector Queen regarded his son for some time. Then he rose and sighed: "Come along, Thomas."

Sergeant Velie growled something about some people always spoiling other people's fun and why the hell did he ever have to become a cop; but he got up and obediently followed the Inspector.

Mr. Queen nibbled his fingernails and avoided Miss Paris's accusing eyes.

The second inning was uneventful. Neither side scored.

As the Giants took the field again, an usher came running down the concrete steps and whispered into Jim Connor's ear. The Song-and-Dance Man blinked. He rose slowly. "Excuse me, Judy."

Judy grasped the rail. "It's Bill. Jimmy, tell me."

"Now, Judy—"

"Something's happened to Bill!" Her voice shrilled, and then broke. She jumped up. "I'm going with you."

Connor smiled as if he had just lost a bet, and then he took Judy's arm and hurried her away.

Paula Paris stared after them, breathing hard.

Mr. Queen beckoned the redcoat. "What's the trouble?" he demanded.

"Mr. Tree passed out. Some young doc in the crowd tried to pull him out of it up at the office, but he couldn't, and he's startin' to look worried—"

172

"I knew it!" cried Paula as the man darted away. "Ellery Queen, are you going to sit here and do *nothing?*"

But Mr. Queen defiantly set his jaw. Nobody was going to jockey him out of seeing this battle of giants; no, ma'am!

There were two men out when Frank Crosetti stepped up to the plate for his second time at bat and, with the count two all, plastered a wicked single over Ott's head.

And, of course, Sergeant Velie took just that moment to amble down and say, his eyes on the field: "Better come along, Master Mind. The old man wouldst have a word with thou. Ah, I see Frankie's on first. Smack it, Red!"

Mr. Queen watched Rolfe take a ball. "Well?" he said shortly. Paula's lips were parted.

"Big Bill's just kicked the bucket. What happened in the second inning?"

"He's . . . *dead?*" gasped Paula.

Mr. Queen rose involuntarily. Then he sat down again. "Damn it," he roared, "it isn't fair. I won't go!"

"Suit yourself. Attaboy, Rolfe!" bellowed the Sergeant as Rolfe singled sharply past Bartell and Crosetti pulled up at second base. "Far's I'm concerned, it's open and shut. The little woman did it with her own little hands."

"Judy *Starr?*" said Miss Paris.

"Bill's wife?" said Mr. Queen. "What are you talking about?"

"That's right, little Judy. She poisoned his hot dog." Velie chuckled. "Man bites dog, and—zowie."

"Has she confessed?" snapped Mr. Queen.

"Naw. But you know dames. She gave Bill the business, all right. C'mon, Joe! And I gotta go. What a life."

Mr. Queen did not look at Miss Paris. He bit his lip. "Here, Velie, wait a minute."

DiMaggio hit a long fly that Leiber caught without moving in his tracks, and the Yankees were retired without a score.

"Ah," said Mr. Queen. "Good old Hubbell." And as the Giants trotted in, he took a fat roll of bills from his pocket, climbed onto his seat, and began waving greenbacks at the spectators in the reserved seats behind the box. Sergeant Velie and Miss Paris stared at him in amazement.

"I'll give five bucks," yelled Mr. Queen, waving the

173

money, "for every autograph Bill Tree signed before the game! In this box right here! Five bucks, gentlemen! Come and get it!"

"You nuts?" gasped the Sergeant.

The mob gaped, and then began to laugh, and after a few moments a pair of sheepish-looking men came down, and then two more, and finally a fifth. An attendant ran over to find out what was the matter.

"Are you the usher who handled the crowd around Bill Tree's box before the game, when he was giving autographs?" demanded Mr. Queen.

"Yes, sir. But, look, we can't allow—"

"Take a gander at these five men. . . . You, bud? Yes, that's Tree's handwriting. Here's your fin. Next!" and Mr. Queen went down the line, handing out five-dollar bills with abandon in return for five dirty scorecards with Tree's scrawl on them.

"Anybody else?" he called out, waving his roll of bills.

But nobody else appeared, although there was ungentle badinage from the stands. Sergeant Velie stood there shaking his big head. Miss Paris looked intensely curious.

"Who didn't come down?" rapped Mr. Queen.

"Huh?" said the usher, his mouth open.

"There were six autographs. Only five people turned up. Who was the sixth man? Speak up!"

"Oh." The redcoat scratched his ear. "Say, it wasn't a man. It was a kid."

"A boy?"

"Yeah, a little squirt in knee pants."

Mr. Queen looked unhappy. Velie growled: "Sometimes I think society's takin' an awful chance lettin' you run around loose," and the two men left the box. Miss Paris, bright-eyed, followed.

"Have to clear this mess up in a hurry," muttered Mr. Queen. "Maybe we'll still be able to catch the late innings."

Sergeant Velie led the way to an office, before which a policeman was lounging. He opened the door, and inside they found the Inspector pacing. Turk, the thug, was standing with a scowl over a long, still thing on a couch covered with newspapers. Jimmy Connor sat between the two women; and none of the three so much as stirred a foot. They were all pale and breathing heavily.

"This is Dr. Fielding," said Inspector Queen, indicating an elderly white-haired man standing quietly by a window. "He was Tree's physician. He happened to be in the park watching the game when the rumor reached his ears that Tree had collapsed. So he hurried up here to see what he could do."

Ellery went to the couch and pulled the newspaper off Bill Tree's still head. Paula crossed swiftly to Judy Starr and said: "I'm horribly sorry, Mrs. Tree," but the woman, her eyes closed, did not move. After a while Ellery dropped the newspaper back into place and said irritably: "Well, well, let's have it."

"A young doctor," said the Inspector, "got here before Dr. Fielding did, and treated Tree for fainting. I guess it was his fault—"

"Not at all," said Dr. Fielding sharply. "The early picture was compatible with fainting, from what he told me. He tried the usual restorative methods—even injected caffeine and picrotoxin. But there was no convulsion, and he didn't happen to catch that odor of bitter almonds."

"Prussic!" said Ellery. "Taken orally?"

"Yes. HCN—hydrocyanic acid, or prussic, as you prefer. I suspected it at once because—well," said Dr. Fielding in a grim voice, "because of something that occurred in my office only the other day."

"What was that?"

"I had a two-ounce bottle of hydrocyanic acid on my desk—I sometimes use it in minute quantities as a cardiac stimulant. Mrs. Tree," the doctor's glance flickered over the silent woman, "happened to be in my office, resting in preparation for a metabolism test. I left her alone. By a coincidence, Bill Tree dropped in the same morning for a physical check-up. I saw another patient in another room, returned, gave Mrs. Tree her test, saw her out, and came back with Tree. It was then I noticed the bottle, which had been plainly marked DANGER—POISON, was missing from my desk. I thought I had mislaid it, but now . . ."

"I didn't take it," said Judy Starr in a lifeless voice, still not opening her eyes. "I never even saw it."

The Song-and-Dance Man took her limp hand and gently stroked it.

"No hypo marks on the body," said Dr. Fielding dryly. "And I am told that fifteen to thirty minutes before Tree collapsed he ate a frankfurter under . . . peculiar conditions."

"I didn't!" screamed Judy. "I didn't do it!" She pressed her face, sobbing, against Connor's orchid.

Lotus Verne quivered. "She made him pick up her frankfurter. I saw it. They both laid their frankfurters down on that empty seat, and she picked up his. So he had to pick up hers. She poisoned her own frankfurter and then saw to it that he ate it by mistake. Poisoner!" She glared hate at Judy.

"Wench," said Miss Paris *sotto voce,* glaring hate at Lotus.

"In other words," put in Ellery impatiently, "Miss Starr is convicted on the usual two counts, motive and opportunity. Motive—her jealousy of Miss Verne and her hatred—an assumption—of Bill Tree, her husband. And opportunity both to lay hands on the poison in your office, Doctor, and to sprinkle some on her frankfurter, contriving to exchange hers for his while they were both autographing scorecards."

"She hated him," snarled Lotus. "And me for having taken him from her!"

"Be quiet, you," said Mr. Queen. He opened the corridor door and said to the policeman outside: "Look, McGillicuddy, or whatever your name is, go tell the announcer to make a speech over the loud-speaker system. By the way, what's the score now?"

"Still one to skunk," said the officer. "Them boys Hubbell an' Gomez are hot, what I mean."

"The announcer is to ask the little boy who got Bill Tree's autograph just before the game to come to this office. If he does, he'll receive a ball, bat, pitcher's glove, and an autographed picture of Tree in uniform to hang over his itsybitsy bed. Scram!"

"Yes, sir," said the officer.

"King Carl pitching his heart out," grumbled Mr. Queen, shutting the door, "and me strangulated by this blamed thing. Well, Dad, do you think, too, that Judy Starr dosed that frankfurter?"

"What else can I think?" said the Inspector absently. His ears were cocked for the faint crowd shouts from the park.

"Judy Starr," replied his son, "didn't poison her husband any more than I did."

Judy looked up slowly, her mouth muscles twitching. Paula said gladly: "You wonderful man!"

"She didn't?" said the Inspector, looking alert.

176

"The frankfurter theory," snapped Mr. Queen, "is too screwy for words. For Judy to have poisoned her husband, she had to unscrew the cap of a bottle and douse her hot dog on the spot with the hydrocyanic acid. Yet Jimmy Connor was seated by her side, and in the only period in which she could possibly have poisoned the frankfurter a group of Yankee ball players was *standing before her* across the field rail getting her autograph. Were they all accomplices? And how could she have known Big Bill would lay his hot dog on that empty seat? The whole thing is absurd."

A roar from the stands made him continue hastily: "There was one plausible theory that fitted the facts. When I heard that Tree had died of poisoning, I recalled that at the time he was autographing the six scorecards, *he had thoroughly licked the end of a pencil* which had been handed to him with one of the cards. It was possible, then, that the pencil he licked had been poisoned. So I offered to buy the six autographs."

Paula regarded him tenderly, and Velie said: "I'll be a so-and-so if he didn't."

"I didn't expect the poisoner to come forward, but I knew the innocent ones would. Five claimed the money. The sixth, the missing one, the usher informed me, had been a small boy."

"A kid poisoned Bill?" growled Turk, speaking for the first time. "You're crazy from the heat."

"In spades," added the Inspector

"They why didn't the boy come forward?" put in Paula quickly. "Go on, darling!"

"He didn't come forward, not because he was guilty but because he wouldn't sell Bill Tree's autograph for anything. No, obviously a hero-worshiping boy wouldn't try to poison the great Bill Tree. Then, just as obviously, he didn't realize what he was doing. Consequently, he must have been an innocent tool. The question was—and still is—of whom?"

"Sure Shot," said the Inspector slowly.

Lotus Verne sprang to her feet, her eyes glittering. "Perhaps Judy Starr didn't poison that frankfurter, but if she didn't then she hired that boy to give Bill—"

Mr. Queen said disdainfully: "Miss Starr didn't leave the box once." Someone knocked on the corridor door and he opened it. For the first time he smiled. When he shut the door they saw that his arm was about the shoulders of a boy with brown hair and quick clever eyes. The boy was clutching a scorecard tightly.

"They say over the announcer," mumbled the boy, "that I'll get a autographed pi'ture of Big Bill Tree if . . ." He stopped, abashed at their strangely glinting eyes.

"And you certainly get it, too," said Mr. Queen heartily. "What's your name, sonny?"

"Fenimore Feigenspan," replied the boy, edging toward the door. "Gran' Concourse, Bronx. Here's the scorecard. How about the picture?"

"Let's see that, Fenimore," said Mr. Queen. "When did Bill Tree give you this autograph?"

"Before the game. He said he'd only give six—"

"Where's the pencil you handed him, Fenimore?"

The boy looked suspicious, but he dug into a bulging pocket and brought forth one of the ordinary yellow pencils sold at the park with scorecards. Ellery took it from him gingerly, and Dr. Fielding took it from Ellery, and sniffed its tip. He nodded, and for the first time a look of peace came over Judy Starr's still face and she dropped her head tiredly to Connor's shoulder.

Mr. Queen ruffled Fenimore Feigenspan's hair. "That's swell, Fenimore. Somebody gave you that pencil while the Giants were at batting practice, isn't that so?"

"Yeah." The boy stared at him.

"Who was it?" asked Mr. Queen lightly.

"I dunno. A big guy with a coat an' a turned-down hat an' a mustache, an' big black sunglasses. I couldn't see his face good. Where's my pi'ture? I wanna see the game!"

"Just where was it that this man gave you the pencil?"

"In the—" Fenimore paused, glancing at the ladies with embarrassment. Then he muttered: "Well, I hadda go, an' this guy says—in there—he's ashamed to ask her for her autograph, so would I do it for him—"

"What? What's that?" exclaimed Mr. Queen. "Did you say 'her'?"

"Sure," said Fenimore. "The dame, he says, wearin' the red hat an' red dress an' red gloves in the field box near the Yanks' dugout, he says. He even took me outside an' pointed down to where she was sittin'. Say!" cried Fenimore, goggling. "That's her! That's the dame!" and he leveled a grimy forefinger at Judy Starr.

Judy shivered and felt blindly for the Song-and-Dance Man's hand.

"Let me get this straight, Fenimore," said Mr. Queen softly. "This man with the sunglasses asked you to get this lady's autograph for him, and gave you the pencil and scorecard to get it with?"

"Yeah, an' two bucks too, sayin' he'd meet me after the game to pick up the card, but—"

"But you didn't get the lady's autograph for him, did you? You went down to get it, and hung around waiting for your chance, but then you spied Big Bill Tree, your hero, in the next box and forgot all about the lady, didn't you?"

The boy shrank back. "I didn't mean to, honest, Mister. I'll give the two bucks back!"

"And seeing Big Bill there, your hero, you went right over to get *his* autograph for *yourself,* didn't you?" Fenimore nodded, frightened. "You gave the usher the pencil and scorecard this man with the sunglasses had handed you, and the usher turned the pencil and scorecard over to Bill Tree in the box—wasn't that the way it happened?"

"Y-yes, sir, an' . . ." Fenimore twisted out of Ellery's grasp, "an' so I—I gotta go." And before anyone could stop him he was indeed gone, racing down the corridor like the wind.

The policeman outside shouted, but Ellery said: "Let him go, officer," and shut the door. Then he opened it again and said: "How's she stand now?"

"Dunno exactly, sir. Somethin' happened out there just now. I think the Yanks scored."

"Damn," groaned Mr. Queen, and he shut the door again.

"So it was Mrs. Tree who was on the spot, not Bill," scowled the Inspector. "I'm sorry, Judy Starr. . . . Big man with a coat and hat and mustache and sunglasses. Some description!"

"Sounds like a phony to me," said Sergeant Velie.

"If it was a disguise, he dumped it somewhere," said the Inspector thoughtfully. "Thomas, have a look in the Men's Room behind the section where we were sitting. And Thomas," he added in a whisper, "find out what the score is." Velie grinned and hurried out. Inspector Queen frowned. "Quite a job finding a killer in a crowd of fifty thousand people."

"Maybe," said his son suddenly, "maybe it's not such a job after all. . . . What was used to kill? Hydrocyanic acid. Who was intended to be killed? Bill Tree's wife. Any

179

connection between anyone in the case and hydrocyanic acid? Yes—Dr. Fielding 'lost' a bottle of it under suspicious circumstances. Which were? That Bill Tree's wife could have taken that bottle . . . *or Bill Tree himself.*"

"Bill Tree!" gasped Paula.

"Bill?" whispered Judy Starr.

"Quite! Dr. Fielding didn't miss the bottle until *after* he had shown you, Miss Starr, out of his office. He then returned to his office with your husband. Bill could have slipped the bottle into his pocket as he stepped into the room."

"Yes, he could have," muttered Dr. Fielding.

"I don't see," said Mr. Queen, "how we can arrive at any other conclusion. We know his wife was intended to be the victim today, so obviously she didn't steal the poison. The only other person who had opportunity to steal it was Bill himself."

The Verne woman sprang up. "I don't believe it! It's a frame-up to protect *her,* now that Bill can't defend himself!"

"Ah, but didn't he have motive to kill Judy?" asked Mr. Queen. "Yes, indeed; she wouldn't give him the divorce he craved so that he could marry *you.* I think, Miss Verne, you would be wiser to keep the peace. . . . Bill had opportunity to steal the bottle of poison in Dr. Fielding's office. He also had opportunity to hire Fenimore today, for he was the *only* one of the whole group who left those two boxes during the period when the poisoner must have searched for someone to offer Judy the poisoned pencil.

"All of which fits for what Bill had to do—get to where he had cached his disguise, probably yesterday; look for a likely tool; find Fenimore, give him his instructions and the pencil; get rid of the disguise again; and return to his box. And didn't Bill know better than anyone his wife's habit of moistening a pencil with her tongue—a habit she probably acquired from *him?*"

"Poor Bill," murmured Judy Starr brokenly.

"Women," remarked Miss Paris, "are *fools.*"

"There were other striking ironies," replied Mr. Queen. "For if Bill hadn't been suffering from a hay-fever attack, he would have smelled the odor of bitter almonds when his own poisoned pencil was handed to him and stopped in time to save his worthless life. For that matter, if he hadn't been Fenimore Feigenspan's hero, Fenimore would

180

not have handed him his own poisoned pencil in the first place.

"No," said Mr. Queen gladly, "putting it all together, I'm satisfied that Mr. Big Bill Tree, in trying to murder his wife, very neatly murdered himself instead."

"That's all very well for *you*," said the Inspector disconsolately. "But *I* need proof."

"I've told you how it happened," said his son airily, making for the door. "Can any man do more? Coming, Paula?"

But Paula was already at a telephone, speaking guardedly to the New York office of the syndicate for which she worked, and paying no more attention to him than if he had been a worm.

"What's the score? What's been going on?" Ellery demanded of the world at large as he regained his box seat. "Three to three! What the devil's got into Hubbell, anyway? How'd the Yanks score? What inning is it?"

"Last of the ninth," shrieked somebody. "The Yanks got three runs in the eighth on a walk, a double, and DiMag's homer! Danning homered in the sixth with Ott on base! Shut up!"

Bartell singled over Gordon's head. Mr. Queen cheered.

Sergeant Velie tumbled into the next seat. "Well, we got it," he puffed. "Found the whole outfit in the Men's Room—coat, hat, fake mustache, glasses and all. What's the score?"

"Three-three. Sacrifice, Jeep!" shouted Mr. Queen.

"There was a rain check in the coat pocket from the sixth game, with Big Bill's box number on it. So there's the old man's proof. Chalk up another win for you."

"Who cares? . . . *ZOWIE!*"

Jeep Ripple sacrificed Bartell successfully to second.

"Lucky stiff," howled a Yankee fan nearby. "That's the breaks. See the breaks they get? See?"

"And another thing," said the Sergeant, watching Mel Ott stride to the plate. "Seein' as how all Big Bill did was cross himself up, and no harm done except to his own carcass, and seein' as how organized baseball could get along without a murder, and seein' as how thousands of kids like Fenimore Feigenspan worship the ground he walked on—"

"Sew it up, Mel!" bellowed Mr. Queen.

"—and seein' as how none of the newspaper guys know

181

what happened, except that Bill passed out of the picture after a faint, and seein' as everybody's only too glad to shut their traps—"

Mr. Queen awoke suddenly to the serious matters of life. "What's that? What did you say?"

"Strike him out, Goofy!" roared the Sergeant to Señor Gomez, who did not hear. "As I was sayin', it ain't cricket, and the old man would be broke out of the force if the big cheese heard about it. . . ."

Someone puffed up behind them, and they turned to see Inspector Queen, red-faced as if after a hard run, scrambling into the box with the assistance of Miss Paula Paris, who looked cool, serene, and star-eyed as ever.

"Dad!" said Mr. Queen, staring. "With a murder on your hands, how can you—"

"Murder?" panted Inspector Queen. "What murder?" And he winked at Miss Paris, who winked back.

"But Paula was telephoning the story—"

"Didn't you hear?" said Paula in a coo, setting her straw straight and slipping into the seat beside Ellery's. "I fixed it all up with your dad. Tonight all the world will know is that Mr. Bill Tree died of heart failure."

They all chuckled then—all but Mr. Queen, whose mouth was open.

"So now," said Paula, "your dad can see the finish of your precious game just as well as *you*, you selfish oaf!"

But Mr. Queen was already fiercely rapt in contemplation of Mel Ott's bat as it swung back and Señor Gomez's ball as it left the Señor's hand to streak towards the plate.

Long Shot

"ONE MOMENT, dear. My favorite fly's just walked into the parlor," cried Paula Paris into her ashes-of-roses telephone. "Oh, Ellery, do sit down! . . . No, dear, you're fishing. This one's a grim hombre with silv'ry eyes, and

I have an option on him. Call me tomorrow about the Monroe excitement. And I'll expect your flash the moment Debbie springs her new coiffure on palpitating Miss America."

And, the serious business of her Hollywood gossip column concluded, Miss Paris hung up and turned her lips pursily towards Mr. Queen.

The poor fellow gave Miss Paris an absent peck, after which he rubbed the lipstick from his mouth.

"No oomph," said Miss Paris critically, holding him off and surveying his gloomy countenance. "Ellery Queen, you're in a mess again."

"Hollywood," mumbled Mr. Queen. "The land God forgot. No logic. Disorderly creation. The abiding place of chaos. Paula, your Hollywood is driving me c-double-o-ditto!"

"You poor imposed-upon Wimpie," crooned Miss Paris, drawing him onto her spacious maple settee. "Tell Paula all about the nasty old place."

So, with Miss Paris's soft arms about him, Mr. Queen unburdened himself. It seemed that Magna Studios ("The Movies Magnificent"), to whom his soul was chartered, had ordered him as one of its staff writers to concoct a horse-racing plot with a fresh patina. A mystery, of course, since Mr. Queen was supposed to know something about crime.

"With fifty writers on the lot who spend all their time —and money—following the ponies," complained Mr. Queen bitterly, "of course they have to pick on the one serf in their thrall who doesn't know a fetlock from a wither. Paula, I'm a sunk scrivener."

"You don't know *anything* about racing?"

"I'm not interested in racing. I've never even *seen* a race," said Mr. Queen doggedly.

"Imagine that!" said Paula, awed. And she was silent. After a while Mr. Queen twisted in her embrace and said in accusing despair: "Paula, you're thinking of something."

She kissed him and sprang from the settee. "The wrong tense, darling. I've *thought* of something!"

Paula told him all about old John Scott as they drove out into the green and yellow ranch country.

Scott was a vast, shapeless Caledonian with a face as craggy as his native heaths and a disposition not less dour.

183

His inner landscape was bleak except where horses breathed and browsed; and this vulnerable spot had proved his undoing, for he had made two fortunes breeding thoroughbreds and had lost both by racing and betting on them.

"Old John's never stood for any of the crooked dodges of the racing game," said Paula. "He fired Weed Williams, the best jockey he ever had, and had him blackballed by every decent track in the country, so that Williams became a saddlemaker or something, just because of a peccadillo another owner would have winked at. And yet —the inconsistent old coot!—a few years later he gave Williams's son a job, and Whitey's going to ride Danger, John's best horse, in the Handicap next Saturday."

"You mean the $100,000 Santa Anita Handicap everybody's in a dither about out here?"

"Yes. Anyway, old John's got a scrunchy little ranch, Danger, his daughter Kathryn, and practically nothing else except a stable of also-rans and breeding disappointments."

"So far," remarked Mr. Queen, "it sounds like the beginning of a Class B movie."

"Except," sighed Paula, "that it's not entertaining. John's really on a spot. If Whitey doesn't ride Danger to a win in the Handicap, it's the end of the road for John Scott. . . . Speaking about roads, here we are."

They turned into a dirt road and plowed dustily towards a ramshackle ranch house. The road was pitted, the fences dilapidated, the grassland patchy with neglect.

"With all his troubles," grinned Ellery, "I fancy he won't take kindly to this quest for Racing in Five Easy Lessons."

"Meeting a full-grown man who knows nothing about racing may give the old gentleman a laugh. Lord knows he needs one."

A Mexican cook directed them to Scott's private track, and they found him leaning his weight upon a sagging rail, his small buried eyes puckered on a cloud of dust eddying along the track at the far turn. His thick fingers clutched a stopwatch.

A man in high-heeled boots sat on the rail two yards away, a shotgun in his lap pointing carelessly at the head of a too well-dressed gentleman with a foreign air who was talking to the back of Scott's shaggy head. The well-

184

dressed man sat in a glistening roadster beside a hard-faced chauffeur.

"You got my proposition, John?" said the well-dressed man, with a toothy smile. "You got it?"

"Get the hell off my ranch, Santelli," said John Scott, without turning his head.

"Sure," said Santelli, still smiling. "You think my proposition over, hey, or maybe somethin' happen to your nag, hey?"

They saw the old man quiver, but he did not turn; and Santelli nodded curtly to his driver. The big roadster roared away.

The dust cloud on the track rolled towards them and they saw a small, taut figure in sweater and cap perched atop a gigantic stallion, black-coated and lustrous with sweat. The horse was bounding along like a huge cat, his neck arched. He thundered magnificently by.

"Two-o-two and four-fifths," they heard Scott mutter to his stopwatch. "Vulcan's Forge's ten-furlong time for the Handicap in '49. Not bad . . . Whitey!" he bellowed to the jockey, who had pulled the black stallion up. "Rub him down good!"

The jockey grinned and pranced Danger towards the adjacent stables.

The man with the shotgun drawled: "You got more company, John."

The old man whirled, frowning deeply; his craggy face broke into a thousand wrinkles and he engulfed Paula's slim hand in his two paws. "Paula! It's fine to see ye. Who's this?" he demanded, fastening his cold keen eyes on Ellery.

"Mr. Ellery Queen. But how is Katie? And Danger?"

"You saw him." Scott gazed after the dancing horse. "Fit as a fiddle. He'll carry the handicap weight of a hundred twenty pounds Saturday an' never feel it. Did it just now with the leads on him. Paula, did ye see that murderin' scalawag?"

"The fashion plate who just drove away?"

"That was Santelli, and ye heard what he said might happen to Danger." The old man stared bitterly down the road.

"Santelli!" Paula's serene face was shocked.

"Bill, go look after the stallion." The man with the shotgun slipped off the rail and waddled towards the stable. "Just made me an offer for my stable. Hell,

185

the dirty thievin' bookie owns the biggest stable west o' the Rockies—what's he want with my picayune outfit?"

"He owns Broomstick, the Handicap favorite, doesn't he?" asked Paula quietly. "And Danger is figured strongly in the running, isn't he?"

"Quoted five to one now, but track odds'll shorten his price. Broomstick's two to five," growled Scott.

"It's very simple, then. By buying your horse, Santelli can control the race, owning the two best horses."

"Lassie, lassie," sighed Scott. "I'm an old mon, an' I know these thieves. Handicap purse is $100,000. And Santelli just offered me $100,000 for my stable!" Paula whistled. "It don't wash. My whole shebang ain't worth it. Danger's no cinch to win. Is Santelli buyin' up all the other horses in the race, too?—the big outfits? I tell ye it's somethin' else, and it's rotten." Then he shook his heavy shoulders straight. "But here I am gabbin' about my troubles. What brings ye out here, lassie?"

"Mr. Queen here, who's a—well, a friend of mine," said Paula, coloring, "has to think up a horse-racing plot for a movie, and I thought you could help him. He doesn't know a thing about racing."

Scott stared at Mr. Queen, who coughed apologetically. "Well, sir, I don't know but that ye're not a lucky mon. Ye're welcome to the run o' the place. Go over an' talk to Whitey; he knows the racket backwards. I'll be with ye in a few minutes."

The old man lumbered off, and Paula and Ellery sauntered towards the stables.

"Who is this ogre Santelli?" asked Ellery with a frown.

"A gambler and bookmaker with a national hook-up." Paula shivered a little. "Poor John. I don't like it, Ellery."

They turned a corner of the big stable and almost bumped into a young man and a young woman in the lee of the wall, clutching each other desperately and kissing as if they were about to be torn apart for eternity.

"Pardon *us*," said Paula, pulling Ellery back.

The young lady, her eyes crystal with tears, blinked at her. "Is—is that Paula Paris?" she sniffled.

"The same, Kathryn," smiled Paula, "Mr. Queen, Miss Scott. What on earth's the matter?"

"Everything," cried Miss Scott tragically. "Oh, Paula, we're in the most awful trouble!"

Her amorous companion backed bashfully off. He was a slender young man clad in grimy, odoriferous overalls.

186

He wore spectacles floury with the chaff of oats, and there was a grease smudge on one emotional nostril.

"Miss Paris—Mr. Queen. This is Hank Halliday, my—boy friend," sobbed Kathryn.

"I see the whole plot," said Paula sympathetically. "Papa doesn't approve of Katie's taking up with a stablehand, the snob! and it's tragedy all around."

"Hank *isn't* a stablehand," cried Kathryn, dashing the tears from her cheeks, which were rosy with indignation. "He's a college graduate who—"

"Kate," said the odoriferous young man with dignity, "let me explain, please. Miss Paris, I have a character deficiency. I am a physical coward."

"Heavens, so am I!" said Paula.

"But a man, you see . . . I am particularly afraid of animals. Horses, specifically." Mr Halliday shuddered. "I took this—this filthy job to conquer my unreasonable fear." Mr. Halliday's sensitive chin hardened. "I have not yet conquered it, but when I do I shall find myself a real job. And then," he said firmly, embracing Miss Scott's trembling shoulders, "I shall marry Kathryn, Papa or no Papa."

"Oh, I hate him for being so mean!" sobbed Katie.

"And I—" began Mr. Halliday somberly.

"Hankus-Pankus!" yelled a voice from the stable. "What the hell you paid for, anyway? Come clean up this mess before I slough you one!"

"Yes, Mr. Williams," said Hankus-Pankus hastily, and he hurried away with an apologetic half-bow. His lady love ran sobbing off towards the ranch house.

Mr. Queen and Miss Paris regarded each other. Then Mr. Queen said: "I'm getting a plot, b'gosh, but it's the wrong one."

"Poor kids," sighed Paula. "Well, talk to Whitey Williams and see if the divine spark ignites."

During the next several days Mr. Queen ambled about the Scott ranch, talking to Jockey Williams, to the bespectacled Mr. Halliday—who, he discovered, knew as little about racing as he and cared even less—to a continuously tearful Kathryn, to the guard named Bill—who slept in the stable near Danger with one hand on his shotgun—and to old John himself. He learned much about jockeys, touts, racing procedure, gear, handicaps, purses, forfeits, stewards, the ways of bookmakers, famous races and horses and owners and tracks; but the divine spark perversely refused to ignite.

So, on Friday at dusk, when he found himself unaccountably ignored at the Scott ranch, he glumly drove up into the Hollywood hills for a laving in the waters of Gilead.

He found Paula in her garden soothing two anguished young people. Katie Scott was still weeping and Mr. Halliday, the self-confessed craven, for once dressed in an odorless garment, was awkwardly pawing her golden hair.

"More tragedy?" said Mr. Queen. "I should have known. I've just come from your father's ranch, and there's a pall over it."

"Well, there should be!" cried Kathryn. "I told my father where *he* gets off. Treating Hank that way! I'll never speak to him as long as I live! He's—he's *unnatural!*"

"Now, Katie," said Mr. Halliday reprovingly, "that's no way to speak of your own father."

"Hank Halliday, if you had one spark of manhood—!"

Mr. Halliday stiffened as if his beloved had jabbed him with the end of a live wire.

"I didn't mean that, Hankus," sobbed Kathryn, throwing herself into his arms. "I know you can't help being a coward. But when he knocked you down and you didn't even—"

Mr. Halliday worked the left side of his jaw thoughtfully. "You know, Mr. Queen, something happened to me when Mr. Scott struck me. For an instant I felt a strange —er—lust. I really believe if I'd had a revolver—and if I knew how to handle one—I might easily have committed murder then. I saw—I believe that's the phrase —red."

"Hank!" cried Katie in horror.

Hank sighed, the homicidal light dying out of his faded blue eyes.

"Old John," explained Paula, winking at Ellery, "found these two cuddling again in the stable, and I suppose he thought it was setting a bad example for Danger, whose mind should be on the race tomorrow; so he fired Hank, and Katie blew up and told John off, and she's left his home forever."

"To discharge me is his privilege," said Mr. Halliday coldly, "but now I owe him no loyalty whatever. I shall *not* bet on Danger to win the Handicap!"

"I hope the big brute loses," sobbed Katie.

"Now, Kate," said Paula firmly, "I've heard enough of this nonsense. I'm going to speak to you like a Dutch aunt."

Katie sobbed on.

"Mr. Halliday," said Mr. Queen formally, "I believe this is our cue to seek a slight libation."

"Kathryn!"

"Hank!"

Mr. Queen and Miss Paris tore the lovers apart.

It was a little after ten o'clock when Miss Scott, no longer weeping but facially still tear-ravaged, crept out of Miss Paris's white frame house and got into her dusty little car.

As she turned her key in the ignition lock and stepped on the starter, a harsh bass voice from the shadows of the back seat said: "Don't yell. Don't make a sound. Turn your car around and keep going till I tell you to stop."

"Eek!" screeched Miss Scott.

A big leathery hand clamped over her trembling mouth.

After a few moments the car moved away.

Mr. Queen called for Miss Paris the next day and they settled down to a snail's pace, heading for Arcadia eastward, near which lay the beautiful Santa Anita race course.

"What happened to Lachrymose Katie last night?" demanded Mr. Queen.

"Oh, I got her to go back to the ranch. She left me a little after ten, a very miserable little girl. What did you do with Hankus-Pankus?"

"I oiled him thoroughly and then took him home. He'd hired a room in a Hollywood boardinghouse. He cried on my shoulder all the way. It seems old John also kicked him in the seat of his pants, and he's been brooding murderously over it."

"Poor Hankus. The only honest male I've ever met."

"I'm afraid of horses, too," said Mr. Queen hurriedly.

"Oh, you! You're detestable. You haven't kissed me once today."

Only the cooling balm of Miss Paris's lips, applied at various points along U.S. Route 66, kept Mr. Queen's temper from boiling over. The roads were sluggish with traffic. At the track it was even worse. It seemed as though every last soul in Southern California had converged upon Santa Anita at once, in every manner of conveyance, from the dusty Model T's of dirt farmers to the shiny metal monsters of the movie stars. The magnificent stands seethed with noisy thousands, a wriggling mosaic of color and movement. The sky was blue, the sun warm, zephyrs blew, and the track was fast. A race was being run, and the sleek animals were small and fleet and sharply focused in the clear light.

"What a marvelous day for the Handicap!" cried Paula, dragging Ellery along. "Oh, there's Bing, and Dean Martin, and Bob Hope! . . . Hello! . . . And Joan and Clark and . . ."

Despite Miss Paris's overenthusiastic trail-breaking, Mr. Queen arrived at the track stalls in one piece. They found old John Scott watching with the intentness of a Red Indian as a stablehand kneaded Danger's velvety forelegs. There was a stony set to Scott's gnarled face that made Paula cry: "John! Is anything wrong with Danger?"

"Danger's all right," said the old man curtly. "It's Kate. We had a blow-up over that Halliday boy an' she ran out on me."

"Nonsense, John. I sent her back home last night myself."

"She was at your place? She didn't come home."

"She didn't?" Paula's little nose wrinkled.

"I guess," growled Scott, "she's run off with that Halliday coward. He's not a mon, the lily-livered—"

"We can't all be heroes, John. He's a good boy, and he loves Katie."

The old man stared stubbornly at his stallion, and after a moment they left and made their way towards their box.

"Funny," said Paula in a scared voice. "She couldn't have run off with Hank; he was with you. And I'd swear she meant to go back to the ranch last night."

"Now, Paula," said Mr. Queen gently. "She's all right." But his eyes were thoughtful and a little perturbed.

Their box was not far from the paddock. During the preliminary races, Paula kept searching the sea of faces with her binoculars.

"Well, well," said Mr. Queen suddenly, and Paula became conscious of a rolling thunder from the stands about them.

"What's the matter? What's happened?"

190

"Broomstick, the favorite, has been scratched," said Mr. Queen dryly.

"Broomstick? Santelli's horse?" Paula stared at him, paling. "But why? Ellery, there's something in this—"

"It seems he's pulled a tendon and can't run."

"Do you think," whispered Paula, "that Santelli had anything to do with Katie's . . . not getting . . . home?"

"Possible," muttered Ellery. "But I can't seem to fit the blinking thing—"

"Here they come!"

The shout shook the stands. A line of regal animals began to emerge from the paddock. Paula and Ellery rose with the other restless thousands, and craned. The Handicap contestants were parading to the post!

There was High Tor, who had gone lame in the stretch at the Derby two years before and had not run a race since. This was to be his comeback; the insiders held him in a contempt which the public apparently shared, for he was quoted at 50 to 1. There was little Fighting Billy. There was Equator, prancing sedately along with Buzz Hickey up. There was Danger! Glossy black, gigantic, imperial, Danger was nervous. Whitey Williams was having a difficult time controlling him and a stablehand was struggling at his bit.

Old John Scott, his big shapeless body unmistakable even at this distance, lumbered from the paddock towards his dancing stallion, apparently to soothe him.

Paula gasped. Ellery said quickly: "What is it?"

"There's Hank Halliday in the crowd. Up there! Right above the spot where Danger's passing. About fifty feet from John Scott. And Kathryn's not with him!"

Ellery took the glasses from her and located Halliday.

Paula sank into her chair. "Ellery, I've the queerest feeling. There's something wrong. See how pale he is. . . ."

The powerful glasses brought Halliday to within a few inches of Ellery's eyes. The boy's glasses were steamed over; he was shaking, as if he had a chill; and yet Ellery could see the globules of perspiration on his cheeks.

And then Mr. Queen stiffened very abruptly.

John Scott had just reached the head of Danger; his thick arm was coming up to pull the stallion's head down. And in that instant Mr. Hankus-Pankus Halliday fumbled in his clothes; and in the next his hand appeared clasping a snub-nosed automatic. Mr. Queen very nearly cried out. For, the short barrel wavering, the automatic in Mr. Halliday's trembling hands pointed in the general direction of John Scott, there was an explosion, and a puff of smoke blew out of the muzzle.

Miss Paris leaped to her feet, and Miss Paris did cry out.

"Why, the crazy young fool!" said Mr. Queen dazedly.

Frightened by the shot, which had gone wild, Danger reared. The other horses began to kick and dance. In a moment the place below boiled with panic-stricken thoroughbreds. Scott, clinging to Danger's head, half-turned in an immense astonishment and looked inquiringly upwards. Whitey struggled desperately to control the frantic stallion.

And then Mr. Halliday shot again. And again. And a fourth time. And at some instant, in the spaces between those shots, the rearing horse got between John Scott and the automatic in Mr. Halliday's shaking hand.

Danger's four feet left the turf. Then, whinnying in agony, flanks heaving, he toppled over on his side.

"Oh, gosh; oh, *gosh*," said Paula biting her handkerchief.

"Let's go!" shouted Mr. Queen, and he plunged for the spot.

By the time they reached the place where Mr. Halliday had fearfully discharged his automatic, the bespectacled youth had disappeared. The people who had stood about him were still too stunned to move. Elsewhere, the stands were in pandemonium.

In the confusion, Ellery and Paula managed to slip through the inadequate track-police cordon hastily thrown about the fallen Danger and his milling rivals. They found old John on his knees beside the black stallion, his big hands steadily stroking the glossy, veined neck. Whitey, pale and bewildered-looking, had stripped off the tiny saddle, and the track veterinary was examining a bullet wound in Danger's side, near the shoulder. A group of track officials conferred excitedly nearby.

"He saved my life," said old John in a low voice to no one in particular. "He saved my life."

The veterinary looked up. "Sorry, Mr. Scott," he said grimly. "Danger won't run this race."

"No. I suppose not." Scott licked his leathery lips. "Is it—mon, is it serious?"

"Can't tell till I dig out the bullet. We'll have to get him out of here and into the hospital right away."

An official said: "Tough luck, Scott. You may be sure we'll do our best to find the scoundrel who shot your horse."

The old man's lips twisted. He climbed to his feet and looked down at the heaving flanks of his fallen thoroughbred. Whitey Williams trudged away with Danger's gear, head hanging.

A moment later the loud-speaker system proclaimed that Danger, Number 5, had been scratched, and that the Handicap would be run immediately the other contestants could be quieted and lined up at the stall barrier.

"All right, folks, clear out," said a track policeman as a hospital van rushed up, followed by a hoisting truck.

"What are you doing about the man who shot this horse?" demanded Mr. Queen, not moving.

"Ellery," whispered Paula nervously, tugging at his arm.

"We'll get him; got a good description. Move on, please."

"Well," said Mr. Queen slowly, "I know who he is, do you see."

"Ellery!"

"I saw him and recognized him."

They were ushered into the Steward's office just as the announcement was made that High Tor, at 50 to 1, had won the Santa Anita Handicap, purse $100,000, by two and a half lengths . . . almost as long a shot, in one sense, as the shot which laid poor Danger low, commented Mr. Queen to Miss Paris, *sotto voce.*

"Halliday?" said John Scott with heavy contempt. "That yellow-livered pup try to shoot me?"

"I couldn't possibly be mistaken, Mr. Scott," said Ellery.

"I saw him, too, John," sighed Paula.

"Who is this Halliday?" demanded the chief of the track police.

Scott told him in monosyllables, relating their quarrel of the day before. "I knocked him down an' kicked him. I guess the only way he could get back at me was with a gun. An' Danger took the rap, poor beastie." For the first time his voice shook.

"Well, we'll get him; he can't have left the park," said the police chief grimly. "I've got it sealed tighter than a drum."

"Did you know," murmured Mr. Queen, "that Mr.

193

Scott's daughter Kathryn has been missing since last night?"

Old John flushed slowly. "You think—my Kate had somethin' to do—"

"Don't be silly, John!" said Paula.

"At any rate," said Mr. Queen dryly, "her disappearance and the attack here today can't be a coincidence. I'd advise you to start a search for Miss Scott immediately. And, by the way, send for Danger's gear. I'd like to examine it."

"Say, who the devil are you?" growled the chief.

Mr. Queen told him negligently. The chief looked properly awed. He telephoned to various police headquarters, and he sent for Danger's gear.

Whitey Williams, still in his silks, carried the high small racing saddle in and dumped it on the floor.

"John, I'm awful sorry about what happened," he said in a low voice.

"It ain't your fault, Whitey." The big shoulders drooped.

"Ah, Williams, thank you," said Mr. Queen briskly. "This *is* the saddle Danger was wearing a few minutes ago?"

"Yes, sir."

"Exactly as it was when you stripped it off him after the shots?"

"Yes, sir."

"Has anyone had an opportunity to tamper with it?"

"No, sir. I been with it ever since, and no one's come near it but me."

Mr. Queen nodded and knelt to examine the empty-pocketed saddle. Observing the scorched hole in the flap, his brow puckered in perplexity.

"By the way, Whitey," he asked, "how much do you weigh?"

"Hundred and seven."

Mr. Queen frowned. He rose, dusted his knees delicately, and beckoned the chief of police. They conferred in undertones. The policeman looked baffled, shrugged, and hurried out.

When he returned, a certain familiar-appearing gentleman in too-perfect clothes and a foreign air accompanied him. The gentleman looked sad.

"I hear some crackpot took a couple o' shots at you, John," he said sorrowfully, "an' got your nag instead. Tough luck."

There was a somewhat quizzical humor behind this ambiguous statement which brought old John's head up in a flash of belligerence.

"You dirty, thievin'—"

"Mr. Santelli," greeted Mr. Queen. "When did you know that Broomstick would have to be scratched?"

"Broomstick?" Mr. Santelli looked mildly surprised at this irrelevant question. "Why, last week."

"So that's why you offered to buy Scott's stable—to get control of Danger?"

"Sure." Mr. Santelli smiled genially. "He was hot. With my nag out, he looked like a cinch."

"Mr. Santelli, you're what is colloquially known as a cock-eyed liar." Mr. Santelli ceased smiling. "You wanted to buy Danger not to see him win, but to see him lose!"

Mr. Santelli looked unhappy. "Who is this," he appealed to the police chief, "Mister Wacky himself?"

"In my embryonic way," said Mr. Queen, "I have been making a few inquiries in the last several days and my information has it that your bookmaking organization covered a lot of Danger money when Danger was five to one."

"Say, you got somethin' there," said Mr. Santelli, suddenly deciding to be candid.

"You covered about two hundred thousand dollars, didn't you?"

"Wow," said Mr. Santelli. "This guy's got idears, ain't he?"

"So," smiled Mr. Queen, "if Danger won the Handicap you stood to drop a very frigid million dollars, did you not?"

"But it's my old friend John some guy tried to rub out," pointed out Mr. Santelli gently. "Go peddle your papers somewheres else, Mister Wack."

John Scott looked bewilderedly from the gambler to Mr. Queen. His jaw muscles were bunched and jerky.

At this moment a special officer deposited among them Mr. Hankus-Pankus Halliday, his spectacles awry on his nose and his collar ripped away from his prominent Adam's apple.

John Scott sprang towards him, but Ellery caught his flailing arms in time to prevent a slaughter.

"Murderer! Scalawag! Horse-killer!" roared old John. "What did ye do with my lassie?"

Mr. Halliday said gravely: "Mr. Scott, you have my sympathy."

The old man's mouth flew open. Mr. Halliday folded his scrawny arms with dignity, glaring at the policeman who had brought him in. "There was no necessity to manhandle me. I'm quite ready to face the—er—music. But I shall not answer any questions."

"No gat on him, Chief," said the policeman by his side.

"What did you do with the automatic?" demanded the chief. No answer. "You admit you had it in for Mr. Scott and tried to kill him?" No answer. "Where is Miss Scott?"

"You see," said Mr. Halliday stonily, "how useless it is."

"Hankus-Pankus," murmured Mr. Queen, "you are superb. You don't know where Kathryn is, do you?"

Hankus-Pankus instantly looked alarmed. "Oh, I say, Mr. Queen. Don't make me talk. Please!"

"But you're expecting her to join you here, aren't you?"

Hankus paled. The policeman said: "He's a nut. He didn't even try to make a getaway. He didn't even fight back."

"Hank! Darling! Father!" cried Katie Scott; and, straggle-haired and dusty-faced, she flew into the office and flung herself upon Mr. Halliday's thin bosom.

"Katie!" screamed Paula, flying to the girl and embracing her; and in a moment all three, Paula and Kathryn and Hankus, were weeping in concert, while old John's jaw dropped even lower and all but Mr. Queen, who was smiling, stood rooted to their bits of Space in timeless stupefaction.

Then Miss Scott ran to her father and clung to him, and old John's shoulders lifted a little, even though the expression of bewilderment persisted; and she burrowed her head into her father's deep, broad chest.

In the midst of this incredible scene the track veterinary bustled in and said: "Good news, Mr. Scott. I've extracted the bullet and, while the wound is deep, I give you my word Danger will be as good as ever when it's healed." And he bustled out.

And Mr. Queen, his smile broadening, said: "Well, well, a pretty comedy of errors."

"Comedy!" growled old John over his daughter's golden

curls. "D'ye call a murderous attempt on my life a comedy?" And he glared fiercely at Mr. Hank Halliday, who was at the moment borrowing a handkerchief from the policeman with which to wipe his eyes.

"My dear Mr. Scott," replied Mr. Queen, "there has been no attempt on your life. The shots were not fired at you. From the very first Danger, and Danger only, was intended to be the victim of the shooting."

"What's this?" cried Paula.

"No, no, Whitey," said Mr. Queen, smiling still more broadly. "The door, I promise you, is well guarded."

The jockey snarled: "Yah, he's off his nut. Next thing you'll say *I* plugged the nag. How I could be on Danger's back and at the same time fifty feet away in the grandstand? A million guys saw this screwball fire those shots!"

"A difficulty," replied Mr. Queen, bowing, "I shall be delighted to resolve. Danger, ladies and gentlemen, was handicapped officially to carry one hundred and twenty pounds in the Santa Anita Handicap. This means that when his jockey, carrying the gear, stepped upon the scales in the weighing-out ceremony just before the race, the combined weight of the jockey and gear had to come to exactly one hundred and twenty pounds; or Mr. Whitey Williams would never have been allowed by the track officials to mount his horse."

"What's that got to do with it?" demanded the chief, eyeing Mr. Whitey Williams in a hard, unfeeling way.

"Everything. For Mr. Williams told us only a few minutes ago that he weighs only a hundred and seven pounds. Consequently the racing saddle Danger wore when he was shot must have contained various lead weights which, combined with the weight of the saddle, made up the difference between a hundred and seven pounds, Mr. Williams's weight, and a hundred twenty pounds, the handicap weight. Is that correct?"

"Sure. Anybody knows that."

"Yes, yes, elementary, in Mr. Holmes's imperishable phrase. Nevertheless," continued Mr. Queen, walking over and prodding with his toe the saddle Whitey Williams had fetched to the office, "when I examined this saddle *there were no lead weights in its pockets.* And Mr. Williams assured me no one had tampered with the saddle since he had removed it from Danger's back. But this was impossible, since without the lead weights Mr. Wil-

197

liams and the saddle would have weighed out at less than a hundred and twenty pounds on the scales.

"And so I knew," said Mr. Queen, "that Williams had weighed out with a different saddle, that when he was shot Danger was wearing a different saddle, that the saddle Williams lugged away from the wounded horse was a different saddle; that he secreted it somewhere on the premises and fetched here on our request a *second* saddle —this one on the floor—which he had prepared beforehand with a bullet hole nicely placed in the proper spot. And the reason he did this was that obviously there was something in that first saddle he didn't want anyone to see. And what could that have been but a special pocket containing an automatic, which in the confusion following Mr. Halliday's first signal shot, Mr. Williams calmly discharged into Danger's body by simply stooping over as he struggled with the frightened horse, putting his hand into the pocket, and firing while Mr. Halliday was discharging his three other futile shots fifty feet away? Mr. Halliday, you see, couldn't be trusted to hit Danger from such a distance, because Mr. Halliday is a stranger to firearms; he might even hit Mr. Williams instead, if he hit anything. That's why I believe Mr. Halliday was using blank cartridges and threw the automatic away."

The jockey's voice was strident, panicky. "You're crazy! Special saddle. Who ever heard—"

Mr. Queen, still smiling, went to the door, opened it, and said: "Ah, you've found it, I see. Let's have it. In Danger's stall? Clumsy, clumsy."

He returned with a racing saddle; and Whitey cursed and then grew still. Mr. Queen and the police chief and John Scott examined the saddle and, surely enough, there was a special pocket stitched into the flap, above the iron hoop, and in the pocket there was a snub-nosed automatic. And the bullet hole piercing the special pocket had the scorched speckled appearance of powder burns.

"But where," muttered the chief, "does Halliday figure? I don't get him a-tall."

"Very few people would," said Mr. Queen, "because Mr. Halliday is, in his modest way, unique among bipeds."

"Huh?"

"Why, he was Whitey's accomplice—weren't you, Hankus?"

Hankus gulped and said: "Yes. I mean no. I mean—"

"But I'm sure Hank wouldn't—" Katie began to cry.

"You see," said Mr. Queen briskly, "Whitey wanted a setup whereby he would be the last person in California to be suspected of having shot Danger. The quarrel between John Scott and Hank gave him a ready-made instrument. If he could make Hank seem to do the shooting, with Hank's obvious motive against Mr. Scott, then nobody would suspect his own part in the affair.

"But to bend Hank to his will he had to have a hold on Hank. What was Mr. Halliday's Achilles' heel? Why, his passion for Katie Scott. So last night Whitey's father, Weed Williams, I imagine—wasn't he the jockey you chased from the American turf many years ago, Mr. Scott, and who became a saddlemaker?—kidnaped Katie Scott, and then communicated with Hankus-Pankus and told him just what to do today if he ever expected to see his beloved alive again. And Hankus-Pankus took the gun they provided him with, and listened very carefully, and agreed to do everything they told him to do, and promised he would not breathe a word of the truth afterward, even if he had to go to jail for his crime, because if he did, you see, something terrible would happen to the incomparable Katie."

Mr. Halliday gulped, his Adam's apple bobbing violently.

"An' all the time this skunk," growled John Scott, glaring at the cowering jockey, "an' his weasel of a father, they sat back an' laughed at a brave mon, because they were havin' their piddling revenge on me, ruining me!" Old John shambled like a bear towards Mr. Halliday. "An' I am a shamed mon today, Hank Halliday. For that was the bravest thing I ever did hear of. An' even if I've lost my chance for the Handicap purse, through no fault of yours, and I'm a ruined maggot, here's my hand."

Mr. Halliday took it absently, meanwhile fumbling with his other hand in his pocket. "By the way," he said, "who did win the Handicap, if I may ask? I was so busy, you see—"

"High Tor," said somebody in the babble.

"Really? Then I must cash this ticket," said Mr. Halliday with a note of faint interest.

"Two thousand dollars!" gasped Paula, goggling at the ticket. "He bet two thousand dollars on High Tor at fifty to one!"

"Yes, a little nest egg my mother left me," said Mr. Halliday. He seemed embarrassed. "I'm sorry, Mr. Scott. You made me angry when you—er—kicked me in the

199

pants, so I didn't bet it on Danger. And High Tor was such a beautiful name."

"Oh, Hank," sobbed Katie, beginning to strangle him.

"So now, Mr. Scott," said Hankus-Pankus with dignity, "may I marry Katie and set you up in the racing business again?"

"Happy days!" bellowed old John, seizing his future son-in-law in a rib-cracking embrace.

"Happy days," muttered Mr. Queen, seizing Miss Paris and heading her for the nearest bar.

Heigh, Danger!

Mind Over Matter

PAULA PARIS found Inspector Richard Queen of the Homicide Squad inconsolable when she arrived in New York. She understood how he felt, for she had flown in from Hollywood expressly to cover the heavyweight fight between Champion Mike Brown and Challenger Jim Coyle, who were signed to box fifteen rounds at the Stadium that night for the championship of the world.

"You poor dear," said Paula. "And how about you, Master Mind? Aren't you disappointed, too, that you can't buy a ticket to the fight?" she asked Mr. Ellery Queen.

"I'm a jinx," said the great man gloomily. "If I went, something catastrophic would be sure to happen. So why should I want to go?"

"I thought witnessing catastrophes was why people *go* to fights."

"Oh, I don't mean anything gentle like a knockout. Something grimmer."

"He's afraid somebody will knock somebody off," said the Inspector.

"Well, doesn't somebody always?" demanded his son.

"Don't pay any attention to him, Paula," said the Inspector impatiently. "Look, you're a newspaperwoman. Can you get me a ticket?"

"You may as well get me one, too," groaned Mr. Queen.

So Miss Paris smiled and telephoned Phil Maguire, the famous sports editor, and spoke so persuasively to him that he picked them up that evening in his cranky little sports roadster and they all drove uptown to the Stadium together to see the brawl.

"How do you figure the fight, Maguire?" asked Inspector Queen respectfully.

"On this howdedo," said Maguire, "Maguire doesn't care to be quoted."

"Seems to me the champ ought to take this boy Coyle."

Maguire shrugged. "Phil's sour on the champion," laughed Paula. "Phil and Mike Brown haven't been cuddly since Mike won the title."

"Nothing personal, y'understand," said Phil Maguire. "Only, remember Kid Berès, the Cuban boy? This was in the days when Ollie Stearn was finagling Mike Brown into the heavy sugar. So this fight was a fix, see, and Mike knew it was a fix, and the Kid knew it was a fix, and everybody knew it was a fix and that Kid Berès was supposed to lay down in the sixth round. Well, just the same Mike went out there and sloughed into the Kid and half-killed him. Just for the hell of it. The Kid spent a month in the hospital and when he came out he was only half a man." And Maguire smiled his crooked smile and pressed his horn gently at an old man crossing the street. Then he started, and said: "I guess I just don't like the champ."

"Speaking of fixes . . ." began Mr. Queen.

"Were we?" asked Maguire innocently.

"If it's on the level," predicted Mr. Queen gloomily, "Coyle will murder the champion. Wipe the ring up with him. That big fellow wants the title."

"Oh, sure."

"Damn it," grinned the Inspector, "who's going to win tonight?"

Maguire grinned back. "Well, you know the odds. Three to one on the champ."

When they drove into the parking lot across the street from the Stadium, Maguire grunted: "Speak of the devil." He had backed the little roadster into a space beside a huge twelve-cylinder limousine the color of bright blood.

"Now what's that supposed to mean?" asked Paula Paris.

201

"This red locomotive next to Lizzie," Maguire chuckled. "It's the champ's. Or rather, it belongs to his manager, Ollie Stearn. Ollie lets Mike use it. Mike's car's gone down the river."

"I thought the champion was wealthy," said Mr. Queen.

"Not any more. All tangled up in litigation. Dozens of judgments wrapped around his ugly ears."

"He ought to be hunk after tonight," said the Inspector wistfully. "Pulling down more than a half million bucks for his end!"

"He won't collect a red cent of it," said the newspaperman. "His loving wife—you know Ivy, the ex-strip-tease doll with the curves and detours?—Ivy and Mike's creditors will grab it all off. Come on."

Mr. Queen assisted Miss Paris from the roadster and tossed his camel's-hair topcoat carelessly into the back seat.

"Don't leave your coat there, Ellery," protested Paula. "Someone's sure to steal it."

"Let 'em. It's an old rag. Don't know what I brought it for, anyway, in this heat."

"Come on, come on," said Phil Maguire eagerly.

From the press section at ringside the stands were one heaving mass of growling humanity. Two bantamweights were fencing in the ring.

"What's the trouble?" demanded Mr. Queen alertly.

"Crowd came out to see heavy artillery, not popguns," explained Maguire. "Take a look at the card."

"Six prelims," muttered Inspector Queen. "And all good boys, too. So what are these muggs beefing about?"

"Bantams, welters, lightweights, and one middleweight bout to wind up."

"So what?"

"So the card's too light. The fans came here to see two big guys slaughter each other. They don't want to be annoyed by a bunch of gnats—even good gnats. . . . Hi, Happy."

"Who's that?" asked Miss Paris curiously.

"Happy Day," the Inspector answered for Maguire. "Makes his living off bets. One of the biggest plungers in town."

Happy Day was visible a few rows off, an expensive Borsalino resting on a fold of neck fat. He had a puffed face the color of cold rice pudding, and his eyes

202

were two raisins. He nodded at Maguire and turned back to watch the ring.

"Normally, Happy's face is like a raw steak," said Maguire. "He's worried about something."

"Perhaps," remarked Mr. Queen darkly, "the gentleman smells a mouse."

Maguire glanced at the great man sidewise, and then smiled. "And there's Mrs. Champ herself. Ivy Brown. Some stuff, hey, men?"

The woman prowled down the aisle on the arm of a wizened, wrinkled little man who chewed nervously on a long green cold cigar. The champion's wife was a full-blown animal with a face like a Florentine cameo. The little man handed her into a seat, bowed elaborately, and hurried off.

"Isn't the little guy Ollie Stearn, Brown's manager?" asked the Inspector.

"Yes," said Maguire. "Notice the act? Ivy and Mike Brown haven't lived together for a couple of years, and Ollie thinks it's lousy publicity. So he pays a lot of attention in public to the champ's wife. What d'ye think of her, Paula? The woman's angle is always refreshing."

"This may sound feline," murmured Miss Paris, "but she's an overdressed harpie with the instincts of a she-wolf who never learned to apply make-up properly. Cheap —very cheap."

"Expensive—very expensive. Mike's wanted a divorce for a long time, but Ivy keeps rolling in the hay—and Mike's made plenty of hay in his time. Say, I gotta go to work."

Maguire bent over his typewriter.

The night deepened, the crowd rumbled, and Mr. Ellery Queen, the celebrated sleuth, felt uncomfortable. Specifically, his six-foot body was taut as a violin string. It was a familiar but always menacing phenomenon. It meant that there was murder in the air.

The challenger appeared first. He was met by a roar, like the roar of a river at flood tide bursting its dam.

Miss Paris gasped with admiration. "Isn't he the one!"

Jim Coyle was the one—an almost handsome giant six feet and a half tall, with preposterously broad shoulders, long smooth muscles, and a bronze skin. He rubbed his unshaven cheeks and grinned boyishly at the frantic fans.

His manager, Barney Hawks, followed him into the

ring. Hawks was a big man, but beside his fighter he appeared puny.

"Hercules in trunks," breathed Miss Paris. "Did you ever see such a body, Ellery?"

"The question more properly is," said Mr. Queen jealously, "can he keep that body off the floor? That's the question, my girl."

"Plenty fast for a big man," said Maguire. "Faster than you'd think, considering all that bulk. Maybe not as fast as Mike Brown, but Jim's got height and reach in his favor, and he's strong as a bull. The way Firpo was."

"Here comes the champ!" exclaimed Inspector Queen.

A large ugly man shuffled down the aisle and vaulted into the ring. His manager—the little wizened, wrinkled man—followed him and stood bouncing up and down on the canvas, still chewing the unlit cigar.

"Boo-oo-oo!"

"They're booing the champion!" cried Paula. "Phil, why?"

"Because they hate his guts," smiled Maguire. "They hate his guts because he's an ornery, brutal, crooked slob with the kick of a mule and the soul of a pretzel. That's why, darlin'."

Brown stood six feet two inches, anatomically a gorilla, with a broad hairy chest, long arms, humped shoulders, and large flat feet. His features were smashed, cruel. He paid no attention to the hostile crowd, to his taller, bigger, younger opponent. He seemed detached, indrawn, a subhuman fighting machine.

But Mr. Queen, whose peculiar genius it was to notice minutiae, saw Brown's powerful mandibles working ever so slightly beneath his leathery cheeks.

And again Mr. Queen's body tightened.

When the gong clamored for the start of the third round, the champion's left eye was a purple slit, his lips were cracked and bloody, and his simian chest rose and fell in gasps.

Thirty seconds later he was cornered, a beaten animal, above their heads. They could see the ragged splotches over his kidneys, blooming above his trunks like crimson flowers.

Brown crouched, covering up, protecting his chin. Big Jim Coyle streaked forward. The giant's gloves sank into

Brown's body. The champion fell forward and pinioned the long bronze merciless arms.

The referee broke them. Brown grabbed Coyle again. They danced.

The crowd began singing "The Blue Danube," and the referee stepped between the two fighters again and spoke sharply to Brown.

"The dirty double-crosser," smiled Phil Maguire.

"Who? What d'ye mean?" asked Inspector Queen, puzzled.

"Watch the payoff."

The champion raised his battered face and lashed out feebly at Coyle with his soggy left glove. The giant laughed and stepped in.

The champion went down.

"Pretty as a picture," said Maguire admiringly.

At the count of nine, with the bay of the crowd in his flattened ears, Mike Brown staggered to his feet. The bulk of Coyle slipped in, shadowy, and pumped twelve solid, lethal gloves into Brown's body. The champion's knees broke. A whistling six-inch uppercut to the point of the jaw sent him toppling to the canvas.

This time he remained there.

"But he made it look kosher," drawled Maguire.

The Stadium howled with glee and the satiation of blood-lust. Paula looked sickish. A few rows away Happy Day jumped up, stared wildly about, and then began shoving through the crowd.

"Happy isn't happy any more," sang Maguire.

The ring was boiling with police, handlers, officials. Jim Coyle was half-drowned in a wave of shouting people; he was laughing like a boy. In the champion's corner Ollie Stearn worked slowly over the twitching torso of the unconscious man.

"Yes, sir," said Phil Maguire, rising and stretching, "that was as pretty a dive as I've seen, brother, and I've seen some beauts in my day."

"See here, Maguire," said Mr. Queen, nettled. "I have eyes, too. What makes you so cocksure Brown just tossed his title away?"

"You may be Einstein on Centre Street," grinned Maguire, "but here you're just another palooka, Mr. Queen."

"Seems to me," argued the Inspector in the bedlam, "Brown took an awful lot of punishment."

"Oh, sure," said Maguire mockingly. "Look, you boobs.

205

Mike Brown has as sweet a right hand as the game has ever seen. Did you notice him use his right on Coyle tonight—even once?"

"Well," admitted Mr. Queen, "no."

"Of course not. Not a single blow. And he had a dozen openings, especially in the second round. And Jimmy Coyle still carries his guard too low. But what did Mike do? Put his deadly right into cold storage, kept jabbing away with that silly left of his—it couldn't put Paula away!—covering up, clinching, and taking one hell of a beating. . . . Sure, he made it look good. But your ex-champ took a dive just the same!"

They were helping the gorilla from the ring. He looked surly and tired. A small group followed him, laughing. Little Ollie Stearn kept pushing people aside fretfully. Mr. Queen spied Brown's wife, the curved Ivy, pale and furious, hurrying after them.

"It appears," sighed Mr. Queen, "that I was in error."

"What?" asked Paula.

"Hmm. Nothing."

"Look," said Maguire. "I've got to see a man about a man, but I'll meet you folks in Coyle's dressing room and we'll kick a few gongs around. Jim's promised to help a few of the boys warm up some hot spots."

"Oh, I'd love it!" cried Paula. "How do we get in, Phil?"

"What have you got a cop with you for? Show her, Inspector."

Maguire's slight figure slouched off. The great man's scalp prickled suddenly. He frowned and took Paula's arm.

The new champion's dressing room was full of smoke, people, and din. Young Coyle lay on a training table like Gulliver in Lilliput, being rubbed down. He was answering questions good humoredly, grinning at cameras, flexing his shoulder muscles. Barney Hawks was running about with his collar loosened handing out cigars like a new father.

The crowd was so dense it overflowed into the adjoining shower room. There were empty bottles on the floor and near the shower-room window, pushed into a corner, five men were shooting craps with enormous sobriety.

The Inspector spoke to Barney Hawks, and Coyle's manager introduced them to the champion, who took one look at Paula and said: "Hey, Barney, how about a little privacy?"

206

"Sure, sure. You're the champ now, Jimmy-boy!"

"Come on, you guys, you got enough pictures to last you a lifetime. What did he say your name is beautiful? Paris? That's a hell of a name."

"Isn't yours Couzzi?" asked Paula coolly.

"Socko," laughed the boy. "Come on, clear out, guys. This lady and I got some sparring to do. Hey, lay off the liniment, Louie. He didn't hardly touch me."

Coyle slipped off the rubbing table, and Barney Hawks began shooing men out of the shower room, and finally Coyle grabbed some towels, winked at Paula, and went in, shutting the door. They heard the cheerful hiss of the shower.

Five minutes later Phil Maguire strolled in. He was perspiring and a little wobbly.

"Heil, Hitler," he shouted. "Where's the champ?"

"Here I am," said Coyle, opening the shower-room door and rubbing his bare chest with a towel. There was another towel draped around his loins. "Hya, Phil-boy. Be dressed in a shake. Say, this doll your Mamie? If she ain't, I'm staking out my claim."

"Come on, come on, champ. We got a date with Fifty-second Street."

"Sure! How about you, Barney? You joining us?"

"Go ahead and play," said his manager in a fatherly tone. "Me, I got money business with the management." He danced into the shower room, emerged with a hat and a camel's-hair coat over his arm, kissed his hand affectionately at Coyle, and lumbered out.

"You're not going to stay in here while he dresses?" said Mr. Queen petulantly to Miss Paris. "Come on—you can wait for your hero in the hall."

"Yes, sir," said Miss Paris submissively.

Coyle guffawed. "Don't worry, fella. I ain't going to do you out of nothing. There's plenty of broads."

Mr. Queen piloted Miss Paris firmly from the room. "Let's meet them at the car," he said in a curt tone.

Miss Paris murmured: "Yes, sir."

They walked in silence to the end of the corridor and turned a corner into an alley which led out of the Stadium and into the street. As they walked down the alley Mr. Queen could see through the shower-room window into the dressing room: Maguire had produced a bottle and he, Coyle, and the Inspector were raising glasses. Coyle in his athletic underwear was—well . . .

Mr. Queen hurried Miss Paris out of the alley and across the street to the parking lot. Cars were slowly driving out. But the big red limousine belonging to Ollie Stearn still stood beside Maguire's roadster.

"Ellery," said Paula softly, "you're such a fool."

"Now, Paula, I don't care to discuss—"

"What do you think I'm referring to? It's your topcoat, silly. Didn't I warn you someone would steal it?"

Mr. Queen glanced into the roadster. His coat was gone. "Oh, that. I was going to throw it away, anyway. Now look, Paula, if you think for one instant, that I could be jealous of some oversized . . . Paula! What's the matter?"

Paula's cheeks were gray in the brilliant arc light. She was pointing a shaky forefinger at the blood-red limousine.

"In—in there . . . Isn't that—Mike Brown?"

Mr. Queen glanced quickly into the rear of the limousine. Then he said: "Get into Maguire's car, Paula, and look the other way."

Paula crept into the roadster, shaking.

Ellery opened the rear door of Stearn's car.

Mike Brown tumbled out of the car to his feet, and lay still.

And after a moment the Inspector, Maguire, and Coyle strolled up, chuckling over something Maguire was relating in a thick voice.

Maguire stopped. "Say. Who's that?"

Coyle said abruptly: "Isn't that Mike Brown?"

The Inspector said: "Out of the way, Jim." He knelt beside Ellery.

And Mr. Queen raised his head. "Yes, it's Mike Brown. Someone's used him for a pin cushion."

Phil Maguire yelped and ran for a telephone. Paula Paris crawled out of Maguire's roadster and blundered after him, remembering her profession.

"Is he . . . is he—" began Jim Coyle, gulping.

"The long count," said the Inspector grimly. "Say, is that girl gone? Here, help me turn him over."

They turned him over. He lay staring up into the blinding arc light. He was completely dressed; his hat was still jammed about his ears and a gray tweed topcoat was wrapped about his body, still buttoned. He had been stabbed ten times in the abdomen and chest, through his topcoat. There had been a great deal of bleeding; his coat was sticky and wet with it.

"Body's warm," said the Inspector. "This happened just

a few minutes ago." He rose from the dust and stared unseeingly at the crowd which had gathered.

"Maybe," began the champion, licking his lips, "maybe—"

"Maybe what, Jim?" asked the Inspector, looking at him.

"Nothing, nothing."

"Why don't you go home? Don't let this spoil your night, kid."

Coyle set his jaw. "I'll stick around."

The Inspector blew a police whistle.

Police came, and Phil Maguire and Paula Paris returned, and Ollie Stearn and others appeared from across the street, and the crowd thickened, and Mr. Ellery Queen crawled into the tonneau of Stearn's car.

The rear of the red limousine was a shambles. Blood stained the mohair cushions, the floor rug, which was wrinkled and scuffed. A large coat button with a scrap of fabric still clinging to it lay on one of the cushions, beside a crumpled camel's-hair coat.

Mr. Queen seized the coat. The button had been torn from it. The front of the coat, like the front of the murdered man's coat, was badly bloodstained. But the stains had a pattern. Mr. Queen laid the coat on the seat, front up, and slipped the buttons through the buttonholes. Then the bloodstains met. When he unbuttoned the coat and separated the two sides of the coat the stains separated, too, and on the side where the buttons were the blood traced a straight edge an inch outside the line of buttons.

The Inspector poked his head in. "What's that thing?"

"The murderer's coat."

"Let's see that!"

"It won't tell you anything about its wearer. Fairly cheap coat, label's been ripped out—no identifying marks. Do you see what must have happened in here, Dad?"

"What?"

"The murder ocurred, of course, in this car. Either Brown and his killer got into the car simultaneously, or Brown was here first and then his murderer came, or the murderer was skulking in here, waiting for Brown to come. In any event, the murderer wore this coat."

"How do you know that?"

"Because there's every sign of a fierce struggle, so fierce Brown managed to tear off one of the coat buttons of his

209

assailant's coat. In the course of the struggle Brown was stabbed many times. His blood flowed freely. It got all over not only his own coat but the murderer's as well. From the position of the bloodstains the murderer's coat must have been buttoned at the time of the struggle, which means he wore it."

The Inspector nodded. "Left it behind because he didn't want to be seen in a bloody coat. Ripped out all identifying marks."

From behind the Inspector came Paula's tremulous voice. "Could that be *your* camels-hair coat, Ellery?"

Mr. Queen looked at her in an odd way. "No, Paula."

"What's this?" demanded the Inspector.

"Ellery left his topcoat behind in Phil's car before the fight," Paula explained. "I told him somebody would steal it, and somebody did. And now there's a camel's-hair coat—in this car."

"It isn't mine," said Mr. Queen patiently. "Mine has certain distinguishing characteristics which don't exist in this one—a cigarette burn at the second buttonhole, a hole in the right pocket."

The Inspector shrugged and went away.

"Then your coat's being stolen has nothing to do with it?" Paula shivered. "Ellery, I could use a cigarette."

Mr. Queen obliged. "On the contrary. The theft of my coat has everything to do with it."

"But I don't understand. You just said—"

Mr. Queen held a match to Miss Paris's cigarette and stared intently at the body of Mike Brown.

Ollie Stearn's chauffeur, a hard-looking customer, twisted his cap and said: "Mike tells me after the fight he won't need me. Tells me he'll pick me up on the Grand Concourse. Said he'd drive himself."

"Yes?"

"I was kind of—curious. I had a hot dog at the stand there and I—watched. I seen Mike come out and climb into the back—"

"Was he alone?" demanded the Inspector.

"Yeah. Just got in and sat there. A couple of drunks come along then and I couldn't see good. Only seemed to me somebody else come over and got into the car after Mike."

"Who? Who was it? Did you see?"

The chauffeur shook his head. "I couldn't see good. I

don't know. After a while I thought it ain't my business, so I walks away. But when I heard police sirens I come back."

"The one who came after Mike Brown got in," said Mr. Queen with a certain eagerness. "That person was wearing a coat, eh?"

"I guess so. Yeah."

"You didn't witness anything else that occurred?" persisted Mr. Queen.

"Nope."

"Doesn't matter, really," muttered the great man. "Line's clear. Clear as the sun. Must be that—"

"What are you mumbling about?" demanded Miss Paris in his ear.

Mr. Queen stared. "Was I mumbling?" He shook his head.

Then a man from Headquarters came up with a dudish little fellow with frightened eyes who babbled he didn't know nothing, nothing, he didn't know nothing; and the Inspector said: "Come on, Oetjens. You were heard shooting off your mouth in that gin mill. What's the dope?"

And the little fellow said shrilly: "I don't want no trouble, no trouble. I only said—"

"Yes?"

"Mike Brown looked me up this morning," muttered Oetjens, "and says to me, he says, 'Hymie' he says, 'Happy Day knows you, Happy Day takes a lot of your bets,' he says, 'so go lay fifty grand with Happy on Coyle to win by a K.O.,' Mike says. 'You lay that fifty grand for *me*, get it?' he says. And he says, 'If you shoot your trap off to Happy or anyone else that you bet fifty grand for me on Coyle,' he says, 'I'll rip your heart out and break your hands and give you the thumb,' he says, and a lot more, so I laid the fifty grand on Coyle to win by a K.O. and Happy took the bet at twelve to five, he wouldn't give no more."

Jim Coyle growled: "I'll break your neck, damn you."

"Wait a minute, Jim—"

"He's saying Brown took a dive!" cried the champion. "I licked Brown fair and square. I beat the hell out of him fair and square!"

"You thought you beat the hell out of him fair and square," muttered Phil Maguire. "But he took a dive, Jim. Didn't I tell you, Inspector? Laying off that right of his—"

211

"It's a lie! Where's my manager? Where's Barney? They ain't going to hold up the purse on this fight!" roared Coyle. "I won it fair—I won the title fair!"

"Take it easy, Jim," said the Inspector. "Everybody knows you were in there leveling tonight. Look here, Hymie, did Brown give you the cash to bet for him?"

"He was busted," Oetjens cringed. "I just laid the bet on the cuff. The payoff don't come till the next day. So I knew it was okay, because with Mike himself betting on Coyle the fight was in the bag—"

"I'll cripple you, you tinhorn!" yelled young Coyle.

"Take it easy, Jim," soothed Inspector Queen. "So you laid the fifty grand on the cuff, Hymie, and Happy covered the bet at twelve to five, and you knew it would come out all right because Mike was going to take a dive, and then you'd collect a hundred and twenty thousand dollars and give it to Mike, is that it?"

"Yeah, yeah. But that's all, I swear—"

"When did you see Happy last, Hymie?"

Oetjens looked scared and began to back away. His police escort had to shake him a little. But he shook his head stubbornly.

"Now it couldn't be," asked the Inspector softly, "that somehow Happy got wind that you'd laid that fifty grand not for yourself, but for Mike Brown, could it? It couldn't be that Happy found out it was a dive, or suspected it?" The Inspector said sharply to a detective: "Find Happy Day."

"I'm right here," said a bass voice from the crowd; and the fat gambler waded through and said hotly to Inspector Queen: "So I'm the sucker, hey? I'm supposed to take the rap, hey?"

"Did you know Mike Brown was set to take a dive?"

"No!"

Phil Maguire chuckled.

And little Ollie Stearn, pale as his dead fighter, shouted: "Happy done it, Inspector! He found out, and he waited till after the fight, and when he saw Mike laying down he came out here and gave him the business! That's the way it was!"

"You lousy rat," said the gambler. "How do I know you didn't do it yourself? He wasn't taking no dive you couldn't find out about! Maybe you stuck him up because of that fancy doll of his. Don't tell *me*. I know all about you and that Ivy broad. I know—"

"Gentlemen, gentlemen," said the Inspector with a satisfied smile, when there was a shriek and Ivy Brown elbowed her way through the jam and flung herself on the dead body of her husband for the benefit of the press.

And as the photographers joyously went to work, and Happy Day and Ollie Stearn eyed each other with hate, and the crowd milled around, the Inspector said happily to his son: "Not too tough. Not too tough. A wrap-up. It's Happy Day, all right, and all I've got to do is find——"

The great man smiled and said: "You're riding a dead nag."

"Eh?"

"You're wasting your time."

The Inspector ceased to look happy. "What am I supposed to be doing, then? You tell me. You know it all."

"Of course I do, and of course I shall," said Mr. Queen. "What are you to do? Find my coat."

"Say, what *is* this about your damn coat?" growled the Inspector.

"Find my coat, and perhaps I'll find your murderer."

It was a peculiar sort of case. First there had been the ride to the Stadium, and the conversation about how Phil Maguire didn't like Mike Brown, and then there was the ringside gossip, the preliminaries, the main event, the champion's knockout, and all the rest of—all unimportant, all stodgy little details . . . until Mr. Queen and Miss Paris strolled across the parking lot and found two things—or rather, lost one thing—Mr. Queen's coat—and found another—Mike Brown's body; and so there was an important murder case, all nice and shiny.

And immediately the great man began nosing about and muttering about his coat, as if an old and shabby topcoat being stolen could possibly be more important than Mike Brown lying there in the gravel of the parking space full of punctures, like an abandoned tire, and Mike's wife, full of more curves and detours than the Storm King highway, sobbing on his chest and calling upon Heaven and the New York press to witness how dearly she had loved him, poor dead gorilla.

So it appeared that Mike Brown had had a secret rendezvous with someone after the fight, because he had got rid of Ollie Stearn's chauffeur, and the appointment must have been for the interior of Ollie Stearn's red limousine. And whoever he was, he came, and got in with Mike, and there was a struggle, and he stabbed Mike almost a dozen times with something long and sharp, and then fled, leaving his camel's-hair coat behind, because with blood all over its front it would have given him away.

That brought up the matter of the weapon, and everybody began nosing about, including Mr. Queen, because it was a cinch the murderer might have dropped it in his flight. And, sure enough, a radio-car man found it in the dirt under a parked car—a long, evil-looking stiletto with no distinguishing marks whatever and no fingerprints except the fingerprints of the radio-car man. But Mr. Queen persisted in nosing even after that discovery, and finally the Inspector asked him peevishly: "What are you looking for now?"

"My coat," explained Mr. Queen. "Do you see anyone with my coat?"

But there was hardly a man in the crowd with a coat. It was a warm night.

So finally Mr. Queen gave up his queer search and said: "I don't know what you good people are going to do, but, as for me, I'm going back to the Stadium."

"For heaven's sake, what for?" cried Paula.

"To see if I can find my coat," said Mr. Queen patiently.

"I told you you should have taken it with you!"

"Oh, no," said Mr. Queen. "I'm glad I didn't. I'm glad I left it behind in Maguire's car. I'm glad it was stolen."

"But why, you exasperating idiot?"

"Because now," replied Mr. Queen with a cryptic smile, "I have to go looking for it."

And while the morgue wagon carted Mike Brown's carcass off, Mr. Queen trudged back across the dusty parking lot and into the alley which led to the Stadium dressing rooms. And the Inspector, with a baffled look, herded everyone—with special loving care and attention for Mr. Happy Day and Mr. Ollie Stearn and Mrs. Ivy Brown—after his son. He didn't know what else to do.

And finally they were assembled in Jim Coyle's dressing room, and Ivy was weeping into more cameras, and Mr. Queen was glumly contemplating Miss Paris's red straw hat, which looked like a pot, and there was a noise at the door and they saw Barney Hawks, the new champion's manager, standing on the threshold in the company of several officials and promoters.

"What ho," said Barney Hawks with a puzzled glance about. "You still here, champ? What goes on?"

"Plenty goes on," said the champ savagely. "Barney, did you know Brown took a dive tonight?"

"What? What's this?" said Barney Hawks, looking around virtuously. "Who says so, the dirty liar? My boy won that title on the up and up, gentlemen! He beat Brown fair and square."

"Brown threw the fight?" asked one of the men with Hawks, a member of the Boxing Commission. "Is there any evidence of that?"

"The hell with that," said the Inspector politely. "Barney, Mike Brown is dead."

Hawks began to laugh, then he stopped laughing and sputtered: "What's this? What's this? What's the gageroo? Brown dead?"

Jim Coyle waved his huge paw tiredly. "Somebody bumped him off tonight, Barney. In Stearn's car across the street."

"Well, I'm a bum, I'm a bum," breathed his manager, staring. "So Mike got his, hey? Well, well. Tough. Loses his title and his life. Who done it, boys?"

"Maybe you didn't know my boy was dead!" shrilled Ollie Stearn. "Yeah, you put on a swell act, Barney! Maybe you fixed it with Mike so he'd take a dive so your boy could win the title! Maybe—"

"There's been another crime committed here tonight," said a mild voice, and they all looked wonderingly around to find Mr. Ellery Queen advancing toward Mr. Hawks.

"Hey?" said Coyle's manager, staring stupidly at him.

"My coat was stolen."

"Hey?" Hawks kept gaping.

"And, unless my eyes deceive me, as the phrase goes," continued the great man, stopping before Barney Hawks, "I've found it again."

"Hey?"

"On your arm." And Mr. Queen gently removed from Mr. Hawks's arm a shabby camel's-hair topcoat, and unfolded it, and examined it. "Yes. My very own."

Barney Hawks turned green in the silence.

Something sharpened in Mr. Queen's silver eyes, and he bent over the camel's-hair coat again. He spread out the sleeves and examined the armhole seams. They had burst. As had the seam at the back of the coat. He looked up and at Mr. Hawks reproachfully.

"The least you might have done," he said, "is to have returned my property in the same condition in which I left it."

"Your coat?" said Barney Hawks damply. Then he shouted: "What the hell is this? That's my coat! My camel's-hair coat!"

"No," Mr. Queen dissented respectfully, "I can prove this to be mine. You see, it has a telltale cigarette burn at the second buttonhole, and a hole in the right-hand pocket."

"But—I found it where I left it! It was here all the time! I took it out of here after the fight and went up to the office to talk to these gentlemen and I've been—" The manager stopped, and his complexion faded from green to white. "Then where's my coat?" he asked slowly.

"Will you try this on?" asked Mr. Queen with the deference of a clothing salesman, and he took from a detective the bloodstained coat they had found abandoned in Ollie Stearn's car.

Mr. Queen held the coat up before Hawks; and Hawks said thickly: "All right. It's my coat. I guess it's my coat, if you say so. So what?"

"So," replied Mr. Queen, "someone knew Mike Brown was broke, that he owed his shirt, that not even his lion's share of the purse tonight would suffice to pay his debts. Someone persuaded Mike Brown to throw the fight tonight, offering to pay him a large sum of money, I suppose, for taking the dive. That money no one would know about. That money would not have to be turned over to the clutches of Mike Brown's loving wife and creditors. That money would be Mike Brown's own. So Mike Brown said yes, realizing that he could make more money, too, by placing a large bet with Happy Day through the medium of Mr. Oetjens. And with this double nest egg he could jeer at the unfriendly world.

"And probably Brown and his tempter conspired to meet in Stearn's car immediately after the fight for the payoff, for Brown would be insistent about that. So Brown sent the chauffeur away, and sat in the car, and the tempter came to keep the appointment—armed not with the payoff money but with a sharp stiletto. And by using the stiletto he saved himself a tidy sum—the sum he'd promised Brown—and also made sure Mike Brown would never be able to tell the wicked story to the wicked world."

Barney Hawks licked his dry lips. "Don't look at me,

mister. You got nothing on Barney Hawks. I don't know nothing about this."

And Mr. Queen said, paying no attention whatever to Mr. Hawks: "A pretty problem, friends. You see, the tempter came to the scene of the crime in a camel's-hair coat, and he had to leave the coat behind because it was bloodstained and would have given him away. Also, in the car next to the murder car lay, quite defenseless, my own poor camel's-hair coat, its only virtue the fact that it was stained with no man's blood.

"We found a coat abandoned in Stearn's car and my coat, in the next car, stolen. Coincidence? Hardly. The murderer certainly took my coat to replace the coat he was forced to leave behind."

Mr. Queen paused to refresh himself with a cigarette, glancing whimsically at Miss Paris, who was staring at him with a soul-satisfying worship. Mind over matter, thought Mr. Queen, remembering with special satisfaction how Miss Paris had stared at Jim Coyle's muscles. Yes, sir, mind over matter.

"Well?" said Inspector Queen. "Suppose this bird did take your coat? What of it?"

"But that's exactly the point," murmured Mr. Queen. "He took my poor, shabby, worthless coat. Why?"

"Why?" echoed the Inspector blankly.

"Yes, why? Everything in this world is activated by a reason. Why did he take my coat?"

"Well, I—I suppose to wear it."

"Very good," applauded Mr. Queen, playing up to Miss Paris. "Precisely. If he took it he had a reason, and since its only function under the circumstances could have been its wearability, so to speak, he took it to wear it." He paused, then murmured: "But why should he want to wear it?"

The Inspector looked angry. "See here, Ellery—" he began.

"No, Dad, no," said Mr. Queen gently. "I'm talking with a purpose. There's a point. *The* point. You might say he had to wear it because he'd got blood on his suit *under* the coat and required a coat to hide the bloodstained suit. Or mightn't you?"

"Well, sure," said Phil Maguire eagerly. "That's it."

"You may be an Einstein in your sports department, Mr. Maguire, but here you're just a palooka. No," said Mr. Queen, shaking his head sadly, "that's not it. He couldn't possibly have got blood on his suit. The coat shows that at the time he attacked Brown he was wearing it buttoned. If the topcoat was buttoned, his suit didn't catch any of Brown's blood."

"He certainly didn't need a coat because of the weather," muttered Inspector Queen.

"True. It's been warm all evening. You see," smiled Mr. Queen, "what a cute little thing it is. He'd left his own coat behind, its labels and other identifying marks taken out, unworried about its being found—otherwise he would have hidden it or thrown it away. Such being the case, you would say he'd simply make his escape in the clothes he was wearing *beneath* the coat. But he didn't. He stole another coat, my coat, for his escape." Mr. Queen coughed gently. "So surely it's obvious that if he stole my coat for his escape, he *needed* my coat for his escape? That if he escaped without my coat he would be *noticed?*"

"I don't get it," said the Inspector. "He'd be noticed? But if he was wearing ordinary clothing—"

"Then obviously he wouldn't need my coat," nodded Mr. Queen.

"Or—say! If he was wearing a uniform of some kind—say he was a Stadium attendant—"

"Then still obviously he wouldn't need my coat. A uniform would be a perfect guarantee that he'd pass in the crowds unnoticed." Mr. Queen shook his head. "No, there's only one answer to this problem. I saw it at once, of course." He noted the Inspector's expression and continued hastily: "And that was: If the murderer had been wearing clothes—*any* normal body-covering—beneath the bloodstained coat, he could have made his escape in those clothes. But since he didn't, it can only mean that he *wasn't* wearing clothes, you see, and that's why he needed a coat not only to come to the scene of the crime, but to escape from it as well."

There was another silence, and finally Paula said: "Wasn't wearing clothes? A . . . naked man? Why, that's like something out of Poe!"

"No," smiled Mr. Queen, "merely something out of the Stadium. You see, we had a classification of gentlemen in the vicinity tonight who wore no—or nearly no—clothing. In a word, the gladiators. Or, if you choose, the pugilists. . . . Wait!" he said swiftly. "This is an extraordinary case, chiefly because I solved the hardest part of it almost the instant I knew there was a murder. For the instant I discovered that Brown had been stabbed, and that my coat had been stolen by a murderer who left his own behind, I knew that the murderer could have been *only one of thirteen men* . . . the thirteen living prize-fighters left after Brown was killed. For you'll recall there were fourteen fighters in the Stadium tonight—twelve distributed among six preliminary bouts, and two in the main bout.

"Which of the thirteen living fighters had killed Brown? That was my problem from the beginning. And so I had to find my coat, because it was the only concrete connection I could discern between the murderer and his crime. And now I've found my coat, and now I know which of the thirteen murdered Brown."

Barney Hawks was speechless, his jaws agape.

"I'm a tall, fairly broad man. In fact, I'm six feet tall," said the great man. "And yet the murderer, in wearing my coat to make his escape, burst its seams at the arm-holes and back! That meant he was a big man, a much bigger man than I, much bigger and broader.

"Which of the thirteen fighters on the card tonight were bigger and broader than I? Ah, but it's been a very light card—bantamweights, welterweights, lightweights, middleweights! Therefore none of the twelve preliminary fighters could have murdered Brown. Therefore only one fighter was left—a man six and a half feet tall, extremely broad-shouldered and broad-backed, a man who had every motive—the greatest motive—to induce Mike Brown to throw the fight tonight!"

And this time the silence was ghastly with meaning. It was broken by Jim Coyle's lazy laugh. "If you mean me, you must be off your nut. Why, I was in that shower room taking a shower at the time Mike was bumped off!"

"Yes, I mean you, Mr. Jim Coyle Stiletto-Wielding Couzzi," said Mr. Queen clearly, "and the shower room was the cleverest part of your scheme. You went into the shower room in full view of all of us, with towels, shut the door, turned on the shower, slipped a pair of trousers over your bare and manly legs, grabbed Barney Hawks's camel's-hair coat and hat which were hanging on a peg in there, and then ducked out of the shower-room window into the alley. From there it was a matter of seconds to the street and the parking lot across the street. Of course, when you stained Hawks's coat during the commission of your crime, you couldn't risk coming back in it. And you had to have a coat—a buttoned coat—to cover your nakedness for the return trip. So you stole mine, for which I'm very grateful, because otherwise—Grab him, will you? My right isn't very good," said Mr. Queen, employing a dainty and beautiful bit of footwork to escape Coyle's sudden homicidal lunge in his direction.

And while Coyle went down under an avalanche of flailing arms and legs, Mr. Queen murmured apologetically to Miss Paris: "After all, darling, he *is* the heavyweight champion of the world."

Trojan Horse

"Whom," demanded Miss Paula Paris across the groaning board, "do you like, Mr. Queen?"

Mr. Queen instantly mumbled: "You," out of a mouthful of Vermont turkey, chestnut stuffing, and cranberry sauce.

"I didn't mean that, silly," said Miss Paris, nevertheless pleased. "However, now that you've brought the subject up—will you say such pretty things when we're married?"

Mr. Ellery Queen paled and, choking, set down his weapons. His precious liberty faced with this alluring menace, Mr. Queen now choked over the luscious Christmas dinner which Miss Paris had cunningly cooked with her own slim hands and served *en tête-à-tête* in her cosy maple and chintz dining room.

"Oh, relax," pouted Miss Paris. "I was joking. What makes you think I'd marry a creature who studies cutthroats and chases thieves for the enjoyment of it?"

"Horrible fate for a woman," Mr. Queen hastened to agree. "Besides, I'm not good enough for you."

"Darned tootin' you're not! But you haven't answered my question. Do you think Carolina will lick USC next Sunday?"

"Oh, the Rose Bowl game," said Mr. Queen, discovering

his appetite miraculously. "More turkey, please! . . . Well, if Ostermoor lives up to his reputation, the Spartans should breeze in."

"Really?" murmured Miss Paris. "Aren't you forgetting that Roddy Crockett is the whole Trojan backfield?"

"Southern California Trojans, Carolina Spartans," said Mr. Queen thoughtfully, munching. "Spartans versus Trojans . . . Sort of modern gridiron Siege of Troy."

"Ellery Queen, that's plagiarism or—or something! You read it in my column."

"Is there a Helen for the lads to battle over?" grinned Mr. Queen.

"You're *so* romantic, Queenikins. The only female involved is a very pretty, rich, and sensible coed named Joan Wing, and she *isn't* the kidnaped love of any of the Spartans."

"Curses," said Mr. Queen, reaching for the brandied plum pudding. "For a moment I thought I had something."

"But there's a Priam of a sort, because Roddy Crockett is engaged to Joan Wing, and Joanie's father, Pop Wing, is just about the noblest Trojan of them all."

"Maybe you know what you're talking about, beautiful," said Mr. Queen, "but *I* don't."

"You're positively the worst-informed man in California! Pop Wing is USC's most enthusiastic alumnus, isn't he?"

"Is he?"

"You mean you've never heard of Pop Wing?" asked Paula incredulously.

"Not guilty," said Mr. Queen. "More plum pudding, please."

"The Perennial Alumnus? The Boy Who Never Grew Up?"

"Thank you," said Mr. Queen. "I beg your pardon."

"The Ghost of Exposition Park and the L.A. Coliseum, who holds a life seat for all USC football games? The unofficial trainer, rubber, water boy, pep-talker, Alibi Ike, booster, and pigskin patron-in-chief to the Trojan eleven? Percy Squires 'Pop' Wing, Southern California '04, the man who sleeps, eats, breathes only for Trojan victories and who married and, failing a son, created a daughter for the sole purpose of snaring USC's best fullback in years?"

"Peace, peace; I yield," moaned Mr. Queen, "before the

crushing brutality of the characterization. I now know Percy Squires Wing as I hope never to know anyone again."

"Sorry!" said Paula, rising briskly. "Because directly after you've filled your bottomless tummy with plum pudding we're going Christmas calling on the great man."

"No!" said Mr. Queen with a shudder.

"You want to see the Rose Bowl game, don't you?"

"Who doesn't? But I haven't been able to snag a brace of tickets for love or money."

"Poor Queenie," purred Miss Paris, putting her arms about him. "You're *so* helpless. Come on watch me wheedle Pop Wing out of two seats for the game!"

The lord of the château whose towers rose from a magnificently preposterous parklike estate in Inglewood proved to be a flat-bellied youngster of middle age, almost as broad as he was tall, with a small bald head set upon small ruddy cheeks, so that at first glance Mr. Queen thought he was viewing a Catawba grape lying on a boulder.

They came upon the millionaire seated on his hams in the center of a vast lawn, arguing fiercely with a young man who by his size—which was herculean—and his shape—which was cuneiform—and his coloring—which was coppery—could only be of the order *footballis,* and therefore Mr. Wing's future son-in-law and the New Year's Day hope of the Trojans.

They were manipulating wickets, mallets, and croquet balls in illustration of a complex polemic which apparently concerned the surest method of frustrating the sinister quarterback of the Carolina eleven, Ostermoor.

A young lady with red hair and a saucy nose sat cross-legged on the grass nearby, her soft blue eyes fixed on the brown face of the young man with that naked worshipfulness young ladies permit themselves to exhibit in public only when their young men have formally yielded. This, concluded Mr. Queen without difficulty, must be the daughter of the great man and Mr. Roddy Crockett's fiancée, Joan Wing.

Mr. Wing hissed a warning to Roddy at the sight of Mr. Queen's unfamiliar visage, and for a moment Mr. Queen felt uncomfortably like a spy caught sneaking into the enemy's camp. But Miss Paris hastily vouched for his devotion to the cause of Troy, and for some time there were Christmas greetings and introductions, in the course of which Mr. Queen made the acquaintance of two persons whom he recognized instantly as the hybrid genus *house-guest perennialis*. One was a bearded gentleman with high cheekbones and a Muscovite manner (pre-Soviet), entitled the Grand Duke Ostrov; the other was a thin, dark, whiplike female with inscrutable black eyes who went by the mildly astonishing name of Madame Mephisto.

These two barely nodded to Miss Paris and Mr. Queen; they were listening to each word that dropped from the lips of Mr. Percy Squires Wing, their host, with the adoration of novitiates at the feet of their patron saint.

The noble Trojan's ruddiness of complexion, Mr. Queen pondered, came either from habitual exposure to the outdoors or from high-blood pressure; a conclusion which he discovered very soon was accurate on both counts, since Pop Wing revealed himself without urging as an Izaak Walton, a golfer, a Nimrod, a mountain climber, a polo player, and a racing yachtsman; and he was as squirmy and excitable as a small boy.

The small-boy analogy struck Mr. Queen with greater force when the Perennial Alumnus dragged Mr. Queen off to inspect what he alarmingly called "my trophy room." Mr. Queen's fears were vindicated; for in a huge vaulted chamber presided over by a desiccated, gloomy, and monosyllabic old gentleman introduced fantastically as "Gabby" Huntswood, he found himself inspecting as heterogeneous and remarkable an assemblage of junk as ever existed outside a small boy's dream of Paradise.

Postage-stamp albums, American college banners, mounted wild-animal heads, a formidable collection of matchboxes, cigar bands, stuffed fish, World War trench helmets of all nations . . . all were there; and Pop Wing beamed as he exhibited these priceless treasures, scurrying from one collection to another and fondling them with such ingenuous pleasure that Mr. Queen sighed for his own lost youth.

"Aren't these objects too—er—valuable to be left lying around this way, Mr. Wing?" he inquired politely.

"Hell, no. Gabby's more jealous of their safety than I am!" shouted the great man. "Hey, Gabby?"

"Yes, sir," said Gabby; and he frowned suspiciously at Mr. Queen.

"Why, Gabby made me install a burglar-alarm system. Can't see it, but this room's as safe as a vault."

"Safer," said Gabby, glowering at Mr. Queen.

"Think I'm crazy, Queen?"

"No, no," said Mr. Queen, who meant to say "Yes, yes."

"Lots of people do," chuckled Pop Wing. "Let 'em. Between 1904 and 1924 I just about vegetated. But something drove me on. Know what?"

Mr. Queen's famous powers of deduction were unequal to the task.

"The knowledge that I was making enough money to retire a young man and kick the world in the pants. And I did! Retired at forty-two and started doing all the things I'd never had time or money to do when I was a shaver. Collecting things. Keeps me young! Come here, Queen, and look at my *prize* collection." And he pulled Mr. Queen over to a gigantic glass case and pointed gleefully, an elder Penrod gloating over a marbles haul.

From his host's proud tone Mr. Queen expected to gaze upon nothing less than a collection of the royal crowns of Europe. Instead, he saw a vast number of scuffed, streaked, and muddy footballs, each carefully laid upon an ebony rest, and on each a legend lettered in gold leaf. One that caught his eye read: "Rose Bowl, 1930. USC 47-Pitt 14." The others bore similar inscriptions.

"Wouldn't part with 'em for a million dollars," confided the great man. "Why, the balls in this case represent every Trojan victory for the past fifteen years!"

"Incredible!" exclaimed Mr. Queen.

"Yes, sir, right after every game they win the team presents old Pop Wing with the pigskin. What a collection!" And the millionaire gazed worshipfully at the unlovely oblate spheroids.

"They must think the world of you at USC."

"Well, I've sort of been of service to my Alma Mater," said Pop Wing modestly, "especially in football. Wing Athletic Scholarship, you know; Wing Dorm for varsity athletes; and so on. I've scouted prep schools for years, personally; turned up some mighty fine varsity material. Coach is a good friend of mine. I guess," and he drew a happy breath, "I can have just about what I damn well ask for at the old school!"

"Including football tickets?" said Mr. Queen quickly, seizing his opportunity. "Must be marvelous to have that kind of drag. I've been trying for days to get tickets for the game."

The great man surveyed him. "What was your college?"

"Harvard," said Mr. Queen apologetically. "But I yield to no man in my ardent admiration of the Trojans. Darn it, I did want to watch Roddy Crockett mop up those Spartan upstarts."

"You did, huh?" said Pop Wing. "Say, how about you and Miss Paris being my guests at the Rose Bowl Sunday?"

"Couldn't think of it—" began Mr. Queen mendaciously, already savoring the joy of having beaten Miss Paris, so to speak, to the turnstiles.

"Won't hear another word." Mr. Wing embraced Mr. Queen. "Say, long as you'll be with us, I'll let you in on a little secret."

"Secret?" wondered Mr. Queen.

"Rod and Joan," whispered the millionaire, "are going to be married right after the Trojans win next Sunday!"

"Congratulations. He seems like a fine boy."

"None better. Hasn't got a cent, you understand—worked his way through—but he's graduating in January and . . . shucks! he's the greatest fullback the old school ever turned out. We'll find something for him to do. Yes, sir, Roddy's last game . . ." The great man sighed. Then he brightened. "Anyway, I've got a hundred-thousand-dollar surprise for my Joanie that ought to make her go right out and raise another triple-threat man for the Trojans!"

"A—how much of a surprise?" asked Mr. Queen feebly.

But the great man looked mysterious. "Let's go back and finish cooking that boy Ostermoor's goose!"

New Year's Day was warm and sunny; and Mr. Queen felt strange as he prepared to pick up Paula Paris and escort her to the Wing estate, from which their party was to proceed to the Pasadena stadium. In his quaint Eastern fashion, he was accustomed to don a mountain of sweater, scarf, and overcoat when he went to a football game; and here he was en route in a sports jacket!

"California, thy name is Iconoclast," muttered Mr. Queen, and he drove through already agitated Hollywood streets to Miss Paris's house.

"Heavens," said Paula, "you can't barge in on Pop Wing that way."

"What way?"

"Minus the Trojan colors. We've got to keep on the old

225

darlin's good side, at least until we're safely in the stadium. Here!" And with a few deft twists of two lady's handkerchiefs Paula manufactured a breast-pocket kerchief for him in cardinal and gold.

"I see you've done yourself up pretty brown," said Mr. Queen, not unadmiringly; for Paula's figure was the secret envy of many better-advertised Hollywood ladies, and it was clad devastatingly in a cardinal-and-gold creation that was a cross between a suit and a dirndl, to Mr. Queen's inexperienced eye, and it was topped off with a perky, feathery hat perched nervously on her blue-black hair, concealing one bright eye.

"Wait till you see Joan," said Miss Paris, rewarding him with a kiss. "She's been calling me all week about *her* clothes problem. It's not every day a girl's called on to buy an outfit that goes equally well with a football game and a wedding." And as Mr. Queen drove off towards Inglewood she added thoughtfully: "I wonder what that awful creature will wear. Probably a turban and seven veils."

"What creature?"

"Madame Mephisto. Only her real name is Suzie Lucadamo, and she quit a dumpy little magic and mind-reading vaudeville act to set herself up in Seattle as a seeress—you know, 'We positively guarantee to pierce the veil of the Unknown'? Pop met her in Seattle in November during the USC-Washington game. She wangled a Christmas-week invitation out of him for the purpose, I suppose, of looking over the rich Hollywood sucker field without cost to herself."

"You seem to know a lot about her."

Paula smiled. "Joan Wing told me some—Joanie doesn't like the old gal nohow—and I dug out the rest . . . well, you know, darling, I know everything about *everybody*."

"Then tell me," said Mr. Queen. "Who exactly is the Grand Duke Ostrov?"

"Why?"

"Because," replied Mr. Queen grimly, "I don't like His Highness, and I do like—heaven help me!—Pop Wing and his juvenile amusements."

"Joan tells me Pop likes you, too, the fool! I guess in his adolescent way he's impressed by a real, live detective. Show him your G-man badge, darling." Mr. Queen glared, but Miss Paris's gaze was dreamy. "Pop may find it handy having you around today, at that."

"What d'ye mean?" asked Mr. Queen sharply.

"Didn't he tell you he had a surprise for Joan? He's told everyone in Los Angeles, although no one knows what it is but your humble correspondent."

"And Roddy, I'll bet. He did say something about a 'hundred-thousand-dollar surprise.' What's the point?"

"The point is," murmured Miss Paris, "that it's a set of perfectly matched star sapphires."

Mr. Queen was silent. Then he said: "You think Ostrov—"

"The Grand Duke," said Miss Paris, "is even phonier than Madame Suzie Lucadamo Mephisto. *His* name is Louie Batterson, and he hails from the Bronx. Everybody knows it but Pop Wing." Paula sighed. "But you know Hollywood—live and let live; you may need a sucker yourself some day. Batterson's a high-class deadbeat. He's pulled some awfully aromatic stunts in his time. I'm hoping he lays off our nostrils this sunny day."

"This," mumbled Mr. Queen, "is going to be one heck of a football game, I can see that."

Bedlam was a cloister compared with the domain of the Wings. The interior of the house was noisy with decorators, caterers, cooks, and waiters; and with a start Mr. Queen recalled that this was to be the wedding day of Joan Wing and Roddy Crockett.

They found their party assembled in one of the formal gardens—which, Mr. Queen swore to Miss Paris, outshone Fontainebleau—and apparently Miss Wing had solved her dressmaking problem, for while Mr. Queen could find no word to describe what she was wearing, Mr. Roddy Crockett could, and the word was "sockeroo."

Paula went into more technical raptures, and Miss Wing clung to her gridiron hero, who looked a little pale; and then the pride of Troy went loping off to the wars, leaping into his roadster and waving farewell with their cries of good cheer in his manly, young, and slightly mashed ears.

Pop Wing ran down the driveway after the roadster, bellowing: "Don't forget that Ostermoor defense, Roddy!"

And Roddy vanished in a trail of dusty glory; the noblest Trojan of them all came back shaking his head and muttering: "It ought to be a pipe!"; flunkies appeared bearing mounds of canapés and cocktails; the Grand Duke, regally Cossack in a long Russian coat gathered

at the waist, amused the company with feats of legerde-
main—his long soft hands were very fluent—and Madame
Mephisto, minus the seven veils but, as predicted, wearing
the turban, went into a trance and murmured that she
could see a "glorious Trojan vic-to-ree"—all the while
Joan Wing sat smiling dreamily into her cocktail and Pop
Wing pranced up and down vowing that he had never
been cooler or more confident in his life.

And then they were in one of Wing's huge seven-pas-
senger limousines—Pop, Joan, the Grand Duke, Madame,
Gabby, Miss Paris, and Mr. Queen—bound for Pasadena
and the fateful game.

And Pop said suddenly: "Joanie, I've got a surprise
for you."

And Joanie dutifully looked surprised, her breath coming a little faster; and Pop drew out of the right-hand
pocket of his jacket a long leather case, and opened it,
and said with a chuckle: "Wasn't going to show it to you
till tonight, but Roddy told me before he left that you
look so beautiful I ought to give you a preview as a re-
ward. From me to you, Joanie. Like 'em?"

Joan gasped: *"Like* them!" and there were exclama-
tions of "Oh!" and "Ah!" and they saw lying upon black
velvet eleven superb sapphires, their stars winking royally
—a football team of perfectly matched gems.

"Oh, *Pop!*" moaned Joan, and she flung her arms about
him and wept on his shoulder, while he looked pleased
and blustery, and puffed and closed the case and returned
it to the pocket from which he had taken it.

"Formal opening tonight. Then you can decide whether
you want to make a necklace out of 'em or a bracelet or
what." And Pop stroked Joan's hair while she sniffled
against him; and Mr. Queen, watching the Grand Duke
Ostrov, *né* Batterson, and Madame Mephisto, *née* Lucadamo, thought they were very clever to have concealed so
quickly those startling expressions of avarice.

Surrounded by his guests, Pop strode directly to the
Trojans' dressing room, waving aside officials and police
and student athletic underlings as if he owned the Rose
Bowl and all the multitudinous souls besieging it.

The young man at the door said: "Hi, Pop," respectfully, and admitted them under the envious stares of the
less fortunate mortals outside.

"Isn't he grand?" whispered Paula, her eyes like stars;
but before Mr. Queen could reply there were cries of:

"Hey! Femmes!" and "Here's Pop!" and the coach came over, wickedly straight-arming Mr. Roddy Crockett, who was lacing his doeskin pants, aside, and said with a wink: "All right, Pop. Give it to 'em."

And Pop very pale now, shucked his coat and flung it on a rubbing table; and the boys crowded round, very quiet suddenly; and Mr. Queen found himself pinned between a mountainous tackle and a behemoth of a guard who growled down at him: "Hey, you, stop squirming. Don't you see Pop's gonna make a speech!"

And Pop said, in a very low voice: "Listen, gang. The last time I made a dressing-room spiel was in '33. It was on a January first, too, and it was the day USC played Pitt in the Rose Bowl. That day we licked 'em thirty-three to nothing."

Somebody shouted: "Yay!" but Pop held up his hand.

"I made three January first speeches before that. One was in '32, before we knocked Tulane over by a score of twenty-one to twelve. One was in 1930, the day we beat the Panthers forty-seven to fourteen. And the first in '23, when we took Penn State by fourteen to three. And that was the first time in the history of Rose Bowl that we represented the Pacific Coast Conference in the intersectional classic. There's just one thing I want you men to bear in mind when you dash out there in a few minutes in front of half of California."

The room was very still.

"I want you to remember that the Trojans have played in four Rose Bowl games. And I want you to remember that the Trojans have *won* four Rose Bowl games," said Pop.

And he stood high above them, looking down into their intent young faces; and then he jumped to the floor, breathing heavily.

Hell broke loose. Boys pounded him on the back; Roddy Crockett seized Joan and pulled her behind a locker; Mr. Queen found himself pinned to the door, hat over his eyes, by the elbow of the Trojan center, like a butterfly to a wall; and the coach stood grinning at Pop, who grinned back, but tremulously.

"All right, men," said the coach. "Pop?" Pop Wing grinned and shook them all off, and Roddy helped him into his coat, and after a while Mr. Queen, considerably the worse for wear, found himself seated in Pop's box directly above the fifty-yard line.

And then, as the two teams dashed into the Bowl across the brilliant turf, to the roar of massed thousands, Pop Wing uttered a faint cry.

"What's the matter?" asked Joan quickly, seizing his arm. "Aren't you feeling well, Pop?"

"The sapphires," said Pop Wing in a hoarse voice, his hand in his pocket. "They're gone."

Kick-off! Twenty-two figures raced to converge in a tumbling mass, and the stands thundered, the USC section fluttering madly with flags . . . and then there was a groan that rent the blue skies, and deadly, despairing silence.

For the Trojans' safety man caught the ball, started forward, slipped, the ball popped out of his hands, the Carolina right end fell on it—and there was the jumping, gleeful Spartan team on the Trojans' 9-yard line, Carolina's ball, first down, and four plays for a touchdown.

And Gabby, who had not heard Pop Wing's exclamation, was on his feet shrieking: "But they can't *do* that! Oh, heavens— Come *on*, USC! Hold that line!"

Pop glanced at Mr. Huntswood with bloodshot surprise, as if a three-thousand-year-old mummy had suddenly come to life; and then he muttered: "Gone. Somebody's— picked my pocket."

"*What!*" whispered Gabby; and he fell back, staring at his employer with horror.

"But theese ees fantastic," the Grand Duke exclaimed.

Mr. Queen said quietly: "Are you positive, Mr. Wing?"

Pop's eyes were on the field, automatically analyzing the play; but they were filled with pain. "Yes, I'm sure. Some pickpocket in the crowd . . ."

"No," said Mr. Queen.

"Ellery, what do you mean?" cried Paula.

"From the moment we left Mr. Wing's car until we entered the Trojan dressing room we surrounded him completely. From the moment we left the Trojan dressing room until we sat down in this box, we surrounded him completely. No, our pickpocket is one of this group, I'm afraid."

Madame Mephisto shrilled: "How dare you! Aren't you forgetting that it was Mr. Crockett who helped Mr. Wing on with his coat in that dressing room?"

"You—" began Pop in a growl, starting to rise.

Joan put her hand on his arm and squeezed, smiling at him. "Never mind her, Pop."

230

Carolina gained two yards on a plunge through center. Pop shaded his eyes with his hand, staring at the opposing lines.

"Meester Queen," said the Grand Duke coldly, "that ees an insult. I demand we all be—how you say?—searched."

Pop waved his hand wearily. "Forget it. I came to watch a football game." But he no longer looked like a small boy.

"His Highness's suggestion," murmured Mr. Queen, "is an excellent one. The ladies may search one another; the men may do the same. Suppose we all leave here together —in a body—and retire to the rest rooms?"

"Hold 'em," muttered Pop, as if he had not heard. Carolina gained 2 yards more on an off-tackle play; 5 yards to go in two downs. They could see Roddy Crockett slapping one of his linesmen on the back.

The lines met, and buckled. No gain.

"D'ye see Roddy go through that hole?" muttered Pop.

Joan rose and, rather imperiously, motioned Madame and Paula to precede her. Pop did not stir. Mr. Queen motioned to the men. The Grand Duke and Gabby rose. They all went quickly away.

And still Pop did not move. Until Ostermoor rifled a flat pass into the end zone, and a Carolina end came up out of the ground and snagged the ball. And then it was Carolina 6, USC 0, the big clock indicating that barely a minute of the first quarter's playing time had elapsed.

"Block that kick!"

Roddy plunged through the Spartan line and blocked it. The Carolina boys trotted back to their own territory, grinning.

"Hmph," said Pop to the empty seats in his box; and then he sat still and simply waited, an old man.

The first quarter rolled along. The Trojans could not get out of their territory. Passes fell incomplete. The Spartan line held like iron.

"Well, we're back," said Paula Paris. The great man looked up slowly. "We didn't find them."

A moment later Mr. Queen returned, herding his two companions. Mr. Queen said nothing at all; he merely shook his head, and the Grand Duke Ostrov looked grandly contemptuous, and Madame Mephisto tossed her turbaned head angrily. Joan was very pale; her eyes crept

231

down the field to Roddy, and Paula saw that they were filled with tears.

Mr. Queen said abruptly: "Will you excuse me, please?" and left again with swift strides.

The first quarter ended with the score still 6 to 0 against USC and the Trojans unable to extricate themselves from the menace of their goal post . . . pinned back with inhuman regularity by the sharp-shooting Mr. Ostermoor. There is no defense against a deadly accurate kick.

When Mr. Queen returned, he wiped his slightly moist brow and said pleasantly: "By the way, Your Highness, it all comes back to me now. In a former incarnation—I believe in that life your name was Batterson, and you were the flower of an ancient Bronx family—weren't you mixed up in a jewel robbery?"

"Jewel robbery!" gasped Joan, and for some reason she looked relieved. Pop's eyes fixed coldly on the Grand Duke's suddenly oscillating beard.

"Yes," continued Mr. Queen, "I seem to recall that the fence tried to involve you, Your Highness, saying you were the go-between, but the jury wouldn't believe a fence's word, and so you went free. You were quite charming on the stand, I recall—had the courtroom in stitches."

"It's a damn lie," said the Grand Duke thickly, without the trace of an accent. His teeth gleamed wolfishly at Mr. Queen from its thicket.

"You thieving four-flusher—" began Pop Wing, half-rising from his seat.

"Not yet, Mr. Wing," said Mr. Queen.

"I have never been so insulted—" began Madame Mephisto.

"And you," said Mr. Queen with a little bow, "would be wise to hold your tongue, Madame Lucadamo."

Paula nudged him in fierce mute inquiry, but he shook his head. He looked perplexed.

No one said anything, until near the end of the second quarter, Roddy Crockett broke loose for a 44-yard gain, and on the next play came to rest on Carolina's 26-yard line.

Then Pop Wing was on his feet, cheering lustily, and even Gabby Huntswood was yelling in his cracked, un-oiled voice: "Come on, Trojans!"

"Attaboy, Gabby," said Pop with the ghost of a grin. "First time I've ever seen you excited about a football game."

Three plays netted the Trojans 11 yards more: first down on Carolina's 15-yard line! The half was nearly over. Pop was hoarse, the theft apparently forgotten. He groaned as USC lost ground, Ostermoor breaking up two plays. Then, with the ball on Carolina's 22-yard line, with time for only one more play before the whistle ending the half, the Trojan quarterback called for a kick formation and Roddy booted the ball straight and true between the uprights of the Spartan's goal.

The whistle blew. Carolina 6, USC 3.

Pop sank back, mopping his face. "Have to do better. That damn Ostermoor! What's the matter with Roddy?"

During the rest period Mr. Queen, who had scarcely watched the struggle, murmured: "By the way, Madame, I've heard a good deal about your unique gift of divination. We can't seem to find the sapphires by natural means; how about the supernatural?"

Madame Mephisto glared at him. "This is no time for jokes!"

"A true gift needs no special conditions," smiled Mr. Queen.

"The atmosphere—scarcely propitious—"

"Come, come, Madame! You wouldn't overlook an opportunity to restore your host's hundred-thousand-dollar loss?"

Pop began to inspect Madame with suddenly keen curiosity.

Madame closed her eyes, her long fingers at her temples. "I see," she murmured, "I see a long jewel case . . . yes, it is closed, closed . . . but it is dark, very dark . . . it is in a, yes, a dark place. . . ." She sighed and dropped her hands, her dark lids rising. "I'm sorry. I can see no more."

"It's in a dark place, all right," said Mr. Queen dryly. "It's in my pocket." And to their astonishment he took from his pocket the great man's jewel case.

Mr. Queen snapped it open. "Only," he remarked sadly, "it's empty. I found it in a corner of the Trojans' dressing room."

Joan shrank back, squeezing a tiny football charm so hard it collapsed. The millionaire gazed stonily at the parading bands blaring around the field.

233

"You see," said Mr. Queen, "the thief hid the sapphires somewhere and dropped the case in the dressing room. And we were all there. The question is: Where did the thief cache them?"

"Pardon me," said the Grand Duke. "Eet seems to me the theft must have occurred in Meester Wing's car, after he returned the jewel case to his pocket. So perhaps the jewels are hidden in the car."

"I have already," said Mr. Queen, "searched the car."

"Then in the Trojan dressing room!" cried Paula.

"No, I've also searched there—floor to ceiling, lockers, cabinets, clothes, everything. The sapphires aren't there."

"The thief wouldn't have been so foolish as to drop them in an aisle on the way to this box," said Paula thoughtfully. "Perhaps he had an accomplice—"

"To have an accomplice," said Mr. Queen wearily, "you must know you are going to commit a crime. To know that you must know there will be a crime to commit. Nobody but Mr. Wing knew that he intended to take the sapphires with him today—is that correct, Mr. Wing?"

"Yes," said Pop. "Except Rod— Yes. No one."

"Wait!" cried Joan passionately. "I know what you're all thinking. You think Roddy had—had something to do with this. I can see it—yes, even you, Pop! But don't you see how silly it is? Why should Rod steal something that will belong to him, anyway? I *won't* have you thinking Roddy's a—a thief!"

"I did not," said Pop feebly.

"Then we're agreed the crime was unpremeditated and that no accomplice could have been provided for," said Mr. Queen. "Incidentally, the sapphires are not in this box. I've looked."

"But it's ridiculous!" cried Joan. "Oh I don't care about losing the jewels, beautiful as they are; Pop can afford the loss; it's just that it's such a mean dirty thing to do. Its very cleverness makes it dirty."

"Criminals," drawled Mr. Queen, "are not notoriously fastidious, so long as they achieve their criminal ends. The point is that the thief has hidden those gems somewhere— the place is the very essence of his crime, for upon its simplicity and later accessibility depends the success of his theft. So it's obvious that the thief's hidden the sapphires where no one would spot them easily, where they're unlikely to be found even by accident, yet where he can safely retrieve them at his leisure."

234

"But heavens," said Paula, exasperated, "they are not in the car, they're not in the dressing room, they're not on any of us, they're not in this box, there's no accomplice ... it's impossible!"

"No," muttered Mr. Queen. "Not impossible. It was done. But how? How?"

The Trojans came out fighting. They carried the pigskin slowly but surely down the field toward the Spartans' goal line. But on the 21-yard stripe the attack stalled. The diabolical Mr. Ostermoor, all over the field, intercepted a forward past on third down with 8 yards to go, ran the ball back 51 yards, and USC was frustrated again.

The fourth quarter began with no change in the score; a feeling that was palpable settled over the crowd, a feeling that they were viewing the first Trojan defeat in its Rose Bowl history. Injuries and exhaustion had taken their toll of the Trojan team; they seemed dispirited, beaten.

"When's he going to open up?" muttered Pop. "That trick!" And his voice rose to a roar. "Roddy! Come on!"

The Trojans drove suddenly with the desperation of a last strength. Carolina gave ground, but stubbornly. Both teams tried a kicking duel, but Ostermoor and Roddy were so evenly matched that neither side gained much through the interchange.

Then the Trojans began to take chances. A long pass—successful. Another!

"Roddy's going to town!"

Pop Wing, sapphires forgotten, bellowed hoarsely; Gabby shrieked encouragement; Joan danced up and down; the Grand Duke and Madame looked politely interested; even Paula felt the mass excitement stir her blood.

But Mr. Queen sat frowning in his seat, thinking and thinking, as if cerebration were a new function to him.

The Trojans clawed closer and closer to the Carolina goal line, the Spartans fighting back furiously but giving ground, unable to regain possession of the ball.

First down on Carolina's 19-yard line, with seconds to go!

"Roddy, the kick! The kick!" shouted Pop.

The Spartans held on the first plunge. They gave a yard on the second. On the third—the inexorable hand of the big clock jerked towards the hour mark—the Spartans' left tackle smashed through USC's line and smeared the

235

play for a 6-yard loss. Fourth down, seconds to go, and the ball on Carolina's 24-yard line!

"If they don't go over next play," screamed Pop, "the game's lost. It'll be Carolina's ball and they'll freeze it. ... *Roddy!*" he thundered. *"The kick play!"*

And, as if Roddy could hear that despairing voice, the ball snapped back, the Trojan quarterback snatched it, held it ready for Roddy's toe, his right hand between the ball and the turf. ... Roddy darted up as if to kick, but as he reached the ball he scooped it from his quarterback's hands and raced for the Carolina goal line.

"It worked!" bellowed Pop. "They expected a place kick to tie—and it worked! *Make it, Roddy!*"

USC spread out, blocking like demons. The Carolina team was caught completely by surprise. Roddy wove and slithered through the bewildered Spartan line and crossed the goal just as the final whistle blew.

"We win! We win!" cackled Gabby, doing a war dance.

"Yowie!" howled Pop, kissing Joan, kissing Paula, almost kissing Madame.

Mr. Queen looked up. The frown had vanished from his brow. He seemed serene, happy.

"Who won?" asked Mr. Queen genially.

But no one answered. Struggling in a mass of worshipers, Roddy was running up the field to the 50-yard line; he dashed up to the box and thrust something into Pop Wing's hands, surrounded by almost the entire Trojan squad.

"Here it is, Pop," panted Roddy. "The old pigskin. Another one for your collection, and a honey! Joan!"

"Oh, Roddy."

"My boy," began Pop, overcome by emotion; but then he stopped and hugged the dirty ball to his breast.

Roddy grinned and, kissing Joan, yelled: "Remind me that I've got a date to marry you tonight!" and ran off towards the Trojan dressing room followed by a howling mob.

"Ahem!" coughed Mr. Queen. "Mr. Wing, I think we're ready to settle your little difficulty."

"Huh?" said Pop, gazing with love at the filthy ball. "Oh." His shoulders sagged. "I suppose," he said wearily, "we'll have to notify the police—"

"I should think," said Mr. Queen, "that that isn't necessary, at least just yet. May I relate a parable? It seems that the ancient city of Troy was being besieged by the

236

Greeks, and holding out very nicely, too; so nicely that the Greeks, who were very smart people, saw that only guile would get them into the city. And so somebody among the Greeks conceived a brilliant plan, based upon a very special sort of guile; and the essence of this guile was that the Trojans should be made to do the very thing the Greeks had been unable to do themselves. You will recall that in this the Greeks were successful, since the Trojans, overcome by curiosity and the fact that the Greeks had sailed away, hauled the wooden horse with their own hands into the city and, lo! that night, when all Troy slept, the Greeks hidden within the horse crept out, and you know the rest. Very clever, the Greeks. May I have that football, Mr. Wing?"

Pop said dazedly: "Huh?"

Mr. Queen, smiling, took it from him, deflated it by opening the valve, unlaced the leather thongs, shook the limp pigskin over Pop's cupped hands . . . and out plopped the eleven sapphires.

"You see," murmured Mr. Queen, as they stared speechless at the gems in Pop Wing's shaking hands, "the thief stole the jewel case from Pop's coat pocket while Pop was haranguing his beloved team in the Trojan dressing room before the game. The coat was lying on a rubbing table and there was such a mob that no one noticed the thief sneak over to the table, take the case out of Pop's coat, drop it in a corner after removing the sapphires, and edge his way to the table where the football to be used in the Rose Bowl game was lying uninflated. He loosened the laces surreptitiously, pushed the sapphires into the space between the pigskin wall and the rubber bladder, tied the laces, and left the ball apparently as he had found it.

"Think of it! All the time we were watching the game, the eleven sapphires were in this football. For one hour this spheroid has been kicked, passed, carried, fought over, sat on, smothered, grabbed, scuffed, muddied—with a king's ransom in it!"

"But how did you know they were hidden in the ball," gasped Paula, "and who's the thief, you wonderful man?"

Mr. Queen lit a cigarette modestly. "With all the obvious hiding places eliminated, you see, I said to myself: 'One of us is a thief, and the hiding place must be accessible to the thief after this game.' And I remembered a parable and a fact. The parable I've told you, and the fact was that after every winning Trojan game the ball is presented to Mr. Percy Squires Wing."

"But you can't think—" began Pop, bewildered.

"Obviously you didn't steal your own gems," smiled Mr. Queen. "So you see, the thief had to be someone who could take equal advantage with you of the fact that the winning ball is presented to you. Someone who saw that there are two ways of stealing gems: to go to the gems, or to make the gems come to you.

"And so I knew that the thief was the man who, against all precedent and his taciturn nature, has been volubly imploring the Trojan team to win this football game; the man who knew that if the Trojans won the game the ball would immediately be presented to Pop Wing, and who gambled upon the Trojans; the man who saw that, with the ball given immediately to Pop Wing, he and he exclusively, custodian of Pop's wonderful and multifarious treasures, could retrieve the sapphires safely unobserved—grab the old coot, Your Highness!—Mr. Gabby Huntswood."

More Suspense Thrillers from SIGNET

☐ **THE SMITH CONSPIRACY by Richard Neely.** From the author of **THE WALTER SYNDROME** comes the suspenseful novel of a man and woman fighting against an intrigue that could spiral a whole nation into hell.
(#T5012—75¢)

☐ **THE PAPER DOLLS by L. P. Davies.** This highly acclaimed suspense novel explores the mind of a twelve-year-old English schoolboy possessing extraordinary and potentially evil powers.
(#Q4866—95¢)

☐ **HAIL, HAIL, THE GANG'S ALL HERE by Ed McBain.** In this 87th Precinct Mystery all of Ed McBain's detectives come together for the first time, and they're all kept hopping. Some of the stories are violent, some touching, some ironic, but all are marked by the masterful McBain touch . . . the "gang" has never been better.
(#T5063—75¢)

☐ **THE WALTER SYNDROME by Richard Neely.** A psychopathic rapist who calls himself The Executioner terrorizes all New York, as one after another violated and grotesquely mutilated female corpse is found. You are invited to discover the strange and terrible secret of his identity—if your nerves and stomach can take it! "An eerie thriller . . . even the most hardened reader will feel its impact."—**The New York Times**
(#Y4766—$1.25)

☐ **THE MEPHISTO WALTZ by Fred Mustard Stewart.** A masterpiece in suspense and quiet (the most deadly) horror. Only the strongest will resist its subtly diabolic power.
(#Q4643—95¢)

Other SIGNET Books You'll Want to Read